THE

CANAAN LEGACY

THE
CANAAN
LEGACY

Michael A. Kahn

 LYNX BOOKS
New York

Library of Congress Cataloging-in-Publication Data

Kahn, Michael A., 1952-
  The Canaan legacy.

  I. Title.
PS3561.A375C36   1988   813'.54   88-6795
ISBN 1-55802-156-6

First Edition

This book is published by Lynx Books, a division of Lynx Communications, Inc., 41 Madison Avenue, New York, New York, 10010. The name "Lynx" together with the logotype consisting of a stylized head of a lynx is a trademark of Lynx Communications, Inc.

Printed in the United States of America

0 9 8 7 6 5 4 3 2 1

For Margi

*A special thanks to Toni Mendez
and Jeanne Bernkopf*

All nature is but art unknown to thee,
All chance, direction which thou canst see.

—Alexander Pope

Luck is the residue of design.

—Branch Rickey

THE
CANAAN
LEGACY

Preamble

THERE WERE, OF COURSE, AT least two of him. There usually are.

There was first the public Graham Anderson Marshall III. Choate, Barrett College, Yale Law School. Tall, trim, square-jawed, salt-and-pepper hair, piercing blue eyes. Captain in the United States Marines—two years in South Korea. Three years in the Antitrust Division of the Justice Department. An Undersecretary of State during the Ford administration. Now the senior antitrust partner at Abbott & Windsor, the third oldest and second largest law firm in Chicago. A trustee of Barrett College and a member of the boards of directors of eleven corporations and two charitable foundations. A decent tennis player, an excellent squash player, and a legendary practical joker. (Marshall was the reputed mastermind of the 1950's heist of the Sirena statue from Barrett College.) A home in Kenilworth: oak trees, two-car garage (a BMW and a Country Squire), swimming pool, sauna off the master bathroom. A summer place perched on a gentle green slope overlooking Lake Geneva. Married to the former Julia Emerson Harrison (Chatham Hall, Smith College). Two children: a daughter at Mount Holyoke, a son (also Choate, Barrett College, and Yale Law) at Sullivan & Cromwell.

In sum, a powerful corporate lawyer in his prime, with clients from the first two columns of the Fortune 500, each of whom paid Abbott & Windsor $350 for every hour of Marshall's time. "The best bargain in town," according to the general counsel of a large Chicago steel company on whose behalf Marshall had appeared in the United States Supreme Court just six days before he died.

According to the obituaries in the Chicago newspapers and *The New York Times*, the public Graham Anderson Marshall suffered a massive coronary occlusion at approximately 10:15 P.M. on July 11 "while working on an appellate brief in the LaSalle Street offices of Abbott & Windsor." He was rushed to Northwestern Memorial Hospital, "where efforts to revive him were unsuccessful." The public Graham Anderson Marshall was pronounced dead of apparent heart failure at 11:07 P.M.

A heart attack is not an unusual way for a fifty-two-year-old partner in a major law firm to die. But those on duty at the emergency entrance of Northwestern Memorial Hospital will not soon forget the manner in which one of Chicago's most powerful attorneys filed his penultimate appearance.

Which brings us to the private Graham Anderson Marshall, also pronounced dead of heart failure at 11:07 P.M. on that same sweaty July evening. The orderly who met the ambulance had yanked open the back door, peered inside, and straightened up with a leer.

"My, my. What have we here?" he said, his face flashing crimson from the revolving ambulance light. "Looks to me like ol' Jack Coostow here had hisself too much of that fine mermaid pussy."

The dead lawyer was wearing an orange skin-diving suit, unsnapped at the crotch. A pale thread of semen trailed from the tip of his penis. A black flipper covered one foot; the other foot was bare.

The missing flipper still lay on the Oriental rug in the living room of a condominium on the eighteenth floor of Shore Drive Tower. Cindi Reynolds owned that condominium, and the private Graham Anderson Marshall visited her on alternate Wednesday nights to indulge his devotion to rubber and his preference for fellatio. Ms. Reynolds was lovely, leggy, and lissome. A typical evening of her time cost $900 ($1,100 with videotape) and generally included violations of several municipal ordinances and the commission of at least two of Illinois's infamous crimes against nature, one of which she was performing on Graham Anderson Marshall at the moment his heart gave out.

Although students of contract law might argue that Marshall did not receive the full benefit of his bargain that evening, no one could fault Ms. Reynolds's efforts to mitigate consequential damages. Her first telephone call was to the hospital. Her second call was to the managing partner of Abbott & Windsor, who promptly brought into play the forces necessary to ensure that the private Graham Anderson Marshall would be silently and safely interred long before the morning editions went to press.

The public Graham Anderson Marshall was buried four days later, with propriety and restraint, in a well-kept Lake Forest cemetery. The upper reaches of the corporate, legal, and political hierarchies of Chicago were well represented at the graveside ceremony. By the time the first clods of dirt clattered down onto the ebony coffin, the private Graham Anderson Marshall had disappeared without a trace. Well, almost without trace: the *Tribune*'s obituary did quote the chairman of the Antitrust Law Section of the American Bar Association, who praised Marshall as "one of our era's most accomplished and dedicated practitioners of the oral skills."

What follows in these pages, however, is an account of neither the public nor the private Graham Anderson Marshall. The former is profiled in the October issue of *The American Lawyer*; the latter was captured briefly on a videotape that Ms. Reynolds prudently erased after the paramedics carried Marshall out of her condominium on a stretcher.

Instead, what follows here concerns a third Graham Anderson Marshall—or at least the possibility of a third Graham Anderson Marshall. Unfortunately, the trail was already months, possibly years cold when Graham Anderson Marshall died. Footprints had faded, broken twigs had decayed to dust, flattened bushes had grown full again. The evidence is, at best, circumstantial.

Whether this third Graham Anderson Marshall existed, and for how long, are ultimately questions of fact about which reasonable men and women might differ.

ABBOTT & WINDSOR
MEMORANDUM

TO: Harlan Dodson
FROM: Ishmael Richardson
RE: ESTATE OF GRAHAM A. MARSHALL III

I received the attached in connection with the above-referenced matter. It is a troubling addition to what has been a most difficult situation. Please destroy it after you have reviewed it.

1

"PLEASE CALL ME ISHMAEL," HE said, studying the menu. "The fish here is generally quite good. I prefer the jumbo whitefish."

"Is the chef named Queequeg?" I asked.

"What's that?" Ishmael Richardson looked up from the menu. "No," he said, frowning. "I believe he is French. A nice chap."

We were seated at a window table in Cathedral Hall, the enormous dining room on the ninth floor of the University Club of Chicago. I had first eaten here as a third-year law student, flown out by Abbott & Windsor for a job interview. After joining the firm I came here frequently, usually as the lunch guest of Graham Anderson Marshall and always to discuss some aspect of *In re Bottles & Cans.* This was my first time back since leaving Abbott & Windsor two years ago.

There are more exclusive downtown clubs than

the University Club—and Ishmael Richardson is a member of most of them. But none could boast a more stunning or ludicrous main dining room. Cathedral Hall is a dead-serious replica of a medieval Gothic cathedral, built at the turn of the century by Chicago bankers and lawyers eager for respectability. The results are impressive: stained glass, gray stone walls, and massive fluted columns rising three stories to a vaulted timber ceiling. Chicago's cathedral of capitalism.

As I looked over the menu I wondered again why I was here as the Monday lunch guest of A & W's managing partner. The invitation had been delivered over the telephone last Friday by one of Richardson's secretaries. At the time, I had been reviewing the terms of a proposed divorce settlement with my client, the soon-to-be ex-wife of the Reverend Horace Bridges. Three months earlier she had arrived at my office, grim and revengeful, the morning after she had discovered her husband—unfrocked and speaking in tongues—between the plump thighs of a young Sunday-school teacher at his Baptist church. I had offered sympathy. She had instructed me to visit the wrath of the Lord on Reverend Bridges. And the resulting property settlement read, at least in part, as if it had been drafted by the God of the Old Testament.

My telephone started ringing just as Mrs. Bridges asked if her husband's large organ could be treated as marital property even though he had owned it prior to the marriage.

"He taught me how to use it," she had said, her fists clenched in the lap of her flower-print ankle-length dress, "and it has given me great pleasure over the years. After what he did to me, I don't think the Lord would want him to keep it."

"Excuse me," I said, fumbling for the telephone. "I'll have to answer this."

After I accepted the luncheon invitation, Mrs. Bridges resumed her request and, in response to my questions, revealed that her husband's instrument of pleasure was the product of the Hammond Organ Company and not the result of genetic largess. I added her husband's organ to the list of demands and told Mrs. Bridges we should meet again once her husband's attorney responded.

Now I sat gazing out the window while Ishmael Richardson placed our orders. Down below, across Michigan Avenue, young secretaries and clerks were sitting on the grass near the Art Institute, eating their take-out lunches or just lolling in the sun. Off in the distance—beyond the dark high-rise condominiums and the sluggish traffic on Lake Shore Drive—Lake Michigan sparkled under the glare of the August sun. A rainbow of sailboats bobbed in the waters of the Monroe Street Harbor.

"A pleasant view," said Richardson.

"Tempting," I answered.

"Occasionally," he said with a smile. Ishmael Richardson is made to order for the role of managing partner of a major corporate law firm. His face is tanned and deeply lined, his white hair is thick and wavy, and his eyes are a pale gray. "How is your practice, Rachel?"

"I'm busy enough," I answered.

"Wonderful," he said as he unfolded his napkin and placed it on his lap.

A silver-haired man in a gray pinstripe suit walked over to our table.

"Hello, Ishmael," he said.

"Hello, Charles. Good to see you."

"Who is this beautiful young lady?"

"Rachel Gold. Ms. Gold, this is Charles Winthrop. Mr. Winthrop is president of the Lake Michigan Bank."

"Hello, Miss Gold. Pleased to meet you."

"Same here."

We shook hands.

"Ms. Gold is a former associate of ours, Charles. She was part of our Bottles and Cans team. She is now out on her own."

Winthrop smiled at me. "Isn't that nice." He turned to Richardson. "You'll be at the board meeting this afternoon, won't you?"

"I will be there, Charles."

"We're going to take a hard look at the merger." He smiled at me. "Nice to meet you, young lady. Good luck in your practice."

I forced a "Thanks" and a smile. I was twenty-nine years old, a member of the Illinois bar, and the veteran of more than a dozen federal and state jury trials and appellate arguments. To Charles Winthrop I was still a girl.

Winthrop walked back to his table across the dining room. Most of the tables were occupied—lawyers and bankers and corporate executives cutting deals and plotting strategy over steaks and salads in a mock cathedral.

Ishmael Richardson lifted the club slip off the white tablecloth and removed a gold fountain pen from the inside pocket of his suit jacket. "Have you decided on lunch?"

"I'll go with your recommendation of the broiled whitefish. And I'll have a small salad. House dressing. Iced tea."

"Good choice," he said. He jotted down our orders and signaled for the waitress.

Ishmael Harrison Richardson had joined the

firm of Abbott, Windsor, Harrison, & Reynolds in 1939 after graduating, according to legend, with the fourth highest grade-point average in the history of Harvard Law School. The firm had consisted of six lawyers at the time. Now—almost a half century later and two names shorter—Abbott & Windsor had more than four hundred lawyers, with branch offices in Washington, D.C., Los Angeles, London, Taipei, and Riyadh. Eight years ago Richardson had been named managing partner—the law firm's equivalent of chairman of the board. He had turned seventy last April. The birthday party was held at the Union League Club, and the list of attendees included the Chief Justice of the United States Supreme Court, a former Vice-President of the United States, and the chief executive officers of several multinational corporations. The guest list took up half of Kup's column in the next day's *Sun-Times*.

Although he is the oldest active partner in the firm, Richardson looks and acts far younger than his age. During my last year with Abbott & Windsor, Ishmael Richardson had outlasted a fifty-year-old partner and two young associates from the New York firm of Milbank, Tweed, Hadley, & McCloy during marathon negotiations over the refinancing of a loan to one of Richardson's clients, Argentina. The three Wall Street lawyers had staggered out of the main conference room at 10:15 P.M. Richardson had remained in the conference room for an hour dictating the final modifications to the refinancing papers, and then had had his driver drop him off at his weekly poker game. They played poker every Wednesday night—Richardson and five name partners from Chicago's largest firms.

"Rachel," he said after the waitress had taken the club slip with our orders, "I asked you here to discuss a somewhat peculiar legal problem that has arisen. A rather sensitive matter." He pinched the knot of his club tie. His gold cuff links were initialed IHR in Old English script. "The Executive Committee of Abbott and Windsor has authorized me to retain you in connection with a matter we are handling."

"Should I be flattered or suspicious?"

"The former." Richardson smiled. "You still have many admirers at our firm. I happen to be one of them."

"Is it a conflicts problem?" I asked. Occasionally, large firms are prevented from representing several defendants in the same lawsuit because of a potential conflict of interest between some of the parties. In those situations, the firm will represent the best client—i.e., the largest corporation or the highest-ranking corporate officer—and refer the other clients to another law firm, preferably a firm too small to steal the referred client. Every large Chicago firm has a stable of small firms—usually composed of former members of the large firm—which it uses for conflicts matters. Abbott & Windsor had sent me two conflict cases during the past year.

"I suppose it does involve a potential conflict of interest, but not in the ordinary sense of the term," Richardson said. "Let me explain. It involves Graham Marshall. You are aware of his death?"

"I saw the obituary last month. I was shocked."

"So were we all." Richardson slowly shook his head. "A tragic loss."

We sat in silence for a moment.

"Did an associate find him?"

Richardson looked up, his gray eyes narrowing. "Why do you ask?"

"The obituary said he died in his office at night." I shrugged. "Just morbid curiosity, I suppose. I remember that Bill Phillips found Jean Huber."

Richard relaxed. "No, I don't believe an associate discovered him."

The salads arrived. Richardson paused until the waiter left. "As I was explaining, this matter involves Mr. Marshall. More precisely, it involves his estate. It is a rather unusual problem."

"Didn't the firm handle his will?"

"We did. Harlan Dodson prepared the will. There seems to be no problem there. However, Mr. Marshall executed a codicil to his will two years ago. Apparently without our knowledge. Certainly without our advice." He paused, leaning forward slightly. "Rachel, what I am about to describe is quite confidential. It is known to no one other than the members of the Executive Committee and Harlan Dodson, who is handling the estate."

I nodded.

"This codicil to Mr. Marshall's will establishes a forty-thousand dollar trust fund for the care and maintenance of a gravesite in a cemetery called Wagging Tail Estates."

"What kind of name is that for a cemetery?"

He paused. "It's a pet cemetery."

"A pet cemetery?" I kept a straight face.

Richardson frowned. "I am afraid so."

"Who's buried there?"

"That is your assignment."

"What do you mean?"

"The pet's name is Canaan, according to the codicil."

"A dog?"

"We don't know." Richardson shook his head. "Frankly, we have no idea. Harlan Dodson has asked Marshall's widow and children about the codicil. None of them knows a thing about it. None of them has ever heard of Canaan. Julia Marshall is quite allergic to dog and cat hair. The family has never owned a pet."

"Can't you just challenge the trust?"

"We could. It is what is known as an honorary trust, and it can be broken. But this particular trust has some features that make a court challenge, well, somewhat unattractive. For example, the codicil names me as co-trustee with Marshall's widow. More precisely, the co-trustee is to be the managing partner of the firm at the time of Marshall's death. The codicil instructs the managing partner not only to provide for the general care and maintenance of the gravesite but also to arrange for delivery of flowers to the grave—two dozen long-stemmed white roses—on four specified days each year." Richardson sighed and slowly shook his head. "I am to be paid at twice my normal hourly rate for these services. The trust remains in force until twenty-one years after the death of the last attorney who was a member of the Executive Committee at the time of Marshall's death."

"What happens then?"

"The remaining principal is to be paid to Abbott & Windsor."

I let it all sink in. "That's a weird trust," I finally said.

Richardson nodded. "It is indeed."

"It really puts the firm behind the eight ball."

"We are placed in a most awkward position. We are, of course, representing the Marshall family in winding up the estate. However, since my firm is the ultimate beneficiary of the trust, a challenge to the trust would benefit *only* the firm. An order voiding the trust would result in the trust funds being paid to the firm. Although forty thousand dollars is an insignificant amount for a firm with annual revenues of eighty-seven million dollars, I will not tolerate even the appearance that my firm would somehow profit at the expense of the Marshall family."

"You could solve that problem by transferring the trust moneys to the family," I said.

"Which is exactly what we would do, of course. If it comes to that. But to reach that stage may require us to first seek a court order voiding the trust."

"And a court order could mean a nasty story in the *Sun-Times*."

"Precisely." Richardson rested his fork on the salad plate. "There is another significant factor that must be considered: Mr. Marshall's desires. As eccentric as that trust may be, it is still his trust. Until we can ascertain what is in that grave and why he buried it in that pet cemetery, Mr. Marshall's wishes are entitled to respect."

"And you want me to find out what is in the grave," I said.

"Yes. And, if possible, why he buried it there. We need to determine the facts behind this peculiar codicil. Then we will be in a better position to evaluate the matter and advise the family."

"Why me?" I finally asked.

Richardson took a sip of his wine and set the glass back on the table. "This matter will require some investigation into the underlying facts." He smiled. "Excuse the pun. In any event, the Executive Committee feels it would be inappropriate to have one of our own associates intrude in the private affairs of one of our most senior partners. Similarly, we were uncomfortable turning the matter over to a complete outsider."

"And I'm more like a member of the clan."

"Precisely. You were with the firm, you worked extensively with Mr. Marshall in the Bottles and Cans litigation. We are confident you will handle the matter competently and with discretion." Richardson paused. "Frankly, Rachel, I view you more as my attorney on this matter. After all, I am co-trustee of this Canaan legacy. In addition, I am the individual designated by the codicil to oversee the care and maintenance obligations. For those reasons, the Executive Committee deferred to my selection of outside counsel. I recommended that you be retained." He took another sip of wine. "I was quite impressed with the way you handled that Anderson custody battle last summer."

The Anderson custody battle. Melanie Anderson had come to me three years after her divorce from a prominent North Shore real estate developer. Her ex-husband had decided to launch a custody war over their two children, and he hired the toughest domestic relations law firm in Chicago to wage his battle. Their mission was to overturn the original custody decree on the grounds that my client was unfit as a mother. The trial lasted five weeks, and was filled with allegations of lesbianism, child abuse, and drug addiction. The local media loved it, and *The New York Times* ran a story with two photos: one of Melanie and me entering the courtroom, and the other of her husband striding into the courtroom with his entourage of four male attorneys. One of my strategies was to fight fire with fire, but my investigator failed to turn up any dirt on her ex-husband. During the second week of trial, however, I received a midnight tip from an acquaintance in the FBI. I followed it up on my own over the weekend, and the next week was able to force her ex-husband to take the Fifth Amendment seven times in a row on cross-examination in response to my questions about his cocaine habit. I won the case, and the judge's verdict was affirmed on appeal. Melanie and her two children are still trying to put their lives back together. It was my first, and it will be my last, custody case.

"That's kind of you," I said. "Somehow I didn't think you were the type to follow a custody battle."

"Melanie Anderson is my niece," he said slowly.

"Oh."

"I told her to hire you, Rachel."

"I see," I finally said.

"And that is why I have come to you on this matter. Are you willing to take it on?"

The waiter removed our salad plates and set down the whitefish. I thought it over. The case didn't sound hard, and it was just weird enough to break up the monotony. I decided to accept it.

"Well, Mr. Richardson—"

"Ishmael."

"Okay . . . Ishmael." I smiled. "I'll give it a try."

"Excellent."

"Where is this Wagging Tail Estates?"

"It is located on the southwest side."

"I can get out there this afternoon. I'll see what I can dig up."

"Fine." Richardson smiled and reached into his suit jacket. "We need to have all the material facts before we advise Mrs. Marshall." He placed a cream-colored envelope on the table next to my plate. "This is a retainer in the amount of six thousand dollars."

"That's a lot of money."

"Perhaps. I assume you will bill us at your normal hourly rate and refund the balance, if any. Treat us as you would any client."

"I hope I can wrap it up in a few days."

"If so, fine. But this matter may take longer. As I explained, our preliminary investigation yielded nothing. We have had one telephone communication with the cemetery owner, but that was not fruitful. Perhaps you will have better luck with her. We prefer that you focus your inquiries on those outside of the immediate family. However, you may contact family members if you deem it necessary. As you can understand, Mrs. Marshall finds this topic somewhat distressing, particularly so soon after the loss of her husband." Richardson paused. "Graham Marshall was a respected member of our firm and our community. We feel a profound obligation toward him and his family. I am aware of your clashes with some of our partners during your years with us, but the Executive Committee shares my belief that you will handle this matter in a thorough and professional manner."

Ishmael Richardson lifted his fork and turned his attention to the whitefish. We spent the rest of the lunch searching without success for a conversational common ground. I left him in the lobby of the University Club after he agreed to send me a copy of Marshall's will and codicil.

The Yellow Pages listed an address and telephone number for Wagging Tail Estates. Someone named

Maggie Sullivan answered the phone on the third ring and told me she could see me that afternoon. I called my secretary and told her I'd be out most of the afternoon.

"A pet cemetery?" she said.

"Honest."

"Too bad. I thought old Ishmael was going to ask you out on a date."

"Come on, Mary."

"Hey, I think that old geezer had the hots for you back when we were at A and W."

"Mary, the only thing that turns him on are debentures. Any messages?"

"Nothing that can't wait till tomorrow."

I checked my wallet, flagged a Yellow Cab, and settled back in the seat as the cab lurched into traffic on Michigan Avenue. Three years ago I was working with Graham Anderson Marshall on the international antitrust case of *In re Bottles & Cans*. Now I was heading out to visit his pet's grave. A young lawyer's career on the rise. You're really moving up in the world, kiddo.

2

THE ENTRANCE TO WAGGING TAIL Estates is guarded
by two cement hunting dogs. They sit at eye level
on a pair of squat Doric columns that flank the
pathway into the cemetery. The dogs gaze aloofly
at the plumbing supplies store across the street
from the cemetery.

The main path into the cemetery branches off
into gravel footpaths between rows and rows of
granite tombstones and bronze grave markers. In
the middle of the cemetery stands a little New England chapel the size and shape of a two-car garage, with a small steeple on top. The chapel is
white, with the black silhouette of a dog painted
on the steeple. Beyond the chapel, at the far end
of the cemetery, a statue of Christ stands on a
grassy knoll. Above the statue's outstretched arms
the highway traffic rumbles by. Just off the main
path to my right an elderly couple were holding

hands in front of a grave marker. There were flowers on the grave.

I was a few minutes early, so I wandered down one of the footpaths. To a casual observer the place seemed like a human cemetery—a human cemetery, that is, where the dead preferred to be remembered by their nicknames. Each tombstone and grave marker bore the name of the pet (Pugs, Blackie, Cutie, Laddy), its dates of birth and death, an epitaph, and the names of its owners. Near the main path stood a large granite tombstone with the following legend:

BABY PRINCESS

7/2/76   11/30/84

Till we meet again,
We will be faithful and true,
'Cause no one in the whole wide world
Was loved as much as you.

MOMMY AND DADDY BROWN

I walked along the path, reading the epitaphs: "He Gave So Much and Asked So Little"; "Always a Lady"; "Our Beloved Baby"; "Mommy's Sweetie and Daddy's Boy—Our Little Boss"; "A Little Gentleman: Ever Loving and Faithful"; "So Small, So Sweet, So Soon"; "Momma's Itty-Bitty Poopie."

Some of the tombstones were crowned with miniature statues of the pets. A bronze beagle sat on top of a large slab of black marble; etched in the marble was a poem to the memory of Pugs:

As the chapel chimes softly ring,
Hark, hear those happy barks,

Pugs plays now where angels sing,
And pain's no longer in his heart.

There were framed photographs of the deceased on several tombstones and grave markers. Judging from the photographs, Wagging Tail Estates was the final resting place not just for dogs but also for cats, birds, a turtle, and a Shetland pony.

I checked my watch. It was time to meet Wagging Tail's owner and operator. She had told me her office was in the back of the chapel, just beyond something called the Slumber Room.

Following the pawprints in the cement pathway that led to the chapel, I tried to imagine what possibly could have brought Graham Anderson Marshall to Wagging Tail Estates. It was like finding a LaSalle Street trust officer at a professional wrestling match, standing on a folding chair and waving a Hulk Hogan pennant. I've owned pets, and I know the grief that can lead to a pet cemetery. But men like Graham Anderson Marshall don't bury pets in Wagging Tail Estates.

I walked through the front door of the chapel and into the Slumber Room. In the center of the darkened room a tiny black casket rested on a small wooden bier. The casket was open. Inside, a miniature poodle was arranged on a silk cushion, a white ribbon on its head and a rubber fire hydrant between its forepaws. One milky eye was open. I shuddered and moved on to the door at the back of the room. I knocked softly.

"It's open!" a hearty voice shouted from within.

I walked into the cluttered office, squinting in the bright light. A beefy woman was sitting behind the desk, slitting open her mail with what appeared to be a Bowie knife. She gave me a big grin.

"You must be the lawyer, right?"

I introduced myself and we shook hands. She had a strong grip.

"Well, glad to meet you, Rachel" she said. "I'm Maggie Sullivan. This here is my place. You get a chance to look around some?" She had bright green eyes, high cheekbones, and the beginnings of a double chin. Her frosted hair was set in that ubiquitous short-bouffant style of middle-aged mothers.

"I did. You have quite a place here."

She smiled and stood up. "I'm proud of it. Our tenth anniversary will be this October. We've come a long way since we buried my little girl out there ten years ago."

"Your little girl?"

"Patty. A cocker spaniel. A real sweetie. Carl and I looked around for a nice place to bury her. Didn't like what we saw. Too damn stuffy. So we started our own place out here. We love it. My Carl, bless his soul, joined her four years ago."

"Your husband is buried out there?" My God.

"He and two other folks. Don't look so shocked, honey. Nine families have bought plots out there. It's happening more and more. Check around and you'll see. Pat Blosser over at Paw Print Gardens— she's sold plenty of family plots. Hell, I'll be joining Carl and my little girl out there someday too. But not for a while. This old gal's in no hurry." She laughed and sat back down. "So I take it you didn't come out here to buy yourself a plot, huh?"

"No, not this time."

"Do you have a pet?"

"A golden retriever."

"Nice animal."

"The best."

"Well, what can I do for you?"

"I'm trying to find some information on a pet you may have buried out here. The name is Canaan. C-a-n-a-a-n."

"Canaan, huh? Sure is a lotta interest in that grave lately."

"What do you mean?"

"I've had two other calls on it this month."

Two? One must have been from someone at Abbott & Windsor; Ishmael Richardson had mentioned it. But who was the second caller?

"From whom?" I asked aloud.

"They wouldn't say."

"What did they want to know?"

"What was in the grave. When it was buried. What kind of records I had on it. That kind of stuff."

"What did you tell them?"

"That I didn't give out that kind of information over the phone. Especially to strangers. That's one of my rules. If they want to find out more, they have to come on down to my office."

"Did they?"

"Nope. Never heard from either guy again."

"Both were men?"

"Yep."

I frowned. "That's odd."

"Well, not really. I get a few calls like that each year."

"About Canaan?"

"Oh, no. About other graves. I get all kinds of calls. Someone wants to complain about the condition of the gravesite. Someone's ex-husband wants to know if the dog was wearing the diamond collar when it was buried." She chuckled. "Last winter a poor old man called after he read an article about cloning. He wanted to dig up his cat, cut off one of her legs, and try to find a scientist who could clone the cells and grow a perfect copy of her."

"Good heavens."

"I had him come down here."

"And?"

Maggie shook her head, smiling. "I talked him out of it, and then I called the local pet store. I found him a cute little kitten. He's happy as a clam these days."

I smiled. "That's sweet."

"Yeah." She paused to light a Camel cigarette with a kitchen match. "So what do you want to find out?"

"Whatever you know about Canaan. It was buried here by a Mr. Marshall. Graham Anderson Marshall."

"Just a sec." She reached up behind her and lugged a large blue ledger book off the shelf. "I got over six hundred pets out there. Let's see what I got on Canaan."

She leafed through the ledger book, running a thick forefinger slowly down each page. I stood up and walked over to the display shelves on the side wall. There were two rows of little coffins and a row of cremation urns. The sample coffins ranged from a simple Styrofoam box to a sleek stainless-steel model which was, according to the manufacturer's display card, "airtight, waterproof, and guaranteed until the Judgment Day." The urns included a little doghouse and a pint-size red fire hydrant. The back wall was decorated with news clippings, awards, letters of gratitude, certificates—all mounted and framed. Apparently, Maggie Sullivan had been president of the National Association of Pet Cemeteries several years back.

"Here we go," she said. "Marshall, Graham A."

"Pardon?"

"The grave. You're right. A Mr. Graham A. Marshall bought the plot. Oh, yeah, I remember that guy."

"What do you mean?" I asked.

She frowned. "Tell me something. What are you doing out here?"

"I've been asked to collect some facts about the pet."

"By him?"

"Well, indirectly," I answered. "By his partners."

"And what's that mean?"

"It's kind of complicated to explain. And very personal. I had hoped I could just come down here and—"

"Forget I asked." She rolled her eyes and chuckled. "Lawyers."

I smiled. "All I need to know is what's buried out there."

"It's not that easy. This Marshall guy—he's a real fruitcake."

"How so?" I asked.

"Real secretive. Wouldn't let me see his pet. Wouldn't even tell me what it was. He just showed up one day." She looked at the ledger book. "Back in May of 1986. Asked a lot of questions. Wanted to know what happened if I died or sold the place. What would happen to the grave and all. I explained the whole thing—about the NAPC and their rules and regulations, about how it would always be a pet cemetery. About the laws and all." She stubbed out the cigarette in the ashtray on her desk. "Well, he finally bought a casket—our top-of-the-line model. Asked me if it was waterproof. Then he asked me to show him the warranty." She shook her head and grinned. "Damn lawyers. Well, he finally bought it. But he took it with him. That was the weird part. Our clients either bring us the pet or have us pick it up. We have our own pickup service, you know. But this guy, this Marshall, he takes off with the casket and brings it back the next day, sealed shut. Wouldn't let that casket out of his sight. Watched us bury it. Didn't want a ceremony." She looked at me, puzzled, and then shook her head. "Never seen him since. Never visits the grave. But every year he sends me three hundred bucks for the care and maintenance of that grave. Between you and me, honey, I don't think that guy's got all his oars in the water."

"You really don't know what kind of pet it is?"

"Don't know a damn thing. I asked him when he first came out. Wouldn't tell me."

"Do you know where the grave is?"

"Sure. Let's see." She looked back in her book. "Number two thirty-nine. That would be . . . back and over . . . right. It's halfway down the first row to your right behind the chapel. What's up, sweetheart?"

I turned around to see a teenaged girl standing at the door, her hands in the back pockets of her faded blue jeans.

"The Johnsons just called, Mom. They'll be here tomorrow morning at nine."

"Good. That means I can get over to the zoo this afternoon." She turned back to me. "Brookfield Zoo. One of their hippos died on Saturday. You know, Gus the Hippo. It was in yesterday's papers. He had lots of fans. I called the zoo this morning and told them Wagging Tail would be honored to be his final resting place. Kind of took them by surprise. They've never had a funeral for one of their animals. I told them I'd handle all the arrangements. They're going to think it over and present it to their board. I'm going to go out there now to give them a goose. Wouldn't that be something?" She leaned forward, her eyes wide. "A hippo at Wagging Tail. What a catch!"

"Where do they have Gus now?" I asked.

"In a meat locker in Cicero. They offered him to the museum, to stuff and mount him for an exhibit. But I don't think the museum needs another hippo." She smiled. "I think I have the inside track on Gus. Can you imagine the media coverage this cemetery would get?"

"Front page, and the ten o'clock news." I was grinning.

"You better believe it, honey."

We both stood up.

"Good luck with the zoo, Maggie. And thanks for your time."

"No problem. That guy Marshall—he's an odd duck, that one. Sorry I wasn't more help."

I gave her my business card and told her to call me if she remembered anything else. She walked me to the back door, shook my hand, and slapped me on the back as I walked out.

My back was still smarting when I reached the gravesite. There was a small block of granite, on which was carved the following:

CANAAN
1985
A Nickname for Providence
Graham Anderson Marshall III

3

THE LAW FIRM OF ABBOTT & Windsor occupies the top six floors of the Lake Michigan Bank Building, one of the many modern skyscrapers on or near LaSalle Street that have transformed the less-is-more catechism of modern architecture into a more-or-less blight of steel and glass.

I took the express elevator to the forty-first floor and stepped out onto the beige carpeting of the main reception area. Everything looked familiar except the receptionist behind the large oak desk. When I left Abbott & Windsor, the receptionist was a former Playboy bunny. The senior partners eventually decided that her provocative torso clashed with the subdued decor of the reception area. No such problems with the bunny's replacement: Her gray hair was wrapped tightly in an unforgiving bun, and her breasts were bound and gagged beneath the protective camouflage of a suit jacket the same color as the carpeting.

Graham Marshall's secretary had apparently left word with the receptionist that I was to be sent down when I arrived. I had called her from the pet cemetery, explained that I was working for the firm, and told her I needed to take a look through Graham Marshall's office. The receptionist buzzed her to announce my arrival, and then waved me on after I said I knew my way around.

I walked down the long, carpeted corridor past the secretaries in their little cubicles. Some of them smiled at me with vague recollection. One of the partners—Hamilton Frederick—came out of his office as I walked past.

"Ah, Miss Gold," he said, pausing to light his pipe with a gold Dunhill lighter. "I haven't seen you on our floor for some time. I've been meaning to speak with you."

"Really?" I said. "About what?"

"It's that Carter case." He took the pipe out of his mouth and tamped it with a gold pipe tool. He'd put on a few pounds since I last saw him: the middle button on his navy-blue vest had already given way. "You'll be quite interested to know that we've decided to move for summary judgment on the fraud count." He obviously thought I still worked at Abbott & Windsor. "I'd like you and another associate to start working on the brief right away."

"Summary judgment?" This was fun. "That case is a loser, Ham." He hated that name. "Why don't you quit churning the file and settle that dog? Give the client a break."

"What!"

One of the secretaries giggled.

"Gotta run, Ham." I left him standing there, sputtering.

I rounded the corner and headed toward Marshall's corner office. The corridor walls were hung with the usual collection of abstract paintings, art show posters, and Andy Warhol ripoffs that have become *de rigueur* for corporate law firms.

Helen Marston was standing in the doorway of Graham Marshall's office. A tall, angular widow with short gray hair, she had been Graham Marshall's secretary for at least twenty years.

"Hello, Rachel." Helen smiled at me. Although she looked like the stern elementary-school teacher who patrolled the lunchroom with a ruler clenched in a bony fist, she was actually quite nice, in a formal sort of way.

"Hi, Helen." I paused. "I'm awful sorry about Mr. Marshall."

"Thank you, Rachel. You're very kind."

I looked around. "It's been a while."

"That it has. We miss you."

"I was afraid I wouldn't get here before five. I was out on the southwest side."

"I would have been willing to wait for you. I've stayed down late over the years more times than I care to remember. Come on inside. I'm afraid his things are already packed in boxes."

We went into Marshall's office. I walked over to the large window behind his oval glass-and-chrome desk. The sidewalks below were jammed with commuters and the streets were clogged with fat yellow cabs.

"Can I be of some help, Rachel?" Helen Marston stood by the couch.

"I'm working with the firm on some estate matters for Mr. Marshall. Very confidential, Helen.

Something to do with a pet called Canaan. Do you remember anything like that?"

She frowned in concentration. "Canaan? I'm not aware that Mr. Marshall ever owned a pet. I believe his wife is quite allergic to them."

"That's what I've been told. Maybe it was a friend's pet."

"Perhaps. He certainly never discussed any pet with me."

I glanced at the credenza. "I see they've already taken his computer." The dark outline of the terminal base was still visible on the wood surface of the credenza.

"They removed it three weeks ago."

Graham Marshall had been an early convert to the value of computer-based litigation support and had helped pioneer the law firm's use of computers in complex lawsuits. His own terminal had been tied in directly to the main Bottles & Cans computer. One of my stronger memories of the countless late nights I had spent at Abbott & Windsor during my years with the firm is the image of Marshall's terminal screen glowing green in his empty, darkened office.

"Who has it now?" I asked.

"I'm not sure. So far as I know, Calvin Pemberton has the only other terminal linked to the Bottles and Cans computer. Perhaps they'll give Mr. Marshall's terminal to Mr. Charles."

"Did you pack his things?" I asked.

"Yes. It was really quite sad." She sighed. "All those years." She ran her hand across the corner of his empty desk.

We were silent for a few moments.

"Would you mind if I looked through the boxes, Helen? Maybe there's a clue."

"Certainly."

"I promise to put everything back in order."

"Oh, you needn't worry. It's been a bit slow here. I'm just wrapping things up."

"Will you stay on?" I asked. I couldn't imagine her working for anyone else.

"I don't think so. I've been asked to stay on, but I can't imagine starting all over again with someone new." She smiled. "Mr. Marshall was more than enough for one lifetime." Helen moved to the door. "Well, I'll be out at my desk, Rachel. At least until six o'clock."

"Thanks, Helen."

"Did you find anything unusual while you were packing?" I asked.

She turned. "No. It's all there except for a few items. I found a few motions, some correspondence, and a draft of that brief he was working on the night he . . . the night he passed away. I sent them on to other lawyers who were working on the cases with him. His correspondence hasn't been unusual. He wasn't one for saving things. Very neat and orderly. He was quite proud of that."

"I remember," I said.

She left the room, and I sat down on the couch before the cardboard boxes. There were seven of them. I pulled open the first box. It was filled with framed photographs. There was one of Marshall, tuxedoed and grinning, shaking hands with Richard Nixon; it was signed, "To Graham Marshall—a fine American and first-rate attorney—Dick—3/15/70." In another photograph Marshall and Gerald Ford were huddled in conversation: Marshall was wearing a dark suit, and Ford, pipe in hand, was in shirtsleeves with his tie loosened. There was a recent family portrait: Marshall and his two children in tennis whites, grinning and holding rackets; his wife in a lavender sundress and gold necklace, looking vaguely attractive and very expensive. There were other photographs—Marshall shaking hands with Chief Justice Warren Burger, toasting Senator Charles Percy, playing golf with Congressman Daniel Rostenkowski. Not a hint of a pet.

The next five boxes contained books—law books, history books, books of quotations, a dictionary. I flipped through several. Nothing unusual.

The final box apparently contained the contents of his desk: pencils, pens, a tin of Dunhill pipe tobacco, three pipes, scissors, stapler, legal pads, letter opener, and the like.

As I sorted through the boxes, I thought again about that peculiar gravestone: "A Nickname for Providence." And that name. Canaan? Promised land? An odd name for a pet. I reached into the second box and pulled out Marshall's dictionary, an old leather-bound edition. I flipped to the entry for "Canaan":

> **Canaan** (Kā′ nən). **1.** The fourth son of Ham and the grandson of Noah. **2.** In biblical times, the part of Palestine between the Jordan River and the Mediterranean Sea; the Promised Land. **3.** A small village in Massachusetts, founded in 1679 by Reverend Winthrop Marvell and disbanded in 1698.

I copied the definitions onto a sheet of yellow legal paper, folded the sheet, and put it into my briefcase.

"Rachel?" Helen Marston was at the door.

I gestured at the boxes. "Not much help here."

"I've been sitting at my desk," she said, "trying to remember."

"And?"

"I still don't remember a pet, but I think Mr. Marshall had a client named Canaan."

"Really?"

"Perhaps. I can't seem to recall who it was. But I remember working on something involving something called Canaan."

"What do you remember?" I asked.

"Almost nothing. This was a few years back. Let's see . . . 1984 or 1985, I believe. Mr. Marshall devoted many hours to it. There were evenings, weekends."

"Is there a file on it?"

"I have no idea." She studied me. "There was something about that project that seemed fishy."

"In what way?"

"Mr. Marshall handled *everything* on that matter himself. If there was a file, he kept it in his office. I may have typed a few things for it, but everything went back to him. He specifically instructed me to keep no copies of anything pertaining to Canaan." She paused. "Mr. Marshall always was high-handed. As you know, he made his own rules. But these Canaan procedures were quite irregular even for him."

"Is there a way to check if there's a file on this Canaan?"

"I'll ask the Inactive Files Department tomorrow. A file that old is probably in the warehouse. But they should be able to locate it with the computer. I'll ask first thing tomorrow."

"Terrific, Helen. I'd appreciate it. But try to make your inquiries sort of vague. Ishmael Richardson told me he wants this investigation confidential."

"Of course, dear. I should have an answer by noon."

"I'll check in then. While you're at it, Helen, ask them to look for a file on Maggie Sullivan. There might be a connection."

Helen nodded and went back to her desk. I stood up and took one last look around the large office. No doubt the next partner in line was packed and ready to move in. The death of a senior partner was the starting signal for the Abbott & Windsor version of musical chairs. Several lawyers below the rank of the dead partner would lurch one space closer to the goal: a corner office with a view of the lake. By the end of this week some mid-level associate would be leaving his windowless "inside" office and moving into an "outside" office with one narrow window facing the dull tangle of expressways and warehouses of the west side of Chicago. That "outside" office would have been vacated by a senior associate or junior partner in favor of a slightly larger office with two windows facing the north side or south side. And that office, in turn, would have been vacated by a senior-level partner who would now lay claim to the treasured corner office of Graham Anderson Marshall, to have and hold until death do them part.

It was a nice office, with a view of Lake Michigan and Buckingham Fountain. I moved to the large window. From forty-one stories up, the giant Calder sculpture down in Federal Plaza looked like a discarded rusting paper clip.

4

I LEFT GRAHAM MARSHALL'S OFFICE. On my way down
the hall I passed Calvin Pemberton's office. Kent
Charles was standing by the door.

"Well, look who's here," he said with a smile,
"the Miss Illinois of the American Bar Association."

"Hi, Kent."

"Haven't seen you for a long time, Rachel. Not
since you left us. How you been?"

"Not bad."

"Cal and I were just talking about your favorite
case. Bottles and Cans. You have a minute?"

"I guess."

I followed Kent into Cal's office. Cal Pemberton
was sitting on the couch.

"Hi, Cal."

"Hello, Rachel."

I sat down on the chair facing the desk and scooted it around toward the couch.

Cal Pemberton was wearing a brown three-piece suit, vest buttoned, and a dark bow tie. Kent had his suit jacket off and his club tie loosened.

"So you two are going to run Bottles and Cans?" I asked.

"We're going to give it a try," Kent said as he walked behind the desk and sat against the credenza. He rested his arm on top of Cal's computer terminal. "Cal and I were just going over some strategies for the next round of depositions."

Kent Charles and Cal Pemberton were the two young heavy-hitters in the litigation department. Both specialized in antitrust litigation, although Kent also had a growing practice in white-collar crime. Kent was in his early forties; Cal was in his late thirties. Although paired together under Graham Marshall on the Bottles & Cans litigation for more than a decade—long enough for people to think of them as a unit, like Siamese twins—they were an odd couple.

Kent Charles was a dark and athletic study in aggression. He had played linebacker for the University of Illinois football team. He was first-string his junior and senior years, even though his height and weight—six feet, 195 pounds—made him one of the smallest linebackers in the Big Ten. Illini fans at Abbott & Windsor claimed he had been a ferocious hitter with a reputation for head-spearing running backs and clothes-lining receivers.

He had that reputation in his law practice too. Kent thrived on combat, and sought it out even in otherwise friendly lawsuits—by noticing motions to be heard on the day after Thanksgiving or Christmas (thereby ruining his opponent's holiday), by objecting to routine requests for extensions of court deadlines, by overwhelming opponents with interrogatories and document requests, by antagonizing witnesses and attorneys during depositions. He was savvy enough to pull it off—no easy task considering the number of lawyers in Chicago who were just waiting for the chance to get even with Kent Charles. Most would never get the chance. Kent Charles combined a total commitment to trial preparation with an uncanny ability to find his opponent's jugular vein in a lawsuit while disguising his own. Clients, of course, loved him—as clients love any litigator who provides a vicarious outlet for their own aggression. Kent Charles was the quintessential hired gun.

By contrast, Cal Pemberton was the crafty schemer. If Kent Charles went for the jugular with a switchblade, Cal Pemberton dissected capillaries with a surgical laser. To Cal Pemberton, a lawsuit was a game of chess. He could sit alone in his office for hours, staring out the window, idly twisting a lock of his unkept hair as he plotted moves and countermoves months and even years into the future. He rarely explained the purpose behind the obscure research assignments he gave to younger associates; as a result, the confused and frustrated associate would spend days in the firm's library researching an issue that seemed to bear no relation to the lawsuit. But then, two years later, during the fourth day of a deposition, while Cal's opponent stifled a yawn and checked his watch for the tenth time that hour, Cal would elicit a series of answers from an unsuspecting deponent which, when coupled with the earlier research project, would permanently alter the course of the lawsuit, and always to the advantage of Cal's client. It took clients a long time to warm up to Cal Pemberton and his labyrinthine strategies, but once they did they insisted that he handle all of their cases.

Like any good commander, Graham Marshall had exploited the best that Cal and Kent had to offer. To Cal Pemberton, the bespectacled and brilliant loner, he assigned the byzantine litigation strategies that turned on subtle points of law and seemingly insignificant facts. To Kent Charles, the poor boy from Joliet who had battled his way into the rarefied atmosphere of the large corporate law firm, Marshall assigned the toughest depositions, the nastiest motions, the angriest clients. Kent Charles was clearly Marshall's favorite, his loyal and enthusiastic disciple. Batman and Robin, the firm's pundits called Kent Charles and Graham Marshall—never to their faces. If Cal Pemberton was jealous, he never let on.

Their personal lives were a study in contrasts also. Kent Charles played handball every day at the Union League Club; Cal Pemberton played bridge Wednesday evenings at the Tavern Club. Cal lived in the western suburbs with his shy, plain housewife and his shy, plain son. He was twenty pounds overweight and his curly brown hair was receding on top and usually in need of a trim everywhere else. Kent Charles lived alone in a highrise on the Gold Coast. His second wife—a stewardess—had been killed three years before in a midair collision over San Diego. After a remarkably brief period of mourning—which included according to the firm's rumor mill, intimate ministrations from the wife of a tax partner who was out of town for a few days after the funeral—Kent had become again one of Chicago's most eligible and active bachelors. That he was a widower seemed to make him even more alluring.

And Kent was, I had to admit, a hunk: dark blue eyes; thick black hair combed straight back; tanned face; dark mustache; even, white teeth. As I turned toward him, I felt—as always—that I was in the den of a charming but hungry carnivore.

"I hear you're working on Graham Marshall's estate," Kent said, glancing at my legs.

"And I hear you're dating the weather girl on Channel Nine," I answered quickly, trying to mask my surprise. How did he know about my assignment already?

Kent grinned. "Rumors. I've never even met her."

"Guess you can't believe everything you hear these days," I said.

Cal squinted. "Is there a problem with Mr. Marshall's estate?"

I shrugged. "Not that I know of," I said, glancing at Kent.

"Let me explain," Kent said. "Someone saw you today at lunch with Ishmael Richardson over at the University Club. Four hours later you're here in Graham's office looking through his personal belongings." Kent smiled and raised his hands. "We're not spying on you, Rachel. It's just that Hamilton Frederick stormed into my office thirty minutes ago demanding that I—how did he put it?—demanding that I reprimand you for failing to show proper respect to a partner. He claims you refused a drafting assignment from him. Worse yet, he said you were insolent."

I feigned shock. "Me? Insolent?"

Kent chuckled. "That pompous clown thinks you still work here. Since I'm on the associate compensation committee, he wanted to register a complaint. I'm afraid you're no longer within my jurisdiction."

"Be sure to tell Ham that I'm sorry I can't help him on that case," I said with a smile as I got up to leave.

"If you have any questions about Graham," Kent said, "give either one of us a call. Graham meant a lot to both of us."

I walked back toward the main reception area. A few secretaries were still at their desks, earning overtime. Most of the lawyers were still in their offices. Like most large law firms, Abbott & Windsor never closes down. There are lawyers there at all hours of the night and day. The word processing department and the copy center run on three shifts around the clock. A special typing pool starts work at eight o'clock at night. In a closet off the coffee room there are five rollaway beds. There is a private shower on each floor, stocked with shampoo, deodorant, shaving cream, disposable razors, and fresh towels. I was glad to be leaving.

While waiting for the elevator I studied the piece of metal that "graced" the forty-first floor entrance to Abbott & Windsor. Art dealers in Chicago view senior partners of law firms as easy marks; over the years they have solemnly unloaded their garbage on them at exorbitant prices. Walk into any big Chicago law firm and you will find a large piece of tortured stainless steel, complete with bronze plaque, squatting in the lobby.

"Hey, gorgeous!" The voice was unmistakable.

"What are you doing loose?" I said, turning around. "Don't tell me you made bail on that morals charge?"

"Bail? Shit, Rachel, you think that sheep is going to testify against me? Believe me, she felt the earth move."

We were both grinning.

"How are you doing, Benny?" I asked.

"Same old shit, Rachel. You know the story."

"I know."

"Where you going?" he asked.

"Back to my office," I said.

"Wanna grab a bite to eat?"

"Sure. Let me just stop by my office for phone messages. You never know. General Motors may have finally seen the light and decided to hire a good lawyer."

"I'll keep you company. This place is driving me crazy," he said.

"I know the feeling."

"And anyway, I got some weird info on Graham Marshall that might interest you."

"Not you too. I thought everything was hush-hush."

Benny gave me a big grin. "Rachel, the omnipresent Benny Goldberg knows all. How do you think I've survived with these goyim? And anyway"—he winked—"I've got something on Marshall you're gonna love."

5

BENNY AND I WALKED DOWN Monroe Street to Dearborn. The sun was to our backs, and there was a cool breeze coming off the lake. The last of the commuters brushed past us hurrying toward the train stations, squinting into the setting sun. We turned north on Dearborn and walked by the First National Plaza. The outdoor café on the Plaza was filled with young couples sipping wine coolers. In the shadows of the Plaza the Chagall mosaic looked like a giant slab of moldy cream cheese, splotched with pastel greens and blues.

"When are you going to marry me, Rachel?"

"Benny, don't start that again. You know my mother wants me to marry a nice Jewish doctor."

"Hey, I'm a juris doctor. What's that? Chopped liver?"

Benny Goldberg was an anomaly at Abbott & Windsor, a chubby Jew among tall, athletic Wasps.

Unlike the typical Abbott & Windsor lawyer, whose language complied with the television networks' code of decency, Benny's profanity was astonishing, apparently inspired by his chronic bowel disorders.

Benny also had a first name that sounded like a first name and a last name that sounded like a last name. This, too, put him in the minority at Abbott & Windsor, where most of the lawyers had interchangeable first and last names. The firm's letterhead included Sterling Grant, Hamilton Frederick, Ishmael Richardson, Porter Edwards, Hayden James, Baker Scott, Townsend Ward, and—until recently—Graham Marshall. And centered at the top of the letterhead, the long-dead founding partners: Kendall Abbott and Evans Windsor.

Benny had been with Abbott & Windsor since he graduated near the top of his class at Columbia Law School six years ago. His longevity at the firm was due to a Mexican standoff between the firm's need for Benny's brain and the firm's discomfort with everything that housed, fed, and transported that brain. Up until Graham Marshall's death, the equilibrium had started shifting in the firm's favor as Benny began approaching partnership age. Under ordinary circumstances Benny had no future at Abbott & Windsor beyond his thirtieth birthday. An Ishmael Richardson or a Townsend Ward would shudder at the prospect of introducing Benny to a client as "my partner, Ben Goldberg."

But Marshall's death had shifted the odds. Benny now knew more about *In re Bottles & Cans* than anyone else at the firm, with the possible exception of Marshall's two aides-de-camp, Kent Charles and Calvin Pemberton. At least until some other senior associate could get up to speed in that litigation—a lawsuit which brought more than $6,000,000 a year in fees to the firm—Benny's position was secure.

"I don't have any illusions," Benny said as we crossed Madison Street. "Someone like Richardson would rather be proctoscoped with an electric cattle prod than have me as a partner. Believe me, they'll figure out some way to make sure my shoes aren't shined."

The shoeshine was another Abbott & Windsor tradition. Twice a week Harold (the shoeshine "boy") made his rounds of the partners' offices, providing one of the perks of partnership. Each spring, during a secret meeting, the partners selected the new partners from among the ranks of the seventh-year associates. Harold would be notified later that evening. Word of the meeting usually leaked by nine o'clock the next morning, and all seventh-year associates would begin the nervous vigil known as "waiting for Harold." If you were up for partnership that year, the appearance of Harold at your office door, smiling and asking whether you needed a shine, was the Abbott & Windsor equivalent of divine grace. During my last year at Abbott & Windsor, one high-strung senior tax associate cracked up after Harold, eyes averted, passed his office. Three associates had to wrestle him away from the window he was trying to break with his briefcase.

"I wouldn't worry about that, Benny," I said. "You wear Hush Puppies, anyway."

"Shit, I'm not worried, Rachel," Benny said. "My résumé is on the street, anyway. I think I may even get an offer from DePaul. They really liked that law review article I wrote for them last year."

By the time we got to the elevator of my building

I had decided I wanted to tell Benny about my assignment from Ishmael Richardson and my trip to the cemetery. I knew I wasn't supposed to tell anyone, but I needed someone to talk to about it—and that someone wasn't Ishmael Richardson. Anyway, I swore Benny to secrecy and briefly filled him in during the ride up to my floor.

I unlocked the door and we walked through the tiny reception area to my office. Mary had already gone home. Benny plopped down on the couch while I leafed through the phone messages on my desk. Nothing important. I looked out the window down on the Daley Plaza, where the rust-brown Picasso sculpture stood, huge and isolated. It looked less like a work of art than a bizarre spoof on Soviet technology: an early Russian attempt to mass-produce IUDs, eventually abandoned due to impracticalities of size.

"So," I said, turning back to Benny, "your turn. What's your scoop on Marshall?"

"Did you read the obituaries?"

"Uh-huh."

"Did they mention where he died?"

"In the office."

"Yep. Well, Lou Cohen is a resident over at Northwestern Memorial. The cardiac emergency unit. We grew up together. Next-door neighbors." Benny had grown up in South Orange, New Jersey.

"Okay. So?"

"He saw the obituary too. And it didn't jibe with what he knows about Abbott and Windsor."

"What didn't jibe?" I asked.

Benny was grinning. "Lou didn't think that partners at Abbott and Windsor come to work in skin-diving suits."

"What are you talking about, Goldberg?" I asked.

"You heard me."

"Are you telling me Marshall was wearing a rubber suit when they brought him to the hospital?"

"You got it, Rachel. And judging from the evidence, he wasn't working on a brief when he died."

"Oh?"

"Nope. He was getting laid. Getting his goddamn ashes hauled in an orange rubber suit."

"You've got to be kidding me, Benny." We were both laughing. "Marshall in a rubber suit? My God, that's like . . . like Charles Bronson in fishnets and spike heels."

Benny nodded his head. "It's the truth. Lou saw the obituary and then he went back to check the ambulance log. They didn't pick him up at the office. They got him over at Shore Drive Tower."

"From whom?" I asked.

"Someone named Reynolds. C. Reynolds."

I jotted it down on a yellow legal pad.

"Rachel, this stuff is confidential. Lou swore me to secrecy."

"No promises, Benny."

"Screw you. Anyway, I thought you might find it interesting."

"Do you know this Reynolds's first name?" I asked.

"Nope. Probably some chick."

"First name starts with a C, huh?"

"That's what he said."

I picked up the telephone directory and flipped to the listings for Reynolds. There was a listing for Reynolds, C., at Shore Drive Tower. I jotted down the number.

"Think she had a pet named Canaan?" Benny asked, running his fingers through his curly black hair. He stood up, walked over to my bookshelf, and picked up the dictionary. "It means Promised Land, I think." He sat back down with the dictionary open on his lap. "Here it is. Let's see. Canaan. 'The fourth son of Ham and the grandson of Noah.' What kind of name is Ham for a nice Jewish boy?"

"Read on," I said.

"Okay. Here we go: 'In biblical times, the part of Palestine between the Jordan River and the Mediterranean Sea; the Promised Land.' Some name for a mutt, huh?"

"Keep reading," I said.

"That's it."

"No. There should be one more definition."

"Not here," said Benny, handing me the dictionary.

I read the definitions slowly. "Wait a minute." I reached into my briefcase and pulled out my notes.

"What are you talking about?" asked Benny.

"I checked the definitions over at Abbott and Windsor. Marshall's dictionary. I even wrote them down."

"So?"

"There was a third definition in Marshall's dictionary. Listen." I read from my notes: " 'A village in Massachusetts, founded in 1679 by Reverend Winthrop Marvell and disbanded in 1698.' "

"Big deal," said Benny. "Different dictionary, different definitions."

"Same word, though."

"Maybe you copied the wrong definition, Rachel."

"I don't think so." I frowned. "I'll check it tomorrow. I'm supposed to drop by the firm around noon."

"Read me that definition again," said Benny.

I read it to him.

"Canaan, Massachusetts?" said Benny. "Never heard of it. I knew a couple of preppies from *New* Canaan, Connecticut. Real douche bags. But I never heard of a Canaan." Benny walked to the window. "It's a weird name for a pet."

"You still hungry?" I asked.

"Still hungry? I'm starving. Let's get out of here. I'm ready to put on the feed bag."

I put my notes into my briefcase, turned out the lights, and locked up. We flagged a cab and headed up to the Oxford Pub for a hamburger and beer.

Once we placed our orders, I went over to the pay phone and called C. Reynolds at Shore Drive Tower. She answered on the third ring, sounding pleasant but a little distracted. I introduced myself, vaguely explained my relationship to Graham Marshall and Abbott & Windsor, and asked if I could have thirty minutes of her time tomorrow morning to ask a few questions.

She hesitated, I persisted, and finally she agreed. "Suit yourself, lady," she said. "Drop by around ten tomorrow morning. I can give you fifteen minutes."

6

ON MY WAY DOWN TO Shore Drive Tower Tuesday morning I stopped at a bookstore on Michigan Avenue. I found an atlas in the travel section and studied the maps of New England. There were Canaans all over the East—in Connecticut, New Hampshire, Vermont, Maine, and New York. There was even a Canaan in Mississippi. But no Canaan in Massachusetts. I wandered over to the history section and skimmed the indexes of several books on Colonial America. No mention of Canaan, Massachusetts. I checked every dictionary in the bookstore. No reference to Canaan, Massachusetts.

I walked across Grant Park toward Shore Drive Tower, squinting in the bright morning sun. A couple was playing tennis on the center court. The woman, her back to me, was built like Harmon Killibrew, and she swung her racket, two-fisted, as if it were a Louisville Slugger. Her opponent chased her wild shots with the stiff-legged gait of middle age. Leaning against a lamppost, I watched them play for a few minutes. A pigeon strutted past, its head bobbing.

About thirty yards away, a fat Park District employee methodically stabbed paper cups and other litter with a steel pole and deposited his catch in a black plastic bag. I watched the tennis couple volley until she hit a shot off the handle into the next court, and then I walked on to Shore Drive Tower.

The guard inside called C. Reynolds on the house phone, spoke briefly, and then buzzed me in. I took the mirrored elevator to the eighteenth floor and stepped off into the carpeted hallway. The elevator door slid closed behind me with a muffled sigh. I rang the bell to Apartment 18B.

She opened the door and I introduced myself. We shook hands. She was beautiful—gorgeous—in a Midwest cheerleader sort of way. Pug nose, freckles, pouty lips, perfect white teeth. Her blue eyes were still puffy from sleep, and her blond hair was partially covered by a red and white bandanna. She was in her mid-twenties.

"Well, come on in, Miss Gold," she said, smiling stiffly. "Make yourself at home."

She was wearing an old blue terry-cloth robe that was at least two sizes too big. Her bare feet showed below the bottom of the robe. We walked through the small foyer into her living room.

"I'm gonna get some coffee," she said. "Want some?"

"Sure. Thanks."

"How do you take it?"

"Black. And you can call me Rachel."

She stared at me, and her face relaxed just a little. "Okay. And I'm Cindi. With an *i* at the end."

She left me in the living room and walked into the modern white kitchen. A butcher-block countertop bar separated the two rooms. The living room was bright and cheerful. There were two healthy Boston ferns hanging in front of the large picture window and a pair of areca palms flanking a cream-colored couch. The off-white walls were decorated with chrome-framed prints of art exhibits.

"This is a lovely place," I said, looking out the window at the scalloped beaches along the Gold Coast.

I sat down on the love seat opposite the couch and scanned the magazines spread out on the glass and chrome coffee table. She had eclectic tastes. There was a *New Republic*, a *Vogue*, a *Penthouse*, a *Newsweek*, a *Daedelus*, a *New Yorker*, an *American Scholar*, and a *Harvard Law Review*.

"Here you go." She came in carrying two steaming mugs and handed me one.

"Thanks."

She sat down on the couch, took a sip from her mug, and rested it on the table. Leaning back, she shoved her hands into the deep pockets of her robe.

"Did you work with Graham?" she asked.

"For a while."

"Bottles and Cans?"

"As a matter of fact, yes. How did you know?"

"Graham specialized in litigation." She shrugged and reached for her mug. "I know many litigators." She took another sip of coffee and settled back with the mug on her lap. "Sometimes they talk to me about their cases, and occasionally I listen." She turned her head toward the window.

"He was here the night he died?"

She turned back and stared at me. "Is that a question?"

I shrugged. "Only partly. The hospital records indicate he was picked up here."

She turned again toward the window. "Well, that's true. He was here. I called the ambulance."

"I take it your relationship with him was . . . uh . . . professional," I said.

"That's correct," she said. Her large eyes were a deep blue, almost violet.

"Did he ever talk about his personal life?"

"Not much," she said. "That's why I told you I didn't think I'd be much help."

"Would you mind if I asked you some questions anyway? We're trying to wrap up a few loose ends."

Cindi sighed. "Sure. Go ahead." She lifted her long slender legs and rested them on the table. "Tell me, are you still with Abbott and Windsor?"

"Only as far as this matter is concerned. I left the firm a few years back."

"How come?"

"Hard to say," I said. "It seemed like the right thing to do."

"What do you mean?"

"There were a lot of little things."

"Like what?"

"The clients. All those big corporations fighting over money." I shrugged. "It seemed kind of trivial. So I decided to go into practice on my own."

"Sounds very noble. And not very true," she said, smiling. She had dimples.

I smiled too. "You're right, I guess." I took a sip

of coffee. "Mostly, I was just bored. Do you know the saying, You're either on the bus or off the bus?"

"Sure."

"Well, around my fourth year at Abbott and Windsor I realized I was off the bus. Some people like it that way—sitting by the side of the road, joking about all the bozos on the buses that go rumbling by." I sighed. "But it's not a good way to live. You end up playing to an audience of one: yourself. It gets depressing real quick. Well, when I realized I was off the bus"—I shrugged—"I decided to find another one."

"Did you?" Cindi asked.

"I think so. I have a nice practice—interesting work, decent clients, and I don't have to put up with the usual BS from senior partners. It's not quite a bus, yet. More like a sub-compact."

Cindi smiled. "Any regrets?"

"Some. Everything's a tradeoff." I worked on my coffee. "Sometimes I wish I had some young associate to do the legal research. But I like being on my own. Particularly when I'm in a case up against a firm like Abbott and Windsor."

She nodded her head, smiling. "Good for you." She took another sip of coffee and then frowned. "So, why are you here?"

"Abbott and Windsor is handling Marshall's estate. They've retained me to clear up a few things. For one, how long did you know Marshall?"

"About two years."

"How many times did you two . . . er . . . see each other?"

She thought for a moment. "Approximately twice a month for the last six months or so. Alternate Wednesdays. Before that, maybe once a month."

"What kind of things did you talk about?"

She smiled. "Well, other than the particular logistics for the evening's events, just the usual stuff. The weather, the Bears, the news. He sometimes would talk about one of his lawsuits in a vague way—a deposition, an appellate argument, some motion pending in *In re Bottles and Cans*."

"Did he ever mention something called Canaan?"

"Canaan?" She frowned in thought. "No, not that I remember."

"A pet?"

"No."

"Have you ever had a pet named Canaan?"

She shook her head. "I've never heard of Canaan."

"Anything else that you remember talking about? Anything at all?" I asked.

"No, I don't think so." She paused. "When we first met he used to ask me about the pageant. I don't know why he kept harping on it."

"What pageant?"

She blushed. "The beauty pageant. Ms. United States."

"I don't understand."

"I was in it, Rachel. Back in 1985. Back before I met Graham. You're talking to the third runner-up."

"No kidding."

"Yep. I was Ms. Illinois, 1985." She grinned.

"Congratulations."

"It seems like another lifetime."

"You enter many pageants?"

"Not anymore." She finished her coffee. "I

started my glorious career at six months. I was named cutest baby in Peoria. You know, one of those baby-picture contests the newspapers sponsor. Bare tush and a big toothless grin."

"Great."

Cindi stood up. "I'm gonna grab some yogurt and fruit. You hungry?"

"No, thanks."

She paused, and then smiled. "Let me give you something to look at." She walked into the bedroom and returned with a well-worn scrapbook, which she set on the coffee table. Her name was engraved in gold leaf on the cover: Cynthia Ann Reynolds. She leaned over and opened it to the first page.

"Feast your eyes," she said, pointing to the first page. "I'll be right back."

I leaned forward to look at the faded newspaper clipping from the Peoria *News*. BABY CYNTHIA—THIS YEAR'S CUTEST TYKE read the headline over the photograph of a smiling baby lying on her stomach, wearing nothing but a ribbon around her neck. Next to the clipping someone had hand-printed the following: "3/12/63—P.N.—Cynthia has won her first contest! Only the beginning for my cute little princess!"

Cindi returned carrying a cup of plain yogurt and an apple. She took a large bite out of the apple as she sat back down on the couch, tucking a leg under her. She smoothed her robe over her lap.

"My mother," Cindi explained, pointing to the writing. "The last of the great pageant mothers. She totally planned my career. Tap-dancing lessons at five, for the talent competitions. Dermatologists, dance classes, charm school, music lessons, modeling class—you name it. Bedtime stories about pageants to come." Cindi shook her head. "We were a real pair of clichés, my mother and I. She kept this scrapbook, filling it with newspaper clippings. When she died last year, I brought it back with me."

"She must have been proud."

"Sure. I was the beautiful princess she never could be." There was a trace of bitterness in her voice. "Classic textbook case, right? Klutzy fathers make jocks out of their sons. Homely mothers make their daughters beauty queens."

"My mother wanted me to be the wife of a nice Jewish doctor," I said. "Still does. And my father wants me to learn how to cook a tzimmes like his mother."

I flipped slowly through the scrapbook. Little Miss Peoria—five years old in a short dress, patent leather shoes, and a sunbonnet. Camp Wallawalla Queen for a Day. Homecoming Queen, Peoria High School. And then the big time. Miss Southern Illinois, Miss Cornbelt, Miss Heartland, University of Illinois Homecoming Queen, and then Ms. Illinois. News clippings for each, and hand-printed notes by her mother, loaded with exclamation marks— "We did it! My princess was wonderful! The judges loved her!"

"This is impressive," I said. "Did you really tap-dance for the talent part?"

"Sure. When I was little it was perfectly adorable. And once I reached puberty the male judges loved it. Lots of jiggling."

I turned to the last page. Ms. United States. The headline read: NEW MS. UNITED STATES CROWNED; MISS ILLINOIS THIRD RUNNER-UP. In the picture Cindi was hugging the newly crowned queen. The defeat had been hard on her mother. No notes, no exclama-

tion marks. Just the essentials: "7/28/85 C.H.T.—
Third Runner-up."

"What does C.H.T. mean?"

"*Chicago Herald Tribune*. That's where the article's from. The July twenty-eighth edition of the
Herald Tribune."

"That's my birthday." I read the article. "Third
runner-up. That's not bad."

"I was lucky it wasn't fourth runner-up after the
way I screwed up."

"What happened?"

"I made it to the finals. Then came the part
where each of us was asked one question. The idea
is to see who has grace under pressure, or some
baloney like that. Which is ridiculous, anyway,
since you give the same answer no matter what
you're asked."

"I don't follow."

"You plan your answer ahead of time. Something really patriotic and tear-jerking."

"Did you?"

"Sure. Mine was the social-worker-in-the-cancer-
ward-of-a-children's hospital shtick. Then, no matter what I would be asked, that was the answer. If
they asked me what my future plans were, I'd say
I wanted to be a social worker in the blah, blah,
blah. If they asked me what I'd do to make this
country better, I'd say I'd train social workers and
put them in blah, blah, blah. If they asked me what
I'd do during my reign as Ms. United States, I'd
say I'd spend my days visiting the cancer wards of
children's hospitals, blah, blah, blah. Get the idea?
Total bullshit delivered in a trembling voice."

"Okay," I said, smiling. "So what happened?"

"Well, the emcee called my name and I walked
over to the microphone. He said a few cutesy

things and then he held up the card and read the questions. 'Cynthia,' he said, 'if an alien from outer space landed in the center of your hometown and asked to see the one thing that typified the spirit of Peoria, what would you show him?' The question was a cinch. And I had the answer ready. You know, I'd take the alien to the cancer ward in the children's hospital, blah, blah, blah. But I didn't say anything at first." She frowned, crinkling her nose. "It was weird. Have you ever been talking with someone and suddenly become aware of your own voice? Like you've stepped out of yourself and you're watching yourself talk, and your voice sounds odd, and the words stop making any sense? Or maybe someone is talking to you and you suddenly are noticing the hairs sticking out of his nose or the perspiration on his upper lip, or you even begin to watch yourself standing there listening to him?"

"Sure."

"Well, something like that happened. I started thinking, which, believe me, is never a good thing to do when you're one of the finalists. I realized how my whole life had been leading up to this stupid question from this little jerk. All those years, all those pageants, all the pep talks from my mother, all those hours of smiling and saying cute things and giggling and wiggling my tush. Suddenly the whole thing seemed kind of ludicrous. And then I realized he had stopped talking and was staring at me in a funny way. And I couldn't remember what he had asked. Something about outer space. If I asked him to repeat it, I was dead. Every judge knows that's the oldest ploy for killing time while you're trying to think of an answer. So I just launched into an answer to what I thought he might have asked. 'If I was an astronaut and landed on another planet,' I said, 'I would establish a cancer ward in a children's hospital and spend my life as a social worker for those little aliens and tell them how wonderful life was back in America.' "

"And?" We were both laughing.

"Oh, he paused and gave me a weird look. And then he said, 'Isn't that wonderful. Thank you, Cynthia.' I looked over at the judges and I knew what they were thinking: This broad is either deaf or crazy or both. So . . ." She shrugged. "I lost."

"Well, at least you beat one of the five. After all, you were third runner-up."

"Yeah, I guess." She grinned. "Imagine how rotten the fourth runner-up must have felt when she realized that I beat her."

I closed the scrapbook and leaned back. "You know it's so . . . uh . . ."

"Right. How did a nice girl like me get into a job like this?"

"It's none of my business."

"You're absolutely right, Rachel. It isn't any of your business." She smiled. "But I bet you'd love to know, eh?"

"Well, I was sort of wondering."

"My downfall was nothing special, believe me. I had moved to Chicago a year before the pageant and was doing some modeling with an agency here in town. About three months after the pageant the agency was sued for unfair competition, or something like that. Some of the models were going to be witnesses at the trial. The agency's lawyer met with me the day before my deposition to prepare me. He was a good-looking guy, about fifty-five. He asked me out for dinner. We went to dinner and afterward I invited him up for a drink. He spent the night and left the next morning before I got up. I guess he had to hightail it home and work up some explanation for his wife. When I woke up I found two crisp one-hundred-dollar bills on the other pillow."

"Jesus."

"Yeah. I couldn't believe it. I mean, I had done it, you know, just for fun. No one had ever paid me. I didn't know whether to be hurt or what. I just left the money on my dresser. A couple of days later another lawyer from this guy's law firm calls up and asks if I'm free that night. I asked him how he got my name and he told me the first guy had recommended me. I said no to that guy, and no to the next guy. But they kept calling. And I kept saying no. At least for the next several months. Well, I was getting bored with modeling. I hadn't been getting many assignments, anyway. They said my boobs were too big." She shrugged. "To make a long story short, I finally agreed to have lunch with one of the ones who called. We just had lunch. He was charming. And clean-looking. His wife didn't understand him, he'd just lost a big trial. The usual stuff. I felt kind of sad for him, and finally agreed to sleep with him. It was actually kind of nice. And the poor guy was so grateful. He paid me two hundred dollars. Two hundred dollars for three hours! Where else could a tap-dancing English major make that kind of money? Well, he had friends, and his friends had friends, and before long I was working four nights a week at five hundred dollars a night. Of course, that was two years ago. I'm up to nine hundred these days, but that's partly because of inflation." She smiled. "Also, I'm better."

"Do you work every night?"

"God, no. I keep it to two or three nights a week. That's my limit, believe me."

"How much longer will you keep at it?"

"Not much longer. I've saved plenty of money. Believe it or not, I've even been thinking about law school. Listen, when you screw three lawyers a week, it starts to rub off."

"Really? Law school?"

"Yeah. I did pretty well in college. Graduated with honors." She shrugged. "If people will pay good money to screw me, they ought to pay me good money to screw someone else." She paused for a spoonful of yogurt. "If you think about it, Rachel, you and I are just in different lines of the same business. I sell my body and hang on to my brains. You sell your brains and hang on to your body. You tell me who's got the better deal." She shrugged. "I might take the law boards this fall."

"Where do you want to go?"

"Sometimes I think I'd like to stay in Chicago. But then I think, why not try for the best? Who knows, maybe I can get into Harvard. If I get a high enough score on the LSATs, I'll apply there. If I need extra money up there, it shouldn't be a problem. If those professors are anything like their former students, I'll find plenty of work."

We both laughed.

She stopped laughing and frowned. "This Graham Marshall thing. God, it really shook me up." She looked down at her apple, turning it slowly in her hand. "I didn't really like him that much at first. He could really be a cold bastard. But you don't have that sort of relationship with a guy for that long without developing some feelings."

"It must have been a terrible experience."

"It wasn't a picnic, Rachel. He looked terrible

lying there on the floor. And his eyes. I'll never forget those eyes. He was so scared." She shook her head slowly. "Like a little boy."

She pulled a handkerchief out of one of the pockets of the robe and blew her nose. I stood up and walked over to the window. Cindi concentrated on her yogurt, spooning it out slowly.

"Jesus, Rachel," she finally said, "can you imagine what they thought at the hospital when Marshall arrived in that rubber suit?"

I turned toward her. She was smiling. Her eyes were red.

I smiled too. "I can imagine." I walked back and sat down across from her. "I've been wondering about that. Did he always wear that outfit?"

"A lot of the time. He liked rubber."

"Isn't that a little odd?" I asked.

She smiled. "Actually, it's not that odd for a Yale graduate."

"Oh, really?"

"From my experience, Yalies are into that sort of stuff. They're a kinky crew. They seem to like rubber."

"Just Yalies?" I asked.

"Well," she said, smiling, "each law school has its tendencies. I've noticed patterns."

"Like what?"

"Where'd you go to law school?"

"Harvard," I said.

"Perfect example," she said. "They like English."

"English?"

"Whips, chains, S and M. From my experience, Harvard men are into humiliation."

"Must be the side effects of three years of the Socratic method."

"Yeah. I don't know what they do to those poor guys in Cambridge. Listen." She leaned forward, her eyes twinkling. "I have one Harvard man—a senior partner downtown—he comes up here with his own suitcase full of bondage equipment. He likes me to tie him up."

"He's from Harvard?"

"Yep. I can't tell you his name—hooker-client privilege, you know." She winked.

"How about Michigan?"

"Michigan, Michigan . . . let's see . . . I've had about five clients from there."

"And?"

"Well, I'd have to say most of them have been quick-draw artists."

"I'm afraid to ask."

"Premature ejaculators."

I laughed.

"Rachel, I'm serious. You name the law school, I'll tell you their quirks. I've seen it all."

"You should write a book."

"No, thanks. What about you? You have any lovers who are lawyers?"

"Not since law school."

"Probably a good idea not to."

"Do you do anything during the day?" I asked.

"I read some. And I still do some modeling. Boobs are in again these days. Which reminds me. I gotta kick you out of here. I have an appointment at a modeling agency in an hour. They're interviewing for a swimsuit layout. Sorry."

We both stood up. "Thanks, Cindi. I appreciate your taking the time."

"No problem, Rachel." She handed me my legal pad. "Was I any help?"

"Sure. Anything I can find out about Marshall

might help." I snapped my briefcase shut and followed her to the door.

"Well, give me a buzz if you need any more help." She smiled and opened the door. "I enjoyed it. I really did."

"So did I. Take care, Cindi."

"You too, Rachel."

7

My next stop was Abbott & Windsor. I called my secretary from the telephone in the reception area.

"I just got here," I told Mary. "Any messages?"

"A few. Most can wait. But that Maggie Sullivan called twice. She sounds upset."

"About what?"

"She wouldn't say. I told her she might be able to reach you at A and W."

"Okay. I should be back in an hour."

Helen Marston was waiting for me at her desk with a manila folder in her hand.

"Any luck?" I asked.

"As a matter of fact, I believe so," she answered. I followed her into Marshall's office.

"What turned up?" I asked.

"The filing department ran my request on the computer. Nothing under Maggie Sullivan. But this"—she held out the manila folder—"apparently was filed under Canaan. I don't know what to make of it."

I opened the folder and lifted out a single page of lime and white striped computer paper. Centered at the top of the page in block letters were the words *Canaan log*. Below that heading, in a single column of computer print, was the following:

```
3-20-CN-17-3
7-28-CHT-4-3
9-12-CP-23-6
11-30-CHT-4-2
```

"This is all?" I asked.

"I'm afraid it is. I've already had them double-check the files."

"Some sort of code, I guess. Helen, could you make me a copy of this?"

"Certainly." She took the page. "I'll be right back."

After she left, I remembered the dictionary. I opened the box I had placed it in last night. It wasn't there. I looked around the room. No dictionary. I checked the other six boxes. No dictionary.

"Here, Rachel." Helen handed me a photocopy of the computer printout.

I looked at it again, still baffled.

So was Helen. She nodded at the printout. "I've never seen that before." She paused. "But even after all those years of working for him, that man was still a mystery to me."

"I wish I knew what this means," I said, studying the printout. "By the way, did you take the dictionary out of this office? The one that was here yesterday?"

"No. It isn't there?"

"I don't see it anywhere in here. I checked each of these boxes."

"Hmm, I can't imagine what happened. Perhaps someone borrowed it. Does it matter?"

"I don't know." I shrugged. "Maybe I'm starting to get paranoid. There was something odd about that dictionary. It had three definitions for Canaan and mine has only two."

"Isn't that peculiar? Let's check mine." She walked out to her desk and returned with her dictionary. "Here," she said, handing it to me.

I found the entry for Canaan. Just two definitions. No mention of Canaan, Massachusetts.

"Helen, could you see who might have borrowed Graham's dictionary? It could be important."

"I'll ask around." She paused. "But be careful, Rachel. I have a feeling you could find out more about Mr. Marshall than either of us wants to know."

"I'm afraid I already have," I said to her just as Benny Goldberg strolled in.

"Greetings and salutations, Mrs. Marston," he said.

Helen nodded curtly at him and walked out.

Benny waited until she was out of earshot and then, gesturing with his head in her direction, said, "She's one of my biggest fans. All I have to do is smile at her and her colon goes into vapor-lock for a week." He closed the door and sat down behind the desk. He had left his suit jacket back in his office. The sleeves of his white shirt were rolled up to his elbows, and the shirttail was hanging out of the back of his pants. *"Nu?* What's happening with you and Captain Kink's little pet?"

"Take a look at this." I tossed him the photocopied computer printout and explained how Helen Marston found it.

"Looks like a code." He studied the numbers and letters. "I don't recognize the pattern. Checking account? License plates? Beats the shit out of me, Rachel."

"This whole thing is getting strange," I said. "And now Marshall's dictionary is missing. The one with the extra definition for Canaan. Someone borrowed it, or just took it. Helen is going to try to track it down. Say, aren't you supposed to be in a deposition? Wasn't it this morning?"

"Oy, what a disaster. The other lawyer was a cretin. The deposition lasted only ten minutes before he stormed out with his client."

"What happened?"

"He tells the witness not to answer one of my questions. So I turn to the witness and explain that under the rules of procedure he can decide whether or not to follow his lawyer's instruction not to answer my question."

"That's proper," I said.

"Wait. So then I say to the witness, it's up to you. You decide whether you want to answer my question or whether you'd prefer to follow the advice of that colostomy bag you call your lawyer. Well, his lawyer went ape-shit. He screams at me, I yell back at him, and then he stomps out of the deposition with his client."

"Who's the partner on the case?" I asked.

"Don't ask. Kent Charles. He was real pleased when I reported it all to him." Benny rolled his eyes. "This place is driving me nuts." He took a pack of Life Savers out of his shirt pocket and offered me one.

"No, thanks."

"I gotta go over to the public library this afternoon," he said, crunching on his candy. "One of the Bottles and Cans plaintiffs filed a new claim. Listen to this: copyright infringement. They're pissed about some advertising materials some of our clients allegedly copied."

"Copyright?" I said. "God, that case is the Black Hole of litigation."

"No kidding. Anyway, I'm going to the library to find the magazine ads they base their copyright claim on. While I'm there, I'm gonna see what I can dig up on Canaan, Massachusetts. It's got me a little curious. I'll just bill the time to Bottles and Cans. No one will ever know the difference."

"Thanks, Benny. I kind of doubt that some seventeenth-century Puritan village has anything to do with Marshall's pet. But I'm curious about it, anyway."

There was a shout from the other side of the door. "Out of my way, grandma!"

The door flew open and Maggie Sullivan stomped into the office, red-faced and angry. "Listen, you," she started, her voice rising in volume, "did you have anything to do with it? 'Cause if you did, I'll get you thrown in jail!"

"What are you talking about, Maggie?" I asked.

"That grave, dammit!" Her hands were resting on her broad hips, fists clenched. "That's my property. There's laws out there that protect it too. And if you had anything—"

"Wait a minute," I said. "What are you talking about?"

She stood there glaring at me, breathing heavily.

Helen Marston was behind her, standing slack-jawed at the door.

"The Canaan grave," Maggie finally said. "It's been dug up."

"What?"

"Last night, I guess. Someone must have come out in the middle of the night and dug it up. There's just a big hole in the ground, and the coffin is gone!"

BY THE TIME MAGGIE AND I reached my office, I had convinced her that I had nothing to do with the grave robbery. Mary was at her desk leafing through a *Cosmopolitan* as we walked in. She handed me my telephone messages and I introduced her to Maggie. Maggie grunted a hello as she walked into my office. I followed her, pausing at the door to look back at Mary, who was staring with raised eyebrows. I shrugged and closed the door.

Maggie was pacing back and forth. "I'm really pissed off," she said. "Someone sneaks onto *my* property in the middle of the night, digs up one of *my* graves, and walks off with the coffin. I'm so angry, I can't tell you. And it's not just the trespassing and the theft that gets me. I run a pet cemetery. A damn fine pet cemetery. And I got people buried out there too. Including my Carl, rest his soul." She stopped pacing and shook her head. "Word of this leaks out and I'm in big trouble. All pet cemeteries are in trouble. People get spooked by grave robbers. The least they can expect is that when they bury their pet out there, it stays buried. You buy a plot out there, you bury your pet—or your husband, for chrissakes—and you expect them to stay put. You have any idea what this does to people?"

"What are you going to do?" I asked.

"I've been thinking about it." Maggie paused to light a cigarette with a kitchen match. "I can't go to the cops. First of all, they're not going to do anything about it. They'll send out two bozos in a squad car, and they'll clomp around and write up a report and that's the last I'll hear from them. Second of all, it might get into the papers. *That's* the real problem. I don't want publicity for this. It's not just that it's bad for future business, including that hippo out at Brookfield Zoo, which I might just nab, knock on wood. But it's just terrible, *I mean terrible,* for all the people, for all the poor families that have pets out there." Maggie shook her head and took a drag on her cigarette. She exhaled the smoke through her nose. "I have some sweet old ladies who'll have a stroke if they hear about it. The high point of their week is their visit to Wagging Tail. I have to look out for them too. For their peace of mind." She stared at me for a moment and then sat down on the couch. "Which brings me to you."

"Me?"

"You. Just what is it you're doing with this Canaan stuff?"

"Up until an hour ago, I was trying to figure out what was in that grave."

"And now?"

"And now—well, I guess I'll advise the client and—"

"Who's the client? That Marshall fellow?"

"No." I paused. "Marshall's dead. His law firm retained me to see what I could find out about Canaan."

"Why?"

"Some estate matters they're looking into."

"What does that mean?" Maggie asked.

"Before we get to that, let's talk about what you plan to do."

"I don't know. I'm not sure. Maybe I'll hire a private eye, or maybe a lawyer. Maybe you."

It might work, I thought. The law firm wanted to keep this Canaan matter quiet, and so did Maggie. Abbott & Windsor certainly wouldn't want Maggie hiring some outsider to start snooping around, bugging Marshall's family, asking questions.

"Why me?" I asked.

Maggie studied me. "I'm not sure. I don't know any good lawyers, and I don't know any private eyes. I wouldn't know how to find a good one. If that big law firm is happy with you, I guess you can't be all bad. But I got to know more about your job on this case."

"So do I," I said. "I'm going to let the firm know about the theft and see if they want me to continue working on the case. If not, I might be able to work for you, assuming they have no genuine objection."

"And if they want you to still work on it?"

"Then I'll stick with it," I answered.

"And what about me?"

"Well, up to a certain point your interests and

the law firm's interests are the same. But there is a possible conflict down the road."

"And what's that?" she asked.

"Well, it relates to future payments for care and maintenance of the gravesite—"

"Look, I don't care about the maintenance money." Maggie stood up and started pacing again. "That money isn't what bothers me. I got an empty hole in the ground out there, and that could hurt my cemetery bad. I want you to find that coffin and get it back to me. Period. And I'm willing to pay you for it."

"Let me first check with the firm," I said. "Then I'll get back to you."

"Good." She sat back down."

"How are things going with the zoo?" I asked.

"Hard to tell," she said, shaking her head. "I'm going to see them again today and tell them it's time to piss or get off the pot. The museum turned them down yesterday. I think I have a chance. Their only other option is to sell it to a rendering plant." Maggie stood up and started for the door. "Give me an answer today."

"I will. And good luck with the zoo."

After she left, Mary stuck her head into the office.

"So that's the cemetery lady?" she asked.

"Yep. Someone stole Canaan."

"My God. You're kidding!"

"I wish I were. This case is bizarre."

"What are you going to do?" she asked.

"Well, I'll tell Ishmael Richardson what happened and see if he wants me to keep on it." I started flipping through the earlier telephone messages.

"I have another message for you," Mary said.

"Mr. Marshall's widow called back. She said she could meet you at two-thirty at her home. Do you need her address?"

"No. I have it."

"Jesus, Rachel, why would anyone rob a pet cemetery? How long was the pet buried there?"

"Since 1986."

"Weird."

Mary was out getting our lunches when a messenger from Abbott & Windsor arrived with a large thick envelope for me. Inside was a copy of the last will and testament of Graham Anderson Marshall III, a copy of the first codicil to the last will and testament of Graham Anderson Marshall III, and a short cover note from one of Ishmael Richardson's secretaries: "Mr. Richardson requested that I send you the enclosed."

The will was thirty-two pages long and printed on legal-size paper. It seemed to sag under the leaden jargon of the trust and estates lawyer. In the belt-and-suspenders world of a will drafter, it is hardly sufficient for the testator merely to give his stamp collection to his son; instead, he must give, devise, bequeath, surrender, assign, settle upon, convey, transfer, set over, and otherwise direct that said collection of postage stamps, as hereinbefore described hereinabove, be delivered, free and clear of any and all claims, liens, and encumbrances, to said male issue. In other words, take the damn stamps.

I skimmed through the various provisions of the will, most of them boilerplate, pausing to underline a $50,000 bequest, grant, devise, etc., to Barrett College and a $50,000 bequest to the Massachusetts Historical Society.

The codicil was just three pages long. It had all the odd provisions Ishmael Richardson had described: the appointment of the managing partner as co-trustee of the trust, the request that the co-trustee supervise the care and maintenance of the gravesite, the direction to pay Abbott & Windsor a fee of twice the standard hourly rate for the managing partner's services, the provision terminating the trust twenty-one years after the death of the last attorney who was a member of the Executive Committee of Abbott & Windsor at the time of Marshall's death—a provision needed for compliance with the ancient and virtually incomprehensible (to a litigator, at least) rule against perpetuities.

I reread the provision governing the delivery of flowers to the grave four times a year: on March 19, July 27, September 11, and November 29. I stared at those dates and then copied them onto a yellow legal pad.

The closing paragraph of the codicil must have given Ishmael Richardson pause. Marshall "implored" his law firm "to honor and carry out my simple but heartfelt requests, as expressed in this, my codicil. Even if the civil law does not make binding the terms of this trust, I hope and pray that my partners, and especially the managing partner, will deem as binding the moral obligations I hereby call upon them to honor. I seek only to memorialize the small role I played in the eternal life of Canaan."

I read that last sentence a second time, aloud.

The codicil was dated July 15, 1986, and was witnessed by two file room clerks at Abbott & Windsor. I recognized both names. No doubt Marshall called them into his office, had them witness his signature, and then had them sign as witnesses. Neither one would have any idea of what he had been asked to witness.

The telephone rang. It was Kent Charles. He said he had a new case he wanted to discuss with me in person. I agreed to meet him for drinks tomorrow at five at the Yacht Club.

I called directory assistance in New York and asked for the telephone number of the publisher of the *American Language Dictionary*. I dialed the number and asked for the customer relations department. Someone named Ralph Pinchley answered. Posing as the newly appointed purchasing agent for several large Chicago law firms, I asked him for information about their latest edition of the dictionary. I told him that I had two copies of their dictionary on my desk. Although the two copies appeared identical, I had made a random check and discovered that the definitions for *Canaan* were different. I read him the definitions in my dictionary and then I read, from my notes, the definitions in Graham Marshall's dictionary. He must have had his own copy of the dictionary before him, because he sounded confused when I reached the reference to Canaan, Massachusetts.

"Would you read that last definition again," he said. "Slowly."

I did.

"And you say that's from our dictionary, ma'am?"

I said it was.

There was a pause. "Well, uh, I'll have to check with the dictionary division."

"Certainly," I answered. "Before I place my orders, I'd like to know if that dictionary is available. The one with the three definitions. My law firm clients prefer the most comprehensive dictionary available."

I then called Ishmael Richardson and told him about the theft and about Maggie's request that I also represent her. After a long pause he told me to continue the investigation. We discussed Maggie's request and agreed that it was better for me to represent Maggie than to force her to turn to someone else. He asked a few general questions about my practice and then ended the conversation by asking whether I had any interest in returning to the firm to work on *In re Bottles & Cans*. I politely declined.

I shuffled through my telephone messages for the second time and then put them back on the desk, reached into the top drawer, and pulled out a cigarette—my second of the day. I was down to four a day. I lit it with a match and leaned back in the chair.

In re Bottles & Cans. To a nonlawyer it sounded like an antilitter statute. But to any of the 132 law firms across the nation involved in it, Bottles & Cans was the motherlode, producing annual legal fees in an amount greater than the gross national products of several member nations of the United Nations.

Bottles & Cans had started thirty-one years before with the filing of a run-of-the-mill six-page civil antitrust complaint in the federal district court for the Eastern District of Missouri. In that complaint—the original of which is now on display in a glass case in the United States Court and Custom House in St. Louis—two Southeast Missouri bottling companies accused a Southern Illinois bottler of attempting to monopolize the regional market. The case, *Ames Bottle, Inc., et al.*

v. King of Peoria Bottling Co., was, in the jargon of the antitrust litigator, just a garden-variety Section 2 claim.

What happened then, however, can best be analogized by that awful moment in any one of dozens of 1950's horror films: The mad scientist has just trudged up the basement stairs to bed, leaving behind the little blob of protoplasm in the petri dish in his subterranean laboratory. As the distant church bells chime midnight, the camera moves in tight on the petri dish. The little blob has started to quiver and glow. Cue the organist.

The case was just three months old when a Kansas bottling company intervened in the lawsuit, accusing the two plaintiffs of predatory pricing. Then a Nebraska canner entered the battle, accusing the others of a group boycott and joining two more bottlers as defendants. Two Indiana canners joined next, alleging violations of the Robinson-Patman Act. By the end of the first year there were sixteen parties in the lawsuit. In succeeding years scores of bottling and canning companies have entered the case, switched sides, or settled out. In 1974 the case was officially recaptioned *In re Bottles & Cans*. At last count there were eighty-one plaintiffs, ninety-three defendants, and over nine hundred pages of claims, counterclaims, cross-claims, and third-party claims alleging virtually every antitrust violation, unfair trade practice, and business tort invented by modern capitalism.

In re Bottles & Cans is now the largest civil lawsuit in American legal history. After more than thirty years it is still in the preliminary discovery stages. More than one billion documents have been exchanged and over eight hundred depositions have been taken. Optimists predict the trial might begin in about a decade. Pessimists are fond of quoting a recent article on the lawsuit which appeared in the *University of Virginia Law Review:* "At its current pace, the tail end of this brontosaurus of a lawsuit will drag past the bench seventy-five years after the snout first appeared at the courtroom door."

In re Bottles & Cans has made four trips to the Supreme Court and more than two dozen trips to the appellate courts. During my last year at Harvard Law School the reading list for a Harvard seminar in advanced civil procedure consisted entirely of the appellate opinions in *In re Bottles & Cans.* Indeed, an entire generation of professors of civil procedure earned tenure at the trough of *In re Bottles & Cans.* At last count, 723 law review articles, notes, and comments have been written about the litigation.

Of course, the real battle of *In re Bottles & Cans* has been waged not in the courtroom but in three cavernous warehouses in Cedar Rapids, Iowa, and two giant warehouses on the outskirts of Fort Worth, Texas. The plaintiffs' documents are stored in Iowa, the defendants' in Texas. Eight hours a day, six days a week, dozens of paralegals and young lawyers from across the nation sifts through mountains of documents, preparing abstracts of each one. Thirty-two computer programmers take those abstracts and type them onto computer terminals that are connected with the main computer in Chicago.

Presiding over this Gargantua of a lawsuit is District Judge Harold Greenman. Judge Greenman heard the first motion in the case thirty years ago, and has lived with the litigation throughout its entire history.

Three years ago, after Judge Greenman suffered a mild stroke and thereby introduced the dreaded wild card of his mortality into the proceedings, the defendants' central steering committee held a special meeting. Three hours into the meeting the committee members realized that no one in the room really knew what the case was about anymore. Accordingly, they asked the head programmers to instruct the computers to examine all the stored information and produce a summary of the most significant and material facts in the litigation. Twenty-three lawyers crowded in the hallway outside the terminal, waiting for the results. The computer hummed and whirred for two hours, and then began to print. And print. And print. For ten hours straight. The result numbered close to five thousand pages.

An associate from Abbott & Windsor—a highly regarded young associate—was assigned to read and summarize the results. That associate spent two months alone in a windowless office plowing through the seemingly endless printout. The result was a 212-page memorandum which she gave to Graham Anderson Marshall ten minutes before she handed in her resignation. That young associate was me.

The telephone rang just as I was leaving the office to travel to Kenilworth to meet with Marshall's widow. It was Ralph Pinchley again from the *American Language Dictionary*. He sounded even more confused. There was only one version of the dictionary, and its definition of Canaan did not include a town in Massachusetts. The editorial staff had double-checked their manuscript, galleys, and research files. They found no reference to Canaan, Massachusetts.

"Are you sure you have *our* dictionary there?" he asked.

"Absolutely," I said.

"Well, I'm somewhat confused. Perhaps you could send me a copy of that page and, in the meantime, we'll keep looking here. Maybe we have something in our archives."

I thanked him for his help, listened to a sales pitch for the dictionary and other resource materials of great interest to lawyers, and hung up.

9

THE WIDOW MARSHALL WAS DRESSED in black. A black Catalina swimsuit, that is. A black beach towel, folded on a deck chair nearby, carried through the motif.

A uniformed maid—a heavyset black woman in her fifties—had met me at the door and led me through the house to the large pool out back. Julia Marshall was reclining on a chaise by the pool, the chair angled toward the afternoon sun. There was a tall glass with ice cubes on the small table near her elbow. She was wearing tortoise-shell sunglasses with oversize round lenses and was reading what appeared to be a textbook on business administration.

I suppose I had expected the Hollywood version of the Widow: in an upstairs room, shades drawn, wrinkled black dress, crumpled lace handkerchief, sagging shoulders, red eyes, limp hair. Instead, I saw a tanned and manicured North Shore matron, the kind that would draw furtive stares from teen-aged boys as she stepped out on the diving board at the country club pool or bent over to retrieve a tennis ball on the courts. The lilac polish on her fingernails matched the shade on her toenails. Her lightly frosted hair, parted in the middle, ended just above her shoulders. She was probably in her late forties, although her figure looked at least a decade younger.

Her husband had been dead for more than a month. Life must go on, I thought.

I introduced myself.

"Hello, dear," she said, sitting up and raising her sunglasses. The skin around her large hazel eyes seemed just a tad too taut. Her chin and neck were probably the next items on her plastic surgeon's agenda. "Ruby," she said, "bring us a pitcher of vodka tonics." She turned to me. "Would you like some cheese and crackers?"

"No, thanks."

"Just the drinks, Ruby."

"Yes, ma'am."

We started off talking about the weather. She admired my necklace and asked where I had found it. In one of the care packages my mother sent me from St. Louis once a month. I admired her business administration textbook and asked why she had it. For one of the courses she had signed up for at Northwestern. Ruby returned with a pitcher of vodka tonics and two tall glasses on a tray. Julia told her to place it on the umbrella table, and we both moved over there. She had good, strong features—handsome but not beautiful.

"So," Julia Marshall said as she poured our drinks, "you're here about Canaan."

"Yes, I am."

She shrugged. "I can tell you what I told Harlan Dodson. I have no idea what Graham put in that grave. None whatsoever. I assume he's already told you that."

"Ishmael Richardson did. I haven't spoken with Mr. Dodson yet."

She settled back in her chair and rested her elbows on the armrests, her hands crossed in her lap. "I'm not the best source of information on my husband's extracurricular activities." She reached for her drink." Harlan says I should just forget about it. Let him break the trust and go about my life."

"That's not bad advice," I said.

"It's rotten advice. You don't just forget about something like that." She studied me, her head tilted slightly. "What do you think he buried in that coffin?"

"I don't know. That's what I'm supposed to find out."

"I want to know as soon as you have something. I've got to know what this is all about. I have a right to know."

"You do. And when I find out, I'll tell you about it myself."

"Good." She took a sip of her drink. "Are you a litigator?"

"I used to be. I used to work for your husband."

"Oh." She seemed to size me up . . . and down. "Well, if you worked for him, you must be tough. And you must be a good investigator. Graham didn't talk to me about his work"—there was a trace of bitterness—"but I often heard him brag to others that his assistants had balls and knew how to get out of the law library to dig up facts."

"I don't know about the balls part."

She laughed.

"But he sure taught me to get out of the library. My first month he had me on a plane to Little Rock to interview three ex-employees of a bottling plant down there."

"Ah, that sounds like Bottles and Cans," she said. "God, what a bore that case must be." She reached for the pitcher of vodka tonics. "More?"

"No, thanks." I waited until she filled her glass. "Do you recall anything unusual about your husband's activities back in 1985?"

Julia Marshall frowned in concentration. "Actually," she finally said, "that was a normal year for him. At least as far as I remember. He worked late, traveled a lot, worked weekends. I didn't see him much, and when I did, he seemed distracted." She sighed. "I'm sorry to say that was a typical year for him. At least compared to the year before and the year after. Those were definitely unusual."

"What do you mean?"

"Graham almost died in 1984."

"I do remember he spent some time in a hospital. Was that in 1984?"

"Yes. Down in Houston. He had open heart surgery to replace a valve in his heart with an artificial one. His heart disease wasn't all that advanced, and it was supposed to be fairly routine."

"But it wasn't?"

"It was terrifying. He had a heart attack during the surgery. That's very unusual, but it does happen. Then he had an allergic reaction to the anesthesia. Apparently an extremely rare reaction, according to the doctor. Anyway, he barely survived the operation and was in a coma for three days."

"God."

Julia gazed at the pool. "It changed him. I noticed it when we came back from Houston. He felt like he'd been brought back from the edge of the grave. Which he had." She was still looking at the pool. "I guess everyone reacts differently. You know, someone else might drop out and go live on a mountaintop, or change careers, or something like that. For Graham, though, it just seemed to make him even more determined to throw himself into his work with all his energy." She paused. "I had hoped it might bring us closer together." She turned to me. "It didn't."

"I'm sorry."

She ran her fingers through her hair. "My husband was a very manipulative man." She drew an index finger down the condensation on the outside of her glass. "I suppose all lawyers are manipulative, at least to a certain degree. But nothing like Graham." She gave me a rueful smile. "I think he was happiest during his years at the State Department. He loved all those behind-the-scenes maneuvers, the cloak-and-dagger part of foreign policy. He'd have been perfect for the CIA."

"He seemed right at home in complex lawsuits," I said. "He loved to plot strategies."

Julia Marshall sighed. "My husband had a powerful need to control events . . . and the people caught up in them. It could be terrifying." She paused. "Ten years ago I finally extricated myself from his grasp." She looked at me. "To outsiders we still were the perfect couple. Graham was a master at keeping up appearances." She turned toward the pool. "It worked quite well. He left early in the morning and came home late at night. Unless we were going to a social function, we rarely ate together. We slept in separate bedrooms." She turned to me with a shrug. "Except for a few times a year when we were both drunk. The all-American couple."

"I'm sorry, Mrs. Marshall."

Her eyes narrowed. "The firm hired you to investigate the Canaan grave, correct?"

I nodded.

"And the firm represents me in that matter?"

"They do."

"So in a sense you're my lawyer too."

"I suppose I am."

"Good. I want you to have that coffin dug up."

I looked down at my legal pad. "It may not be that easy," I said.

"I told you I want to know what's in that coffin. He took forty thousand dollars of my money and sunk it in that box. I want to know whose pet it was. Dig it up."

"There are probably rules and regulations covering animal burials," I said.

"Then find out what they are. If you can exhume a human corpse, you can surely dig up a dead dog."

"I'll look into it," I said, keeping it vague.

"See if you can get it publicized too," she said, her voice rising. "Maybe that'll force one of his little bimbos to come forward to claim it. She must be something special to rate forty thousand dollars for her dead pet."

"You don't want that, Mrs. Marshall. Your husband is dead. That kind of publicity would only embarrass you and your children."

Julia Marshall stared at me, her features gradually relaxing. "Don't humor me."

"Never," I said. "I know how painful this Canaan thing must be, especially so soon after your husband died. I'm going to try to find out what's in that coffin. For the firm's sake, and yours." Assuming, of course, that I could ever find the coffin.

We were both silent for a while. I watched a fat bumblebee crawl across a yellow mum in a flowerpot on the pool deck.

"My husband had a keen sense of irony," she said finally. "Wherever he is now, he must be enjoying the cause of his death."

"I'm not following you," I said, hoping I wasn't. I didn't want her to ask me about Cindi.

"Graham told me that when he died, I'd have the goddamnedest wrongful death case in the history of Illinois. He'd even talked to a couple of big personal injury lawyers about it."

"I'm definitely not following you."

She smiled. It was a sad smile. "In the spring of 1986 he received some terrible news about the artificial valve in his heart. Several of them had malfunctioned. The FDA launched an investigation and eventually forced the manufacturer to recall all the valves in one of the lots. There were about two hundred out there, most still on the shelves. But about twenty were in people's hearts. One of them was in Graham's heart."

"My God. How awful."

"Believe it or not, that wasn't the first time there's been a valve recall. There've been others since, too."

"What did he do?"

"He flew down to Houston and met with his surgeon. Apparently there was a ten-percent failure rate with those valves. One in ten. Based on Graham's first heart surgery, his doctor told him he might have only a fifty percent chance of surviving another operation. Graham went with the odds."

"He left it in?"

"He decided the odds were better. If the valve didn't malfunction, he could live for years. If it did malfunction, well, he'd be dead."

"That's Russian roulette for life."

"Exactly. He was walking around with a time bomb in his chest, except he didn't know if or when it would explode. Frankly, I don't know how he could stand it."

"Are you going to sue?"

She laughed. "That's what I meant about Graham's sense of irony. The valve never malfunctioned. When they did the autopsy, they discovered the valve had nothing to do with the heart attack. That valve was in perfect working condition. That goddamn valve outlived—" Her voice cracked, but she quickly regained control.

"I'm sorry," I said softly.

She waved her hand. "The only part of that man's heart that worked was artificial. I didn't need a coroner to tell me that." She took a deep breath and slowly exhaled. "So," she said, "what else can I tell you?"

Looking down the list of topics on my legal pad, I mentally crossed most of them off. "Well, two quick questions, if you don't mind."

"Fire away."

"I noticed in his will he left some money to Barrett College."

"His alma mater," she said. "He was very active in alumni affairs."

"He also left some money to the Massachusetts Historical Society."

"Yes. Graham believed that his ancestors dated back to the Puritans. It was his family's gospel. But he was never able to get any confirmation in the records. He even hired a genealogist a few years back, but he could trace the family back only to the beginning of the nineteenth century. I guess Graham left money to the Historical Society because they'd tried to help him with the search."

"Who was the ancestor?" I asked.

"I don't remember."

She frowned in thought.

We talked a few minutes more, mostly about her children and her studies at Northwestern. I wished her luck.

10

I WAS BACK IN MY office a little after five. Mary was just leaving for the day. She handed me a message from Maggie Sullivan.

I called Maggie, who was ecstatic, having just been awarded the burial rights to the zoo's hippopotamus. The funeral was set for one week from this Saturday.

"Why so long?" I asked.

"You think it's easy to bury a five-ton hippo? I gotta arrange for a crane and two backhoes. And then I have to find some carpenters who can build me a coffin the size of a Ford pickup. Gus can wait. Hell, it'll take two days to thaw him out. And I think they're going to do an autopsy on him. That'll take a few days too."

We both realized the importance—to her, to Graham Marshall, and to Abbott & Windsor—of keeping the grave robbery out of the press. But I wanted to explain to her the potential conflict between her interest in protecting her property rights and the law firm's possible interest in voiding the trust fund.

"Listen, I want you to take the case. I know you'll be straight with me, Rachel. I could tell when I first met you. We're a couple of tough broads, you and me. Just find the coffin."

"I'll try."

"By the way, my brother-in-law was out here today. Carl's brother. He used to be a cop. Now he's a security guard over at one of the plants down here. He took a real careful look around. He said it was a professional job. No footprints, no tire tracks, no nothing. No clues."

I told her I had a few leads I was running down. We agreed to talk again tomorrow.

I dictated a few letters into my machine, stuffed some court papers in my briefcase, and locked up. Benny Goldberg and I had agreed to meet for dinner at the Heartland Cafe in East Rogers Park. I reached the subway platform at State Street just as the northbound train rumbled into the station. I found a window seat, the hinged doors rattled shut, and the train lurched forward with a dull metallic groan. I settled back as the train screamed through the dark tunnel under the Loop and the Chicago River. The naked tunnel lights flickered by outside my window.

The el train rumbled into the Morse Station. I got off and walked to the north end of the platform and down the stairs to Lunt Avenue. Heartland Cafe is on the corner of Lunt, just across the narrow street that runs parallel to the el tracks. Benny wasn't there yet. I took the last open table in the outdoor courtyard.

Ten minutes later Benny pulled into a parking space in front of the restaurant and beeped the horn of his 1970 Chevy Nova as he climbed out. He was wearing sandals, blue jeans, and a red T-shirt with the white-lettered message, PLEASE HELP ME— I AM AN ENDOMORPH. His T-shirt was untucked in front, exposing a broad expanse of hairy flesh.

"You stop off at home?" I asked.

"You better believe it, Rachel." Benny sat down across the table. "I was down in the bowels of the Chicago Public Library all afternoon, sweating my butt off. What a pit! No air-conditioning, no ventilation. By the time I left there, I think I had the cure for cancer growing in my armpits." He looked around the restaurant and then picked up the menu. "A real chic place you got here, Rachel. Look at this menu. Nutburgers? What the hell's that? They got any ham hocks here?"

"Try the chicken or the fish."

He finally settled on the chicken with fresh dill. I picked lentil soup and mushroom quiche. After we placed our orders, Benny summarized his research efforts that afternoon.

"I think the dictionary definition must have been a misprint, Rachel. I couldn't find anything on Canaan, Massachusetts. Nothing. I even had one of the librarians check too. The place never existed."

"This whole thing is crazy," I said. "Nothing hangs together."

"What do you have so far?"

"Just a lot of apparently unrelated junk. Graham Marshall buries something called Canaan in a pet cemetery. He puts up a tombstone with an odd epitaph. The tombstone has just one date: 1985. But Marshall buried it in May of '86. No one knows what's in the grave, including the owner of the cemetery."

"That's Maggie Sullivan, that big babe?"

"Yep. And then Marshall sets up a trust fund for the care and maintenance of the grave. Sets it up in a secret codicil even though the firm did his will. Nothing happens until five weeks after he dies and one day after Abbott and Windsor retains me and I visit the grave. Then someone digs up the grave in the middle of the night and steals the coffin. Meanwhile, Marshall's secretary vaguely remembers working on a secret project involving Canaan for Marshall back in 1985. But she doesn't know what it was about, because he handled even the filing himself. She just knows she never heard him mention a pet. She ran a search through the firm's files for anything having to do with Canaan and turned up one page from a computer printout. The one I showed you today." I paused while the waitress put down our food. "I visited Cindi Reynolds today. You were right. She was with Marshall when he died. She's actually very nice. Smart too."

"Do you have the paper?" Benny asked.

"What paper?"

"That computer printout."

I pulled my copy out of my briefcase and smoothed it onto the table. "I've been studying it on and off all afternoon," I said. "Something's familiar about it, but nothing's clicked yet."

"Let's take them one at a time," Benny said. Three, dash, twenty, dash, CN, dash, seventeen, dash, three." He studied the list. "Each line has the same pattern: two numbers, then two or three letters, then two more numbers. They aren't license plate numbers—at least not Illinois license plate numbers. Wait a minute, maybe they have something to do with the dog. Don't you need a license for your dog? Maybe these are the dog's license numbers?"

"I already thought of that. I had Mary check with City Hall. No luck. Dog licenses don't have that pattern of numbers and letters. And anyway, there are four rows of stuff on this page. He didn't bury four pets in that coffin."

"What else have you thought of?" Benny asked between bites of his chicken. "You know, this stuff isn't bad."

I ran through my list of possibilities: check numbers, charge numbers, bank account numbers, safety deposit box numbers. All the while I was looking down the list of entries on the computer printout:

```
3-20-CN-17-3
7-28-CHT-4-3
9-12-CP-23-6
11-30-CHT-4-2
```

Suddenly it clicked. "That's it!" I said. "I've got it."

"You've got what?"

"Look at the second row. Read it."

"Okay. Seven, dash, twenty-eight, dash, CHT, dash, four, dash, three. Yeah?"

"It's my birthday."

"Mazel tov, Rachel. Happy birthday."

"No, no. Look at it, you clown. Seven, dash, twenty-eight. July twenty-eighth. That's my birthday. And then CHT. Don't you see? It's the newspaper. The *Chicago Herald-Tribune*. Get it? Something appeared in the *Chicago Herald-Trib-*

une on July twenty-eight. On July 28, 1985. And I think I know what that something is."

"Wait a minute. Where do you get 1985?"

"A hunch," I said. "Remember I told you about Cindi Reynolds's scrapbook? Each newspaper clipping had the date and the name of the newspaper. One of those dates stuck in my head because it was on my birthday. July twenty-eighth. That was the article about the Ms. United States Pageant. July 28, 1985. In the *Chicago Herald-Tribune*. It's gotta be 1985. Everything points to 1985. The tombstone, Helen Marston's memories, the newspaper article."

"What about the last two numbers?" Benny asked. "Four, dash, three?"

"I don't know. We'll have to see the article."

"I think you're on to something. Look at the rest of the entries," Benny said. "Three, dash, twenty. March twentieth. What about CN?"

"*Chicago News,*" I said.

"Maybe so. Then CP. Uh, *Chicago Post*?"

"Might be."

"Wow!" said Benny. "I think that's it, Rachel."

"Finish your meal and let's get out of here. Loyola's library is still open. We can look up the articles."

Benny threaded the microfilm into the reader, advanced the reel to the first frame, and focused the viewer. We were staring at the front page of the *Chicago Herald-Tribune* for Monday, July 22, 1985. Benny pushed the fast-forward button and advanced the film in jerks and blurs to July 28, 1985. Nothing on the first page. He advanced the film slowly, page by page.

"Hold it," I said. "That's it."

Page four of the first section of the *Herald-Tribune* was projected onto the screen. In the middle of the page was the same article I had seen in Cindi Reynolds's scrapbook:

NEW MS. UNITED STATES CROWNED; MS. ILLINOIS THIRD RUNNER-UP

ATLANTA—As a nationwide audience looked on last night, Miss Betty Jo Johnson of Austin, Texas, was crowned Ms. United States at the Ninth Annual Ms. United States Pageant. Ms. Illinois, Cynthia Ann Reynolds (Peoria), was named third runner-up.

"I thank the good Lord for the role He has chosen for me," said the tearful Miss Johnson during the post-crowning press conference. "I hope to spread God's word during my reign as Ms. United States."

Illinois's Miss Reynolds told the *Herald-Tribune* that she had hoped to bring the crown back to Illinois. "But I'm so happy for Betty Jo," she said. "She'll be a wonderful Ms. United States."

The newly crowned Ms. United States is the second Ms. Texas to receive that honor in the nine-year history of the beauty pageant. During the talent portion of the pageant she impressed the judges by singing "The Impossible Dream" while twirling two fire-tipped batons.

"If there's a clue in that," I finally said, "I sure missed it."

"She thanks God." Benny shook his head. "As if God gave two shits who won that pageant."

"Let's figure this out. Read me the entry for this article."

"Okay." Benny unfolded the computer printout. "Let's see . . . seven, dash, twenty-eight. That's July 28, 1985, I guess. CHT. *Chicago Herald-Tribune*. Four, dash, three. Hmmm."

We both studied the article again.

"I've got it!" he said. "It's obvious. Page four, column three."

"You're right. Third column. Fourth page, third column. That's the code. The date, the newspaper, the page, and the column."

"Yep."

"What else is on the list?" I asked, picking up the printout.

"Here's another CHT," Benny said, pointing. "Eleven, dash, thirty. November thirtieth. Page four, second column."

"I'll get it." I walked over to the filing cabinet and found the roll of microfilm for the week of November 24.

"Another beauty pageant?" Benny asked as I threaded the film.

"Who knows. Maybe he's got a thing for beauty queens. You should see Cindi Reynolds," I said.

"Nice, huh?"

"A knockout. Gorgeous." I wound the film forward to November 30 and stopped at page four.

"My God," Benny mumbled.

The headline read TWO KILLED IN PLANE CRASH. The article was short:

ROSEMONT (AP)—Two Carbondale business partners perished yesterday when their single-engine airplane crashed in a soybean field in northwest Illinois. Killed were William Carswell of 2120 Maple Lane and Peter Framingham of 15 Greybridge Avenue.

A spokesman for the National Transportation Safety Board said an investigator from the board's field office in Chicago had been dispatched to look into the crash. Preliminary findings indicate engine failure, according to investigators at the scene.

The victims of the crash were en route from Chicago's Midway Airport to a Rockford trade show when the accident occurred.

"What do you make of it?" Benny asked.

"I don't know." I copied down the names and addresses of the victims. "Maybe Cindi Reynolds knows them. Let's find the rest of these articles."

Benny was studying the computer printout. "*Chicago News*, March twentieth. *Chicago Post*, September twelfth."

He walked over to the file drawers, poked around for a while, and came back with two rolls of microfilm. I threaded the first roll of film and advanced it to the seventeenth page of the March twentieth edition of the *Chicago News*. The headline at the top of the third column read: TYPO CAUSES EMBARRASSMENT. Beneath that headline appeared a five-paragraph story:

CHICAGO (UPI)—The publishers of *For the People*, the autobiography of crusading Congressman Ralph Barnett (D.-Ill.), were red-faced today when they discovered an embarrassing pair of typographical errors in the opening sentence of the just-published autobiography.

As originally written, the autobiography began with the words: "At the age of fourteen, I happily dove, headfirst, into the public arena of Sharon." (Congressman Barnett was born in Sharon, Illinois.) As published, however, the word *public* was printed without the letter *l* and the word *arena* was printed without the letter *n*—i.e., *pubic area.*

The publisher, Athena Publications, Inc., of Oak Park, declined comment. Congressman Barnett could not be reached for his reaction.

Sources at the publishing house said that the initial printing of 10,000 copies of the autobiography is already in the bookstores and that the company will be forced to undertake an expensive recall of those books.

"You can be sure heads will roll at Athena," said one source, who asked that his identity not be disclosed.

"A beauty pageant, a plane crash, and a typographical error," Benny mumbled as he rewound the microfilm and then threaded the next one:

PARK FOREST COUPLE
DISCOVERS $$ IN USED CABINET

Robert and Lois Byron of Park Forest bid $15 for a used filing cabinet at a police auction last Saturday in Evanston. They thought it was a good deal. It turned out to be a good deal more.

On Sunday, Mr. Byron went down to his basement to sand and paint the cabinet. He came back upstairs two hours later with a fat manila envelope he had found taped to the underside of one of the drawers. As his wife looked on in amazement, Mr. Byron opened the envelope and dumped out 142 $100 bills, totaling $14,200.

"Bob and I were absolutely stunned," Mrs. Byron explained. "Just that morning at breakfast we were trying to figure out how we could afford to have a baby if I had to quit my job. And then we discovered $14,200 in that cabinet."

The Byrons contacted the Evanston police later that day. The police have taken temporary custody of the cabinet and the money pending further investigation.

"We've checked our records," stated Detective James Moran, "and it appears that we came into custody of the filing cabinet after the city had condemned an old vacant warehouse on Church Street. This was abandoned property. Unless we discover something unexpected, we will return custody of the property and the money to the Byrons."

"Hell, maybe Cindi was banging Barnett and these two businessmen," Benny said. "This whole thing is getting even weirder."

"Maybe," I mumbled. "I'll see if Cindi knows anything about these stories."

11

I LIVE ON THE TOP floor of a three-story apartment building in East Rogers Park, just a block away from the Heartland Cafe, where Benny had left his car. Benny walked me back from Loyola. On the way I told him about my telephone call from Kent Charles and my agreement to meet him at the Yacht Club tomorrow afternoon.

Benny frowned. "A new case, huh? Well, maybe. If you ask me, I think Kent's just trying to get you in bed. You'd better watch out for that guy, Rachel."

"Don't worry, Benny. I'm a big girl." I kissed him on the cheek.

"So call me tomorrow, Rachel."

"Take care, Benny."

He lumbered down the street into the darkness, and I walked into the entranceway of my building. First the mail. Bills from Illinois Bell and Marshall Field's, a letter from the Harvard Club of Chicago, a *New Yorker,* and a postcard from San Francisco. The front of the postcard was a photograph of Alcatraz Island. I read the message written on the back in that neat and all-too-familiar script:

> Dear Rachel—
> Sorry I missed your B-day. The seminar ended last Wednesday. I'll be home by the time you get this. Maybe?
>
> Love,
Paul

I stuffed the mail into my briefcase, unlocked the inside door, and walked down the hallway to the first-floor apartment. Ozzie must have heard me, because he was already scratching against the other side of the door.

Ozzie is my golden retriever. He spends part of most days with the owners of the building, John and Linda Burns. John plays trombone in the Chicago Symphony Orchestra. Linda was a social worker until she had her first baby five years ago. They have two kids: a five-year-old girl named Katie and a two-year-old boy named Ben. Linda stays home with the kids, and Ozzie keeps them company during the day. It's a nice arrangement for all of us: I have someone to walk Ozzie, Linda has a big friendly dog to help watch the kids, and Ozzie loves all the attention.

"Rachel?" Linda's voice was muffled by the door. "It's me."

The door locks clicked open one by one, and then Linda pulled open the door. Ozzie wedged his way past Linda and jumped up, resting his front paws gently on my bent arms.

"Hey, Oz, how you doing, buddy?"

Ozzie licked my right cheek and then sat down in front of me, his tail flopping.

"Everything okay today?" I asked Linda.

"Great day," she said. Linda had on a red robe. Her long black hair was gathered on top of her head and rolled around an empty orange juice can. "I took the kids and Ozzie down to the beach. Ozzie loved it. He spent the whole morning in the water." She patted Ozzie's head. "Isn't that right, Ozzie?"

Ozzie's tail flopped twice.

"Are the kids asleep?" I asked.

"Ben is. I don't know about Katie. She drew you a picture today and told me she was going to wait up until you came home."

"Let's see if she made it. Do you mind?"

"Heavens, no. Go ahead."

I walked down the hall to Katie's room. She was in her bed, facing the wall with her thumb in her mouth. Her eyes were half closed. On the bedspread was a sheet of construction paper with a stick-figure crayon drawing of a girl and a dog. I bent over and kissed her softly on her nose. "Hello, cutie," I whispered.

Katie rolled slowly onto her back. "Hi, Rachel," she said hoarsely, her thumb still in her mouth.

"Your mommy told me you made me a special picture."

Katie slowly nodded her head, her eyes widening.

"Is this it?" I asked, lifting up the picture.

Katie nodded again.

I sat down on the edge of the bed. "It's beautiful, Katie. I love it. Thank you."

Katie smiled and took her thumb out of her mouth. "Will you put it in your office, Rachel?"

"I sure will. First thing tomorrow. Right next to your other pictures. And I'll tell everyone that my special friend Katie made it for me."

"I wrote my name on it. Katie. See?"

"I do." I bent over, kissed her on the forehead, and then stood up. "Thanks, sweetie. Good night."

"Good night, Rachel." She put her thumb back into her mouth.

I walked back down the hall carrying Katie's picture.

"She was still up," I said, holding up the picture. Linda smiled.

"Is John playing with the symphony at Ravinia?" I asked.

"Every night this week."

"Come on, Ozzie," I said. He scrambled to his feet. "See you tomorrow, Linda."

"Good night, Rachel."

Ozzie and I climbed the two flights of stairs to my apartment. I walked in after Ozzie. Tossing my briefcase on the couch, I stepped out of my shoes and went into the kitchen, where Ozzie was waiting by the pantry.

"Hungry, huh?"

He wagged his tail.

I took out two cans of dog food and emptied them into his bowl. I tossed in a few handfuls of cereal and set the bowl on the hardwood floor. *Bon appetit.* I patted Ozzie on the back.

I went into the bedroom, undressed, slipped on my purple and gold boxing robe (a Valentine's gift from Paul), stopped in the kitchen for a glass of white wine, and walked into the living room. I pulled the postcard out of my briefcase, clicked on the lamp, and settled down on the couch.

I read the postcard again. So he was back home. After teaching his annual one-month summer seminar at Stanford University on the detective in American fiction. "I'll be home by the time you get this. Maybe?" Maybe? Jesus. "Love, Paul." I sailed the postcard across the living room toward the bay window. It bounced off the rubber plant and fluttered to the floor.

Paul Mason. Professor Paul Mason. The dark-haired, green-eyed Young Turk of American literature. We had met last summer, just after Paul had joined the faculty of Northwestern University. I had ridden my bike up to Northwestern's Evanston campus, followed by Ozzie. Ozzie went swimming in the lake and I sat down on the boulders overlooking the water near the observatory. I was reading a Robert Parker mystery when Paul made his move.

"Mind if I share your boulder?"

"Help yourself," I mumbled, looking up from my book.

He was tall, tanned, and—from the look of him in his dark blue tank swimsuit—in excellent shape. Benny Goldberg calls men's tank suits "marble bags." Not so in Paul's case. He hoisted himself up onto the boulder with easy grace. He was wearing aviator sunglasses and had a trim dark beard.

"Beautiful day, huh?" he said, pushing his sunglasses back onto his head, where they almost disappeared in the thick curly hair.

I looked into his dark green eyes and nodded. I was wearing what Paul would later describe as my wet-dream outfit: a snug pink cotton tank top and black satiny jogging shorts cut high on the hips. It had seemed a sensible and comfortable outfit for a hot afternoon—or at least that's what I told myself that morning when I looked at my reflection in the bedroom mirror.

"Is it true?" he asked.

"Is what true?"

"Your shirt."

My T-shirt was a gift from a doctor I had lived with for almost a year while he was a resident at Michael Reese Hospital. He had moved back home to Cleveland to go into private practice after begging me to marry him and settle in Cleveland. It just wasn't the right time for me. I was still the young professional woman with dragons to slay. We gradually lost touch after several increasingly sporadic weekend trips. The T-shirt had a legend on the front: ALL THIS . . . AND BRAINS TOO.

"Absolutely," I said, smiling. "I even have an affidavit from the man who gave it to me."

He laughed.

"Are you a Spenser fan?" he asked, pointing to my Robert Parker mystery.

"Actually, I'm a Hawk fan," I said.

"I like Susan Silverman."

"So you're a mystery fan?"

"Have to be," he said. "Occupational hazard. I teach a seminar at Northwestern on the detective in American literature. My name's Paul Mason."

"Professor, huh?"

"American lit. I was out at U.C.L.A. for the last five years. I just joined the faculty here."

We watched a big yacht pass by. "Are you here alone?" he finally asked.

"No," I said. "I'm here with my friend Ozzie."

"Oh." A flicker of disappointment.

He was a damn good-looking guy. I took special note of the gold *chai* hanging from his neck.

"He's out there swimming." I pointed to where Ozzie was paddling in the lake.

Paul lowered his sunglasses and looked. "Ah." He smiled and then turned back to me, pushing his sunglasses up on his head again. "You thirsty?"

"A little," I said.

"I'm renting a house just across Sheridan. My fridge is stocked with beer. I'm sure I could find some water for your friend."

I looked at him for a moment and then shrugged. "Sounds great."

We walked back to his house. I had a beer, Ozzie knocked off a bowl of water, and I agreed to meet Paul at Dave's Italian Kitchen for dinner. After dinner we walked along the lake and then went back to his house, where—after two more beers— I broke one of my cardinal rules: Never sleep with a man on a first date. I told myself maybe some rules are meant to be broken. Within two weeks I had moved enough of my things to Paul's house to start spending the weekends there.

I loved everything about Paul Mason: his tastes in movies *(Annie Hall, The Big Chill, Chinatown),* his sense of humor, his favorite authors (Jane Austen, Wallace Stevens), his trim muscular torso, his beard, his eyes, his smile, his laugh, his smell, his uncanny sense of the romantic. I was, for the first time, passionately in love. The erotic voltage between us seemed to grow in force with each passing week. One night, at a dull faculty cocktail party, we snuck upstairs and made love, fully dressed, standing up against the tiled wall in the guest bathroom. The mirror was fogged by the time we slumped to the cold floor.

It remained wonderful for almost eight months. And then it happened. Looking back, it seems like a scene lifted—clichés still intact—out of a formula romance novel. Paul had office hours every Thursday morning from ten until noon. He usually held them at his house, and was free the rest of the day. I had decided to give him a romantic surprise one Thursday, when a deposition scheduled for that day was canceled. I walked into the house about twelve-thirty that afternoon, carrying a grocery bag containing a loaf of French bread, a couple of wedges of cheese, and a bottle of chilled white wine. We'd build a fire in the fireplace and start with a picnic on the rug by the fire.

There was a red down jacket and a leather purse on the dining room table, along with a copy of *Moby Dick*. I paused for a moment, but then—trusting to the end—decided Paul's office hours had run over. I put the grocery bag on the kitchen counter, hung my coat up in the closet, and tossed my briefcase onto the couch in the living room. Then I heard the shower. And it all clicked. The shower. Paul's most irritating habit. He took a shower after making love. Always. It could be four in the morning, after we'd come home from a party and had drunkenly made love, half dressed, on the couch. Nevertheless, Paul would stagger into the bathroom for his shower.

I walked slowly up the stairs, the pain turning to rage and then back to pain. I went into the bedroom first, where a terrified college girl with long blond hair was pulling on her faded blue jeans. She was hopping on one leg, her naked breasts wobbling.

"Get out of this house," I said.

She grabbed her blouse and shoes in one hand and, with the other hand covering her breasts, hurried past me and stumbled down the stairs.

I pulled my suitcase out of the closet, heaved it onto the bed, flipped it open, and stomped over to the dresser. I threw my blouses and jeans and sweaters and underwear into the suitcase. Then I went to the closet and, in one sweep, pulled my clothes out of the closet, still on their hangers. Carrying them over one arm, I reached down, picked up my shoes, and tossed them into the suitcase. All the while—even as I was muttering curses under my breath—I knew I was acting out a scene I'd watched performed in dozens of bad movies over the years. Which only made me angrier, and more humiliated.

"Rachel, honey, I can explain."

I spun around. Paul stood at the door, wet and naked, a towel slung around his shoulders. He stepped toward me, his genitals swaying. "It's not what you think," he said, putting a hand on my shoulder.

"Save your breath, you son of a bitch." I slapped him hard across the face and then spun around, picked up my suitcase and other clothes, and stomped out of the house.

He called that night. I hung up as soon as I heard his voice. He called again. And again. Finally, I let him talk. He apologized, told me he'd never do it again, promised he'd change, told me he loved me.

"How many?" I asked.

"How many what?" he responded.

"Office hours. Jesus. How many of those little girls have you screwed in that house?"

"C'mon, Rachel. I promise it'll all be different from now on."

"Listen," I said, my voice rising, "you can do whatever you want. Invite your little coeds over and screw their brains out. But don't you ever call me again, because—"

"But Rachel—"

"Because the next time you do, I'm calling the police. I'll tell them you're harassing me, and they'll throw your butt in jail so fast you won't know what hit you." I slammed down the receiver.

He stopped calling. Eventually, I felt sorry—or, more precisely, embarrassed—about the slap in the face, but not about anything else.

And now the postcard.

I sighed and picked up my book from the coffee table, where it lay facedown, open to where I had left off last night. *Pride and Prejudice.* I read it again every two or three years. Back when Paul and I were together, I used to read him passages aloud. I read for an hour, clicked off the living room light, and went into my bedroom. Slipping off my robe, I stepped over Ozzie (who was asleep on the floor near my bed) and climbed into bed.

I stared at the ceiling, rolled on my side, and then back on my back. "Damn," I mumbled, and got out of bed. I stepped over Ozzie, went back to the living room, picked up the postcard, and walked slowly back to the bedroom.

12

I SAW THE ARTICLE IN the *Tribune* on the ride downtown Wednesday morning. On page three of the
City section:

ZOO TO GIVE POPULAR HIPPO PROPER BURIAL

A spokesperson for the Brookfield Zoo announced yesterday afternoon that the zoo had
decided to bury Gus, the popular hippopotamus who died last Saturday, at Wagging Tail
Estates, a pet cemetery on the southwest side
of Chicago.

"This way Gus's many fans can have the opportunity to pay their last respects to him,"
announced Harmon Brown, assistant keeper
of the suburban zoo.

Final funeral arrangements have not been announced.

"We expect the funeral will take place a week from Saturday," explained Maggie Sullivan, owner of Wagging Tail Estates. "It will be a simple and tasteful ceremony. That's the way Gus would have wanted it."

The hippopotamus died three weeks after his 41st birthday. A team of veterinarians is scheduled to perform an autopsy later in the week. Zoo officials say he was one of the oldest hippopotamuses in captivity.

I was pleased for Maggie's sake, and for mine. The funeral would be a boost for business, and it would keep her mind off the grave robbery, at least until after the funeral.

I spent most of the morning in the courtroom of Judge Harry Wilson on the twenty-second floor of the Federal Courts building. It was the morning motion call, and there were about two dozen lawyers scattered around the courtroom waiting for their cases to be called. Some were skimming their pleadings, some reading newspapers. I took a seat in one of the rows of benches in the gallery. While I waited for my case to be called, I read through Graham Marshall's codicil again. I compared the four dates specified for delivery of flowers to the grave with the four dates of the newspaper articles listed in code on the computer printout. In each case, the flowers were to be delivered one day before the anniversary of the newspaper article. I was baffled for a moment, but then the two sets of dates lined up. It was obvious.

The motion call started at 9:30 A.M. My case was finally called at 10:30 A.M. The arguments lasted fifteen minutes, and the judge granted my motion, ordering my opponent to produce certain medical records within fifteen days.

I called my office from the phone outside the courtroom.

"Any messages?" I asked.

"Benny wants you to meet him for lunch at one at the Bar-Double-R."

"Tell him I'll be there. Do you have Cindi Reynolds's phone number?"

I called Cindi. She said she could meet me down at her condominium pool in fifteen minutes.

"I got the swimsuit layout," she said. "They're going to shoot it down at the Indiana Dunes tomorrow. So I have to catch some rays."

Cindi was on a chaise longue on the pebbled-concrete deck of the condominium pool. Two kids were splashing and shouting in the shallow end of the pool, and an elderly man wearing a black bathing cap and green goggles was swimming laps in slow motion. A middle-aged woman in a red one-piece swimsuit was sitting on a chair on the far side of the pool, smoking a cigarette and reading a paperback.

Cindi was wearing a white string bikini and sunglasses. I pulled up a deck chair and sat down beside her. The sun felt good.

"You models sure have a tough life," I said.

Cindi smiled. "It's a swimsuit layout for a winter resort-wear catalogue. They told me to get a little sun this morning. No more than an hour. All the models have to meet at this motel down in Indiana tonight. They'll start the shooting tomorrow. It might take two days."

"What's it for," I asked, "Frederick's of Hollywood?"

She giggled. "Kind of skimpy, huh?"

I nodded. The bikini top ended just above the nipples, and the bikini bottom was cut high on her hips and scooped low below her belly button.

"They told me no visible tan lines. I wasn't going to lie out here naked. The catalogue is for Carsons, I think. I can't believe they'll have me pose in anything skimpier than this."

"You're probably safe," I said.

Cindi leaned back and put on her sunglasses. "So, what's up?"

"I'm not sure," I said, frowning. "I found a list filed under Canaan at Abbott and Windsor. It turned out to be a code for newspaper articles."

"Newspaper articles?"

"Four of them. All from 1985. I read the articles last night."

"And?"

"And you're in one of them."

"Me?" Cindi raised her sunglasses. "What do you mean?"

"The article about the Ms. United States Pageant. The same one you have in your scrapbook. It was one of the four articles listed in code on the sheet."

"Really?" Cindi sat up.

I nodded. "Along with three other articles having nothing to do with you or beauty pageants."

"Was it Graham's list?"

"It looks that way, but I don't know for sure. His secretary remembered that he worked on something called Canaan back in 1985. But she doesn't know what it was. She had the firm check the files and they turned up just one document. The page with the codes. You can't tell who compiled the list."

"Is it handwritten?"

"No. A computer printout."

"Is it run on an Abbott and Windsor computer?"

"I don't think so," I said. "At least not on the firm's main computer. I've got a hunch, though, and I'm going to get back there tomorrow to see if I can turn up anything."

I checked my notes. "What do you know about two businessmen named Carswell or Framingham? Did you know them?"

She shook her head. "Nope."

"Congressman Barnett? Or a Park Ridge couple named Byron?"

"No. Are they in the other articles?"

I nodded. "The two businessmen died in a plane crash. Private plane. Congressman Barnett's autobiography got published with a big typo on the first page. And the Byrons found a lot of money in an old filing cabinet they bought at a police auction."

Cindi frowned. *Those* were the other articles?"

"Yep."

"What's my article doing in there?"

I shrugged. "I have no idea. But those articles are just about the only clue I have so far."

"And you think they have something to do with this pet, Canaan?"

"I think it's all related somehow." I told her about the codicil.

"I don't get it, Rachel."

"I don't either. But match up the dates. Your article appeared on July twenty-eighth. According to Marshall's codicil, two dozen roses are supposed to be placed on the grave on July twenty-seventh. It's the same with the other three articles. The roses are supposed to be delivered the day before the anniversary of the date the articles appeared."

"Why the day before?"

"That had me stumped at first. But think about it. Each newspaper article appeared the day *after* the event it described. He wanted the roses delivered on the date the event actually occurred. The beauty contest occurred on July twenty-seventh, not the twenty-eighth. As I said, the dates match up. It can't be just a coincidence. Besides, the title of that computer page was Canaan log. And whatever is buried in that grave was named Canaan."

Cindi stared at the pool. "Okay," she finally said. "But what's the relationship between those events and the pet's grave?"

"I don't know. That's why I came back to see you. Maybe you can help. Did you know Marshall before 1985?"

"No. I didn't start seeing him until the summer of 1986."

"Are you sure he never talked to you about anything personal?"

Cindi reached down for her Virginia Slims. She took out a cigarette and lit it with a butane lighter. I waited. She exhaled slowly and turned to me.

"I wasn't totally honest with you yesterday," she said. "I mean, I had just met you and all." She took another drag on her cigarette. "Graham and I weren't close at all the first year. Strictly business. But during the last six months he started opening up a little, sharing things with me. That article about the plane crash—well, it reminded me of something Graham told me a couple of months ago."

"What was it?"

"His sister. She used to be in beauty pageants too. The way he talked about her, I guess she must have been really beautiful. She was two years older than him."

"What happened to her?"

Cindi shook her head. "God, it was terrible. Graham was just eighteen when it happened. During the summer before he started college. It was 1955, I think." Cindi paused to stub out her cigarette. "That summer his mother and sister were killed on their way to a beauty pageant down in Springfield."

"In a plane crash?"

Cindi shook her head. "Not *in* a plane. *By* a plane. A small private plane had engine trouble. The pilot tried to land it on the highway. He landed it right on top of their car as they were going down the highway."

"My God."

Cindi sighed. "Yeah. Everyone was killed. Can you imagine that? Getting killed on a *highway* by a plane dropping out of the sky?"

"Graham told you all this?"

She nodded. "And more. I guess his father never recovered from the shock of it. His dad started drinking heavily that summer and died of a heart attack that winter. It really shook him up. First he loses his mother and his sister. Then he watches his dad disintegrate before his eyes."

"Was she his only sister?"

"Yes. And I could tell he loved her very much. The night he told me—well, he was really choked up by the time he reached the end."

I was genuinely touched by the story, more than I would have imagined. The Graham Marshall I

knew—the arrogant and domineering senior partner—bore no resemblance to the boy who lost his
entire family during his eighteenth year back in
1955.

Cindi wiped her eyes with the back of her hand.
"He never talked about it again. And I was actually kind of relieved. There was one part of the
story that—I don't know—kind of made me uncomfortable."

"What was that?"

Cindi shrugged. "Maybe I read too much into it.
His sister. Her name was Cynthia."

I said nothing.

"He didn't seem to see the connection," she continued. "God, Freud probably makes everyone too
suspicious. I mean, I don't think Graham was into
some kind of incest trip, you know. It's just that I
saw the connection immediately—another beauty
queen named Cynthia." She shook her head. "I've
had some weird requests from my clients. But I
wasn't prepared to play his sister for him. I
couldn't have handled that number. But, like I say,
he never brought it up again."

We were both quiet for a while. "What about the
beauty contest you were in?" I asked. "What exactly did he say about it?"

Cindi held out the pack of Virginia Slims. "Want
one?"

"No, thanks. I'm trying to quit."

"Me too. I quit in January. And in March. And
in May." She paused to light a cigarette. "As I told
you, it was strange the way he brought it up so
often. But the first time he did, he said something
really weird."

"What?"

She blew out a thin stream of smoke that disappeared in the soft breeze. "It was one night after we were, uh, after we were done. Last summer, I think. Graham was standing in front of the mirror in the hallway, knotting his tie. He asked me out of the blue, 'Do you think luck had anything to do with it?' 'With what?' I said. 'The beauty pageant,' he said, 'the other girl winning, you finishing third runner-up.' It sort of caught me off guard. I hadn't really thought much about luck one way or the other. And I was really surprised that he—that Graham Anderson Marshall—would even know who the third runner-up was. Or the winner, for that matter. I sort of shrugged and said, 'I guess it was the luck of the draw.' Well, he turned around and looked at me, his eyes kind of sad. And then he said—and I won't forget these words—he said real slowly, 'It *was* the luck of the draw. I'm sorry about that now. But then again, maybe it brought me you.' Weird, huh?"

"That is odd," I finally said. For a moment I had thought I was on to something, but now I was even more confused.

"Did you enjoy working for him?" she asked.

"Not really," I said. "He was a tough bastard. Very demanding. When he wanted something done, you had to do it. Right away. No excuses. I don't think he ever got used to a woman litigator."

"Did he ever try anything with you?"

"Nope. He wasn't like that." I paused. "In that way he was different. With a lot of male lawyers, particularly partners, there's that undercurrent of sex. The way they look at you when they talk, the jokes they make, the hand on the shoulder."

"Do you have a boyfriend?" Cindi asked.

"Not now."

"Did you just break up?"

"A few months ago."

"I could tell," she said.

"What do you mean?"

"You have your guard up. He must have hurt you."

"He did."

"Another woman, huh?"

I nodded.

"Creeps," she said. "They're like little boys in a candy store. Can't keep their hands off the goodies."

"How about you?" I asked.

"Me?" Cindi smiled and shook her head. "It would be like a busman's holiday. Believe me, I treasure the nights alone. Away from them." She took a drag on her cigarette. "Maybe once I stop all this, maybe then."

I watched the old man swimming laps, his arms slowly heaving out of the water one by one.

"Were you ever married?" Cindi asked.

I shook my head.

"How did you manage?"

"What do you mean?" I asked.

"You're smart, great-looking, nice body. You must have to fight them off."

I shrugged. "For me it's been the wrong guy at the right time or the right guy at the wrong time."

"I don't get it."

"Well, you start off back in high school looking for someone who's cool," I said. "Coolness is what counts. He has to dress cool, talk cool, and be in the in crowd. I had one. The quarterback of the high school team."

"Me too," said Cindi.

"Good-looking, great body, tiny brain."

"And lots of hand jobs."

We both laughed.

"And then you get to college and you want an intellectual," I said. "An intellectual soulmate. Someone you can discuss Sartre with, someone who believes that America is a totalitarian fascist dictatorship. You know the type. And then, if you're lucky enough to outgrow that, you finally realize that what you really want is someone who's—well, who's nice."

Cindi smiled. "Preferably a sweet guy with a cute tush."

"Yeah. A nice guy with a great bod who prefers Robert Lowell to *Car & Driver*."

"You like Robert Lowell too?"

"What do you mean too?" I asked.

"Graham Marshall loved one of his poems."

"You and Marshall read poetry together?"

"Not exactly. Graham brought me an anthology of poems. It was part of his Pygmalion number. He read me 'For the Union Dead.' Then he told me all about Colonel Robert Gould Shaw. Do you know who Shaw was?"

"Not really," I said. "Except that he was a white Civil War soldier who headed an all-black regiment for the North."

"Marshall told me all about him. It's a great story."

"Tell me," I said.

"Shaw was a real Boston blueblood. A New England aristocrat. When the Civil War started, he enlisted. In the spring of 1863 they made him a colonel and asked him to head up the first all-black regiment. He took his blacks to Folly Island that summer. Isn't that perfect: Folly Island. The Union troops attacked Fort Wagner, and Colonel Shaw and his black troops led the charge. Shaw was wounded going up the hill. He reached the top, waved his sword, and died. More than half of his troops died with him. They were all buried—Shaw and his soldiers—in a shallow trench near the sea. A couple of years later the sea washed away the trench and all the bodies, including Shaw's."

"Didn't they build a statue honoring him in Boston?" I asked.

Cindi nodded. "After the war ended, a group of Boston citizens raised money to build the monument. To Colonel Shaw and his men. It took them almost thirty years to do it. I've seen the monument. It's really beautiful." Cindi stubbed out her cigarette. "Isn't it an incredible story?"

"It is," I said.

"And what was just as incredible was the gift Marshall gave me."

"What?"

"Come on upstairs and I'll show it to you," she said, checking her watch. "I've been out here long enough already."

"I'm supposed to meet a guy for lunch," I said to Cindi as we stepped out of the elevator. "Just a friend. From Abbott and Windsor. Why don't you join us? You'd love him. He's really a character, and he knows something about the case."

She unlocked her front door and looked at me.

"I'm serious," I said. "Grab some clothes and come on. It'll be fun."

Cindi paused, her hand on the doorknob. Then she shrugged and said, "Why not? Maybe I will."

She walked into her bedroom, untying the top of her string bikini. She came back into the living room a few minutes later, wearing a pair of lavender bikini panties and a silk blouse which, unbuttoned, wafted open behind her. She was carrying a poster board about the size of a newspaper.

"Marshall gave me this," she said. "I keep it in my bedroom."

Dry-mounted on the poster board was the front page of the *Boston Commonwealth*, dated May 29, 1863. It consisted of ten columns of small, densely packed type with no illustrations.

"I don't know *where* he found it," she said, buttoning her blouse. "But look at this story." She pointed. "I'll go grab some jeans and sandals."

The story was in the middle of the page:

PRESENTATION OF COLORS
TO THE FIFTY-FOURTH REGIMENT

Thursday the 28th of May was a day to be remembered by all Massachusetts men who love liberty and rejoice in its triumphs: for on that day the great stigma of prejudice against color was officially removed.

Led by their valiant young commander, Col. Robert Gould Shaw, the 54th Regiment broke camp at an early hour and marched to the Common, which they reached at half past ten o'clock, stopping before the State House for the officials, who were there to review the troops and present the colors. Gov. Andrew and staff, His Honor Mayor Lincoln, and many officers and civilians of note greeted the regiment.

A great multitude, five or six thousand at least, assembled to witness the ceremony. Among the number we saw the well-known leaders of the Abolitionists—Garrison, Phillips, Quincy, May, Douglass and others, and besides them many names that Boston delights to honor—Lowell, and Putnam, and Jackson, and Cabot.

The men of the colored regiment were well armed with Enfield rifles, were certainly well drilled, and for military bearing and general good appearance certainly would compare well with most new regiments who have passed through this city.

Prayer having been offered by Rev. Mr. Grimes, Gov. Andrew presented the various flags to young Col. Shaw with a lengthy and inspiring speech. The handsome and brave commander of the 54th Regiment responded:

> Your Excellency, we accept these flags with feelings of deep gratitude. They will remind us not only of the cause we are fighting for and of our country, but of our friends we have left behind us. We thank our Lord for the opportunity to show that you have not made a mistake in entrusting the honor of the State to a colored regiment—the first State that has sent one to the war.

The line of the march was then taken up to Battery Wharf, where the troops embarked with little delay on the DeMolay. The Steamer sailed about four o'clock yesterday afternoon.

I leaned the poster board against the couch. What was the reason for Marshall's keen interest in all this? Why had he cared about a black regiment from the Civil War? Cindi seemed to think it was nothing more than an odd little gift from one of her clients. And maybe that's all it was.

The Bar-Double-R Ranch Restaurant is a noisy chili joint sunk in the basement of a city parking garage. The garage butts up against the Woods Theater, whose massive white marquee announced this week's triple feature: *Texas Chainsaw Massacre, Part III, Kung Fu Killers,* and *Return of the Coed Death Squad.*

"You know, I think I was offered a part in *Coed Death Squad,*" Cindi said. "I got some really weird movie offers after that beauty pageant."

Cindi followed me down the stairs into the dimly lit restaurant, past the beeps and thumps of the video games, back to where Benny was sitting. He was at a wooden table next to a tiny stage on which, according to the placard, "The Sundowners, Chicago's finest country-western group, get down to fundamentals each weeknight from sundown to midnight."

I introduced Cindi to Benny, who was momentarily rendered speechless. He struggled to his feet, almost upsetting the small table, and shook her hand, his eyes blinking. Cindi and I got in line, picked up our orders of chili, and returned to Benny's table. He had ordered us each a bottle of Stroh's.

"God, Benny," I said, "how can you eat all that junk?" Spread out on the table before him were two bowls of chili, a hamburger with french fries, and a chili dog.

"This is their Flatus Special," Benny said. "I figure by about three this afternoon I'll be ready for liftoff." He turned to Cindi, who was laughing and choking on a mouthful of beer. "We're a classy group of guys over at Abbott and Windsor."

"So what's the good news?" I asked. "My secretary told me you had some great announcement."

"I can't believe it, Rachel." Benny took a big swallow of beer. "Out of the blue I get a call from the assistant dean of DePaul Law School. First time I heard from them." He turned to Cindi. "I've been trying to get a faculty position. I sent out résumés and copies of my law review articles to every law school in the western hemisphere." He turned back to me. "Anyway, the guy calls me up and offers me a faculty position, starting next January."

"You're kidding!"

"No shit, Rachel. A two-year appointment teaching contract law and a seminar on class actions. Can you believe it? It'll mean a big salary cut, but it's worth it. I said yes on the spot."

"Congratulations, Benny," I said.

"That's super," Cindi added.

"When are you going to leave the firm?" I asked.

"Probably around October first. I'll take a couple of months off before I start teaching. Do something fun for a change. Maybe a long weekend at Myron's House of Latex with the Rockettes."

"How about a month of electroshock therapy at Bellevue Hospital?" I said. I took a sip of beer. "Who knows, maybe Cindi will be one of your law students."

"Cindi?" Benny asked, looking at her.

Cindi shrugged.

"She's thinking about going to law school," I said.

"Good grief," said Benny in mock wonder. "A

beautiful shiksa with brains." He put his hand over his heart and rolled his eyes heavenward. "At last, Lord. You have sent me a sign."

We ate our lunches, making small talk about law schools and the Cubs, who were beginning their annual late-summer swoon.

"Forget the Cubs," I said. "But watch out for my Cardinals. They're going to do it again this year. And this time they'll *win* the World Series."

Benny looked at Cindi and shook his head. "That's Rachel's tragic flaw. She's smart, tough, gorgeous, great legs. All-world legs. But the woman loves the Cardinals. Even named her dog after their shortstop."

"Don't knock it," Cindi said to Benny. "I grew up in Peoria rooting for the Cards. My dad used to take me down to Busch Stadium twice a summer."

"You're both depraved." Benny took a final swig from his beer and ordered another round for all of us. "So, you're helping Rachel with this Canaan thing," Benny said to Cindi.

"A little," she said. "I'm afraid I haven't been much help."

"Benny knows about the heart attack at your apartment," I said.

Benny coughed. "Did you know Jean Huber?" he asked quickly.

"Not, uh, professionally," Cindi said. "But I knew he was at your firm. He really did die of a heart attack in the office, didn't he?"

"Middle of the day," I explained. "He always kept his door shut. His secretary wasn't allowed in his office when the door was closed and he was on the phone."

"He apparently had the heart attack around midmorning," Benny said. "He must have knocked over the phone when he fell. As far as his secretary knew, he was on the phone, because his extension light was lit up on her phone. Around four that afternoon one of the other lawyers knocked on his door and walked in. And there he was, laid out flat on his back, stiff as a carp."

"God," said Cindi.

"Your friend Marshall almost killed Huber with one of his practical jokes," I said to Cindi.

"Marshall was a practical joker?" Cindi asked.

"When he was younger," Benny said. "He was infamous for his practical jokes."

"What did he do to Huber?" Cindi asked.

"Huber and Marshall were down in Kansas City for some sort of court hearing," Benny explained. "They had just checked into the Crown Center Hotel, and the two of them were up in Huber's suite. I guess Huber needed some cash for the night. He told Marshall he was going downstairs to buy a magazine and then he was going to the front desk to cash a check. As soon as Huber leaves the room, Marshall calls downstairs and tells the front desk that he's Jean Huber and that some big guy in a gray suit just broke into his room, beat him up, and stole his wallet and checkbook. Meanwhile, Huber goes down the elevator, stops in the gift shop, and then walks over to the front desk and tells them he wants to cash a check. Two minutes later Huber is surrounded by cops. They handcuff him, take him down to the station, and book him. Huber went berserk. The guy had an absolute shit hemorrhage in jail. Meanwhile, Marshall calls the mayor, who just happens to be an old law school buddy, fills him in on the joke, and then—about two hours later—Marshall goes down to the police station and gets Huber released."

"That's terrible," Cindi said.

"Yeah," Benny said. "But Huber never tried to get even. He was scared to death of Marshall. Most of the partners at Abbott and Windsor were. Marshall had this weird power over them, particularly the younger ones that he'd trained. They were like capons around him."

13

PAUL MASON WAS SITTING IN my outer office chatting with my secretary when I returned from lunch.

"What are *you* doing here?" I asked him. Mary raised her eyebrows and shrugged.

Paul stood up. "I was down in the Loop and thought I'd drop by to say hi. I just flew back from the West Coast."

"And your arms are killing you, huh?"

He forced a laugh. "How are you?"

"Fine." Paul followed me into my office, carrying a gym bag. I sat down behind my desk, and he sat in the chair facing the desk. Paul was wearing a pink Lacoste shirt, khaki slacks, and sandals. He put his gym bag on the carpet by his chair.

"You look great, Rachel."

"You don't look so bad yourself." He looked terrific. Steady, girl. "You screw a lot of California coeds this summer?"

"Jesus, Rachel, that stuff is behind us."

"What do you mean us, kemosabe?"

"I miss you, Rachel. I really do. I've been doing a lot of thinking about us."

"Forget it, Paul. Things were going bad between us long before I caught you giving that private tutorial on the Kama Sutra."

"I know. And it was my fault, Rachel. I accept the blame. I guess I just wasn't ready for that sort of relationship."

"Well, I was. And now I'm not. You killed it, Paul."

"I don't propose we jump right back to where we used to be, Rachel."

"We aren't jumping anywhere. And anyway, this is starting to sound like a bad soap opera."

Paul gave me a sheepish grin. "I know."

Mary buzzed me on the intercom. "Rachel, it's that guy from the dictionary publisher again. He says he has some news on Canaan, Massachusetts."

"Okay, I'll take it." I looked at Paul. "This will take just a sec." I lifted the receiver and said hello.

"Miss Gold, this is Ralph Pinchley from *American Language*."

"How's it going, Ralph?"

"I'm really quite excited, Miss Gold. I think we've finally solved this Canaan mystery."

"Oh?"

"It appears that our 1928 edition did contain an entry for Canaan quite similar to the one you read me. However, it was an erroneous entry. I'm pleased to report to you that the error was caught before the revised edition went to press in 1942. There was no Canaan, Massachusetts, Miss Gold.

Our research files for the 1942 edition confirm that."

"How?"

"Oh. Well, there is a note in the file. Quite, uh, succinct, I might add."

"What does it say?" I asked.

"Well, it says: 'Checked sources; no such place.' "

"What about the 1928 files?"

"I beg your pardon."

I sighed. "Ralph, if there's no such place, then how did it get into the 1928 edition? What's in those files?"

"Oh, dear. I'm afraid those files are gone. They were destroyed in a fire back in 1931."

"Rats."

Undaunted, Pinchley launched into another sales pitch. I listened silently, thanked him again, and hung up.

"Canaan, Massachusetts?" Paul Mason asked.

I shrugged. "An imaginary Puritan village."

"Not necessarily imaginary."

"What does that mean?"

"It's a good story."

"Wait a minute. How do you know anything about Canaan, Massachusetts?"

Paul smiled. "I went to Barrett College. Anyone who went to Barrett College between about 1950 and 1980 has probably heard of Canaan. One of the professors used to give a famous lecture on it each year."

"There really was a Canaan, Massachusetts?"

"Apparently so."

"How come I couldn't find anything on it?"

"It's not in the standard history texts. It was just one of dozens of little towns and villages that failed back in the seventeenth and eighteenth centuries.

But some Colonial historians know about it. And there's been at least one book written about it."

"What book?"

"I'm sure I have a copy of it somewhere. I'll drop it off."

"What's so special about Canaan, Massachusetts?" I asked.

Paul shook his head, grinning. "Read the book first. It's real short. I don't want to spoil the fun. I'll bring it by your place this afternoon. I won't be around tonight, but we can talk about it tomorrow."

I shook my head, smiling despite myself. "This all sounds like a sneaky way to extort another meeting with me."

Paul parodied shock, his hand on his heart. "Me an extortionist? Never."

"All right. Drop off the book and we'll see."

Paul sat back in his seat and studied me with a wry expression. "Does this Canaan thing have anything to do with your work on Graham Marshall's estate?"

I stared at him. "How do you know about my involvement with Marshall's estate?"

Paul chuckled. "Elementary, my dear Gold. You are talking to America's foremost authority on detective fiction. It starts to rub off after a while."

"Don't bullshit me, Paul. How did you find out?"

He shrugged."Your friend Kent Charles told me you were working on the estate." He gestured toward his gym bag, "I played handball with him over the lunch hour."

Back when Paul and I were together, I had dragged him to a few bar association functions. He had met Kent Charles at one of the events, and the two hit it off immediately. We had even double-dated a few times. Paul and Kent played handball together twice a week at the Union League Club.

"What did Kent say?" I asked.

"Not much. He mentioned that he saw you Monday at the firm. And that you looked as gorgeous as ever. An understatement, I might add. He said you were helping the firm on something to do with Marshall's estate. I assume it has to do with that codicil on your desk."

I glanced at my desk and saw the codicil lying faceup on the edge near Paul. The word *Canaan* appeared several times in capital letters on the first page. The caption had Marshall's full name in bold-face type.

"You're getting to be a real snoop," I said.

"I'm sorry. I couldn't help noticing it while you were on the phone with that guy."

"Well, it's supposed to be confidential, Paul. So I'd appreciate it if you keep your mouth shut. Understand?"

He raised his right hand. "I promise."

I glanced at my watch. I was supposed to meet Kent Charles at the Yacht Club in less than an hour.

Paul saw my glance and stood up. "I have to get going," he said. "I'll drop off that book later." He lifted his gym bag and then paused.

"What?" I said.

Paul winked as he unzipped the bag. "I brought back a present from California."

I rolled my eyes. "Paul."

"Don't worry. It's not for you." He handed me a gift-wrapped package. "Tell Ozzie I miss him."

I smiled. "That's sweet. Thanks."

"Tell him it's what all the dogs are into out on the Coast."

After Paul left I unwrapped the gift. Inside was a pair of dog sunglasses—the wraparound Terminator style—and a small package of all-natural dog biscuits from some outfit in Marin County called The Organic Hound.

I sat back in my chair and smiled. Maybe he really had changed.

I met Kent Charles for drinks on the sundeck at the Yacht Club. He got there before me and was flipping through advance sheets when I arrived. His suit jacket was hanging on the back of his chair and he was wearing sunglasses. Just like Ozzie's.

Pausing at the doorway to the sundeck, I had to marvel again at how smoothly Kent Charles had adapted to his present life-style. The fourth son of an East Joliet bricklayer, Kent had been the first and only member of his family to enter college— an achievement made possible through the munificence of the athletic department of the University of Illinois. A four-year football scholarship carried him to a B.A. in economics. A three-year academic scholarship carried him to a J.D. from the University of Illinois College of Law. A combination of hard work, good looks, aggressive smarts, chameleonic adaptability, and a London tailor carried him to junior partnership at Abbott & Windsor— the first graduate of the University of Illinois College of Law to survive that perilous swim upstream. More than one client of Abbott & Windsor had asked Kent where he had prepped. To his credit, he answered truthfully, albeit with a touch of arrogance: East Joliet High.

"Glad you could join me, Rachel," he said, removing his sunglasses and setting them on the table next to his drink.

A waiter in a white jacket arrived just as I sat down.

"I'll have another gin and tonic, John," Kent said. "How 'bout you, Rachel?"

"Bud Light," I said. After the waiter left I gestured toward the harbor. "Is your boat out there?"

Kent pointed. "It's the fourth one on the left, over there."

"I remember going out on it when I was a summer clerk."

Kent smiled. "Yes. You wore a white one-piece, and your boyfriend got seasick as soon as we left the harbor."

"He threw up down in your bathroom." I shook my head. "At least I still have the swimsuit."

"How's your practice?"

"I'm busy," I said.

"Any regrets?"

"None. I guess I'm just not cut out for the big firm culture. I enjoy being on my own."

The waiter arrived with our drinks and a bowl of peanuts.

Kent took a sip of his drink. "Cal and I would like to get you back into Bottles and Cans."

I drank some of my beer. "As I said, I enjoy being on my own."

"And you would be. We have a potential conflict with one of the bottling companies. We'd like you to represent them. It would be easy work, Rachel. We could start you off on one or two of the defendants' subcommittees. Cal is chairing one on pre-1970 market-share surveys. I'm handling the predatory pricing claims, along with a guy from Cravath. It would mean a committee meeting each month, some work with expert witnesses, some drafting work, and attending some of the depositions. The next round of deps starts soon. I can make sure you get some choice assignments. Better yet, your fees are paid out of the joint defense fund. I'm on that subcommittee too." Kent smiled. "We pay all attorneys' bills within thirty days, no questions asked."

I mulled it over. It would mean an easy thousand dollars a month, probably for years to come. Bottles & Cans was an annuity for every lawyer involved. "What's the catch?" I finally asked.

Kent laughed. "No strings attached. Honest, Rachel, we could use the help. And if you don't take the client, we'll just have to refer it to someone else."

"God, I just hate the thought of getting back into that case."

"Might as well get on the gravy train, Rachel. It's an easy fifteen grand a year."

"Who's the client?"

"Mound City Bottling Company."

"In St. Louis?" I asked.

"Right. You're from down there, aren't you?"

"You're making it tempting." I smiled.

"Terrific."

"Wait. I haven't said yes yet. Do you have a file on Mound City Bottling?"

"Sure. I'll have my girl send it over tomorrow."

"Your what?"

"Sorry." Kent laughed. "My secretary."

"That's better, boy."

I asked Kent a few questions about Mound City Bottling, and then we discussed the current status of Bottles & Cans.

Kent pointed to my empty glass. "Another?"

"No, thanks. I have to get back to the office."

Kent checked his watch. "I have a meeting at six. A board meeting of the Shedd Aquarium. It ought to be over by seven. Do you have dinner plans?"

"I do. Thanks, anyway."

Kent smiled. "Maybe some other time."

"Sure. If I decide to represent Mound City, you and Cal can buy me dinner and fill me in on the case." Might as well keep the relationship professional from the start.

"Can I drop you off at your office?" Kent asked as we both stood up.

"No, thanks. In rush hour traffic I can get there quicker on foot. I could use the exercise, anyway."

"You look in great shape to me," Kent said as we passed through the dining area toward the exit.

Outside the Yacht Club one of the car hoppers had pulled Kent's red Mercedes convertible to the front. He handed the keys to Kent.

"I had lunch with Harlan Dodson today," Kent told me. "Harlan said there was a mystery involving Graham Marshall's estate. Is that what they've got you on?"

"Just a loose end they want me to tie up," I said, keeping it vague.

Kent moved close. "Well, Harlan seems really bent out of shape about Ishmael bringing you into the case. He probably drafted the will, and he's hypersensitive about anyone else trying to second-guess him on those things." Kent smiled. "Just a friendly tip."

"Thanks, I'll keep it in mind."

He placed his hand gently around my waist. I could smell his musky cologne. "Listen, if you have trouble tying up that loose end, I'll be happy to tell you whatever I know about Graham. We spent literally hundreds of hours together on out-of-town trips. I probably know more about that man than anyone but his wife. If I can help, give me a buzz."

I almost asked him about Canaan right there, but decided to hold off. I had already told Benny, and I wasn't supposed to tell anyone. "Thanks. I'll give you a call if I have any questions."

Mary had typed my notes of the four newspaper articles listed in code on the computer printout. I read them on the el ride to my apartment.

I got off at the Morse stop in Rogers Park, still mentally shuffling the articles: a beauty pageant, a fatal plane crash, an embarrassing typographical error, and a hidden treasure in a discarded cabinet. I was beginning to sense a pattern somewhere out there on the horizon of my mind, but it was still eluding me.

I knocked on my landlord's door. No one home. It was seven o'clock. Linda probably had taken the kids and Ozzie out for a walk. I left a note on her door and walked upstairs to my apartment.

It was stuffy inside, so I opened a few windows. I put a head of romaine lettuce under the kitchen faucet and went to my bedroom to change. I owed my parents a letter. I'd write them tonight.

I was cutting up a salad when Linda knocked on the door. She had Ozzie with her.

Linda came into the kitchen. "You'll never guess who dropped by an hour ago," she said.

"Who?"

"Mr. Wonderful himself. Professor Mason." She rolled her eyes heavenward. "He was as polite as a boy scout."

"I saw him downtown at the office today."

"Oh?"

"He wants us to give it another try."

"And?"

"I don't know," I said, cutting a tomato into the salad. "He came awful close to begging. And that about killed it for me." I cranked open a can of tuna, pressed the lid to squeeze the water into the sink, and scooped half the tuna on top of the salad.

"Well, he might not be that bad, you know," Linda said. "Look at it from his end. If he really has grown up, then he must feel terrible about what he did."

"I'll see."

"It'll be good for you, Rachel. Just be careful."

"Don't worry."

"Well, Paul dropped this off for you," she said as she handed me a large manila envelope. "He said you'd know what it was all about."

14

AFTER I FINISHED DINNER AND the dishes, I opened the manila envelope and pulled out a slender sheaf of photocopied papers stapled at the upper-left corner. There was a note from Paul Mason paper-clipped to the first page:

> Dear Rachel:
> Here's that Canaan booklet I told you about. It's a Xerox from the rare books collection of the Barrett College library. I'll be having breakfast at the Main Street Cafe tomorrow at 8 if you want to talk about it. I'll be out most of the rest of the day—faculty meetings.
> It was great seeing you today!
>
> Your friend,
> Paul

Faculty meetings? Were they in the same category as his student "conferences"?

I slipped off the note and flipped through the booklet. Thirty-one pages, copied two pages per photocopy. *The Lottery of Canaan*, by Ambrose Springer. Copyrighted 1903 by the Springer Trust. Springer had dedicated his little book to his sister, "As a slight token of the generous sympathy which has cheered me at each stage of this arduous undertaking."

I walked into my bedroom, pulled down the bedspread, and propped up the pillows. Clicking on the reading lamp on my nightstand, I got comfortable on the bed.

In his two-page introduction Springer complained of the difficulties which "bedevil the foolhardy soul who embarks on a mission to rescue from the crypt of time a long-forgotten tale of Colonial America." His mission had taken him "into musty attics in search of old diaries, into the dank storage rooms of old churches in search of the recordations of daily life long ago, and into old burying grounds for a glimpse at faded epitaphs engraved on crumbling tombstones o'ergrown with weeds."

I turned to the first page and began reading:

Perhaps no tale from the earliest days of our young republic is more curious than the brief history of Canaan, Massachusetts. Those in possession of maps of the Commonwealth will search in vain among the cartographer's markings for a sign of that little village. Canaan existed for but a mere quarter of the 17th century, and all references to it were expunged from the Commonwealth's record in

1699 by unanimous vote of the Congregational ministers. All that survives are a handful of sermons and diary entries by Canaan's young minister; a tattered remnant of a hand-printed advertisement; and the faded and besmudged records of that small village's church. This pitiful and tantalizingly incomplete record was rescued from oblivion by your humble author after a fire nearly destroyed the South Hadley home of Jonathan Frye, who claims to trace his ancestry back to Mr. Joseph Frye of Canaan.

Our tale commences in 1675, one year after young Winthrop Marvell graduated from Harvard College with a degree in ministry. Of his youth we know little. He was born in Boston in 1655, the sixth son of Richard and Anne Marvell, who had made the perilous pilgrimage to the New World in 1649.

Young Reverend Marvell settled in Cambridge Village after his graduation from Harvard College. In 1679, some of the inhabitants of that fair village, complaining of the lack of adequate land, announced their desire to leave the banks of the River Charles to set forth to investigate new territory in the wilds of western Massachusetts. Young Marvell consented to accompany them and serve as their minister.

On the morning of May 10, 1679, 119 hardy men and women assembled on the Cambridge common with all their possessions, including seventy head of cattle. After solemn prayer lead by their fervent young minister, they set forth to the beating of the drum which hitherto had summoned them to church. Following ancient Indian trails through the deep forests, they made their way slowly west, driving their cattle before them.

Seven days later, these pioneers reached the banks of the broad Connecticut River. Claiming a gentle hill overlooking the river, they commenced the construction of their small village, which they named Canaan, harking back to the Promised Land of the Hebrews.

Tragedy first struck Canaan in September of 1685. It came in the form of a storm so fierce and relentless as to rival the great Boston storm of 1635. Young Marvell described its terrible onslaught in his diary:

Such a mighty storme of wind & raine as nonne living in these Parts, either English or Indean, ever saw. Being like those Hauricanes that writers make mention of in ye Indeas. It began in ye Morning and came with such Violence in ye beginning, to ye Amasamente of many. It blew downe sundry houses & uncovered others & blew downe many thousands of trees, turning up ye stronger by ye roots and breaking ye higher pines in the middle. Several are ye dead and ye injured. Edmund Barnard lost his gentle wife. . . .

The storm destroyed nearly half the village's buildings, and included in its path of devastation the small church and Reverend Marvell's simple house.

The following evening, the Elders of Canaan met with Reverend Marvell to plan the reconstruction of the church. According to the surviving church records, those in attendance that fateful eve were Richard Bradstreet, Joseph

Frye, Simon Blake, and Benjamin Marshall. By flickering candlelight the Elders of Canaan debated the merits of various means for raising funds to rebuild the church. After many hours the Elders voted to fund the reconstruction by holding a lottery.

Dear reader, please recall that in the early days of our fair republic, lotteries were widespread. Indeed, history records at least one such lottery held years before the lottery of Canaan: the Jamestown lottery. In 1607, the village of Jamestown was founded by the Virginia Company. By 1612, due to disease and famine, the future of that young settlement was in grave peril. The principals of the Virginia Company seized upon the idea of a lottery to finance the expedition, and thereby prolonged the life of that woebegone settlement.

In Colonial America, lotteries raised money for many public improvements. The great colleges of Columbia, Harvard, Dartmouth, and Williams, to name but a few, were built or supported by the proceeds from lotteries. Lest we forget, in 1776 the Continental Congress established a lottery to raise much-needed funds for our Revolution. Alas, the Revolutionary War lottery proved a financial disappointment.

I knew about financial disappointments. I looked up at the Matisse poster on my wall. None of my lottery tickets had ever gotten me to France. I went back to my reading:

That first lottery of Canaan in 1685 proved a success, and the little church was rebuilt before winter. But the curse of Canaan remained, and that February a most ferocious blizzard destroyed the church and killed several villagers. The Canaanites rebuilt again their little church, raising the funds through yet another lottery.

Tragedy struck once more that summer, wounding the young minister most cruelly of all. The prior winter Marvell had married young Rachel Lowell, a fair damsel of sixteen, who had traveled west with her parents. By July 1st, according to the young minister's diary, his pretty wife was already heavy with child. Alas, two weeks later she was dead, the victim of a four-day storm that caused the Connecticut River to overflow its banks. The raging cataract of water swept the young bride down the river to her death. The lamentations of her grieving husband still pluck at the strings of our hearts more than two centuries after he recorded them in his diary:

My dear and loving wife departed this life after we had been married and lived together 7 months and 14 days, whereby I am bereaved of a sweete and pleasante companion & left in a very lonely and solitarie Condition.

Reverend Marvell confided less frequently in his diary during the next few years. His sporadic entries, however, record a most unusual series of tragedies that befell that hapless community. The village knew famine, disease, repeated Indian attacks, fires, and storms. As Reverend Marvell wrote:

I believe never there was a poore village

more pursued by ye wrathe of ye Devil than our poore village. First, ye Indean Powawes moleste our planters. After this, wee have had a continued blaste upon somme of our principal Grain. Herewithal, wasting sicknesses, especiallie Burning and Mortal Agues, have Shot ye Arrows of Death in at our Windows.

But Canaan also knew occasions of supreme felicity: bountiful harvests, miraculous recoveries from fatal diseases, unexpected generosity from neighboring savages.

At first the lotteries of Canaan were simple affairs involving a fortnightly drawing for a prize of grain or butter. But some of the villagers grew discontent with the manner in which their wealthier brethren purchased myriad tickets for each drawing, thereby multiplying their chance of victory. It was Reverend Marvell who introduced the first and, in retrospection, the most profound innovation into the lottery system: two tickets would be drawn, one for a prize and one for a penalty. This elegant solution to the hoarding of tickets injected a new element of risk into the melancholy lives of the Canaanites.

In the beginning, the penalty was a mere fine. As Reverend Marvell notes in his diary entry for May 5, 1690: 'Goodman Phillips drew ye penaltie Ticket and, according to ye day's charte, was ordered to donate 9 stalkes of corne to oure church.' But on July 7, 1690, Richard Pierce drew the penalty ticket, refused to pay the fine, and was forced to sit in the stocks for a day. By March of 1691, the payment of a fine had been eliminated and instead the owner of the unlucky draw was simply ordered to spend a day in the stocks.

The next major change came the following spring. The poorer villagers had complained of the purchase price of the lottery tickets, and some of the wealthier Canaanites had elected to withdraw from the lottery for fear of drawing the unlucky number. The resulting diminution of funds threatened the very existence of the lottery, which by then had become an important element of the village's fragile economy. The Elders of Canaan met with Reverend Marvell and voted to dispense with the requirement of purchasing a ticket. Thenceforth, every adult member of Canaan was enrolled in the lottery and the purchase of tickets was abolished. An annual tax levied on the head of each household supported the lottery.

Reverend Marvell's sermons (and diary) were wont to be written in a fine hand on small pages four by six inches in size. Those sermons that have survived reveal a disquieting preoccupation with biblical lotteries. The one I hold before me quotes the Old Testament (Num. 26:55–56), where the Lord instructed Moses to take a census of the people of Israel and divide the land among them by lot. In this same sermon Reverend Marvell describes how the first king of Israel was selected by lot. In yet another sermon, Reverend Marvell reminds his followers that after the death of Judas Iscariot, a casting of lots determined that Matthias and not Joseph should be named his successor as apostle.

Alas, Reverend Marvell's obsession with lotteries transmogrified into a vision that surely is the dark side of the doctrine of predestination:

And thus it appeareth to me that our Lord hath secreted unto His Scripture a texte which hitherto had not been revealed to me but which tonight hath come cleer, namely, that God doth play dice with His Universe.

From ye Cradle to ye Grave, a Man's life is predetermined in accordance with ye divine Lawe of Chance. Ye application of His Lawe of Chance properly belongs to God; He is ye only Lawemaker. But He hathe given power and gifts to man to interprett his Lawe and to establish on Earthe ye vessels through which His Lawe of Chance can be expressed.

And therefore, an Elder may prescribe ye pleasures and ye penaltyes so long as ye recepients thereof be chosen in accordance with ye Lawe of Chance.

I was startled by the sound of Ozzie barking.

"What's wrong, Oz?" I called out as I put the booklet on my bed and sat up. He barked again.

I found Ozzie in the kitchen, facing the back door. "What do you hear?" I said, patting him on the head.

He wagged his tail and then trotted into the living room. I stared at the back door for a moment and then followed him into the living room. He was standing by the window, his body tense, his head slightly cocked. I peered out the window. The street was empty.

Ozzie looked up at me and then moved over to

the couch. He curled up on the floor, resting his head on his front paws.

I glanced at my briefcase resting against the coffee table. There was work in there, but it could wait.

"C'mon, Oz. Keep me company."

He followed me into the bedroom and settled down by the foot of the bed. I picked up the booklet and found my place:

> The minister found enthusiastic accomplices among the original four Elders who had met with him to establish the first lottery in 1685. The awful vicissitudes of Canaan must have forced each of them to search for an answer to the riddle of their sad village. As Reverend Marvell recorded in his diary:
>
>> Swearing a Solemne Oathe of Secrecy, wee professed ourselves fellow members of Christ, for His worke wee have in hand, it is by mutuall consent through a speciall over-ruleing providence.
>
> By 1694, all lottery drawings were conducted in secret, and the results of the drawings were carried out in secret. No one in Canaan could any longer be sure whether his good luck or misfortune was the work of God or the result of the lottery of Canaan, administered in secrecy by the church Elders. A name would be selected by lot, and then a series of drawings would determine the precise fate of the target of the lottery. According to hints in Reverend Marvell's diary, the lottery drawings for one person could last from midnight until the break of dawn.
>
> Although the church records continued to

record the felicities and ignominies of the Canaanites, no longer do they indicate the cause of the origins of those achievements or punishments. We learn of Richard Brown being publicly whipped, but hear not for what. We learn of Katherine Aimes forced to stand on the church green wearing on her breast the shameful scarlet letter which Hawthorne has so poignantly immortalized in his story about Hester Prynne. But did she commit adultery? And if she did so sin, was she led to sin by her own impurity or by the silent machinations of the Elders of Canaan? The church records are silent and Reverend Marvell's diary contains nary a hint.

Poor men become rich and rich men become poor. Young girls hang from the gallows as witches. A sow dies mysteriously. An old widow discovers a precious gem while digging in her garden. A beautiful succubus visits seven male Canaanites in one week. A midnight conflagration consumes the barn and livestock of John Green, who stands alone on the village common the next morning hurling curses at the unseen lottery. And all the while the forces of nature and the whims of the savage Indians wreak havoc on that tiny community isolated in the wilderness.

The august Cotton Mather paid a brief visit to Canaan on July 30, 1696. His shock at what he saw and his determination to end the blasphemy are recorded in his journal entry for that day:

Wherefore the Devil is now making one attempt more on us; an attempt more difficult, more surprising, more snarl'd with unintelligible circumstances than any that wee have hitherto encountered. Understanding that many, especially of their Elders, gave themselves a Liberty to do things not of good Report, in obedience to the scandalous and secretive Game of Lotterie, I sett myself against their miscarriages and vowed to stoppe this perversion of God's Message.

Cotton Mather returned to Boston and rallied the Congregational ministers against all forms of lottery, and especially against the secret lottery of Canaan. Although the power of the Puritan church was in decline throughout the Commonwealth, Reverend Mather was able to pass a resolution in 1697 condemning the Lottery of Canaan and banishing Reverend Winthrop Marvell from Massachusetts.

Reverend Marvell's last diary entry is dated May 21, 1697:

Ye Elders of Canaan met at ye Church this eve and didst make an oathe to carrie on ye Lotterie into parts knowne and unknowne. Wee must not content ourselves with usuall ordinary meanes whatsoever wee did when wee all lived in Canaan. Ye same must wee do and more allsoe where wee goe. I shall depart on the morrow for ye Territorie west of Ye River. Ye Elders shall carry on in secret without me.

Reverend Marvell left Canaan the next morning and, alas, disappeared forever into the dark forests of western Massachusetts. The Village of Canaan disbanded in 1698, most of the remaining villagers moving on to Northampton, Springfield, or Boston.

Little else is known of the Elders of Canaan

or their lottery. There is a Richard Bradstreet buried in Boston behind the Old South Church. He died in 1711. Is it the same Bradstreet? No one can say. There is a Joseph Frye buried in Springfield, 1714. According to church records in Northhampton, Benjamin Marshall and his family set out for the West. A bill of lading bearing Marshall's name from Fort Pitt, dated April 9, 1720, is still extant. The rest of the Elders seem to have vanished into the sands of time.

Benjamin Marshall? I repeated. Could he have been the ancestor Graham Marshall had tried to trace his own roots to? But then again, it was a common name. There were thousands of Marshalls. Just as there were thousands of Golds. I took a pen off my nightstand, underlined the name, and started reading again:

Echoes of the Lottery of Canaan have reverberated softly through the years. A determined but misguided few persist in the unfounded belief that the Elders spread their blasphemy beyond the Village of Canaan, and that their heirs continue to perform their dark maneuvers in secret, outside the laws of man and God.

Indeed, just a few years back we again heard Canaan uttered in polite society, this time from the mouth of a young ne'er-do-well named Andrew Thompson. Mr. Thompson claims to have been on the Boston Common near the ceremonial platform during the dedication of that inspiring memorial to young Colonel Robert Gould Shaw and his Negro soldiers. Those of us present that glorious day watched with sympathy swelling in our breasts as Shaw's forlorn widow, Anne, burst into tears when the monument was unveiled. The esteemed sculptor of that monument, Augustus Saint Gaudens, placed a comforting arm around her shoulder and said to her, "It was the will of God." According to Mr. Thompson, Anne Shaw looked up at the sculptor with swollen eyes, smiled a bitter smile, and said, "No, sir. Not the will of God. The Lottery of Canaan."

Needless to say, there were others as near to the podium as Mr. Thompson, including your humble author, and all deny Mr. Thompson's incredible tale. And well they should, for the mad scheme of Reverend Marvell died with him somewhere beyond the wilds of the Berkshire Mountains two centuries ago.

But had it? I asked myself.

15

WHAT WAS COLONEL SHAW DOING in Cindi's apartment (compliments of Graham Marshall) and in Ambrose Springer's bizarre little tale? And what did a pet's grave, a computer printout, and four newspaper articles from 1985 have to do with a secret lottery conceived by a mad Puritan minister in a tiny village on the edge of the wilderness of western Massachusetts?

I walked to the kitchen, poured a glass of milk, and sat down at the kitchen table. It was 10:15 P.M. I had to get away from Colonial Massachusetts and someone else's ancestors. I had parents of my own, and I owed them a letter. Though we talked on the telephone every Sunday morning, I still tried to write them every couple of weeks. I knew my father took each of my letters down to the produce company, where he was the bookkeeper. He would read excerpts to the secretaries and salesmen. And then it would be my mother's turn to show it off. Sarah Gold: a brilliant and frustrated woman who came to America from Lithuania at the age of three, never finished high school, and put her older daughter to bed every night with fairy tales about college and medical school. "Someday you'll be a somebody," she would tell me as she kissed me good night, "and not a doormat like your poor father. Dr. Gold, they'll say. Please help me, Dr. Gold."

My younger sister, Ann, was allowed to be the girl of the family. She got as far as her sophomore year at the University of Missouri, married a Z.B.T. from Creve Coeur, worked to put him through dental school, and now lives out in Ladue in a new English Tudor with my niece, Jennifer, my nephew, Cory, and her husband-the-orthodonist (who once made a drunken pass at me at a New Year's Eve party, grabbing me in their modern kitchen, pushing me up against the built-in Amana microwave oven, and stabbing his thick tongue into my mouth—"You have magnificent incisors," he slurred as I pushed him away).

Tonight I got as far as "Dear Mom and Pa" and then crumpled the sheet of stationery and tossed it into the trash can.

"Come on, Ozzie," I said. "Let's take a walk."

Ozzie scrabbled to his feet and was waiting for me when I reached the front door. It was a warm night, and the beach and Loyola Park were crowded with couples enjoying the lake breeze. We walked out on the pier, past the men fishing and the young couples embracing. Standing at the end of the pier, looking south, I could see the red light flashing from the top of the Hancock Building;

looking north, I could make out the squat outline of the observatory at Northwestern. A large sailboat glided by, passing close enough for me to hear a woman's high-pitched laugh.

We walked slowly back to the apartment. Ozzie collapsed on the hardwood floor in the living room and I plopped down on the couch and began leafing through the *Reader*, Chicago's weekly alternative newspaper.

I skimmed the first section and then idly turned to the personals in the third section. This week's crop looked unpromising. Nothing much in the first column. Mostly phone-sex ads in the second column.

And then I spotted it, one column to the right, halfway down the page:

> Canaan 6: Addison-N
> 2:15 a.m., Thursday

I flipped through the rest of the personals. Nothing else. I shuddered, thinking back on Springer's strange booklet.

I turned back to the personals message for Canaan. Addison-N?

I walked to the back door. A procrastinating recycler, I had months and months and months of old *Reader*s, *Tribune*s, and *New Yorker*s stacked on my landing. I started with the three-foot pile of *Reader*s, opening each issue to the personals section. Then I turned to the *Tribune*s, scanning the personals in the classified advertisements section. By the time I was finished my eyes were smarting and my fingers were black with newsprint. Newspapers were strewn all over the back landing.

I had found two other Canaan messages from the past two weeks, and none before that. One was in last week's *Reader*:

Canaan 4: Washington
1:30 a.m., Monday

and the other was in a *Tribune* from eleven days back:

Canaan 6: Jefferson
3 a.m., Saturday

I was in bed and almost asleep when the Canaan personals became clear. "My God," I mumbled as I sat up in bed.

"Washington, Jefferson, Addison," I recited out loud. Of course. They were all el stops. Each message had an el stop, a time, and a day. Addison-N. The Addison stop, north platform. Two-fifteen A.M., Thursday. Tonight was Wednesday night. I checked the digital clock radio. It was no longer Wednesday. It was 1:04 A.M., Thursday.

Was something going to happen on the northbound platform at the Addison el station in one hour and eleven minutes?

I rolled on my side, facing the clock radio. I watched the digital numbers blink to 1:06, 1:07, 1:08. I thought it over. It was too late to call anyone. And who could I call, anyway. Paul? Not yet. Maybe never. Benny? Don't be ridiculous. It's not his case, anyway. 1:10. 1:11. You aren't going to pass this one up, are you? Just because it's the middle of the night and you don't have anyone to go with you? But I do, I told myself. I sat up and stared at Ozzie. 1:13. 1:14.

"Come on, Ozzie," I finally said, pulling back the sheet and getting out of bed. "We're going for a train ride."

16

I PULLED ON A PAIR OF baggy, paint-stained jeans and an old sweatshirt. Rummaging through my dresser drawer for a suitably drab scarf, I found a perfect one (beige with aquamarine flowers), and tied it snugly over my hair. Then I put on my torn high-top basketball shoes and laced them up. I looked at my reflection in the mirror. A real Mata Hari. I put an old pair of sunglasses in the back pocket of my jeans and stuffed four ten-dollar bills and three one-dollar bills into one of the front pockets—enough for subway fare and, if necessary, a long cab ride.

"Let's go, Ozzie," I said.

I stopped in the kitchen and took Ozzie's leash off the hook in the pantry. He was already at the front door, wagging his tail. I patted him on the head. "You're a seeing-eye dog tonight, big guy."

We walked down the empty streets to the Morse

el station. The door was propped open to ease the heat. We stopped in the shadows near the door. I fastened the leash on Ozzie and wound the leash around my hand until it was just about eighteen inches long. I slipped on the sunglasses. We could pass if no one looked closely. My heart was pounding.

An unshaven man in a rumpled raincoat lumbered past us.

I waited outside the station until he was a half block away, and then I took a deep breath. "Okay, Ozzie," I whispered. "Let's pretend we know what we're doing."

I walked slowly into the station and up to the ticket booth. A bearded young man was sitting in the booth, bent over what looked like an electronics textbook. I slid a dollar bill into the slot. He looked up and smiled. I kept my face blank. He leaned forward and saw Ozzie.

"Uh, would you care for a transfer, ma'am?" He spoke loudly and slowly.

"No, thank you." My voice sounded two octaves above normal.

"Here is your change, ma'am."

I slid my hand down the glass to the slot and picked up the dime.

"Are you going south or north?" he asked.

"South."

"Go up the stairs. They are about twenty feet ahead of you. The southbound train is to your left when you reach the top of the stairs."

"Thank you," I said. "Come on, Ozzie."

We squeezed through the turnstile and walked slowly to the stairs. I held Ozzie close to my side with the leash as we went up the stairs to the platform. Fortunately, it was empty. I slid the glasses down low on my nose and we waited. It was 1:33 A.M. At 1:35 I almost turned back. I could feel a drop of sweat trickle down my back.

At 1:39 a southbound train rumbled into the station. Using my hands, I found the door to the first car and stepped in, keeping Ozzie close. Tentatively, slowly, I walked to the front of the car. There were four people in the car: an old man in a tattered shirt and baggy pants mumbling in his sleep; a middle-aged chunky Latino, four rows ahead of the old man, staring blankly out the window; and the two black teenagers, two rows ahead of the Latino, laughing and shoving each other. The teenagers turned to stare at Ozzie and then at me as we passed by. I sat down in the front seat next to the motorman's enclosed compartment, pretending to stare into space. I pressed my hands against my knees to keep them from shaking.

The doors rattled shut and the train lurched forward into the darkness. The train rocked and creaked as it rounded the gentle bend south of Morse and picked up speed. I was facing the front window of the train. An oasis of light became visible in the darkness down the wide band of tracks. The lights grew brighter and gradually resolved into the Loyola station. I turned my head slightly, keeping my face blank. Three people got on: an old man with the jagged walk and unfocused gaze of a mental retardate; a young black dude in an orange jumpsuit; and his woman, teetering on spike heels. The dude wore sunglasses, too, and was carrying a portable stereo the size and shape of a communications satellite. The two of them—the dude and his woman—sat down near the back and soon the car was reverberating with reggae music.

A man with a gray lunch box boarded at Granville. The dude and his woman got off at Lawrence. At the Wilson Station a swaying drunk on the opposite side of the platform was urinating onto the tracks. He lurched forward, almost toppling over the edge as the train pulled out. One of the black teenagers ran to an open window facing the platform and shouted, "Watch out, fool!" His friend burst into laughter, and they slapped each other five.

The train squealed around the curve at Sheridan/Irving Park and pulled into the Addison Station. Holding Ozzie against my side, I groped down the aisle. When we stepped out onto the empty platform, it was 2:03 A.M. I waited until the train pulled out of the station. Raising my sunglasses, I quickly walked down the stairs with Ozzie, across the screened catwalk, and up the stairs to the northbound platform. It was empty too.

I looked down the snarl of train tracks converging in the distance on the Belmont station. No train. Across the el tracks at Addison the gray outline of Wrigley Field loomed above the southbound platform.

What was I doing here? I'm a lawyer, not a detective. I should leave mysteries to Paul.

A CTA bus rumbled along Addison Street below the platform, its air brakes hissing. A police siren wailed in the night—the noise grew louder and louder and then suddenly shut off. The eerie silence was broken by the rasp of heavy footsteps coming up the metal stairs. I turned toward the noise, trying to keep my face blank. I pulled Ozzie closer.

A dark-haired man had reached the top stair. He was wearing khaki workpants and a black T-shirt. He paused, looking at Ozzie and then at me, and stepped out onto the platform. He took up his position about ten yards north of where I was standing. He was a large man with shiny black hair slicked straight back.

We stood there in silence. My sweatshirt was soaked through with perspiration. Ozzie had turned toward the man, his leash taut. Ozzie looked at me and then back at the stranger. I stared straight ahead and the man peered south down the tracks. He had his hands in his pockets and was going up and down on his toes.

I caught the headlights in my peripheral vision before I actually heard the approaching train. As the train slowed, the man walked down the platform toward the front door. Then it happened, so quickly I almost missed it. The train doors opened, the man reached inside, and someone handed him a large manila envelope. The man turned in my direction, holding the envelope, and walked quickly back down the platform to the stairs.

I took two steps toward the train door, as if I were boarding, and then backed away as the man disappeared down the stairs. I waited until the train began moving out of the station, and then I pulled off my glasses. "Come on, Ozzie."

We ran down the stairs and pushed through the turnstile. The man was sitting in a gray Ford station wagon parked in front of the el station. I leaned against the wall, keeping Ozzie close. I was panting. The man was reading something from the manila envelope in the light of the street lamps. Then he started the engine and pulled away.

I ran out in the street. The station wagon was heading east toward Lake Shore Drive. There was a Yellow Cab parked beneath a street lamp, its engine idling. I jumped in with Ozzie.

"Follow that car!" I said, pointing to the station wagon that was now two blocks away.

The cabbie chuckled as he gunned the engine. "Lady, I've been waiting twenty years for someone to say those words. Hang on."

We caught up with the station wagon at the Irving Park entrance to Lake Shore Drive and followed him up the northbound ramp onto the drive.

"Your boyfriend?" the cabbie asked, studying my outfit in the rearview mirror.

"Not exactly," I said.

"Follow that car," he repeated, grinning. He was about fifty years old—short, balding, and chubby. The nails on his stubby fingers were bitten to the quick. His name and photograph were on the license over the meter: Louis M. Farina.

"I once had Red Buttons in this cab," he said, removing an unlit, chewed cigar from his mouth. "A regular guy, that Buttons." He swung the cab into the far left lane following the station wagon.

We followed the station wagon to the end of Lake Shore Drive, where it turned right and sped down Sheridan Road through the canyon of high-rise apartment buildings. It turned onto Devon Avenue and then right onto Western Avenue. We followed the station wagon north on Western and pulled in behind it at the stoplight at Western and Pratt avenues. The huge hot dog on top of Flukey's was dark. The streets were empty. The light turned green and the station wagon pulled ahead on Western. He put on his turn signal as he passed Morse and then turned left at Lunt.

"Give him room," I said as we drove past Indian Boundary Park. "I don't want to spook him."

"Gotcha," the cabbie said. He turned off his headlights.

The station wagon turned right, drove along the boundary of the park, and then turned right again into the dead-end street behind the park.

"Don't turn," I said. "Let's wait right here."

We sat at the corner and watched the station wagon ease into a parking spot at the end of the street across from the park.

"Wait here for me," I said, opening the door.

"You sure you want to go out there alone?"

"I won't be alone." My heart was pounding. "C'mon, Oz."

Indian Boundary Park is one of Chicago's nicer small parks. It has tennis courts, a playground, a big sprinkler, a duck pond, and a mini-zoo that includes goats, rabbits, ducks, geese, two long-legged wolves, a raccoon, and two black bears. I had taken Katie and Ben there a few times this summer. The kids would feed the goats, go on the playground, go under the big sprinkler in their underwear, and end their day at the Baskin-Robbins up the street.

I jogged down the sidewalk past the tennis courts and the backs of the animal cages; Ozzie kept pace at my side. Slowing to a walk at the green chain-link fence enclosing the wolf run, I cut down the path between the wolves' cages and the fenced-in goat and bunny area.

The light inside the station wagon blinked on as the man opened the car door. I crouched by the goats to watch. The man walked around the far side of the goat yard toward the deserted play-ground, which was illuminated by a single lamp-post. I crept closer and stopped against a tree. Ozzie growled at the animal scent.

The man walked past the swings and the jungle gym to the large Cinderella pumpkin carriage, which glowed orange in the dim light. The same carriage I had helped Katie and Ben climb on dozens of times on Sunday afternoons. He stopped in front of the carriage. I ducked back behind the tree as he slowly looked around in all directions.

When I peered around again, he was reaching into the carriage. He pulled out what looked like a grocery bag and walked quickly back to the station wagon. Opening the back door of the station wagon, he set the bag down on the floor and closed the door. Then he got in, started the engine, and clicked on the headlights.

By that time I was sprinting back along the path in front of the animal cages. I didn't want him to spot us on the sidewalk. One of the bears scrambled to his feet as we passed his cage.

Ozzie and I reached the edge of the park just as the station wagon pulled around the corner. I ducked behind the bushes, pulling Ozzie down, until the station wagon passed, and then we ran across the street to the cab. Farina had turned his cab around while he waited for me.

"Good thinking," I said as I hopped into the backseat.

Farina started the cab and we were off down the street in pursuit. "I figured he'd have to come back this way," he said. "I slumped down when he came by. He didn't see nothing, lady."

We followed the station wagon back to Devon. He turned left on Devon and headed back toward the lake. Ozzie had his head out the window, panting in the humid breeze.

"You ain't with the CIA, are you?" Farina asked.

"No, nothing like that. Let's give him a lot of room," I said. "I don't want him to think he's being followed."

The station wagon got back on Lake Shore Drive heading south. We followed the station wagon downtown. It turned off the drive and headed into the underground parking garage of Shore Drive Tower, where I had been with Cindi that morning.

I shoveled a few ten-dollar bills at Farina, and then Ozzie and I hurried down the ramp to the door of the garage. I pushed the button on the wall and the garage door slid up and open with a grinding clatter.

We found the station wagon one level down, parked in one of the visitors' slots. It was empty and locked. The grocery bag was gone. We walked back up to the main level of the garage, and I tried the steel door into the building. Locked. There was a push-button combination security lock over the doorknob, like the dial panel on a push-button telephone. I tried a few random sets of numbers. Nothing.

"Damn," I muttered.

We walked back down to the station wagon and I stared at the license plate, memorizing the number. Maybe he lived at Shore Drive Tower.

I sat down with my back against one of the concrete columns, three rows away from the station wagon, screened from view by a Lincoln Continental. Ozzie rested his head on my lap. We'd wait and see if our quarry came back down.

About an hour later one of the building security guards woke me up. I staggered to my feet. The station wagon was still there.

"You'll have to move on, lady. You and your dog."

I couldn't think of a good explanation to offer as to why he had found me asleep in the garage at 4:30 A.M., or, moreover, why he should let me stay down there with my dog. Given my outfit—baggy jeans, sweatshirt, basketball shoes, and scarf—I doubt he would have believed me, anyway.

"C'mon, Ozzie," I said, and we left.

17

"ENJOY THE BOOK?" PAUL MASON asked. We were both having pancakes and coffee at the Main Street Cafe in Evanston. It was 8:15, Thursday morning. I needed the coffee. Preferably intravenously.

"Is it true?"

Paul shrugged. "Probably only the dull parts. There *was* a Canaan, Massachusetts. It was founded in 1679. Its minister *was* Winthrop Marvell. And it *did* die out at the end of the seventeenth century, like dozens of other Massachusetts villages. The rest of the story, however, has never been confirmed. Most historians treat Springer's booklet as pure fabrication."

"How do you know that?"

Paul was wearing a dark blue Polo shirt and faded olive army pants. I had on a soft cotton blouse and a pleated skirt.

"Because I graduated from Barrett College in

1976," he said. "As I told you, if you attended Barrett College between 1950 and 1980, chances are you either took Henry Abbott's course in Colonial American history or attended his lecture on Canaan, which was the high point of his course. He gave it in Plimpton Chapel, and hundreds of students used to sit in each year."

"What was the Canaan lecture?"

"It was about the dangers of relying on secondary sources. Ambrose Springer's booklet is a secondary source, which means it's an interpretation or description of primary sources—diaries, letters, and the like. The point of Henry Abbott's lecture was that you couldn't write history by relying on secondary sources."

Paul smiled. "A basic lesson for beginning historians," he continued, "but not exactly a titillating topic for a general audience. But Henry Abbott wasn't a typical professor of history, if there is such an animal. He was an enormous, vigorous man, with thick bushy eyebrows and a walrus mustache. His Canaan lecture was mesmerizing. He presented it as a mystery story, with himself cast as the detective. Abbott started by telling Springer's version of the Canaan lottery, including that little Colonel Shaw twist at the end—the suggestion of a lottery surviving through the centuries, operating in secret, controlling the destinies of millions of Americans. Marvelous fodder for college students."

"And?"

Paul chuckled. "Henry Abbott would pause to let the enormity of it all sink in. The audience would be hushed. Most of us who heard it for the first time just sat there stunned, trying to grasp the implications, trying to figure out if and when our lives had been touched by the lottery of Canaan. And then Henry Abbott would destroy the illusion."

"How?"

"Ambrose Springer starts off, if you remember, with a description of the records he found in the attic of the South Hadley home of one Jonathan Frye. In his lecture, Abbott re-created his own search through the South Hadley real estate records. What he discovered was that there never was a Jonathan Frye in South Hadley—never even anyone named Frye who lived in South Hadley. Then Abbott read us the first entry from Reverend Marvell's journal, the excerpt about the storm that destroyed the small church. And then he read it again, or at least that's what we in the audience thought. Only it turned out that the second time he was reading from the journal of Governor Bradford. Springer had apparently copied the entry from Bradford's journal almost word for word, including all the odd spellings. As for the alleged quote from Cotton Mather, it's probably a fabrication. All of Cotton Mather's diaries have been preserved. Although he's known to have visited Canaan, his diaries contain no reference to the village."

"What about the stuff on Colonel Robert Shaw's widow?" I asked.

"Wonderful stuff." Paul conceded. "But very dubious. Henry Abbott would read aloud to us from two different newspaper accounts of the dedication ceremony. He also read us an excerpt from the diary of William James, who was on the platform that day. According to James, Mrs. Shaw was never near the sculptor during the ceremony, and she left the platform on the arm of the governor of Massachusetts. All in all, Professor Henry Abbott's performance was a tour de force. Each year it ended with a standing ovation."

"More coffee?" the waitress asked.

"Please," I said. "But what did Abbott find out about the author? About Ambrose Springer?"

"Apparently not much. It's a good question. I've looked into the whole thing since then. More accurately, I've had some of my students look into it. It's an excellent teaching device. And it gives them a chance to play detective. I hand them a copy of Springer's book cold and tell them to investigate the story. Most of them discover at least one or two of the fabrications Henry Abbott discovered. A few years back one of them tried to dig into Springer's life."

"Did he find anything?" I asked.

"Not much. Springer graduated from Barrett College in 1884. He was a recluse for the rest of his life, living in a small cottage on his family's estate in Quincy, Massachusetts. This was his only book. He published less than fifty copies of it, one of which Henry Abbott had discovered in a secondhand bookstore in Springfield, Massachusetts. When Abbott died, he donated his copy, along with the rest of his books, to Barrett College. As far as I know, no other copy of the original has survived."

"Do you think there's any truth to the lottery?" I asked.

Paul smiled. "I don't know. There are just enough confirmed facts to make it possible. And you know how I love mysteries."

"I don't understand the mechanics of it," I said.

"The mechanics of what?"

"Of the lottery. I understand how they could

draw someone's name. That part's the same as one of those drawings for a door prize. But the rest I don't get. How could a lottery drawing end up with someone's barn burning or a gem being buried in a garden?"

"As I see it," Paul said, "one way would be to have two boxes. In one box would be slips of paper with the names of all the villagers. In the other box would be slips of paper, each with a different scenario or fate. Draw a name from box one and a fate from box two." Paul snapped his fingers. "Just like that. Another way would be more complicated. They'd still have the name box. After they drew the name, though, there could be a series of drawings, or even spins of a wheel to decide things. Would there be a good fate or a bad one? That could be the first draw or spin of the wheel. If a bad fate, would it involve the person himself or someone or something related to the person? That would be another drawing. Et cetera, et cetera. Sort of a Puritan version of *Wheel of Fortune*."

"That could get pretty complicated," I said.

"Well, long, maybe, but still fairly simple. You'd have a series of binary draws. Sort of like computer language. Off, on. Yes, no. Over and over and over until you had reached a specific outcome. You could run that lottery today on a computer with a fairly simple program."

"On a computer," I mused.

"Sure," Paul said. "But what does all this have to do with Graham Marshall?"

"I don't know." I studied Paul. I was definitely in over my head on this Canaan assignment. Paul had plenty of free time. His classes wouldn't start until after Labor Day. He could be useful. Maybe. I decided to take a chance on letting yet another person in on the investigation. "Well, I've been try-ing to solve a mystery."

"Great." He leaned forward. "Tell me about it."

"Only if you can keep your big mouth shut. If this gets back to Ishmael Richardson, he'll be very upset. And you can't go blabbing this to your buddy Kent Charles."

"My lips are sealed."

I was selective about what I told him. I explained the codicil, described the four newspaper articles from 1985, and the little I knew about the grave robbery. But I omitted last night's adventure on the el train. I wanted to mull on that on my own for a while.

"Fantastic," Paul said, his eyes gleaming. "You think Graham Marshall was running his own Canaan lottery?"

"I don't know what to think. It could all be just one of his practical jokes. Take a look at today's newspaper. Or yesterday's. Or any day for that matter. There's at least one freaky event reported each day. Graham could have picked four articles at random and then set up the codicil as a joke. After all, they say he had a pretty perverse sense of humor."

"Maybe," Paul said, leaning back in the booth. He scratched his beard. "But why steal the coffin? And what the hell was in that coffin in the first place?"

"I've got a hunch," I said. "I'm going to run it down. I'll let you know if I come up with any-thing."

"How 'bout a hint?" Paul said.

"Wait."

"Rachel Gold, you're getting to be a real tease."

I snorted. "Serves you right, Casanova. Anyway, I've already told you too much. Give me time."

"How about dinner, then?"

"Paul, let's hold off on any dinners for a while, okay? You help me solve this and dinner will be on me."

"That sounds delightful," Paul said with an impish grin. "Which part of you is dinner going to be on?"

"Very funny." But I knew I had to hold myself in check. We were both behaving as if nothing bad had ever happened between us. As if we were still lovers. I forced myself to remember that shattering moment when I had walked in on that girl in his bedroom. You've been burned once by this guy. Don't forget it, Rachel.

Over his protest, I grabbed both bills.

As we were leaving the restaurant, Paul tried to stifle a big yawn.

"Tired?"

"Yeah," he said. "I didn't get much sleep last night."

"Oh? What's her name?"

"C'mon, Rachel. That's not fair. There's no girl. I have a paper due for a conference in September. My deadline's Monday. I was up all night typing a draft." He peered at me. "You don't exactly look well rested yourself."

I studied him for a moment. "Have you ever tried to sleep on an el train?" I finally said.

"Right," he said, forcing a laugh. But he still looked puzzled when I left him.

18

WHEN I GOT DOWN TO my office, I found a pile of unopened mail and a stack of telephone message slips on my desk. By noon I had plowed through my correspondence, returned most of the telephone calls, and dictated some interrogatories in a copyright case I was handling. For lunch I had two more aspirin with a large mug of coffee. The caffeine helped a little, as did the walk across the Loop. But my head was still throbbing from lack of sleep as I rode the elevator up to the offices of Abbott & Windsor.

My first stop was Helen Marston, who told me Marshall's dictionary was still missing. "I am quite troubled by this, Rachel," she said. "Someone apparently stole it."

I made a mental note to mention the theft to Ishmael Richardson, and headed down two floors to the firm's library. The assistant librarian at the front desk—a new face—told me Lynn was back by the Supreme Court Reports. I walked along the stacks of state and federal case reporters. There was an associate in every study carrel, most behind a bunker of case books, yellow legal pads, and photocopies of court decisions.

The library at Abbott & Windsor is the training ground for new associates, and like the rest of A & W, it's open twenty-four hours a day, 365 days of the year, and there are always dozens of associates at work there, no matter what the hour. Basic training at Abbott & Windsor lasts about four years and consists of thousands of hours researching in the library or reviewing documents in tiny windowless offices.

I found Lynn Rapp walking back down the aisle toward her office. "Rachel Gold! What a wonderful surprise. What brings you back here?"

"A favor, Lynn."

"My pleasure, kiddo. Come on into my office."

I followed behind her. "Hurt your foot?" I asked. She was limping.

"Twisted my ankle again," she said, turning back with a smile. "It's all this darned weight. My doctor told me that if I don't lose fifty pounds by Thanksgiving, he's going to personally enroll me in one of those fat farms."

Lynn Rapp is short and very overweight, although she minimizes both with a cleverly selected wardrobe. She is the firm's head librarian, and has held that position for more than a decade. Cheerful, energetic, and a terrific resource for any research problem, Lynn has always been a favorite among the associates.

She settled herself into the large swivel chair behind her desk. "How've you been, Rachel?" she asked as she pushed her blond bangs back off her forehead. Lynn has large blue eyes and the sort of face that frequently evokes the comment of how pretty she would be if she only lost some weight. She is approaching forty and still lives at home with her mother.

"Things are going well," I said. "I've got enough work to keep me busy, and the firm has been good about sending me referrals."

"They ought to be. You were our best associate, Rachel."

"Don't make me blush." I smiled.

"You survived Mr. Marshall. Not many do." Lynn shook her head. "So what can I do for you, kiddo?"

"I'm helping the firm with a little matter and I need to run down some info on a book and an author."

Lynn picked up a pen and pulled out her pad. "Shoot."

"The book is called *The Lottery of Canaan*. It was copyrighted back in 1903 by the Springer Trust. It's a little book—only thirty-one pages long. The author is Ambrose Springer. What I need is some more information about the book and the author. Who was he? Did he write anything else? That sort of thing. Apparently, Barrett College in Massachusetts has a copy of the book in its rare book collection."

"No problem. I'll get on it right away. Check back in about an hour."

I thanked Lynn and took the spiral staircase up one floor.

My next stop was Harlan Dodson, the partner handling Marshall's estate. On my way down the hall I passed Cal Pemberton, who was standing by the door to one of the conference rooms. He was dressed in his usual state of mild dishevelment: The right side of his shirt was untucked in the front and his bow tie was skewed at a forty-five-degree angle. Apparently lost in thought, he didn't respond to my greeting.

I took the spiral staircase up to Harlan Dodson's office. Harlan is the head of Abbott & Windsor's trusts-and-estates department and occupies a corner office on the firm's top floor—closer to my dearly departed clients, he likes to joke. An office in the sub-basement would better serve that purpose.

Dodson's door was open, and he was on the telephone when I poked my head into the office. He waved me in and pointed to a chair in front of his enormous walnut desk.

Like his desk, Harlan Dodson is squat, massive, and ornate. He looked even fatter than when I had last seen him a couple of years back. The telephone, cradled between his shoulder and neck, was half buried in flesh. Dodson had pinky rings on each hand—a fat diamond on one and a ruby on the other—and a gold chain bracelet around one thick wrist. His black pinstripe suit was freshly pressed, as was the starched white shirt that covered the wide expanse of chest and belly.

The polished effect Dodson strove for with his attire was ruined by an indefatigable set of sweat glands. Dodson perspired constantly and heavily. As I sat there listening to the rasp of his breathing and watching him wipe his shiny face with a handkerchief, I thought of Barney Sonderman, the fat boy who sat across from me in my high school Spanish class—he came to Spanish directly from gym class, unshowered, dripping sweat onto his desk and notebook.

Dodson concluded his telephone conversation and turned to me, forcing a smile. "Hello, Miss Gold. What can I do for you?"

"I have a few questions about Graham Marshall and his will."

Dodson sat forward. "Very well. But before you start, I think it only fair to tell you that I do not share Mr. Richardson's concern over this . . . this ridiculous codicil. The trust can, should, and will be broken. The sooner the better." Dodson flipped through some papers on his desk. He picked up a stapled court document stamped Draft in red on the first page. "I have already prepared the necessary probate papers. As soon as you conclude your investigation, I plan to file them. Today is Thursday. I would like to file the court papers Monday."

"There's been a slight problem," I said.

"Oh?"

"Someone robbed the grave and stole the coffin."

Dodson stared at me from beneath hooded eyelids as he mopped his face with the handkerchief. "All the more reason to break the trust," he finally said. "The whole thing is ludicrous. An embarrassment to Marshall's family, and, frankly, to this firm. A textbook example of why people need attorneys to plan their affairs. No one wants to die. That's a given. They come to me to find a way to cheat death, to control things from the grave. I personally prepared Graham Marshall's will, Miss Gold. That will is impregnable. It achieves exactly what Graham Marshall properly wanted to achieve. And nothing more. And then, after his death, I discover that ridiculous codicil." Dodson shook his head in disgust. "No competent estates lawyer would ever have permitted such a legacy. For a pet's grave? Forty thousand dollars? My God!" Dodson sat back, his breathing labored and raspy.

"I want to wrap it up quickly too, Harlan. But I need some more information. Maybe you can help."

Dodson stared at me and then turned to the window. "Go ahead, then. Ask me."

"Who else knows about the codicil?"

Dodson turned to me. "Just Mr. Richardson, you, and me."

"What about the rest of the Executive Committee?" I asked.

"I seriously doubt that. Mr. Richardson chairs the Executive Committee. I asked Mr. Richardson not to tell anyone else yet. He agreed."

"Kent Charles said you told him."

Dodson's eyes narrowed. "Mr. Charles mentioned that he heard you were working on the estate. I merely confirmed that fact." He paused. "I may have mentioned a problem with a codicil. But I can assure you that I made it quite clear that I had no hand in its preparation."

"How well did you know Graham Marshall?" I asked.

Dodson lifted a pencil and studied it, rotating it between his thick thumb and forefinger. "I spent hours with him on estate planning matters. For him. For his wife." He rapped the pencil on his desk. "People disclose confidential matters when you plan their estates."

"Did he ever talk about his genealogy? About who his ancestors were?"

Dodson stared at me. "Why do you ask?"

"I saw the bequest to the Massachusetts Historical Society."

Dodson frowned. "Graham told me his family traced its roots back to Boston. Back to the time of the Puritans. Back to someone named . . . let's see . . ." Dodson ran his stubby fingers through his sparse brown hair.

"Benjamin Marshall?" I said.

Dodson looked up. He adjusted his tie as he studied me. "Yes, I think that's who it was. Benjamin Marshall. I prepared a bequest to the Massachusetts Historical Society. Fifty thousand dollars. Nothing unusual about that, I assure you. Done all the time."

I asked him a few more questions about the codicil, listened to another diatribe on the importance of getting the matter resolved quickly and quietly, and then stood up. "Thanks for your time, Harlan."

"Very well, Miss Gold. Remember, I want to put this embarrassment behind us. Promptly."

"So do I."

"Are you sure you saw that book?" Lynn Rapp asked me again. I had returned to the library after leaving Harlan Dodson.

"I saw a photocopy. I read it last night."

"Well, I can't find much on the book or the author. First I checked the Chicago Public Library. Nothing. I called the Library of Congress in Washington. My college roommate works in the reference department. They're supposed to have a copy of just about every book ever published. She looked into it and called me back. They have records that show that an Ambrose Springer wrote a book called *The Lottery of Canaan*. It's apparently the only book Springer wrote. And it's the only book copyrighted by the Springer Trust. The Library of Congress doesn't have a copy of the book. I confirmed that the only known copy"—she looked down at her notes—"is at Barrett College in Massachusetts. I talked to the librarian of Barrett's rare books collection. He said they've advertised for additional copies, hoping that a private collector would sell one. They think that some copies are still out there. But no owner has ever come forward." She shrugged. "Sorry I couldn't find anything else about it."

"You found plenty, Lynn. And you helped close some doors."

"Good. Where did you get the book?"

"It was a photocopy of the one at Barrett College."

"Well, I can't add much to that," she said.

"Maybe you can help with something else. Frankly, I wouldn't know where to start. I think it has something to do with Canaan. It's an odd phrase I came across. Maybe it's from a court decision."

"What is it?" Lynn asked, reaching for a pencil.

I recited the epitaph on the Canaan tombstone.

" 'A nickname for Providence'?" Lynn repeated.

"I'd be grateful if you could find what it means, or where it comes from."

Lynn tapped her pencil on her notepad. "Well, I could start by running it through the Lexis terminal. If I don't turn up anything there—" She paused and raised her head, her ears cocked. "I think they just paged you, Rachel."

"Me?"

I listened. A few seconds later I heard it: "Rachel Gold. Please call the switchboard."

"Here," Lynn said, handing me the telephone receiver as she dialed 0. The firm's switchboard operator came on and told me to call my office immediately.

Mary answered. "Good afternoon. This is the law office of Rachel Gold."

"What's up, Mary?"

"Thank God they found you, Rachel. Your neighbor Linda just called. Something's wrong with your dog."

"With Ozzie? What?"

"She doesn't know. She went up after lunch to take him for a walk and she couldn't wake him up."

"Oh, my God. Is he . . . ?"

"No. But he won't wake up. And he isn't breathing right. She's taking him to your vet."

"I'll get over there right away. Thanks."

"Good luck, Rachel."

19

THE THICK FUR ON OZZIE's neck was damp from my tears. He was lying on his side in one of the examining rooms of Dr. Terry Machelski's office. Ozzie's eyes were closed, his mouth was open, and his tongue lolled on the table. He was breathing, though. Thank God he was breathing.

I checked my watch. It had been almost thirty minutes since Terry Machelski had pumped Ozzie's stomach. I scratched Ozzie behind the ear. "It'll be okay, Oz," I whispered, leaning forward to kiss him on the nose.

Terry Machelski walked back in, drying his hands with a paper towel. "He's going to be okay, Rachel," he said, patting Ozzie gently on his ribs. "You gave us a real scare, big fella." Terry leaned over and opened one of Ozzie's eyes with a thick finger.

Everything about Terry Machelski seemed larger

than life. He was as big and broad as a Chicago Bears offensive tackle and had a full, bushy beard as red as the thick, curly hair on his head. When Terry had hugged me as I arrived at his office, I had felt like a waif in those enormous arms.

I met Terry and Peg four years before at a folk-song concert at the Earl of Old Town. My date and I were shown to a small table near the stage, where we squeezed in next to this Kodiak bear of a man and his tiny blond wife. Terry welcomed us like long-lost family members—something Terry does all the time with strangers and stray pets. Two years ago Terry drove me to a kennel out near Union and selected Ozzie from a litter of pups. The owners of the kennel, obviously enchanted by Terry, gave me the pup for half price so long as I promised to make Terry his vet. It's the easiest promise I've ever had to keep.

"What's wrong with Ozzie?" I asked Terry. The sounds of Steve Goodman's "Jazz Man" played over the office speakers.

"Do you take sleeping pills, Rachel?"

"No."

"Do you have any in your apartment?"

"No. Why? Was he drugged?"

Terry scratched his beard. "It looks that way. I've sent samples of his stomach contents to the lab to make sure. But I found this when I pumped his stomach." He reached into the front pocket of his white coat and pulled out a clear plastic bag. Inside was a red capsule.

"What is it?"

"Seconal."

"A sleeping pill?"

Terry nodded. "It's a secobarbital. Prescription only. It's a special type of barbiturate that works

fast and wears off fairly fast. In humans it starts
to work after just ten to fifteen minutes and wears
off after three to four hours."

"You found that in his stomach?"

"I'm afraid so."

"How many were there?"

"I don't know. This is the only one that wasn't
dissolved. Judging from Ozzie's condition, there
were probably several other capsules in the meat."

"Meat?"

"Hamburger. This capsule was inside a chunk
of hamburger. Whoever did this must have stuck
several Seconals into some ground meat and then
fed it to him."

My eyes widened.

Terry nodded, his eyes angry. "Someone broke
into your apartment," he said. "I've called the police. They'll have a squad car waiting there."

My shoulders sagged. "What about Ozzie?"

"He ought to wake up in a few hours. Let me
keep him here for another day or two. For obser-
vation. I want to make sure there aren't any after-
effects." Terry came around the table and placed
a hand on my shoulder. "You can come stay with
us tonight, Rachel. I'll tell Peg to make up the extra bedroom."

I stroked Ozzie. "Thanks. I'll be all right if Ozzie
is. But if the apartment is a wreck, I might just
take you up on it." I stood up.

"You let me know if they find the guy, Rachel,"
he said, his voice growing hard. "Because when
they do, I'm going to visit him in jail."

"Oh?" I said, smiling despite myself.

"After what he did, I'd like to rip off his head
and shit in his lungs."

* * *

"Here's how he got in, ma'am," Officer Tom Casey called from my kitchen. I was in the bedroom with his partner, Officer Sharon Kreusser. Nothing was missing from my jewelry box, and the four twenty-dollar bills were still at the bottom of my sweater drawer.

I followed Officer Kreusser to the kitchen, where Officer Casey was standing by the kitchen counter. "Right through this window here," he said, pointing to the window over the counter with his night-stick. "Looks like it wasn't locked. At least there ain't no sign he had to force it."

I remembered opening that window when I came home the night before. "I guess I forgot to lock it," I said.

"Screen's busted," he said, reaching over and sliding it up. "Latch don't work." He let it drop with a bang.

I looked down at the kitchen floor near his feet. "What is it?" Officer Kreusser asked.

I knelt. A circle of grease was barely visible on the floor. "He must have opened the window and tossed in the meat," I said. "It probably landed here." Ozzie had nearly licked the floor clean. Linda Burns had said she found him asleep by the sink. I thought of Ozzie happily gulping down the drugged hamburger. Rage flooded my veins like adrenaline.

The two cops stayed on for another half hour. I had found signs of the intruder in several places. The papers in and on my desk had been rifled and then replaced in neater stacks than before. A kitchen cabinet was slightly ajar, and the container of peppercorns was now in the front row of spices. The panties in my underwear drawer had been pushed to one side.

But nothing had been stolen.

Officer Kreusser followed me around as I locked all the windows. She told me that one of the detectives would call in the next couple of days.

Linda Burns came up when the cops left. She and the kids were driving up to Ravinia that night to meet John and then they were all going to Wisconsin for a long weekend. I told her Ozzie was all right and assured her that I was too.

Terry Machelski and his wife, Peg, called. I thanked them both for the offer of their extra bedroom, but told them I was okay.

"I'll be fine," I told Peg. "Really." I tried to put some conviction in my voice.

It was still light out. I checked my watch. Six thirty-five P.M.

Maybe he was a real burglar. Hoping to find something more valuable than anything I owned. But it didn't feel like a burglary. After all, the money in my sweater drawer was still there.

I wandered through the empty apartment. Whoever it was had tried to get in and out without my knowing it. According to Terry Machelski, a correct dose would have knocked Ozzie out for just three to four hours. He would have been up and about by the time I got home in the evening.

I thought of my underwear drawer again, of my panties pushed to one side. I shuddered.

I checked my watch. Six-fifty P.M. The sky seemed to be darkening a bit.

I stopped in the living room and stared at the phone. I sat down on the couch and lifted the receiver. I dialed the first three digits of Benny's number and then paused. Much as I loved him, Benny just wasn't the person I wanted to talk to tonight. I hung up and then lifted the receiver again. I dialed the first two digits of a number I still knew by heart. I hesitated, and then, with a sigh, dialed the remaining digits.

On the third ring a male voice answered.

"Uh, is Paul Mason there?" I asked.

"He stepped out for a couple of minutes. Can I take a message?"

"Kent?"

"Yeah? Rachel?"

"It's me."

"How are you?"

"Where's Paul?"

"We just finished playing tennis at Northwestern. He went down to pick up a pizza. He'll be back any minute."

"Oh."

"Is something the matter?"

"No. Well, sort of."

"What is it?"

"Someone broke into my apartment."

"Oh, my God. Are you okay?"

"I'm fine. It happened while I was out."

"Did they steal anything? Have you called the police?"

"The police were here. I don't think anything's missing."

"I'll go get Paul. Sit tight. We'll be right over, Rachel."

"That's okay, Kent. I'll be okay."

"Don't be silly. It's no problem. You're just five minutes away. We'll be right there."

I hung up and frowned, replaying the telephone conversation in my head.

I sat back on the couch. I saw the note from Paul

Mason on the coffee table, the one that had been attached to the copy of *The Lottery of Canaan* he had dropped off last night. It was faceup on the table, in plain view.

20

KENT CHARLES AND PAUL MASON arrived thirty minutes later with a large sausage pizza, a bucket of chicken, and two six-packs of beer. They were both in tennis whites; Paul was carrying a gym bag. I forced my paranoia into a back closet and tried to enjoy them.

It was easier than I hoped. After I satisfied their curiosity—showing them the window I had left unlocked, the grease markings on the kitchen floor— the three of us devoured the pizza and chicken. The fog of fear that had seemed to fill my apartment dissolved in our laughter and conversation, which included Kent's spirited defense of his claim that Arnold Schwarzenegger's *The Terminator* was one of the greatest movies of the decade.

"You guys are great," I said, my eyes watering from a mixture of laughter and emotion. "Thanks for coming by."

Paul smiled. "You're my pal, Rachel. That's what pals are for."

"Hey," Kent said, popping the tab on a beer, "let's not get sentimental. Paul may want his pal, but I'm here just to make sure my new co-counsel is okay." He turned to Paul. "Rachel's coming back on board. She's going to represent one of the defendants in Bottles and Cans."

"Really?" Paul asked me.

I sighed. "I don't think so."

"Why not?" Kent asked.

I poured the rest of my beer into the mug. "It's hard to explain." I paused. "I left Abbott and Windsor to get away from giant cases like that. I want clients I can know, cases I can understand. I don't want to be just another pig at the trough of some huge case."

"It won't be like that," Kent said.

"I like being a trial lawyer, Kent. I like standing up in court on my own, picking my own jury, making my own opening statement, doing my own cross-examination. I want to win on my own." I smiled. "And lose on my own. I want to control my own destiny. That's what it boils down to, I guess. In Bottles and Cans I'd be just another grunt again—for years into the future. And if the case ever went to trial, there probably wouldn't even be room in the courtroom for most of the lawyers." I shrugged. "I appreciate your trying to get me into the case. I know you're only trying to help out. And maybe if things were really bad, I'd be tempted. But fortunately, knock on wood, I have interesting cases. Better yet, I have clients who pay their bills on time."

I thought Kent would be angry. After all, I had just turned down an opportunity to get involved in the biggest case of his career. But he didn't even appear to be irritated. "I think I understand," he said. "I also think you're crazy to pass it up. But I think I understand. I'm just sorry I won't have the chance to work with you on this case. I was looking forward to it."

I smiled. "There'll be other cases, Kent. We'll have other chances."

The three of us talked for another fifteen minutes or so and then Kent got up to go. "I have to be in court at nine-thirty on a big discovery motion. I think I'd better read the court papers first."

I walked him to the door and thanked him again for coming over.

Kent looked back toward the living room. Paul was in the kitchen emptying the chicken bones into the garbage can.

"Give me a buzz if he doesn't treat you right," Kent said with a wink. "Maybe we can still have that dinner."

I was flattered. He really was a hunk. In his tennis whites he looked as though he had just stepped out of the pages of *Gentlemen's Quarterly*. "Thanks," I said. "Have fun with your briefs."

Paul was in the kitchen washing the dishes. I pulled out a dishtowel.

"How do you feel?" he asked.

"Like I've been violated."

He looked over, his eyes sad. "I know. You have."

"He drugs my dog, searches my house. It's creepy."

"Nothing was missing?"

"Not a thing."

"What do you think he was looking for?" Paul asked.

"I wish I knew."

"You think it had to do with Canaan?"

"Maybe. It makes a kind of sense. First they rob the grave. And now this." I dried a plate, thinking it over again. "Someone's trying to cover someone's tracks. But whose tracks I don't know. Whoever it is must not want me to find what was in that coffin. Maybe they searched my place to see if I had come up with any evidence."

"You think Graham Marshall had an accomplice?" Paul asked.

"I don't know. But it sure seems like someone doesn't want me, or anyone else for that matter, to discover what Graham was up to."

Paul ran a soapy sponge around the inside of a beer mug. "Well, if Marshall really had a hand in the stuff in those four newspaper articles, he probably couldn't have done it all by himself. At the very least, he'd need some thugs to help carry it out." Paul set the mug down. "You think one of them is trying to cover this up?"

"You're my mystery expert," I said. "Have you ever read a book involving a blind communication system?"

Paul frowned. "What do you mean?"

"You know, where the bad guy has a way to contact the henchmen without their knowing who he is?"

Paul thought it over and smiled. "You don't need to go to fiction for that. Remember the Barfield murder?"

"Vaguely. Wasn't that about six years ago?"

"Yep. Ted Barfield was a wealthy plumbing contractor from the western suburbs who decided to knock off his wife. He had some mob contacts, and they put him in touch with two enforcers. Except

Barfield never met the hit men face-to-face, and they apparently never even met each other. Barfield communicated with one of them through a post office box, and that guy communicated with the other through some other drop point that Barfield picked. The whole thing took about six months to carry out. It was a great scheme. Perfect plot for a mystery."

"How'd they catch him?"

"The FBI nailed the guy in the middle on some drug offense. They leaned on him, hoping he'd squeal on the drug boss. He didn't, but he told them about this mystery guy who used to contact him through a post office box about killing his wife. He still had a couple of typewritten notes from the guy. The FBI eventually traced the typewriter back to Barfield's office, and Barfield confessed." Paul shook his head. "They never caught the guy who actually killed her." He rinsed out the mug and handed it to me. "Why do you ask?"

I told him about the Canaan personals.

"You actually went up there on the el? Are you nuts, Rachel?"

I shrugged. "It was too late to call anyone. So I took Ozzie."

"Still." Paul shook his head. "At two in the morning?"

I shrugged. "I lived. Ozzie is a good bodyguard."

"Except for himself. Poor Ozzie." Paul leaned back against the kitchen counter. "What a great system," he said. "What do you think they were doing?"

I sighed. "I don't know, Paul. And frankly, I almost don't care. I just want to wrap up this assignment for Ishmael Richardson and get on with my life."

"How can you say that? This is great stuff."

Paul's enthusiasm was irritating. "Look, I'm just a lawyer, Paul. I'm not a cop. I'm not an FBI agent. I'm not some private eye on a mission. That's storybook stuff. Sure I'm curious. Who wouldn't be? But look what's happening to me. I've got strangers breaking into my house. Practically killing my dog, for God's sake. Enough is enough. I want out."

Paul nodded, his eyes bright. "I understand, Rachel. And you're probably right. Once you get what Ishmael Richardson needs, you ought to get out of it. But this newspaper personals angle is terrific stuff. Let me look into it. Maybe I can come up with something."

"Go get 'em, tiger." I put the dishtowel on the counter and rubbed my forehead.

"Headache?" Paul asked.

"Probably from lack of sleep."

He walked over to the cabinet and opened it. "Ah, still keep your aspirin with the spices. Here," he said, handing me two tablets. Paul filled a juice glass with water from the faucet.

"Thanks," I said, taking the two aspirin.

"Go lie down on your bed," he said. "I brought a change of clothes. I can stay with you tonight." He smiled. "On your couch, of course."

"Don't be silly, Paul. Go home. I'll be okay."

"It's no problem, Rachel. Really. I'll get out of these sweaty clothes, take a shower, and hit the sack. I'm bushed myself. It's almost one o'clock in the morning. I even brought my own towel and toothbrush."

"You're sweet."

"Hey, you had a hell of a scare today. It's my pleasure. I mean it." With that—and before it got awkward—he grabbed his gym bag and walked into the bathroom.

I undressed in my bedroom and slipped on a nightgown. I looked at myself in the mirror: It was a sensible, comfortable cotton nightgown that was cut full and reached to my ankles. I studied my reflection for a moment and then walked back to the closet. I pulled the sensible nightgown off over my head and took out a blue silk nightshirt that reached to mid-thigh. Much better, I told myself as I buttoned it up in front of the mirror.

I climbed in bed, pulling up the sheets. My head was throbbing. I yawned. Listening to the sound of the shower, I smiled. It was good to know he'd be here with me tonight. I yawned again. Back in college I could pull all-nighters with ease during finals. You're getting old, kid.

I woke up in the dark. The clock on the nightstand showed 2:10 A.M. I staggered to the bathroom and drank a cup of water. Then I remembered Paul. I must have fallen asleep before he got out of the shower.

I walked softly into the living room. Paul was sound asleep on the couch, wearing nothing but a pair of fitted boxer shorts. I bent over and kissed him lightly on the nose. He grunted but didn't stir.

"Sleep tight, baby," I whispered into his ear.

I got back into bed, pulled up the sheet, and fell right back to sleep.

21

THE TELEPHONE STARTLED ME AWAKE at 7:15 A.M. on Friday.

"Rachel, this is Maggie Sullivan."

I stretched my legs toward the end of the bed. "Hi. What's up?"

"That bastard tried to rob another one of my graves."

I sat up. "Last night?"

"Around dawn, I think. My brother-in-law's dog's been staying with me since the Canaan robbery. A big German shepherd. He started barking around six in the morning. I finally let him out and went out there myself with a shotgun. Whoever was out there was gone by then. I heard a car pull away."

"Did he dig up a grave?"

"Only partway. He got scared off before he got down to the coffin, thank God."

"I'm coming down. Let me throw on some clothes."

I put on my robe and called out to Paul. "You're not going to believe this." He didn't answer. "Paul?" No response.

I walked slowly into the living room. Paul was gone. There was a note taped to the refrigerator:

> Dear Rachel:
>   I had to get back to that paper I'm working on. The deadline is Monday. Hope you had a peaceful sleep. You looked beautiful. And very sexy! I'll talk to you later.
>
> Your pal,
Paul
>
> P.S. There's fresh coffee in the pot.

I put an English muffin into the toaster and poured a cup of coffee. Even with lots of milk, the coffee tasted stale.

Maggie and her brother-in-law were standing by the grave when I arrived. The hole was about two feet deep and roughly rectangular. According to the engraving on the polished face of the small granite tombstone, something named Candy was buried down there—Born February 25, 1974; Died November 16, 1985. To the pet's owner, Candy had been "Mommy's Little Sweetie Pie."

Maggie handled the introductions at the graveside. "Rachel, this here's my brother-in-law, Vern. He's a security guard down at a plant in Hammond. Vern, this here's my lawyer, Rachel Gold."

"Nice to meet you, Vern," I said.

"Ma'am," Vern answered, touching the handkerchief covering his head.

From the waist down Vern was dressed in standard-issue security garb: midnight-blue double-knit slacks disappearing into black knee-high storm-trooper boots. From the waist up Vern looked, well, peculiar: a once-white T-shirt (now tinged gray) stretched tight over a sagging pot belly, a pair of reflector sunglasses resting on a lumpy Mr. Magoo nose, and the white handkerchief covering his close-cropped white hair. There was a large plug of chewing tobacco in his right cheek. Tobacco juice had dribbled from the left side of his mouth down his chin.

"Tell Rachel what you found."

"Not much, ma'am." Vern spit a stream of dark tobacco juice into the grave.

The morning sun was intense. My forehead felt damp.

"My dog musta spooked him good," Vern said. "Looks like the perpetrator grabbed his shovel and lit out. Not many clues."

"Tell her about the prints, Vern," Maggie prompted.

"Looks to me like the perpetrator was wearing sneakers. See them prints?" He pointed at two partial shoe prints in the grave. As he leaned forward, the handkerchief slid off his head. He caught it with his hand. "Looks like a size ten or thereabouts," he said as he placed the handkerchief back on his head.

"Why sneakers?" I asked, trying to ignore the handkerchief.

"No heel prints. Tells me he was wearing flat soles, so I'm guessing sneakers." Vern snorted. "Not much of a clue. Cuts the suspects down to about one million or thereabouts." Vern readjusted his testicles with his right hand, his knees slightly bent.

He leaned over the grave and pointed at the clearer of the two prints. "No heel marks." And with that his handkerchief slid off his head and floated into the open grave, landing on top of a small puddle of tobacco juice. Vern bent over, hands on his knees, and stared at the handkerchief, which now had a brown stain growing in the center. "Well, shit," Vern grunted, and he expectorated the entire wad of tobacco into the grave.

Maybe it was the tension. Or the lack of sleep. Or a combination of the two. Or maybe it was just old Vern all on his own. Whatever the cause, I was having a hard time keeping from laughing. Maggie came to my rescue by sending Vern back to the house.

"Ol' Vern means well," she said, shaking her head, "but he don't exactly have a Sears Die-Hard upstairs. He showed up this morning in his guard outfit waving his gun. I told him I couldn't have him stomping around a half-dug-up grave looking like the Gestapo. He'd scare the daylights out of all my old ladies. I told him to take off his shirt and hat and leave his gun inside." She gestured toward the grave. "You seen enough?"

I stared down at the footprints. Vern was probably right. Last night there must have been tens of thousands of men wearing tennis shoes. Including Kent Charles and Paul Mason. "I've seen enough."

"Let's go up to the house. I'll get one of the gravediggers to fill it back up before folks start arriving. I got a burial at noon."

We were sipping coffee in Maggie's kitchen. She had lugged the blue ledger book in from her office.

It was open to the entry for Plot No. 89, the final resting place of one Yorkshire terrier named Candy. His owner had been an elderly spinster who had died three months after her dog's death. Both had been in the ground several months before Graham Anderson Marshall arrived at Wagging Tail Estates to arrange for the burial of Canaan. The only apparent connection was 1985, the year of Candy's death and the year of Marshall's Canaan lottery.

"You think it's the same guy?" Maggie asked.

"I just don't know."

I told Maggie about the break-in of my apartment.

"My God. How's your dog?"

"He seems okay. The vet wants to keep him another night to be sure."

"The burglar didn't take anything?"

I shook my head. "I think he was searching my apartment for evidence. That's my gut feeling. I think he was looking for something on Canaan. If my instincts are right, the two grave robberies and that break-in are related."

"What in hell did that Marshall bury in that coffin?"

"I've got a hunch," I said. "I'm going down to the law firm to see what I can find. I'll let you know if I turn anything up."

Vern stepped into the kitchen. He had put back on his rent-a-cop shirt and cap, and was strapping his holster around his hips. His sunglasses hung from his shirt pocket.

"I'm gonna hit the sack," he said to Maggie, glancing at me. "I'll be back around seven tonight."

"Come a little earlier, Vern. I'll feed you supper."

"Why, thanks. I might just do that." Vern pulled a pouch of Red Man chewing tobacco out of his back pocket.

"Vern's gonna stand guard tonight," Maggie said to me. "Tomorrow night too. By Monday I'll have my own security guard here. At least until the hippo's buried next Saturday. I don't want anybody at the zoo getting spooked. And with the hippo's funeral scheduled for next weekend, it'll be easier explaining a security guard to folks."

"That's a good idea," I said. I turned to Vern, who was shoving a stringy clump of tobacco into his cheek. "Guard things well, Vern."

"I will, ma'am." His words were muffled by the tobacco. "Be seeing you."

After Vern left, I got up to go. Maggie walked me to my car. "You be careful, Rachel. And let me know if you need some help. It's one thing to have some pervert digging up dead pets. Don't get me wrong. I'm not saying the grave robberies don't matter, 'cause they sure as hell do. But it's a whole new ballgame when they start breaking into your home and drugging your dog. You keep in touch, you hear?"

22

FROM WAGGING TAIL ESTATES I drove downtown to Abbott & Windsor and Litigation Work Room D.

Litigation Work Room D is the size of a racquetball court and is lined on three sides by floor-to-ceiling filing cabinets filled with court pleading files, transcripts of court hearings, and other documents relating to *In re Bottles & Cans*. It is also the site of the main *In re Bottles & Cans* computer terminal and the office of Tyrone Henderson, the head programmer.

I'd come up here on a hunch. Fortunately, Tyrone was in.

"Hey, Tyrone."

Tyrone looked up and gave me a big toothy grin. "Hey, Rachel. What's happening, girl?"

"What did you do with your head, Tyrone?" He had shaved off all his hair. "It looks like an eight ball."

He smiled and ran a hand slowly over his smooth black scalp. "Drives the ladies wild, Rachel."

"Really?"

"You be surprised, girl."

Tyrone Henderson had started at the firm as a messenger, delivering draft contracts and court papers to other law firms in the city. Several years back he had enrolled in night-school courses in computer programming. When a programmer position opened up on the *In re Bottles & Cans* computer team, he applied and got the job. Tyrone started off as a key puncher in a document warehouse in Iowa and gradually worked his way up to his current position as chief programmer. In fact, it was Tyrone who had devised the instructions that produced the many-thousand-page printout that led to my resignation from the firm. For that Tyrone would have my undying gratitude.

"Don't tell me you're coming back to us, Rachel."

"Nope. But I'm working on a weird project for the firm and I came up here on a hunch."

"And I thought it was because you'd finally come to your senses, girl." Tyrone gave me a big grin. "I don't normally truck with white girls, but for a fox like you I can make an exception."

"Well, that all depends. You aren't Jewish, are you?"

"Some of my best friends are."

"Not good enough for my dad."

"Oh, I 'spect you daddy'd be tickled pink if you was to bring home a bad dude like me," he said, exaggerating a ghetto accent that he could turn on or off like a faucet.

"Listen, you big jerk, I came up here because I need you to work some magic with that computer of yours." I closed the door. "I'm trying to find out about something called Canaan. C-a-n-a-a-n. It's very confidential. I had Helen Marston run it through the firm's computer and she didn't turn up much. I thought there might be something in the Bottles and Cans computer."

"Canaan, huh? Don't sound familiar, but let's see what big mama has to say."

Tyrone walked over to the computer table and pulled out the swivel chair. Sitting down in front of the cream-colored keyboard and monitor screen, he flicked on the power. The monitor screen flickered on, and four green bars pulsed on and off on the right side of the screen. I stood behind him and watched over his shoulder.

Tyrone typed some information onto the screen and then pushed the Transmit key on the keyboard. The screen went blank for a moment and then lit up again with a message in green block type:

```
       SIGN ON
       USER ID . . . . . . .
       PASSWORD . . . . . .
       MENU (OPTIONAL)
       LIBRARY . . . . . . .
```

He typed information on each line and then pushed the Transmit key. The screen went blank and then lit up with a row of thirty-five numbered items under the heading Menu. Tyrone typed in a number. The screen flashed a new message:

```
       DATABASE ID SIGN ON
       ENTER DATABASE ID. : . . . . . . . .
```

"You said Canaan?"

"Yep."

Tyrone typed in the letters C-A-N-A-A-N. The screen went blank. After about five seconds the word "Searching" started flashing in green at three-second intervals. We waited and watched.

"C'mon, big mama, keep looking," Tyrone mumbled.

After about a minute, the "Searching" signal stopped and the screen went blank.

"Here it comes, girl."

I held my breath.

A new message unfurled on the screen:

```
YOU HAVE ATTEMPTED TO SIGN ON TO
DATABASE CANAAN. THIS IS A
RESTRICTED-ACCESS DATABASE. PLEASE
ENTER CANAAN ACCESS PASSWORD. . . .
```

"Damn," Tyrone said.

"What's that mean, Ty?"

"We can't get in that Canaan file without the password."

"Do you know the password?" I asked.

"Nope."

"Who does?"

"No way to know."

"Rats. What do we do now?"

Tyrone stared at the screen, his brows knitted in concentration. He ran his hand slowly over his smooth scalp. "Hmm . . . let's try a little breakin' and enterin'." He typed a message in computerese and then leaned back, his arms crossed over his chest.

"What did you do?"

"I ain't just the head programmer, girl. I'm also

the chief of police. I got big mama secretly programmed to keep track of all passwords any Bottles and Cans operator puts in from anywhere in the country. I put together the program two years ago. Made it up myself. It's got every password for the last two years stored in its memory. Helps me keep track of who is doing what in my computer. I just told it to try each one of those passwords and find the one that fits." He pointed to a green rectangle in the lower right corner of the screen, where a blur of words was flashing in rapid succession, far too quickly to read. "It's running through the passwords right there. It's like having a key ring with thousands of keys. It's trying each one to see which one opens the lock."

We waited, both of us staring at the small rectangle. After about thirty seconds the rectangle disappeared, the screen went blank, and then a new message appeared in the middle of the screen:

```
PASSWORD SEARCH COMPLETE.
NO MATCH LOCATED.
```

Tyrone sighed. "Damn."

"How can that be?"

"Means someone set up the Canaan file more than two years ago. Back before I set up this program." Tyrone leaned forward, elbows on the table. He rested his chin between his hands.

"There's got to be a way in, Tyrone."

He straightened up. "Maybe so." He typed a long message in computerese and hit the Transmit key. "If this don't work, nothing will."

"What did you do?"

"I just told big mama to link up with the firm's

main computer. She'll get us access to all the word-processing software, including spell-check."

"What's that?"

"After you input a document in the word-processing department, you can ask it to check for spelling errors. It's got a whole dictionary in its memory. I just told big mama to take a look through that dictionary and test each one as a password."

He pointed to the lower right corner of the monitor screen, where the words were blurring through the green rectangle. We watched and waited.

"How fast is it going?"

"Oh, 'bout five hundred words a second."

I stared at the rectangle. A minute passed. Then the screen went blank. A moment later a new message appeared in the center of the screen.

```
PASSWORD LOCATED.
PASSWORD IS LOTTERY.
```

"Tyrone, you're a genius!" I said, kissing him on his forehead.

He grinned. "Ain't it the truth." He punched up the prior message:

```
PLEASE ENTER CANAAN
ACCESS PASSWORD . . .
```

Tyrone typed in L-O-T-T-E-R-Y and pushed the Transmit key. The screen went blank for an instant, and then a new message appeared, line by line:

```
CANAAN DATABASE ACTIVITY

DATE: 5/9/86
TIME: 11:51 P.M.

BGN TOTAL RECORDS ...... 784
RECORDS ADDED ......... 0
RECORDS REVISED ....... 0
RECORDS PRINTED ...... 784
RECORDS DELETED ...... 784
END TOTAL RECORDS ...... 0

* * * DATABASE DELETED * * *
```

"That don't make much sense." Tyrone leaned to his right and pushed a button on the printer, which stood upright on the floor. The printer whirred for an instant and then rolled up a sheet of lime and white striped paper. Tyrone leaned over, tore it off along the perforated line, and handed it to me. "There's your answer."

I looked at the sheet. It was a printed version of the message on the screen. "What's this mean?"

"I can tell you what it says, but I sure can't tell you what it means." He went line by line. "On May 9, 1986, at 11:51 P.M., somebody printed out the entire contents of the Canaan file—all 784 pages of it—and then erased the whole damn file from the computer's memory. Erased everything but the name of the file. There's nothing else under Canaan in the computer."

He stared at the screen for a moment and then typed in a message:

```
CANAAN DATABASE DELETED BY?
```

The computer answered immediately:

```
USER ID 431
```

Tyrone typed again:

```
WHO IS USER ID 431?
```

The computer came up with the answer almost as quickly as I did:

```
GRAHAM A. MARSHALL III
```

"Mr. Marshall! Shee-it! What's that dude doing messing with my computer?"

It was after five when I left Tyrone Henderson and took the spiral staircase down two flights to the main floor. One of Ishmael Richardson's secretaries was still there, catching up on some filing. She told me Richardson had gone up to his cottage in Michigan for the weekend but would be able to see me on Monday at eleven-thirty.

As I walked down the hallway toward the main lobby and the elevators I passed by Cal Pemberton's office. He was hunched over his Bottles & Cans computer terminal, typing furiously on the keyboard. I watched him for a moment, and then moved on, thinking how nice it would be to have someone like Philip Marlowe on the case with me. Every good clue I followed seemed to lead nowhere. Marshall's dictionary: stolen. The Canaan database: deleted. Ambrose Springer's *The Lottery of Canaan*: a possible fabrication. The coffin: stolen. It was like playing tic-tac-toe with an infallible and invisible opponent. And yet the story—or at least one of the stories—had basically fallen in place. By Monday I ought to be able to tell Ishmael Richardson what was in the coffin. Finding it was another matter—a matter beyond my assignment as far as I was concerned. I'd done what I could. If Ishmael Richardson still wanted to find that coffin—and I doubted he would after I talked to him— he could go out and hire a real Philip Marlowe. And a bodyguard for me.

"Hi, Rachel."

It was Benny Goldberg. He was standing there solemnly, hands in his pockets.

"Hi."

"I feel terrible, Rachel. And I barely even knew her."

"What are you talking about?"

"Have you seen the evening papers?"

"No."

"It's Cindi," he said.

I took a deep breath. "What about her?"

"She's dead."

23

THE GREEN-STREAK EDITION OF THE *Chicago Tribune*
was on the chair in front of Benny's desk. It was
the lead story: a black and white photograph of
Shore Drive Tower, and below that the headline:

BLAST ROCKS HI-RISE CONDO;
BEAUTY QUEEN FEARED DEAD

Two people died today in a condominium in
Shore Drive Tower after an apparent gas-leak
explosion turned an 18th-floor apartment into
a fiery inferno. Police have tentatively identified one of the victims as Cynthia Ann Reynolds, a former Ms. Illinois and the owner of
the condominium. The other victim—a middle-aged male—has not been identified.

The explosion occurred at approximately

11 A.M. The force of the blast shattered the large picture window of the condominium and sent shards of broken glass tumbling to the streets below. No one on the ground was injured.

According to Captain James Howard of the Chicago Fire Department, the explosion and fire were caused by a faulty gas line leading to the condominium's oven.

"Once the place filled up with gas, the slightest spark would have set it off," Captain Howard explained. "Judging from the force of the explosion and the magnitude of the fire, we suspect the decedents may have died from gas inhalation prior to the explosion."

The charred remains of the two victims were taken to the Cook County Morgue, where positive identification awaited receipt of dental records and other relevant data.

I skimmed the rest of the article, which included a photograph of Cindi from the Ms. United States Pageant. My eyes were stinging. I put the newspaper on Benny's desk and rested my hands in my lap.

"I'm sorry, Rachel."

I looked up, my eyes stinging. "I really liked her, Benny. She wasn't at all what I had expected. She was special."

"I know. I could tell."

We sat there in silence. I felt exhausted. "Are you going to take the hoop with you?" I finally asked.

Benny turned around to where a small basketball hoop was anchored to the wall over his chair. He turned back with a weak smile. "Sure." He leaned forward. "Rachel, how's this Canaan thing going?"

I shrugged. "Oh, okay, I guess."

"What's happened to you?"

"What do you mean?"

"C'mon, Rachel. We're buddies, remember. You looked bushed even before I told you about Cindi."

I sighed. "I guess I am. I haven't had much sleep."

"Dammit, tell me what happened. What have you been up to?"

"Well, the night before last I was riding the el trains."

"Late at night?"

I nodded. "Two in the morning. And yesterday someone drugged Ozzie and broke into my apartment."

"Jesus H. Christ, Rachel. Is Ozzie okay?"

"He'll be fine. I can take him home from the vet tomorrow."

"What in hell is going on?"

My shoulders slumped. "That's exactly what I'd like to know. This morning someone tried to rob another grave at Maggie's pet cemetery."

"Holy shit." Benny stood up and started pacing. "What in God's name were you doing up on the el?"

I told him—about the *Reader* personal, about the el ride, about tailing that man to the garage of Cindi's condominium. And I told him about the theft of Marshall's dictionary and *The Lottery of Canaan* and Tyrone Henderson's computer search for the Canaan file. It was a relief to talk to him about it.

"Wow," Benny finally said. "You think there really is a Canaan lottery?" he asked.

"Well, something's definitely going on, Benny. I think I've pieced together part of it. But I still don't have a clue about who took the coffin. Or why. Or who broke into my apartment."

"What have you got so far?"

"Enough to think that Ishmael Richardson probably ought to be the first to hear about it. I'm going to see him Monday morning. And you'll do me a big favor if you don't mention this to anyone."

Benny stood up and grinned. He mimed zipping his lips together. "Listen, you've had a terrible day. You need to get your mind off this stuff. Some guy over at Sidley and Austin told me about a new Mexican restaurant in the Pilsen area. They've got a spicy chili rellenos that'll make your colon sing *Aida*."

I smiled. "Sounds like one of life's great thrills."

"Wanna meet there at seven?" Benny asked.

I shook my head. "I just want to go home tonight."

Benny looked at me, his eyes sad. "I understand. How 'bout lunch tomorrow?"

"Okay."

"Great. I'll pick you up at noon. You better get some sleep tonight, Rachel."

"I plan to." I stood up. "God, Benny, I just feel terrible about Cindi."

"I know. So do I, Rachel." He shook his head and placed an arm around my shoulder. "So do I."

It was drizzling and gloomy when I stepped off the el at Morse Avenue. I leafed through magazines at the newsstand inside the station, waiting for the rain to ease up. Taped to the back of the cash register was an advertisement for the Illinois Lottery: THE LOTTERY—WE MIGHT JUST CHANGE YOUR LIFE . . .

FOREVER. I stared at the sign. Why not? I bought two tickets. I put them into my purse as I walked to the exit. The rain was coming down harder. The guy at the newsstand had told me there was a severe thunderstorm watch until midnight. I pulled a newspaper out of the trash can, held it over my head, and stepped into the rain.

By the time I reached my apartment my skirt and blouse were dripping and my shoes squished. I kicked off my shoes at the front door, stripped off my clothes in the front hall, and padded into the living room. I listened to my messages on the telephone answering machine as I hung my wet clothes over the backs of my kitchen chairs: "Rachel, it's your mother calling to say hello. We'll be home all day tomorrow, sweetie. . . . Click. . . . It's Paul, Rachel. Just calling to make sure you're okay. Talk to you later. . . . Click. . . ." It ended with a dial tone, the last caller having hung up without leaving a message.

I walked into the bathroom and turned on the shower. I stood motionless under the hot water for a long time, struggling to keep my mind blank.

After the shower I put on my boxing robe and walked barefoot into the kitchen. I took a beer out of the refrigerator, stared at it for a moment, then put it back and took a glass out of the cabinet. I clinked four ice cubes into it and poured in some vodka.

Yawning, I walked into the living room, clicked on the television, and plopped onto the couch, splashing some vodka onto my lap in the process. "Damn," I mumbled, and settled back as the local news came on the screen.

The anchorman was joking with the weather girl, who was apologizing for the rain—apparently in the belief that she not only reported the weather but somehow caused it. She promised plenty of sunshine tomorrow, and the anchorman asked her if she'd be out sunbathing on the Oak Street Beach. That broke them both up, and they cut to a commercial.

When they returned from the commercial break, the weather girl was gone—presumably hauled off the set in a straitjacket. The anchorman looked up from his papers and put on his serious face:

"Recapping tonight's top stories. The Tribune Company, owner of the Chicago Cubs, denies a report in the *Chicago Sun-Times* that it is planning to move the team to Phoenix, Arizona. . . . Residents of Shore Drive Tower are still in shock over today's deadly explosion in the apartment of former beauty queen Cynthia Reynolds. . . . The Cubs beat the Dodgers five to two at Wrigley Field this afternoon. The White Sox play tonight in Oakland. . . . Stay tuned for *Family Feud* starring Richard Dawson immediately following this newscast. Have a good evening." I stood up and turned off the television.

I finished my drink in one gulp and walked back to the kitchen for a refill. On the way back I checked the dead-bolt lock on the front door. I stopped at my stereo and put the Temptations' *Greatest Hits* on the turntable.

As I sat back down on the couch, the sky suddenly lit up and there was a crash of thunder. The rain sounded like shotgun pellets on my windows. I thought of Ozzie at the vet's office. How I wished he were here with me tonight.

Get hold of yourself, Rachel. You're a big girl now. There is such a thing as coincidence. Maybe the guy in the station wagon really did live in

Shore Drive Tower. Maybe the gas explosion in Cindi's apartment really was just an accident. If you eliminated the grave robbery and the Canaan personals and the exchange on the el train and the search of my apartment and the second attempted grave robbery, Graham Marshall's odd codicil started to make sense. Assuming Maggie Sullivan confirmed what I was sure was the case, anyway. But you couldn't eliminate the grave robbery, or the Canaan personals, or the incident up on the el train, and all the rest. And you probably couldn't eliminate the gas explosion either. If they could kill Cindi . . .

I stared at the telephone, thinking of Paul. But if I called him and told him about Cindi's death and the attempted grave robbery, he'd be all excited about the possible Canaan connection. And I wasn't in the mood to listen to Paul go over the clues again and spin out possible solutions. Not tonight. My Canaan assignment was almost over. I'd tell Ishmael on Monday what I'd found and let him handle it from there. He could decide whether to bring in the police. Besides, I'd told Paul too much as it was.

A crash of thunder shook the apartment. I glanced at the telephone. Not my parents. Not tonight. I wasn't in the mood for another one of my mother's updates on Dr. Jerome Katzenstein, the latest in a series of nice Jewish doctors she had selected to be my future husband. This one was a urologist, and I was scheduled to meet him at dinner at my parents' house on Rosh Hashanah. My mother said he had strong features, which probably meant that he had a nose the size of one on Mount Rushmore.

The thunderstorm had become even more fierce.

The apartment windows were shuddering from the wind and rain. I pulled my knees up to my chin. Sipping the vodka, I listened to the storm.

I must have dozed off, because I awoke with a start. I checked my watch: the dial—glowing in the darkness—showed ten minutes after one. The storm had passed and the silence was eerie. I realized I was all alone in my apartment. And I realized that what woke me was the sound of footsteps on my back landing.

24

I JUMPED TO MY FEET. There was definitely someone on the back landing. I bolted for the front door to escape. Reaching for the doorknob, I froze. What if they were waiting on the other side of the door? They? Who were *they*? I felt a rivulet of sweat down the middle of my back. I thought of Ozzie and then remembered he was still at the vet. Damn.

Call the police. I dashed back to the living room and grabbed the telephone. It was dead. I grabbed the cord and traced it to the wall. Still connected. Someone was tapping on the back door. I tried to catch my breath.

I walked on wobbly legs into the dark kitchen. The tapping was getting louder. I opened the bottom drawer and reached in. My hand fumbled in the darkness and I pulled out the heavy claw hammer. Someone was now pounding on the back door. I walked to the door. The hand holding the hammer was shaking.

Raising the hammer, I took a deep breath. "Who is it?" I demanded.

"Open up, Rachel." It was a woman's voice. "It's me."

"Who?"

"Cindi. Cindi Reynolds."

"Cindi?"

"Yeah. Please let me in."

I exhaled. This must be a dream. "You're supposed to be dead."

"I know. But it wasn't me. Let me in and I'll explain."

"Are you alone?"

"I promise. Please let me in, Rachel. I'm scared to death and I'm catching pneumonia out here. I'm soaked."

I unlatched the lock and, holding the hammer up with the other hand, I turned the knob. I took a deep breath and yanked open the door.

Cindi was standing barefoot in the yellow light of the porch, her shoulders slumped. Her hair was matted to her head, and her clothes—a cotton pullover shirt and jeans—were soaked. She was holding her sandals in her hand. She stared at me, her eyes blinking and her lips quivering.

"Come in and tell me about it," I said quietly, and held out my hands.

"Oh, Rachel." She lurched forward into my arms, sobbing.

We stood there in the doorway. Cindi clung to me, her head on my shoulders.

She finally lifted her head. "I'm getting you all wet." She smiled.

"That's okay," I said. "But next time give me a

call before you decide to return from the dead. I almost had a stroke in here."

Cindi laughed through her tears and wiped her nose against the back of her arm.

"C'mon," I said. "Let's get you into something warm and dry."

"Then who was she?" I asked.

Cindi was fluffing her hair with a towel. She was wearing my old gray sweatshirt and a pair of my white socks. "Andi Hebner. I've known her for a couple of years. She was a graduate student at the U. of C. She was also a call girl. She had this client—an accountant at Coopers and Lybrand. But both of them—Andi and the guy—live in Harbor Point on the same floor. The guy is married. He doesn't want to risk having his wife see him going into Andi's apartment. So they always go somewhere else. She sees him about once a month, and sometimes she borrows my condo." Cindi sighed. "She was up there with him this morning when it happened."

"When did you find out?"

"Around three o'clock. I was on my way back from that swimsuit layout in the Dunes. It took us two days to finish the photography. When I drove up, there was a police barricade around the whole building. There were fire engines and squad cars and ambulances all over. I asked one of the policemen what had happened. He told me there'd been an explosion up on the eighteenth floor. He wouldn't tell me anything else. One of the gawkers told me that the paramedics had brought out two bodies in those horrible black body bags. Well, I stepped back and looked up and practically passed out when I saw them boarding up my window. I got out of there in a hurry. I was in a daze, Rachel. You can imagine."

"Where'd you go?"

"I walked over to the Hyatt Regency and went to the lounge on the top floor. I just sat by a window staring out at Shore Drive Tower. Drinking gin and tonics. You can't imagine how weird that was. There was a TV behind the bar. I was the lead story on the local news. They had shots of the building and even a film clip of me from the pageant. I went back down to the lobby and bought the evening paper. That's when I really freaked out."

"Why?"

"All that talk of a gas leak. It made me really scared."

"I don't get it."

"There couldn't have been a gas leak, Rachel. My oven hasn't been connected to a gas line for more than a year."

"You're kidding."

Cindi shook her head. "I'd been having all kinds of trouble with it for a couple of years. In the meantime, I was using my toaster oven and my microwave. I finally called in a repairman, and he told me it would cost almost two hundred dollars to fix. I told him to forget it, that I didn't use it, anyway. He told me it was too dangerous to leave it like that because the pilot light wouldn't stay lit and it was leaking gas. So I paid him forty dollars to disconnect the gas and plug up the gas line leading into my condo. He cut off the gas from the main line all the way down the hall past the elevator. There hasn't been a drop of gas in there for more than a year. It couldn't have been a gas leak."

I frowned. "Whatever happened, it was good enough to fool the fire department."

"I know," Cindi said with a shudder. "If they're that good, then they're good enough to find me."

"What did she look like?"

"Who?"

"Your friend. Andi."

"Blond, tall, good-looking."

"How'd she wear her hair?"

"Sort of like mine . . . but a little shorter."

I thought it over. "You're probably safe. At least for a few days. Whoever did it must think you're dead. The police think you're dead too—which means no one in the building told them anything different. What about the doorman?"

"He wouldn't have seen them."

"Why not?"

"They always came in through the garage entrance so no one would see them together. I gave her the combination to the garage door lock so they could get past the doorman."

I nodded. "No one will know it wasn't you until they get your dental records. So you've got at least until Monday. Probably longer. You're not as urgent as the guy. The cops don't have any reason to think it's not your body down in the morgue."

Cindi shuddered. "My God."

"You want something to drink?" I asked.

"No, thanks."

"Why didn't you go to the cops right away?"

"I guess I panicked. And I didn't want to have to explain about Andi and why she was in my condo. I don't know. When you're a hooker"—she shrugged—"you get conditioned to avoid the cops."

"Well, you're going to have to go to them eventually. You can't stay dead forever."

"I know."

"Who would want to kill you?"

"I don't have a clue."

"Do you have any violent or weird clients?" I asked.

Cindi thought for a moment and then shook her head. "No. Not like that."

"Maybe it's just a coincidence, but I followed some guy to your building two nights ago."

Cindi leaned forward. "What do you mean?"

I had to tell her about *The Lottery of Canaan* and the personals in the *Reader* and the *Tribune* and following the guy to her building. Pretty soon I might as well broadcast it. But Cindi's life was involved, and she had a right to know what was happening.

Cindi gasped. "My God."

I said, "Maybe it's just a coincidence. But maybe not. Maybe they think you know something about Canaan." I paused. "There've been some other weird things going on."

"Like what?"

"Someone tried to steal another coffin from the pet cemetery. And yesterday someone broke into my apartment." I told her about Ozzie being drugged and the evidence that someone had searched through my things. "Ozzie's okay," I said. "Thank God. I can pick him up tomorrow morning. But there's definitely something out there called Canaan."

"What are you going to do?"

"I don't know. Yesterday I just wanted out. Period. But now . . . that may not be an option anymore." I checked my watch and stood up. "C'mon.

Let's go to sleep. It's almost three in the morning."
I yawned and stretched. "I've got a queen-size bed.
You can share it with me."

Cindi stood up. "Thanks, Rachel." She gave me
a hug. "You were the only one I thought of turning
to when this happened. I left the Hyatt and wandered down Michigan Avenue toward the Loop,
sneaking in and out of bookstores and clothing
stores. I sat through two kung-fu movies in one of
those horrible theaters in the Loop. It was dis-
gusting. Sticky seats, rats running down the aisles.
I finally left the theater, looking you up in the
phone book, and tried to call, but your line was
dead. I didn't even know if I had the right Gold,
but I had to take a chance. I didn't know where
else to go."

"I'm glad you came, Cindi. God, I'm so happy
you're alive."

I checked the telephone on my way to bed.

"Phone still dead?" Cindi asked.

"Yes."

"The storm must have knocked out the phone
lines. There're big branches all over the streets out
there."

I looked out the back window. An Illinois Bell
Telephone van was parked in the alley, its yellow
light revolving slowly.

"Rachel?"

"Hmmm?" I was almost asleep.

"Being dead was really depressing."

"Um-hmmm."

"I was really bummed listening to that TV news
guy do his thirty-second profile on my life. Ms. Illinois, Third Runner-up in the Ms. United States

Pageant, and now a part-time fashion model. And a high-priced call girl, I thought. I sat there in the darkness in that horrible movie theater thinking about my life. Cindi, I said to myself, you really gotta get your act together. What if you really had died, and that's all you had to show for yourself? I mean, you're different, Rachel. You're a lawyer. A professional. You know?"

"Um-hmmm."

"So I said to myself, you've got to pull yourself together. I'm definitely going to go to law school, Rachel. Or something like that. I mean, I have more going for me than just tits and ass, you know. I have . . ."

I fell asleep to the sound of her voice.

Cindi woke up about an hour later, sitting up and shouting, "No, no, no!"

I touched her on the shoulder and she stopped. She laid back down and snuggled up against me. I held her until her panting slowed to the rhythmic breathing of deep sleep.

25

"You writing a letter?"

"Notes," I said, looking up from the kitchen table. It was Saturday morning. Cindi was leaning against the doorway, arms crossed. She was still wearing my sweatshirt. "Investigation notes on this Canaan matter," I explained. "I'm writing down everything that's happened so far. I'm going to go down to the office this afternoon to use the dictaphone. I want to make sure I've got a complete record of all this." I shrugged. "Just in case."

"Just in case what?"

I shook my head. "I just don't know. Just in case something else happens."

Cindi walked barefoot into the kitchen. "I'm really freaked out," she said as she pulled up a chair.

"Me too," I said, putting down my pen. "Maybe there really was a gas leak in your apartment. Maybe—but not likely. And I guess there's still a possibility that they were after your friend Andi. Or that accountant. But how could they know those two were going to use your place? And even if they did find out, how could they rig a fake gas explosion that quickly? It doesn't fit. It's more likely they were after you."

Cindi shuddered. "God, it gives me the creeps."

"That makes two of us." I shrugged. "You want coffee?"

"That sounds great. What time is it, anyway?"

"Ten o'clock."

I walked over to the kitchen counter, took a mug out of the cabinet, and poured her a cup. "How 'bout some breakfast?" I asked.

"Love some."

"I have a quart of buttermilk. Do you like buttermilk pancakes?"

"Love 'em. Can I help?"

"Nope."

I thoroughly enjoy cooking, even though I don't do it often. Putting together the homemade pancake batter might take my mind off the Canaan situation, at least briefly. Besides, we both needed some hearty food to cheer us up.

I gave Cindi the first two pancakes.

"These are delicious, Rachel. You're in the wrong profession."

"I know."

Cindi smiled. "I can see it now. Three little kids at the table and Mama Gold at the stove cooking up flapjacks."

I smiled too. "That doesn't sound so bad."

Cindi sighed. "I know."

We picked up Ozzie at Terry Machelski's office. Poor Ozzie looked bedraggled from two days in a cage. But Terry said he was showing no after-effects. Certainly no memory loss: Ozzie lapped at my face with his wet tongue and barked for joy. I kissed him on the nose and hugged him. I had his brush in the car. He licked my face as I untangled his coat.

We took the car back home, and then Cindi, Ozzie, and I walked over to the lake. Cindi was wearing her own clothes, which had dried overnight. I had on a pair of cutoffs and a St. Louis Cardinals T-shirt.

The three of us walked halfway down the pier. Ozzie jumped into the water. Cindi and I sat on the concrete with our legs dangling over the edge. I leaned back and closed my eyes. The sun felt good on my face.

"The police ran a trace on the license of the station wagon I followed to your building," I said.

"What did they find?"

"Turns out it was a stolen car. They found it in an alley in Uptown last night. Abandoned."

Cindi sat up and took out a cigarette. "That sure doesn't sound like a resident of Shore Drive Tower."

"Nope."

"You really think they were trying to kill me?" she asked.

"I can't figure out the motive. That's what bothers me. Unless they think you know something about them."

"Marshall didn't tell me a darn thing," Cindi said.

"Where did you keep that newspaper poster? The one about Colonel Shaw?"

"In my bedroom. Why?"

"Anyone ever ask you about it?"

236   MICHAEL A. KAHN

"Once in a while."

"Can you remember who?"

Cindi thought it over.

"No."

"Did they ever ask who gave it to you?"

"I don't think so. And even if they had, I wouldn't have told them. God, you don't think it was one of my clients, do you?"

"I don't know what to think."

We were interrupted by Ozzie, who came padding down the pier after his swim and shook himself all over us.

On the way back I stopped at a telephone booth in Loyola Park to call Maggie Sullivan. Her daughter answered and told me that her mother was out in the cemetery doing a funeral. I gave her my office telephone number and asked her to tell her mother to call me after two.

I hung up and turned to find Cindi. She was about twenty yards away, throwing an old tennis ball for Ozzie to fetch. She had her back to me as Ozzie bounded after the ball. As I walked toward her I noticed a stocky black man leaning against a tree about forty yards beyond where the tennis ball had landed. His arms were crossed over his barrel chest. He wore wraparound sunglasses, a black sleeveless T-shirt, blue jeans, and leather sandals.

Ozzie and I reached Cindi from opposite directions at the same time.

"Good doggie," Cindi said as she patted him on the head.

"Don't look up," I said, "but one of us seems to have an admirer."

Cindi kept patting Ozzie on the head. "Who?"

"The black guy in the shades."

"Good boy," Cindi said as she took a quick look.

I bent over Ozzie and rubbed his head. "Let's see if he means business."

We walked out of Loyola Park and down Sheridan to Morse Avenue. As we stood at the corner of Morse and Sheridan waiting for the light to change, I dropped the tennis ball onto the grass by the sidewalk. As I bent down to pick it up I looked back. He was standing at a park bench twenty yards away, his right foot up on the bench as he adjusted his sandal strap. The light changed and we crossed Sheridan and headed west in silence along Morse. When we reached the Poolgogi Restaurant I said, "Wait here for a sec."

I went into the restaurant, picked up a *Reader* from the stack inside the front door, and walked back out. He was thirty yards behind us on the sidewalk, reading a sign nailed to a telephone pole.

We turned right at Greenview and headed north down the narrow street along the el tracks. As we walked, my anger began to build. This was my neighborhood, and it was broad daylight. "Dammit," I mumbled, and spun around.

The sidewalk was empty. He was gone. I jogged back down to Morse with Ozzie and scanned the scene in both directions. No sign of him anywhere.

"Vanished into thin air," I said when Ozzie and I reached Cindi again.

"Not quite," she said, jerking her head toward the el tracks.

I looked up. He was on the el platform, his back toward us. We watched as a southbound train pulled into the station. He stepped into the train without looking down at us. The train doors clattered shut. Shading my eyes, I watched the train curve down the tracks out of sight.

26

BENNY GOLDBERG WAS WAITING IN the foyer of my apartment building when we returned home. He looked at Cindi, his eyes widening.

"Holy shit," he mumbled.

I grinned. "Benny," I said, "you remember Cindi, don't you?"

"Goddamn, girl. Welcome back!" Benny enveloped her in a bear hug, lifting her off the ground.

Cindi giggled and blushed. "Thanks. It's good to be back."

We went up to my apartment and Cindi filled him in while I gave Ozzie some water and scrambled him two eggs. Good for his coat. I came back into the living room with a beer for Benny and diet colas for Cindi and me. I put the *Abbey Road* album on the stereo and turned to Benny. "Pretty wild, huh?"

"Wild?" said Benny. "More like dangerous as

hell. You've stumbled onto a very dangerous group of men."

"Maybe," I said. "And maybe not." I pulled the tab on my soda and sat down on the floor facing Cindi and Benny, who were on the couch. "The explosion in Cindi's apartment doesn't prove that some Canaan conspiracy tried to kill her. It doesn't even prove that *anyone* tried to kill her. It's just possible that there really was a gas leak. Cindi paid some guy to cut off the gas. Maybe he did a poor job. Or maybe someone else on the floor had some work done on their oven and whoever did the work accidentally reopened Cindi's gas line. It could have happened."

"But what about all the rest?" Cindi asked.

"Some of it you can explain." I shrugged. "Some you can't. Yet. The grave robbery. The messages in the *Reader* and the *Tribune*. The exchange up on the el train. The guy in the station wagon driving to Shore Drive Tower." I smiled sheepishly. "The second grave robbery. And the stolen dictionary. And the search of my apartment."

"Terrific, Rachel," Benny said. "Glad to hear there aren't many loose ends. What are you going to do?"

"I don't know." I shrugged. "I'll think of something."

Benny tried to stifle a belch. "God," he groaned.

"You don't look so hot," I said to him.

"I met my match."

"Who was she?"

"Shit, it wasn't no girl. It was food." Benny leaned back against the couch. He stared at the unopened can of beer and closed his eyes. "Actually, I wouldn't even call it food."

"What was it?" I asked.

Benny shivered. "Smoky links. From that joint that just opened down on Halstead. God! My entire gastrointestinal system has been on red alert since midnight."

"What are smoky links?" asked Cindi.

Benny moaned. "Allegedly, smoked pork sausage. But you should have seen those things. God only knows what was in them."

"Bad, huh?" Cindi asked, giggling.

"Worse. You ever hear of traif?" he asked her.

"No."

"It's the opposite of kosher," Benny said. He smothered another belch. "Well, those smoky links are mega-traif. If a Jewish man eats four of them in one sitting, he'll grow a new foreskin. After just two of them I felt like a toxic waste dump. By midnight I was driving the porcelain bus."

"I take it you're not up for that Mexican place, huh?"

"Ugh. Don't even mention it. I couldn't deal with anything stronger than milk of magnesia." Benny struggled to his feet. "Excuse me, ladies. I seem to be picking up an SOS from my large intestine."

We all decided to skip lunch. Cindi and I were still full from breakfast, and Benny's stomach was rumbling ominously. I made him a cup of weak tea, and then he drove us downtown in his Nova. I wanted to go to my office, and Cindi needed to buy some clothes and a disguise.

It was a beautiful August afternoon. The sky was a deep blue and the lake sparkled in the sunlight as we drove onto Lake Shore Drive at Hollywood. A red Frisbee sailed over the sunbathers as we passed the beach at Foster. Soccer games were in progress on all the fields along Montrose, and Hispanic families were gathered in loose circles around dozens of barbecue grills dotting the park. Farther south, the joggers and bike riders moved slowly where the path narrowed at Belmont Harbor.

Cindi pointed to the sailboats and yachts gently swaying in Belmont Harbor. "I once had a client who took me out on his yacht at high tide," she said. "He paid me two hundred dollars to read him his old college girlfriend's letters and watch him masturbate. Very strange."

"Ah," Benny said. "So we beat off, boats against the current, borne back ceaselessly into the past." He glanced back at me in the rearview mirror.

"Not bad," I said. "Not great, but not bad."

Beyond the Fullerton exit Lake Shore Drive swung into a strange stretch toward the high-rises on Michigan Avenue. The John Hancock Building loomed ahead like the rook in a chess game for giants. Traffic slowed at Oak Street Beach. Benny started moaning. "God, look at those chicks," he said.

"Forget it, Benny," Cindi said. "I know the type. All they want is drugs and kinky sex."

Benny moaned again. "Cocaine and bondage. The staff of life."

Benny dropped his car off at a public garage near my office. Cindi was going to Marshall Field's for some clothes, a black wig, and Lolita sunglasses, and Benny volunteered to keep her company. We agreed to meet back at my office at six o'clock.

My office is in one of the oldest buildings in the loop. The major tenants—law firms and accounting firms—left years ago for loftier quarters in the shimmering office towers along LaSalle Street.

More than half the vacated office space remains empty. I share my floor with a pair of process servers, a podiatrist, an elderly solo practitioner, and a three-woman accounting firm. All of their offices were dark on this Saturday afternoon.

I let myself in and opened a window to air the place out. Mary had typed my draft of a trial brief that was due on Friday. I had six days to get it in shape, and it still needed a lot of editing. I put a tape into my Dictaphone, turned toward the window, put my feet up on the ledge, and started dictating. I stopped after the second sentence and rewound the tape, telling myself that the trial brief could wait.

I had to dictate my Canaan notes. Where to start? At the cemetery: my first meeting with Maggie. No, better to start at the beginning. My meeting with Ishmael Richardson. Dictate everything I could remember. There might be a clue buried there somewhere. I clicked on the Dictaphone and started at the beginning.

About an hour later the telephone rang. It was Maggie Sullivan.

"How are the funeral arrangements going?"

"They're going to start digging on Monday, kid. I found a carpenter for the coffin. He promised it'll be ready by Thursday. They'll load Gus into it Friday morning and haul him out here on a gooseneck truck."

"Have they done the autopsy?" I asked.

"Not yet. They're gonna thaw him out over the weekend and start on Monday."

"I'll be out there on Saturday for the funeral."

"Glad to have you. But get here early. There's going to be a big crowd."

"I assume it was quiet out there last night."

"Yep. I found ol' Vern sound asleep in the Slumber Room this morning."

"Good. Listen, I don't know where that coffin is, but I think I have a pretty good idea what's in it. Do you want to come by my office? I'm here until six."

"I can get there by then."

"Good. Come on down. I have a couple of questions for you now," I said.

"Shoot."

"What does a burial fee buy at your cemetery?"

"The plot of land and the burial."

"What about care and maintenance?"

"That's extra."

"How is that handled?"

"Depends. I give my customers several options. They're printed right on the form contract. They can pay an annual fee or they can buy permanent care and maintenance for a lump sum. The amount depends on what kind of care and maintenance they want. I have a no-frills package and a deluxe package."

"And that's all on the contract?"

"You bet. I always explain it too."

That clinched it. "Thanks, Maggie."

"See you tonight, kiddo."

THIRty minutes later I was staring at the file drawer in the cabinet against the office wall. I had opened it to get my research notes on the trial brief.

Mary handled all the filing, and she was careful to keep each case separate and arranged in alphabetical order by client. The research notes should have been in the Candlelite file; I finally found them in the Frontenac Village one. A quick inspection turned up four other files out of order.

I returned to my desk and pulled out each desk drawer, one at a time, trying to remember what had been where. Had the stapler been in the front of the third drawer? Or had someone put it there after looking through all the papers in the drawer?

I stared at the stapler. My apartment had been searched on Thursday. I hadn't been in the office on Friday. I shook my head. The Canaan investigation was turning me into a paranoid. It was probably just Mary, looking for something in my desk on Friday. And if not Mary, then perhaps the cleaning lady who worked from six P.M. to two A.M.

There was a knock at my outer office door. I slowly closed the desk drawer and waited. It was too early for Cindi and Benny. Another knock. I stood up and walked out of my office into the small reception area. Through the pebbled glass I could see a hulking male figure. I picked up Mary's telephone, ready to dial 911.

"Who is it?" I called.

"Rachel?" the voice said. "It's Kent Charles. Can I come in?"

I put down the phone and opened the door. Kent Charles smiled. "Hi," he said. "Hope I'm not interrupting anything."

"No problem," I said. "C'mon in."

Kent followed me into my office. I took a seat behind my desk and Kent sat on the couch along the side wall.

He was dressed casual. "I've never been here before," he said, looking around the room.

"Well, you just missed the four o'clock tour. There won't be another until Monday."

Kent smiled. "How are you feeling? And how's your dog?"

"Okay," I said. "And Ozzie is fine. I picked him up from the vet this morning."

"Good," he said. "I ran into Harlan Dodson down at the office this morning."

"And?"

"He wants to move in court on that codicil fast. He's gone nuts over that grave robbery."

"He's pressuring me too," I said. "What's wrong with him?"

Kent shook his head. "I guess it's that Ebersoll estate litigation. It's getting messy."

"Getting messy?" I had to laugh. "That thing was messy from day one."

The Ebersoll estate litigation was the final chapter in one of those delicious scandals that newspaper publishers pray for. Two years ago Harold Ebersoll, CEO of a major Chicago plastics manufacturer, married Heather Brindle. It was the first marriage for both. Harold was sixty-eight. Heather was nineteen. Three months later Harold Ebersoll was found dead in the den of his Lincoln Park co-op, wrapped in seventy-five feet of adhesive tape, his genitals exposed, a small puddle of semen on the hardwood floor in front of his chair. The coroner eventually ruled it an accidental death resulting from strangulation during an act of sexual bondage with Heather. The neighborhood druggist provided sufficient corroboration for the verdict: during his three months of marriage, Harold Ebersoll had made weekly purchases of adhesive tape totaling, over that period, more than one thousand feet. Predictably, one of the Chicago newspapers labeled the scandal Mummygate.

The other shoe dropped when his last will and testament, executed three weeks before he died, was unveiled. Harold Ebersoll had left his entire estate—estimated at close to six million dollars—to his young widow. Both of Harold's sisters, major beneficiaries under his prior will, had been cut out completely by the new will.

Harlan Dodson had drafted the new will. Last fall the Ebersoll sisters had filed suit to set aside that will.

"Harlan had his deposition in that case three weeks ago," Kent said.

"How'd it go?"

Kent shook his head. "Cal and I defended it. It was tough."

"Who's the other side's attorney?"

"That asshole Joe Oliver."

Joe Oliver had a well-deserved reputation as one of the toughest lawyers in Chicago.

"Did Joe rake him over the coals?" I asked.

"He tried," Kent said. "I cut off the deposition after Oliver started to suggest that Ebersoll's wife was trading sexual favors for Harlan's assistance in getting a new will drafted." Kent shook his head. "Harlan's been climbing the walls ever since. The next round of his deposition is scheduled for September."

"No wonder Harlan's upset about Graham's codicil."

Kent nodded. "He's afraid of another scandal."

I waited.

Kent smiled. "I didn't come over here *just* because I'm curious as hell. Which I am." He smiled. "I thought I might be able to help you out. As I told you, Graham and I were on the road together constantly on Bottles and Cans. I think I knew him better than most people did."

I thought it over. "When Harlan Dodson mentioned the grave robbery," I asked, "when you heard about a pet's grave, did that ring a bell?"

"Not a pet's grave per se," Kent said. "But I can put two and two together. If you've been called in to investigate it, then I assume that the family knows nothing about the pet."

"And?"

"So that means it was someone else's pet." Kent ran his fingers through his hair. "Frankly, I had the strong impression that Graham had a girlfriend in town. Someone he was seeing on a fairly regular basis." He shrugged. "It could be just a wild-goose chase, but maybe it was her pet he buried out there."

"What makes you think he had a girlfriend?"

"Lots of little things. I'd find him in the partners' washroom at night shaving or splashing on cologne. He was very vague about who he was meeting, where he was going. This was over the last couple of years. After a while I just assumed he was having an affair. He'd had others before, you know. Anyway, that's why I came to you with this. I doubt whether his wife even knew about her. I don't know if anyone knew who she was. But she might be a good lead."

"What was his girlfriend's name?"

Kent frowned. "He never mentioned any names. Like I say, I just sort of put two and two together." Kent paused. "Wait a minute. Maybe he did mention a name. It was about a year ago. We were on the red-eye out of LAX. Graham had a lot to drink on that flight. He didn't come out and say he had a girlfriend. Nothing that direct. But he mentioned a girl's name. Something with an *S*." Kent frowned. "Sandy? Cindy? Sally? Something like that."

"You remember anything else?"

"No. But maybe I will later."

"Give me a call if you do."

"I will," he said. "Are you still having problems with it?"

"With what?"

"The codicil."

"Too early to tell for sure," I said. "I'm going to try to wrap it up by the beginning of next week, and then I'll give my report to Ishmael."

"Who do you think robbed the grave?" Kent asked.

I shook my head. "No idea. Believe it or not, there's been a second grave robbery."

"You're kidding! They stole another coffin?"

"No. A watchdog apparently scared him off before he reached the coffin."

"Weird," Kent said, stroking his mustache. "It could be vandals, you know. That stuff happens. At least in human cemeteries. Have the police been told?"

"Not yet."

I tried to check my watch unobtrusively around 5:30. Cindi and Benny were due back soon. She was still officially dead. I didn't want her to run into Kent Charles. Especially Kent Charles. He was sure to be on the prowl. I wondered if I was getting jealous.

Kent must have seen me check my watch, because he stood up to go. "I have to get back to the office," he said. "I'm getting ready for a week of depositions."

"Bottles and Cans?" I asked.

He smiled. "Of course. Too bad you won't be joining us on the case. Listen, I'll be done by seven-thirty. If you're free, maybe we can grab a bit to eat. There's a terrific Cajun place that just opened on Halsted Street."

"Thanks," I said. "I already have plans for tonight."

Kent shrugged. "Maybe some other time. You're a busy woman."

"Not all the time," I said with a smile.

"Well, I'll just have to keep asking, I guess." He paused at the door. "If I think of anything else on this Canaan thing, I'll give you a buzz."

After Kent left, I picked up my Dictaphone. I tried to get back to the trial brief, but I couldn't concentrate. Instead, I opened another desk drawer and stared again at the contents, trying to remember.

MAGGIE SULLIVAN CALLED AT 6:15 P.M. to tell me she was running late. I put her on hold and told Cindi and Benny, who had walked in a few minutes earlier with armloads of packages from Marshall Field's. Benny—whose lower intestinal tract was now, according to him, in stable condition—suggested the Billy Goat Tavern.

"Can you meet me at the Billy Goat Tavern?" I asked Maggie. "Around seven-thirty?"

"Sure."

"I'll have two other people with me. Both of them know a little about the case."

"They aren't cops, are they?"

"No. Just friends."

"Okay. I'll meet you there."

Cindi put on her wig before we left. She now had long black hair, parted in the middle and ending just below her shoulders.

"Amazing," I said.

"Put her in bell bottoms," Benny said, "and she's a refugee from Woodstock."

Benny, Cindi, and I walked down Washington Street to Michigan Avenue. As we crossed over the Chicago River, one of the sight-seeing boats passed underneath the bridge. Some of the passengers waved, and we waved back.

Just beyond the Wrigley Building we took the stairway down into the perpetual darkness of Lower Michigan Avenue. Fashionable Michigan Avenue—the Magnificent Mile of designer dress shops, art galleries, the Ritz-Carlton, and Neiman-Marcus—runs directly over Lower Michigan Avenue, propped up on huge steel columns that vibrate as the limos and cabs pass overhead. Lower Michigan Avenue is the grande dame stripped of her makeup, jewelry, and Japanese cloth fan. The street is pocked and the air is dank. Cobwebs sag from the columns above, and an occasional rat scurries out to drink from the oily puddles below. Tucked in a corner along Lower Michigan Avenue is the Billy Goat Tavern—a long-time hangout for Chicago journalists.

We pushed past the crowded tables to a small table in the corner at the back of the restaurant, directly below a photograph of the late Mayor Richard J. Daley. We each ordered a beer.

I filled them in on Kent Charles's visit to my office that afternoon. "And you're sure he was never one of your customers?" I asked Cindi.

"Never," she said. "I'm positive."

Benny looked up. "Hey, there's your friend."

I turned toward the front of the restaurant, where Maggie Sullivan was standing at the door in navy-blue double-knit slacks, a pink and blue floral print polyester short-sleeve shirt, and white tennis shoes. I stood up and waved to her. She saw me and started moving through the crowd toward our table, holding her navy-blue vinyl handbag over her head. I caught the waiter's eye and ordered a beer for Maggie.

Maggie hoisted her mug. "Down the hatch." She took two big swallows.

The long table in front of ours was packed with a softball team from one of the big insurance-defense law firms in town. The team members wore blue shirts with the team name—The Fender Benders—in white letters. They had downed a tremendous amount of beer, and several of them had staggered off to the men's room. The shouts and laughter from their table, mixed with the general din of the restaurant, gave us almost total privacy at our small table near the back wall.

We had finished our hamburgers and small talk. Maggie turned to me. "So, what was in the coffin?"

"I'm virtually certain it wasn't an animal," I said. "The tombstone says 1985. But he buried it in June of 1986. That's at least a six-month lag. Who would keep a dead animal that long before burying it?" I paused. "I'm pretty sure what he buried was a computer printout."

I described Tyrone Henderson's computer search for the Canaan file. "The dates match," I explained. "Marshall printed out a seven-hundred-page document from the Canaan file late at night in May 1986. A couple weeks later he has you bury a coffin in your cemetery and erects a tombstone for Canaan."

"But why a pet cemetery?" Maggie asked.

I shrugged. "Ambivalence."

"What do you mean?"

"Let's assume that the Canaan file in the computer contained evidence of something secret that Marshall was heavily involved with in 1985. Something very important to him. So important that he couldn't bear the thought of erasing all evidence of it. So first he prints it out of the computer and then he erases the file. Now he has all the evidence in his own hands. But what does he do with it?"

"Why a pet cemetery?" Cindi asked.

"Why not?" I answered. "A safety deposit box is too obvious, too dull: He dies and his wife opens the box. Where's the excitement? Moreover, what if his wife doesn't understand? Or care? Or tell anyone? Marshall wanted to make sure others found out. A human cemetery is too complicated. You don't just bury an unidentified human corpse. And a coffin that size—a coffin for an infant— would raise more than a few eyebrows. What else fits in a little coffin, he must have asked himself. Of course: a dog or a cat. A pet cemetery. Immortality for his documents and a grave marker that announces, at least to someone out there, that he was Graham Marshall and that he was involved with Canaan back in 1985." I turned to Maggie. "Remember the coffin he picked out? And his question about whether it was watertight?" I shifted to Benny. "Graham Anderson Marshall worrying about whether a dead animal would get wet? No way. It's got to be documents. Water damages documents—and those were documents Marshall didn't want damaged."

Maggie leaned forward. "So you're saying that fruitcake stuck a bunch of documents in a coffin and buried it in my cemetery?"

I nodded.

"Where they'd be safe forever," Cindi said.

"With Marshall's name carved in granite on top," Benny added. "Along with the name Canaan."

"I still don't get it," Maggie said. "What good does it do him in a pet cemetery? Who's gonna ever know it's there? And if none of his friends know it's there, what's it worth to him?"

"Maybe he was looking to the future," Cindi said. "Hundreds of years from now. Someone finds that grave marker and wonders what it was all about. Maybe they dig it up to see what it is. Maybe that's what he was hoping for."

"He was looking to the future," I said, "but probably not much further than his own death."

"What are you getting at, Rachel?" Benny asked.

"He wanted someone to find it," I said. "He made sure of that."

"How?" Cindi asked.

"The codicil," I said. "Something odd like that—a trust fund for the care and maintenance of the grave of a pet no one's ever heard of. First of all, the trust fund was unnecessary." I turned to Maggie. "Tell them what you told me. If someone wants you to take special care of a pet's grave, what do they do?"

"They tell me what option they want," Maggie answered. "It's right on the contract form I give them when they come in for a plot. There's standard care. That cost seventy-five dollars a year. Then there's perpetual care. One thousand dollars. And then there's eternal loving care. Three grand."

"Up front," I said. "Right?"

"Yep."

"See?" I said, looking around the table. "His codicil was totally superfluous. The only thing it could possibly do was arouse the law firm's curiosity. He knew A and W would handle his probate. And he knew that an oddball trust fund for forty thousand dollars would make them curious. No probate lawyer could ignore a trust for a mystery grave in a pet cemetery. Especially where the law firm is one of the beneficiaries of the trust. At the very least, the lawyer's got a fiduciary duty to find out what's in the grave."

"If that's what he wanted," said Benny, "it worked."

"If the grave hadn't been robbed," I said, "I bet the firm would have been forced to have it exhumed. They couldn't break that trust fund without at least finding out what was in the grave."

"Did he leave any other clues?" Cindi asked.

I nodded. "Take the computer data base. He printed out the contents in 1986 and then erased *just* the contents. He left the *name* of the Canaan file in the computer."

We sat in silence for a few moments.

Cindi stubbed out her cigarette in the ashtray and looked up, frowning. "So what was on that printout that he buried?"

I looked around the table. "Fasten your seat belts. It seems that Graham Marshall traced his family back to the Puritans in Massachusetts. In 1679, someone named Benjamin Marshall helped found a village in western Massachusetts. A village named Canaan. Benjamin Marshall was an Elder of the church there. Does Graham Marshall know this? Maybe not till he goes to college. Barrett College. And there he takes a course or hears a lecture about a book. A book by Ambrose Springer called *The Lottery of Canaan.*"

"How do you know all that?" Cindi asked.

"I talked to a faculty member at Northwestern who graduated from Barrett." I turned to Benny. "Paul Mason. He said there was a professor back then who gave a popular lecture on the book and the village of Canaan."

I tried to give some sense of the original lottery of Canaan. "A secret lottery that decides people's fates," I concluded, "that controls people's destinies. It's strangely credible. It bowled me over when I read it. Imagine what it could do to a nineteen-year-old kid who thinks he's hearing the story of one of his ancestors."

I took a sip of beer. "Marshall's secretary said that back in 1985 he worked long hours on some secret matter called Canaan. The tombstone has only one date on it: 1985. No date of birth or death. So we can assume Marshall's involvement with Canaan was in 1985. He apparently used the Bottles and Cans computer in connection with it. It was convenient and safe. He had a terminal right in his office, and there's so much junk in that computer that the Canaan file would be a needle in a haystack."

"What the hell was he doing?" Benny asked me.

"I wish I knew for sure. Based on those newspaper articles you helped me find, it looks like Marshall had something to do with four seemingly random events." I turned to Maggie. "Bear with me on this. I'll explain it later." I looked at Benny and Cindi. "You can find examples of luck or chance in the newspaper every day. Maybe Marshall picked four such events at random, left the clues, buried the coffin, and hoped that whoever was assigned the job of figuring out what was in the coffin would think that Marshall had caused the events."

"That's all?" Benny asked.

"Maybe," I said. "But that doesn't explain what's happened since Monday. Who stole the coffin? At first I thought that maybe Marshall arranged that in advance. Bury an empty coffin, have it stolen after you're dead, and chuckle ahead of time at how crazy you'll make the person who's assigned to figure out what was in the coffin. But where's the payoff for Marshall? Where's the punch line? How does he know who's going to find the coffin? How does he know that the investigator—me—will be able to put it all together with just an empty coffin?"

"Good God," Maggie said, shaking her head. "Eleven pet cemeteries in Chicago to choose from and that Graham cracker had to pick mine. Jeez."

"What bothers me," I said, "is the thought that it wasn't all just a clever little joke. What if it was a clever *big* joke? A cosmic practical joke? What if Graham Marshall decided to honor the three-hundredth anniversary of the lottery of Canaan by setting up his own lottery? What if Graham Marshall *caused* the plane crash? What if Graham Marshall *caused* the typographical error? What if Graham Marshall hid the money in that used filing cabinet? What if Graham Marshall fixed the beauty contest?"

"But why?" Cindi asked.

"Why not?" I answered. "If Benjamin Marshall could do it back in 1685, why couldn't Graham Marshall do it in 1985?" I paused. "Look at it this way. Marshall spent his life as a trial lawyer. Doing a trial is like writing history. What's history but the story of cause and effect? It's the same in a trial. If you're the plaintiff, you try to create a link between the effect—your client's injury—and what you claim is the cause—the defendant's conduct. If you're the defendant, you try to destroy the casual link. But the lawyer—like the historian—gets there *after* the event. He doesn't *cause* it; he just tries to explain it."

I nodded at Benny. "So you see? That could be the appeal of a Canaan lottery. You're not *explaining* history. And you're not stuck depending on the testimony of witnesses outside your control. Instead, you go out there and *create* history on your own. You're the judge. You're the jury. And you're the witness."

"But there's no history if it's all secret," Cindi said.

"But of course there is," I answered. "All that's happened is you've separated the cause and the effect. The effect gets recorded in the newspaper—the plane crash, the beauty queen, the hidden treasure, the costly typo. It's just that no one but Marshall knows the real cause. To the rest of the world it's just fate or luck or chance. Remember the epitaph on the tombstone? A nickname for Providence. You know what the full quote is? The librarian at A and W found it for me. Some French philosopher said it. 'Chance is a nickname for Providence.' Except here, chance is just a nickname for Graham Marshall."

"But the wrong person dug up the coffin," said Cindi.

"Yeah," Benny said. "Who dug it up?"

"And what about the second grave robbery?" Maggie said. "What's that all about?"

"And who broke into your apartment and drugged Ozzie?" Benny asked. "And who tried to kill Cindi? And who the hell was that guy you followed from the el?"

"That's where I'm stumped," I said. "Even Marshall couldn't do that stuff from the grave."

We sat in silence amid the shouting and laughter of the restaurant.

"I've got to admit," Benny said, "I could almost believe that Marshall arranged for all this."

"Even for the recent Canaan personals?" Cindi persisted. "And that crazy stuff in the el trains?" Cindi sat back. "What if there really is a Canaan lottery? Some big secret organization that's still going strong after all these years? God knows, there's enough happening all the time that can't be explained."

"Maybe," I said. "But it's almost too incredible to believe."

"So what do we do?" Maggie asked.

"We wait," I said. "We keep our eyes open. And cross our fingers. Maybe we'll get lucky."

"How?" Benny asked.

"Something else is bound to happen," I said. "And I sure pray it doesn't happen to one of us."

CINDI AND I WERE SIPPING herbal tea at my kitchen table. Both of us were in our nightgowns and ready for bed. Ozzie was asleep on the kitchen floor by my feet.

There had been another message from Paul Mason on my answering machine: "I just wanted to see how you and Ozzie are doing. Give me a call, Rachel. And give Ozzie a hug for me." It was close to midnight, too late to call Paul tonight. I took a sip of tea. Paul was being awfully solicitous these past two days. Don't be so suspicious, I told myself. It's nice to have someone who's concerned for you.

"I keep trying to fit the Graham I knew into the Graham who ran that secret lottery," Cindi said. "A man who could calmly decide that two men should die in a plane crash. Two men he had never

met. Men with wives and children and friends."
She shuddered.

I blew across the top of my mug of steaming tea.
"You knew one Graham Marshall. I knew another.
Neither one of us knew this third one."

"How could he do that?" Cindi said. "How could
anyone just decide to kill two men at random? Just
for the hell of it."

"I don't think he saw it that way." I rubbed my
bare toes against Ozzie's side. "He didn't think he
was murdering those two men in the plane crash.
Graham could have seen it as carrying on his
ancestor's master plan. He was arrogant enough
for that. I'll bet it was almost a religious cause for
him."

"When do you think he first decided to set up a
lottery?"

"In 1984. After he almost died." I told Cindi
about his heart surgery in Houston. "His wife told
me that the experience seemed to have a profound
impact on him. The man was already a huge success. He'd tried and won big lawsuits, he'd argued
major cases in the Supreme Court. What else was
left for him to achieve?" I took a sip of tea. "If he
really believed he was a descendant of one of the
original Elders of Canaan, then 1985—the year after he almost died—would have been a significant
year. Think of it. It was the three hundredth anniversary of the first lottery. And the thirtieth anniversary of the bizarre deaths of his mother and
sister. Talk about luck of the draw." I shook my
head. "You know you can't underestimate the impact of those deaths on him."

Cindi nodded.

"To someone like Graham," I continued, "just
back from his brush with death, 1985 must have

seemed like that rare moment in time—when all the spheres were in perfect alignment. Maybe he thought, why not?"

"But why stop?" Cindi asked.

"What do you mean?"

"He went to all that trouble to set up his lottery and hire those Canaan operatives. Why would he run the lottery for just one year and then stop? Why didn't he keep it going?"

"Maybe it was just too demanding and complicated to run for more than one year. Or maybe he planned from the outset to run it for just one year—to commemorate those anniversaries and then walk away. Or maybe"—I paused—"maybe he didn't stop. Maybe he was still running it up to the day he died."

Cindi frowned. "But then why bury the coffin?"

"Because in 1986 he learned he could die at any moment." I told Cindi about the recall of the defective heart valves and Marshall's decision to leave the valve in his heart.

"How horrible."

I nodded. "He had his own private lottery going on inside his heart. He must have feared that if he died unexpectedly, no one would ever know what he had done. That's why he buried the coffin and set up the secret codicil. To preserve the record of what he had done. Remember the language in that codicil? He said he wanted a memorial of the small role he had played in the eternal life of Canaan. The guy wanted people to know about it." I shrugged. "I guess he was proud."

"God, that's creepy."

"I agree, but it's creepy on an almost cosmic level. What's going on now is down-to-earth creepy."

"What do you mean?"

"On the surface it looks like the same old lottery—messages in the personal columns, exchanges on the subways. The Canaan operatives may even be the same ones Graham used. But I'm convinced whoever is running the show now is up to something different."

"How so?"

"Look at what's happened. A grave robbery, the fake gas explosion, the break into my apartment. Assuming these are all related, someone out there is trying to *eliminate* evidence of what Graham was doing—not preserve it."

"But why kill me?" Cindi asked. "I didn't know a thing."

"Maybe this guy thinks Graham told you about the lottery." I paused, thinking it over. "Maybe Graham told him about the lottery, and he was afraid Graham might have told you too."

"God. Do you think Graham picked a successor?"

"It makes sense, doesn't it? Someone to take over when he died. Or maybe Graham didn't even realize that he had picked a successor. Maybe he got drunk one night and bragged about the lottery to someone, and that someone decided to take it over when Graham died. Whoever he is, he could have worried that Graham told others too. You'd be a likely candidate."

"I don't know," Cindi said. "If this guy's that clever, you'd think he'd first try to find out if I knew anything before he had me killed."

"Maybe," I said. "But maybe that was too risky for him. I don't know. Let me ask you something: How could the killer have known you weren't around the night he had someone go up to your apartment to rig the explosion?"

"That part would be pretty easy," she said. "All he had to do was call the modeling agency to find out my schedule for that week. They would have told him I was out of town on that night."

"Just like that?" I asked.

Cindi smiled. "Oh, he'd have to pose as a potential client of the agency. You know, like some advertising outfit. A lot of them request specific models. When they're scheduling a specific shoot and they want certain models, they call in advance to see which ones are available on what dates. The agency gets those calls all the time."

"So if he asked about you, they would have told him you were going to be out of town last Wednesday."

Cindi nodded.

"That's how he knew you wouldn't be in your condo that night," I said.

"But the explosion killed the wrong people," Cindi said.

"It could have been a time bomb," I said. "Set to go off in the middle of the day—when he thought you'd be around."

We were both quiet for a while.

"You think it's all a cover-up now?" Cindi finally asked.

"I think it's more than just a cover-up," I said. "Whoever's running the lottery now must have his own plans. That's the really creepy part. What if this last week is just a prelude? Whoever this one is seems violent enough for anything. I just hope he isn't as clever as Marshall."

"But what can we do?" Cindi asked.

"Go to the police," I said. "We don't have much

to give them. But we do have you." I smiled. "A living corpse ought to get their attention." I stood up and walked over to the sink with my tea mug. "I'm meeting with Ishmael Richardson on Monday morning to give him my report. He has enough City Hall contacts to get the police involved in a quiet way. He'll want to keep a lid on this."

Cindi and I checked the locks on the doors and all the windows before we got into bed.

Neither of us slept well.

30

I REACHED FOR THE TELEPHONE receiver on the third ring.

"Hello," I croaked, my head still on the pillow.

"Guess what the police just gave me?"

"Maggie?" I turned toward the clock radio on the nightstand. Nine thirty-eight Sunday morning. Sunlight was streaming in through the bedroom window.

"Guess what just got returned?"

"What?"

"That coffin we've been looking for."

"Canaan?"

Cindi sat up in bed.

"Yep," Maggie said. "I matched the serial number on the coffin against my log book. Same one."

"Did you open it?" I asked.

"Didn't have to. The police did before they brought it out."

"And?"

"Bones. Just bones."

"I'm coming right out, Maggie. Don't bury it yet." I hung up and looked at Cindi. "Let's go," I said. "The cops found the Canaan coffin."

We were in Maggie's office in the back of the chapel—Cindi, Maggie, and I. The coffin was on the desk, and the coffin lid was on the carpet in front of the desk.

I was staring at the skeleton inside the coffin. It looked like the skeleton of a small dog. The thin bones were clean and white. Bone-white. One eye socket stared blankly up at me. The skeleton was resting on its side on the satin cushion that lined the bottom and sides of the coffin.

"They found it behind the police station?" I asked again.

"Yep. Out near the back steps," Maggie said. "Someone left it there. I guess they could tell it was mine because of the stamp on the bottom."

I lifted one end of the coffin. Stamped in black ink on the bottom was WAGGING TAIL ESTATES—MARGARET SULLIVAN, PROP., along with the address and telephone number.

"One of the boys at the station dropped it off this morning," Maggie said. "They had already looked inside. They were so relieved it wasn't a human body that they hardly asked me any questions. I made up some story about a client who had decided to transfer her pet from another cemetery to Wagging Tail and lost it in the process. They bought the story." Maggie leaned back. "Well, maybe that Graham Marshall wasn't so crazy after all. It could of been just some punks pulling a prank. The same ones who tried to dig up the other grave."

I didn't answer.

"You two want some coffee?" Maggie asked.

"Sure," Cindi answered.

"Let's go on over to the house and I'll put on a pot." Maggie stood up.

"I'll be along in a minute," I said.

Maggie stopped at the door. "Your pal Benny called here a while ago, Rachel. Said he's been looking for you everywhere. Tried me as a last resort. Said he had something to show you. I gave him the address and told him to come on down."

After Maggie and Cindi left, I stared at the skeleton. It was all too pat.

What happened, Graham? Someone pulled your documents out and replaced them with a skeleton. Was someone on to you, Graham? Was someone afraid of those documents? Did you suspect that back in 1986 when you buried the coffin?

If you did, if you thought someone was on to you, then maybe you knew who that someone was.

I sat back and mulled it over. You bury your secret but set up a bizarre legacy in a codicil to make sure your secret gets discovered after you're dead. What if you are worried that someone else might try to spoil your plan? That someone else might get to the coffin first? That someone else might dig it up, destroy the documents, and bury it again? What do you do?

Maybe you leave a clue for the second one who finds the coffin.

I leaned forward again and looked into the coffin. Where do you leave the clue? In the coffin? Maybe. Before you bury the coffin you hide a clue inside the coffin. You hide it where someone interested in the documents won't think to look.

I reached inside the coffin and, with a shiver, lifted out the frail skeleton and set it on the carpet next to the coffin lid. I put the coffin on my lap. The satin-covered padding that lined the sides of the coffin lifted out in one piece, a rectangular belt of cushion. I checked both sides of the satin covering. Nothing. I squeezed it. It felt like foam rubber. There was a sharp-edged letter opener on Maggie's desk. Using the letter opener, I poked a hole in the satin and ripped off the covering. Nothing inside but foam rubber. I looked along the inner sides of the coffin. Nothing.

I reached inside the coffin and tried to pull out the cushion lining the floor of the coffin. It was glued down. I yanked, and it popped out with a tearing sound. I turned the pillow-sized cushion over. Nothing. A piece of the satin covering had torn off when I pulled out the cushion. I tore off the rest of the covering. Nothing. Just foam rubber. I tossed the cushion onto the floor and looked inside the bare coffin. Two small scraps of satin were still glued to the floor of the coffin.

And then I saw it. In the upper right corner of the floor of the coffin, where it had been hidden under the glued-down cushion. Printed in black ink:

00320-1953

GAM

I picked up the coffin and hurried toward Maggie's house.

Cindi and Maggie were seated at the kitchen table

drinking coffee. I showed Maggie the handwritten code on the inside of the empty coffin.

"Did you write this in here?" I asked.

Maggie frowned and shook her head. "No. Definitely not."

"What is it?" Cindi asked.

I handed her the coffin and turned to Maggie. "You mentioned something about a serial number over the phone," I said. "You said that that was how you knew it was your coffin."

Maggie reached for the coffin and turned it upside down. "This is what I was talking about," she said, pointing to a twelve-digit number stamped on the bottom of the coffin. "The manufacturer stamps a serial number on the bottom of each of the coffins. I always copy it down in my log book next to the name of the pet and the name of the owner. Sometimes I have two burials in the same day. Keeping track of serial numbers is just a precaution, to make sure I don't bury a pet in the wrong hole."

"What does the code mean?" Cindi asked.

"I don't know what the number stands for," I answered, "but I'm sure GAM stands for Graham Anderson Marshall."

There was a knock at the back door. We turned around to see Benny standing there with a newspaper folded under his arm.

"C'mon in," Maggie called. "The door's open."

"Hi, gang," Benny said as he walked in. "I've got something interesting to show you."

"So have we," said Cindi. "Maggie got the coffin back."

"No kidding?"

Maggie explained how the coffin got back to

Wagging Tail Estates, and then I showed Benny what I had found inside it.

"Do you recognize the code?" Benny asked.

"No. There's something familiar about the sequence of numbers, but I can't figure it out."

Benny stared at the numbers, frowning.

"What was your news?" Cindi asked.

Benny looked up and smiled. "Oh, yeah. You guys are going to love this one." He opened the newspaper and laid it flat on the table. "I was reading the Sunday paper this morning," he explained, "and I turned to the classifieds. I've been looking for a roll-top desk, and I wanted to see if there were any available. Then I remembered those Canaan messages you found, Rachel. So I turned to the personals." Benny opened the newspaper, folded it over, and laid it back on the table. "Look what I found." He pointed.

I bent over him and looked where his finger was pointing. "Well," I said. "Another one."

It was another Canaan message:

Canaan 3: Grand-S
1 a.m., Monday

I stared at the message, my thoughts racing. "One A.M. Monday is tonight. After midnight. This is a terrific break."

"What do you mean?" Maggie asked.

"Don't you see? Tonight the Canaan drop point is down at the Grand subway station."

"You're not suggesting that we go down there, are you?" Maggie asked.

I looked at each of them. "Someone has to. We have to find out who's behind all this. How do we know they won't try to kill Cindi again? Or one of us? I'm scared of these people, whoever they are. But I'm also scared to go home at night. I can't go on living like that. If we can find out who these Canaan operatives are, follow one of them to his home, we'll finally have enough to go to the police." I shrugged. "Right now all we have is a lot of weird incidents. We need something more. We need to find the connection."

We were silent for a while. Benny studied the Canaan personal. Cindi lifted the empty coffin and turned it over. Maggie walked over to the coffeepot for a refill.

"I'm going with Rachel tonight," Cindi said, looking at me.

Maggie replaced the coffeepot and looked at Benny. "You going too?"

Benny turned to me and, after a pause, grinned. "What the hell? Subway station, one in the morning. You never know. I might meet some nice chicks down there."

Maggie shook her head. "What kind of shape are you in?" she asked Benny.

He patted his ample belly. "Two hundred and seven pounds of blue twisted steel."

Maggie stared at me. "You're crazy, Rachel," she finally said with a sigh. "But if you cowboys are really going to do it, you ought to do it right. This ain't no Sunday school picnic. Two of you ought to follow the guy who gets the package and two more ought to follow the guy who hands him the package. Maybe both of them are just messengers, but the guy who hands over the package is at least one step closer to the source."

"Are you volunteering?" Benny asked Maggie.

"Well, I got me a Ford pickup parked out front with a tankful of gas. It looks a little beat up, but let me tell you something: You give that baby some gas and she can shit and split."

Benny and Cindi both broke up with laughter.

"You shouldn't feel you have to do this," I said to them. "It could be dangerous."

"Listen, Rachel," Maggie said, "somebody stole a coffin out of my cemetery. And tried to steal another one. If it's just vandals, well, there isn't much I can do about it. But if it's connected with this Canaan, I got some obligations to my clients and their pets."

I looked around the table and smiled. "Thanks, guys."

"We can't go down there unprotected," Cindi said.

"Well," I said, "I can go get Ozzie. Maggie has her brother-in-law's German shepherd."

Benny shook his head. "I don't know. We'd look like a blind circus down there."

"Hang on," Maggie said, getting up from her chair. "I got something that packs a little more wallop than a couple of dogs." She walked out of the kitchen and returned a few minutes later with two handguns and a box of ammunition cradled in her arms. "My Carl collected these things," she said as she laid them on the kitchen table. "Taught me how to use them too. Any of you ever fired one of these?"

I shook my head.

"I have," Cindi said.

"You?" Benny asked her.

Cindi nodded. "I own one. Same model as that Smith and Wesson," she said, pointing to one of Maggie's guns.

Maggie slid it across the table to Cindi. "See how it feels."

31

At 12:40 A.M. Maggie parked her pickup truck a half block from the entrance to the Grand Avenue subway station. Maggie, Cindi, and I climbed down out of the cab of her pickup as Benny pulled his Nova into the space behind the truck. Cindi and I were in jeans and sweatshirts. Maggie was wearing a green double-knit jogging outfit with white piping, and Benny had on a Chicago White Sox T-shirt and baggy khaki slacks.

"Listen, gang," Benny said, "we don't need any heroes tonight. Let's just find out what we can—and run like hell if we have to." He looked at Maggie. "You bring your license for that gun?"

Maggie patted her bulging shoulder bag. "Right here," she said.

Benny grinned at me. "Are we fucking nuts or what?"

I forced a smile. "I hope not." The guns made me queasy.

Walking down the stairs toward the fare booth, we passed a recruiting poster: THE MARINES—WE'RE LOOKING FOR A FEW GOOD MEN.

"And a whole bunch of sadistic bastards," Benny added.

Maggie snorted. "We could sure use a few tonight."

We paid the fare, passed through the turnstiles, and took the stairway down to the tracks. Maggie and Benny waited near the foot of the stairs. Cindi and I walked ahead, stopping about fifty feet away.

"This is creepy," Cindi whispered.

I nodded. Two gray rats waddled along the tracks below us. There was a hollow plunk-plunk-plunk of water somewhere off in the darkness.

Two college-age boys—both pasty-white and fat—were huddled together farther down the platform. One of them pointed at us, and they both grinned. Each had a can of beer in his hand.

I leaned my head toward Cindi. "Here come the men of our dreams," I said.

"Terrific."

They walked single file, stopping about ten feet away. The one in front had curly black hair, a beer belly, and a red football jersey with the number 69 on the front. His buddy peered around him with a gap-toothed leer.

The one in front grinned, raised his can of beer, and belched. "Good evening, girls. How are we tonight?"

"Take a hike, you clowns," Cindi said.

The guy in front winked and turned back toward his buddy. "Sure, girls. But first we'd like you to

THE CANAAN LEGACY 277

meet Red. Go ahead, Pete. Let these girls meet him."

Pete stepped out from behind his buddy, wagging his half-erect penis in his right fist. "Say hello to Red, girls."

"Ignore these bozos," Cindi mumbled as she grasped my elbow to pull me away.

I didn't budge. Instead, I stared at Pete's crotch, and then glanced at Cindi. "Look at that," I said to her, nodding at the display. "It looks just like a penis, only smaller."

Pete's face dropped, followed by his penis. He looked down at his crotch, then back at me, then back at his crotch.

"Poor thing looks undernourished," Cindi said, picking up on my lead.

Pete pushed his penis back into his pants and yanked up the zipper. He turned and walked away, followed by his buddy.

When they were almost twenty yards away, one of them shouted "Bitch!" without looking back at us.

Cindi burst into laughter and held out her palm. I slapped her five.

"That was beautiful, Rachel. Just beautiful."

My smile froze. "Someone's coming."

Cindi turned slowly. Coming down the stairs toward the subway platform was a skinny Hispanic man dressed in a baggy gray suit and a dark brown shirt open at the collar. He brushed past Benny and Maggie, who were still standing at the bottom of the stairs, and walked nervously down the platform with his hands in his pockets. Benny and Maggie looked toward us, and Benny pointed at the man. I nodded and checked my watch. It was 1:01 A.M.

"Think that's him?" Cindi whispered.

I shrugged and checked my pocket for the key. It was still there. Cindi and I were to follow the recipient of the package—and if I was right, the skinny guy was our man. If something got screwed up, Benny had given me an extra key to his car—just in case.

The skinny guy stood with his toes on the yellow warning line at the edge of the platform. He started cutting his nails with a nail clipper. Maggie and Benny had moved down the platform to within twenty feet of him. Cindi and I stood quietly, listening to the click of the nail clipper and the plunk of the water and the rustlings of the rats below.

From off in the distance, in the darkness beyond the north end of the platform, came the sound of an approaching train. It was barely audible at first—a low growl. The noise grew louder, and suddenly the train screamed out of the tunnel and rumbled into the station. It stopped with a squeal of brakes several feet shy of where Cindi and I were standing. It was one of the newer trains—silver with large windows.

The skinny Hispanic had backed up a few steps. He was standing near the front doors of the train as they opened. Cindi and I moved toward him. Out from the train walked the same man I had seen on the el tracks at Addison, the one I had followed to Shore Drive Tower. He was dressed the same: black T-shirt and khaki work pants. He had a thick manila envelope under his left arm. The skinny guy stepped forward and said something to the man with the envelope, who then handed it over. The skinny guy stepped into the train, and Cindi and I followed him in.

THE CANAAN LEGACY 279

He sat down in the first row of seats on the side opposite the door we had entered. Cindi and I sat down two rows back on the side closest to the platform.

I peered out the window as the train lurched forward. The other man was walking at a brisk pace down the platform toward the stairs. Maggie and Benny were following him. I watched them until the train passed beyond the end of the station and plunged back into darkness.

"All systems go," I said to Cindi. "We have lift-off."

Our man got off at the Washington subway station. We followed him across the Loop to the First Illinois Bank Building. We waited across the street from the entrance as he entered the building. He stopped at the security guard's desk for a moment and then moved past the guard toward the elevator banks.

"C'mon," I said to Cindi, and we sprinted across the street.

A gray-haired security guard was behind a desk in the middle of the lobby. He was leaning back in his chair, staring at a miniature television at the edge of the desk. The white plastic sign on the desk stated that all visitors had to sign in.

"Evening," I said as we reached the desk.

The guard looked up and touched his cap. "Evening, girls," he said, and turned back to the television, where the tinny sounds of a gun battle could be heard.

I leaned over the sign-in book and picked up the pen. The last entry was for John Doe at 1:37 A.M. I checked my watch: 1:39 A.M. Under the Destination column John Doe had written Reynolds & Henderson, 42nd floor.

I wrote in Bridgid O'Shaughnessy and Nora Charles, 1:41 A.M.

We walked over to the express elevator bank. I started to reach for the Up button and then stopped.

"What's wrong?" Cindi asked.

"Wait here a sec. I've got a hunch." I walked back to the security guard. "Is there something wrong with the express elevator?" I asked.

The guard looked up from his television. "What's wrong with it?"

"I pushed the button and waited and it never came down."

"Well, we only got one of them in service after midnight. It takes a while sometimes."

"Are you sure it isn't stuck somewhere?"

The guard leaned forward and squinted at a small terminal screen on the desk. "Let's see. That's elevator number four. It's just sitting up there on the thirty-sixth floor. Push that button again and I'll see if it starts coming down."

"Thanks."

I walked back to Cindi and pushed the Up button. Ten seconds later the guard called out, "It's coming down now, lady."

"I think he's on the thirty-sixth floor," I said to Cindi. "Not the forty-second. Let me go up there alone. You stay here. Give me about ten minutes. If I'm not down by then, get that guard and come up after me."

"Are you sure you want to go up there alone, Rachel? You don't even have a gun."

"I wouldn't know what to do with one, anyway."

The elevator doors slid open and I stepped inside. "Don't worry," I said. "I'm not going to confront him. I just want to see what he's up to. Remember, come get me if I'm not down in ten minutes."

"Good luck, Rachel," Cindi said as the doors started closing.

"Thanks," I said as the doors slid shut.

I took a deep breath, and the elevator started its ascent.

32

I STEPPED OUT OF THE elevator onto the 36th floor. Down the hall to my right was the entrance to the law firm of Perrini & Oliver. To my left was the entrance to the real estate investment firm of Krantz, Hedburg, & Disher, Ltd. The glass doors to both were open, and night-shift cleaning carts were in the lighted reception area of both firms. A heavyset woman in a white smock and blue scarf finished dusting the receptionist's desk at Krantz, Hedburg, & Disher and then moved down the hall out of sight. I walked into their empty reception area. From somewhere inside the offices came the muffled sound of a vacuum cleaner. Walking over to the cleaning cart, I pulled out a white rag and a spray bottle of window cleaner.

Five minutes later, as I was pretending to clean the glass entrance door of Krantz, Hedburg, &

Disher, I saw the skinny guy come out of Perrini & Oliver. He was no longer carrying anything.

I waited until he stepped into the elevator, and then I walked into the law offices of Perrini & Oliver.

Oscar Perrini had died of lung cancer about ten years ago, when the law firm consisted of just him, Joe Oliver, and one associate. Since Perrini's death Joe Oliver had built Perrini & Oliver into one of the premier plaintiff's antitrust firms in the Midwest. They have a substantial role in most antitrust cases pending in Chicago and at least some piece of the action in several of the larger antitrust cases in the country, including four of the plaintiffs in *In re Bottles & Cans.*

In the lexicon of corporate litigators, plaintiffs' antitrust lawyers are sharks. Among these sharks Joe Oliver is the Great White. Although he hardly looks the part—a skinny, slouching man with a neatly trimmed goatee, a hawk's-beak nose, and a pair of dark-rimmed glasses pushed back in his bushy gray hair—the mere presence of Joe Oliver on the plaintiff's side doubles the settlement value of the case. Graham Marshall had described him, with grudging respect, as an old river rat.

Like aging predators in most professions, Joe Oliver had become hungry for respectability. Three years ago he had endowed a chair at his alma mater, the Loyola School of Law. Two years ago the Art Institute of Chicago had opened the Joseph P. Oliver Gallery of Mexican Art, featuring a collection of pre-Columbian figurines from the Joseph P. Oliver Collection. When the society pages of the local newspapers covered benefits for the Chicago Symphony or the Field Museum or the Lyric Opera these days, more often than not one of the photographs included a tuxedoed Joe Oliver and his stunning raven-haired second wife, Roxanne. He'd come a long way from stickball on the West Side.

I passed the cleaning woman by the copying machine. She looked up from her vacuum and smiled, obviously used to comings and goings of lawyers at all hours of the night. I stopped at each office, flicked on the light, and scanned the office for the package. It wasn't in the first ten offices. At least not in a visible place. I would quickly check all the offices and the law library. If I didn't see it the first time through, I'd start over again.

I found it the first time through—sitting on the leather chair behind the chrome and glass desk in the corner office of Joseph P. Oliver. Hand-printed in black felt-tip marker on the front of the envelope was the following: TO JOSEPH OLIVER—PERSONAL & CONFIDENTIAL.

I picked up the envelope, sat down in the chair, tore open the flap, and dumped the contents on the glass-top desk. A black videocassette clattered onto the desk. I looked in the envelope and pulled out a sheet of white bond paper. The message was hand-printed in block letters in red marker:

DEAR JOE:
REMEMBER THIS VIDEOTAPE?
WE HAVE COPIES FOR YOUR
WIFE, YOUR DAUGHTER AT STANFORD,
AND YOUR FRIENDS AT THE ART
INSTITUTE, THE FIELD MUSEUM,
LYRIC OPERA AND THE A.B.A.

IF YOU COOPERATE WITH US, WE
WILL RETURN THE ORIGINAL AND ALL
COPIES. WE DO NOT WANT MONEY.

JUST YOUR COOPERATION. WE
WILL EXPLAIN LATER.

UNTIL THEN, SIT TIGHT. AND,
OF COURSE, DO NOT GO TO THE
POLICE. IF YOU DO, WE WILL
HAVE TO DELIVER ALL OF THE
COPIES TO YOUR FRIENDS AND
LOVED ONES.

WE'LL BE IN TOUCH.

I put the message and videocassette back in the envelope and stuffed the envelope into my purse.

The elevator doors opened on an empty lobby. Cindi was gone, and so was the guard. I checked my watch. I'd been up there for almost twenty minutes. Cindi must have gone up after me.

Waiting at the guard's desk, I thought of the videocassette recorder and television in my office, which was just across the street. I had bought the equipment last year in connection with two copyright lawsuits for one of my clients. Maggie and Benny were supposed to meet me back there. With any luck, I could view the videotape before they got there.

I tore a sheet of paper off the guard's log book and wrote Cindi a short note: Everything's okay. I'm at my office. Come on over.

I added my office address and signed my name.

33

I GOT TO MY OFFICE before the others. I flicked on the light, walked across the room, and turned on the television and the videocassette recorder. I slid the videocassette out of its black cardboard jacket, inserted it into the recorder, and pushed the Play button. As the recorder whirred and clicked into gear, I backed up to the edge of my desk to watch.

The snow on the television screen flickered and jumped and then resolved into focus. I was staring at Cindi Reynolds. Not the Miss Illinois Cindi Reynolds. Not the tap-dancing English major. This was the $900-a-night Cindi Reynolds, in black push-up bra, black string-bikini panties, frilly black garter belt, dark stockings, and black spike heels. She was sitting on the edge of her bed, facing the camera, legs crossed.

Cindi tilted back her head, eyes half closed, and ran a bright red fingernail slowly down her long tan neck and into the swollen valley between her breasts. Her eyes opened wider and she pushed the finger into her mouth between puckered lips. Her eyes closed, and then opened as she slowly pulled her finger out.

"Come on over here, Joe," she said into the screen, her voice husky. "Cindi's lonely."

A hairy male body passed in front of the camera and off the screen, reappearing on camera again by her bed. It was Joe Oliver, wearing red briefs and black knee-high socks.

As Cindi tugged down his red briefs I walked over and pushed the Fast Forward button. It became a silent high-speed pornographic movie, the bodies jerking and flopping around the bed. Joe finally collapsed on top of her, panting like a dog. The scene jumped to a head-on shot of Cindi's bathroom shower, both of them naked and visible from the knees up. A series of manic scrubbings and soapings and gropings, and then the shower scene ended and it was back to the bedroom, where Joe Oliver, former campaign chairman for the Catholic Charities of Chicago annual fund-raising drive, was spread-eagled and naked on the bed. Cindi—now wearing a garter belt, nylons, and spike heels—tied his wrists and ankles to the bed posts, her hands a blur of choppy motion. Straddling Oliver on her hands and knees, her bottom to the camera, she worked her way up from his toes. Joe Oliver flopped on the bed like a live fish on a boat deck. As she lowered her round bottom onto his face, I walked over to the recorder and pushed the Stop button. The last image was of Joe Oliver, visible from the neck down, his body arched on the bed as if he were being electrocuted.

I had rewound the videotape, put it back in the

envelope along with the blackmail message, and placed the whole package in my briefcase, when there was a knock on my door. It was Benny and Maggie.

Benny was puffing on a fat cigar. "Greetings and salutations. Where's Cindi?"

"Not back yet. She should be here soon. Well?" I asked.

"Everything went as planned," Benny answered. "How 'bout you? Where'd that skinny guy lead you?"

"To the First Illinois Bank Building," I answered. "I lost him up on the thirty-sixth floor. Cindi must still be over there with the security guard." I didn't want to tell them about the videotape until I talked to Cindi. "How about your guy?"

"You mean Anthony Rossino?" Maggie asked.

"That's his name?"

"Yep. We followed him home," said Benny. "Me and old Hot Rod Sullivan over here."

Maggie laughed. "We didn't lose him, did we?"

"Miss Parnelli Jones here"—Benny jerked his thumb toward Maggie—"could use a refresher course in the Illinois Motor Vehicle Code." They were both grinning.

"What happened?" I asked.

"That guy kept making the lights and we kept missing them," Maggie explained. "He got too far ahead."

"So he turns right way up ahead," Benny said. "He's going north, we're still going west, and both of us are moving along the edge of a country club golf course. Well, this crazy broad tells me to hang on, and then she whips that pickup over the curb, jumps the sidewalk, crashes through a row of hedges, and cuts a diagonal across the back nine holes of the golf course. Shit, we're bouncing through sand traps, skidding over the putting greens, knocking over small trees."

"Hold on, ace," Maggie said. "What's the bottom line? Did we lose him?"

"Nope," Benny answered. "Followed him all the way home."

"Where's home?" I asked.

"Park Ridge," Benny answered, pulling a folded sheet of paper out of his pants pocket. He unfolded the paper. "A three-flat on Asbury. Home of one Anthony Rossino."

"How'd you find out his name?"

"We watched him go into the building," Maggie said.

"A few minutes later the lights flicked on up on the third floor," Benny said. "You could see him walking around up there. I went into the lobby and checked the mailboxes for his name."

"Good work, guys," I said.

There was a knock at the door. "Rachel?" Cindi called.

I unlocked the door and let her in. "Thank God you're okay," she said.

"What happened?" I asked.

"That guy came down ten minutes after you went up. I waited five more minutes. I was going crazy. I got the guard. He was sure you went up to the thirty-eighth floor. I told him it was the thirty-sixth floor. Well, we searched the thirty-eighth floor first and then the thirty-sixth floor. God, I was scared to death. I practically shouted for joy when I saw your note at the guard's desk."

* * *

Benny dropped Cindi and me off at my apartment at 4:30 A.M. The three flights of stairs felt like the west ridge of Mount Everest. Ozzie greeted me with a big wet kiss, obviously relieved that I'd finally come home. I went to get him a dog biscuit.

Cindi followed me into the kitchen and I poured us both a glass of milk.

"I didn't really lose that guy up in the bank building," I said.

Cindi looked confused.

"I wanted you to be the first one to see this." I pulled the thick manila envelope out of my purse. "He left this in Joe Oliver's office." I dropped the envelope on the kitchen table.

Cindi's eyes opened wide as she reached for it. I watched her pull out the videocassette and the note. Her excitement turned to pain as she read the note. "Oh, my God." She covered her face with her hands, shaking her head. When she looked up, her eyes were glistening. "Did you watch it?"

"Some of it."

"Benny and Maggie?"

"No. Just me."

"Poor Joe. My God, that poor man."

"How did they get the tape?"

"I don't know."

"Did all your customers get a videotape?"

"No. It was extra."

"Who filmed that?" I asked, nodding toward the videocassette.

"I did. I set up the camera and got us both into the frame. I had a remote button to start the camera."

I frowned. "What do they do with their videotapes?" I asked, fascinated despite myself.

Cindi shrugged. "Watch them, I guess. I got the

idea from one client who used to take Polaroid shots of me, and of us ... together. You'd be surprised how many of them wanted a videotape."

"Did your customers take their videotapes home with them?"

"Of course." Cindi looked up, frowning, and then her eyes opened wide. "Oh, no!"

"What? What is it?"

"That tape of Joe Oliver was in my apartment."

"When?"

"Up until the end. Until the explosion. Or at least it was there when I left for the Dunes."

"Where?"

"In a safe in the wall. Behind one of the pictures in the living room."

"Why?"

"Joe asked me to keep it for him. For a few weeks. He wanted it somewhere safe. He didn't want it in his office or home."

"Was he the only one?"

"The only one what?"

"The only one who had you keep his videotape?"

"No." Cindi frowned. "It varied. No one ever left a tape with me permanently. Most took the tape with them when they left. But some left them with me for safekeeping for a few weeks. Especially if there was still room on the tape. Those tapes can record for two hours. Sometimes it takes three sessions before the tape is full. Usually for a few weeks they—God, Rachel! Do you think?"

"Probably. It's sure a good enough motive. How many videocassettes were there when you left for the Dunes?"

"Maybe six or seven." She shook her head. "God."

"Do you know their names?" I asked.

"Sure. At least most of them."

"They told you their *real* names?"

"Of course," she snapped. "I insisted. They knew my real name and where I lived. Why shouldn't I know theirs?"

"I'm sort of surprised," I said. "I just assumed they'd use phony names."

"Some tried. But I could tell a phony name right off."

I thought it over.

"Look," she said impatiently, "if your name is Tom and your greatest fantasy is to have some woman tell you you've got a giant cock, it's not going to get you off if she keeps calling you Harry or Joe. And anyway, these were lawyers, for chrissakes. Trial lawyers. You know the type, Rachel. Giant egos. They loved bragging to me about their victories in court. They wanted to impress me, Rachel. It was like foreplay for them. Once they learned to trust me, they had no problem with their real name."

"Who else besides Joe Oliver?" I asked softly.

Cindi was able to name two others. She wasn't sure about the rest. But the two she could remember were an extortionist's vision of nirvana: a litigation partner at a major Chicago law firm and a state appellate judge.

"Boy," I finally said. "They hit the mother lode."

"Those poor men," Cindi said. "They'll be destroyed."

And so will you, I thought. Dumb. All around dumb. The lawyers and Cindi. And now there were at least a half dozen other videocassettes out there. I had been shocked by the videotape. Up until then

Cindi's professional life had seemed little more than an amusing peculiarity, detached from the rest of her. The videotape had changed all that, had driven home the gritty reality of her job. She had decided to leave that life, to move on to a new career. Whatever chance she'd had, she'd never do it if those tapes got out.

"What can we do?" Cindi asked.

"First we have to confirm that they stole all the videocassettes," I said.

"How?"

"I'll have someone check the police inventory from your condo tomorrow."

"What's a police inventory?"

"A list of everything the police found in your place after the explosion. What else was in the safe?"

"Some cash. Some jewelry."

"The police inventory will tell us what's missing."

"Rachel, I think we're in over our heads."

"A little," I said. More like standing on the ocean floor. "I'm going to try to get us some help tomorrow. And I think it's time Cindi Reynolds returned from the dead. At least as far as the police are concerned."

"Whatever you say." Her shoulders were slumped and her head was down.

"Who knew about the safe and the videocassettes?"

"Only the ones who asked me if I knew of a place they could store their tapes."

We got into bed at 5:30 A.M. and I set my alarm for 8:30 A.M. My appointment with Ishmael Richardson was at 11:30.

I thought back to the code in the coffin. The numbers weren't familiar, but the sequence was. I'd know for sure after I saw Tyrone Henderson in the morning.

34

ON MONDAY MORNING I CALLED Detective Kevin Turelli before I left for my office.

"You want the police inventory from the Shore Drive Tower explosion?" he asked. "You mind telling me why, Rachel?"

"I can't, Kevin. At least not yet."

"Well, I'll see what I can find. I know they'll have a copy at the Eighteenth District. There might be one down here. And there's probably a dick from the Bomb and Arson Squad working on it too."

"Thanks, Kevin. I'm especially interested in the contents of her wall safe. Also, could you see if you have any records on someone named Anthony Rossino?"

"Rossino, huh? I'll do what I can."

Mary had a telephone message for me when I walked into my office: Det. Turelli called—he has some info for you.

I dialed his number. Another detective answered and put me on hold.

Kevin Turelli and I had met as first-year associates at Abbott & Windsor. We had shared an office—the twenty-four-year-old graduate of Harvard Law School and the forty-four-year-old ex-cop from the West Side of Chicago who had worked his way through night school at John Marshall Law School. We became good friends.

Kevin had lasted three years at A & W before returning to the Chicago Police Department as a detective under a special fast-track arrangement. He was currently assigned to homicide down at 11th & State—the "smart shop," as Kevin called it.

"Detective Turelli here."

"Hi, Kevin."

"Hi, Rachel. I got the dope."

"And?"

"First, the inventory. I have a copy of it right here. Looks like nothing's missing. One pearl necklace, one gold choker necklace with a large pear-shaped diamond and matching bracelet, two sets of diamond earrings, one gold Lucien Picard wristwatch, one diamond ring, one ruby ring, and three thousand five hundred dollars in assorted denominations, all paper."

Nine hundred dollars a night could add up fast, I thought. "Anything else?"

"Nope. Now, what's the deal with this Rossino, Rachel? Is this guy a client of yours?"

"No. But it's confidential, Kevin. Did you find anything on him?"

"Plenty. I pulled his sheet. The guy's a small-time hood with a string of priors going back to

1972. He served a year in Joliet in 1983. For shy-locking and extortion. The guy's bad news, Rachel. Bad news. When are you going to tell me what's going on?"

"Give me a little more time, Kevin."

"Be careful."

"Don't worry," I said.

"By the way, Mamma wants to know what you're doing for Labor Day. She's having the whole family over for dinner and wants you to come too." Kevin Turelli was the fourth son of an Irish mother and an Italian father. His mother's holiday dinners were wonderful polyglot feasts: corned beef, cabbage, pasta, Irish soda bread, homemade spumoni.

"I'd love to. Tell her I'll be there."

"Okay, kid. Take care."

My first stop at Abbott & Windsor was Tyrone Henderson.

"Ty, can you get access to the firm's billing computer?"

"Baby, I can get access to just about anything these days 'cept you."

"Tyrone," I said, putting my hands on my hips and shaking my head.

He rolled his eyes and turned slowly in his swivel chair to face the terminal. "Shee-it," he signed as he typed in a code, pushed the Transmit button, and turned back to me. "Next?"

"Okay." I pulled out the slip of paper with the code from inside the coffin. "Can you see what this is? Zero zero three two zero dash one nine five three."

Tyrone typed in the numbers as I read them off.

At corporate law firms, the attorneys charge by the hour. Each day each attorney fills out time sheets indicating what he did for each client matter and how much time he spent doing it. At the end of each billing period the computer sorts out the time billed to each client matter and sends a printout to the billing partner responsible for that client matter.

Each client at Abbott & Windsor is assigned a five-digit client number. As the client brings in each new matter (*i.e.*, a lawsuit, a corporate deal, a labor arbitration, a tax problem), it is assigned its own four-digit matter number. The handwritten numerical code in the coffin matched the pattern of a typical client matter at the firm: a five-digit client number (00320) and a four-digit matter number (1953).

"Looks like it's our old friend again," said Tyrone, pointing to the screen, which displayed the following:

```
           NO. 00320-1953
CLIENT: GRAHAM ANDERSON MARSHALL III
   MATTER: MISCELLANEOUS PERSONAL
```

"Bingo," I said.

"Yep. That dude keeps popping up, don't he?"

"Is there any billing record left for that matter?" I asked.

"If there was any time recorded, it'll be in there."

"Can you see?" I asked.

"Sure." Tyrone typed a set of instructions and pushed the Transmit button. The screen went blank for twenty seconds and then the following appeared:

```
FIRST TIME CHARGES: 1/29/85
LAST TIME CHARGED: 10/4/85
ATTORNEYS: CHARLES, KENT R.
           DODSON, HARLAN B.
           GOLDBERG, BENJAMIN J.
           PEMBERTON, CALVIN S.
```

I studied the screen. "So those four worked on the matter," I said, staring at the Goldberg, Benjamin J.

"From January 29, 1985, to October 4, 1985." Tyrone pointed to the four names. "These dudes."

"Can you tell what they did?"

Tyrone typed some more instructions and pushed the Transmit button and then the Print button. "We'll print out the billing records. It'll list every entry for every attorney."

The printer clicked on, advanced the paper in three quick jumps, and then started printing. It stopped two minutes later. Tyrone reached over and tore off the four-page printout. "Here you go, Rachel."

"Thanks, Ty."

I sat on the work table and studied the printout. Cal Pemberton had billed a total of 13.2 hours from January 29, 1985, to February 15, 1985. Kent Charles had billed 16.3 hours from May 4, 1985, to June 26, 1985. Benny had billed 17.2 hours during three days in August 1985. Harlan Dodson had billed 6.1 hours over the first four days of October 1985. The descriptions were vague but no more so than most billing descriptions. Kent, Cal, and Harlan had telephone calls and meetings with various unnamed people and had reviewed documents. Benny had researched and drafted a legal memorandum.

I stared at the printout. What did Benny know about Canaan that I didn't? And why?

35

"Mr. Richardson can see you now."

I stood up. "Thanks," I said, and walked past the secretary's desk into the office of Ishmael Richardson.

Ishmael was seated behind his ornate oak desk jotting something in his calendar as I walked in. He looked up and smiled. "Hello, Rachel. Please have a seat."

I did. "I came over to give you my report on the Canaan matter."

"Excellent." He leaned forward and pushed the intercom button on his telephone. "June, hold my calls until Miss Gold leaves." He leaned back in his high-backed leather chair, rested his elbows on the armrests, and lightly touched his fingertips together beneath his chin. "Tell me what you have found."

"For starters, the coffin. It turned up yesterday,"
I said.

"Wonderful."

"There was a dog's skeleton in it," I continued.
"But I'm reasonably certain there wasn't a dog in
the coffin when Graham Marshall buried it."

Richardson raised his eyebrows.

"It's a long story, Ishmael." I'd managed to use
his first name.

"Let me hear it."

I started by explaining what I had pieced together
about Graham Marshall's Canaan exploits back in
1985. I described Ambrose Springer's little book,
The Lottery of Canaan, and its connection to both
Barrett College and Marshall's ancestor, Benjamin
Marshall. I mentioned the missing dictionary with
the additional definition of Canaan, explained Helen
Marston's recollections about Marshall's secret activities back in 1985, and described the four newspaper articles listed in code on the slip of paper filed
under Canaan. I went into the significance of the year
1985: it was the three hundredth anniversary of the
first Canaan lottery and the thirtieth anniversary of
the bizarre deaths of Marshall's sister and mother.
I explained how Marshall had maintained a Canaan
data bank in the Bottles & Cans computer and had
printed out the contents of the file just before he
buried the coffin.

"Marshall wanted someone to discover what
he'd done," I continued. "He set up that bizarre
codicil to force the firm to investigate and possibly
exhume the coffin. We did exactly what he hoped
we'd do. Except someone beat us to the coffin."

Ishmael Richardson stroked his chin.

I sighed, glancing at the row of three framed Edward Hopper pen and ink sketches on the wall behind his desk. "As for my assignment, it's basically complete—no matter what was originally in the coffin, regardless of whether Mr. Marshall actually was running his own Canaan lottery. The trust fund is superfluous. You can still honor the purpose of the codicil, if the family wants to. Just break the trust and purchase the permanent care and maintenance option from the cemetery. It's a one-time flat fee of a thousand dollars."

I sat back and waited.

Richardson finally cleared his throat. "As I am sure you must realize, Rachel, I find this . . . this Canaan lottery rather difficult to believe. Even if we assume, arguendo, that Graham participated in this criminal scheme, the logistics are rather difficult to envision. He could not possibly have accomplished all of it by himself. How in heaven's name would Graham Marshall know how to sabotage a plane?" Richardson shook his head. "Frankly, the image of him sneaking around an abandoned warehouse and taping an envelope full of money to the bottom of a filing cabinet is, quite frankly, absurd."

"I know," I said. "I agree. But let's assume Marshall recruited some henchmen. Assume he set up a one-way communication system, where he could communicate with them but they didn't know how to contact him, or even who he was. It's been done before. Remember the Barfield murder?"

Richardson nodded. He was staring out his window toward the lake. "It would require substantial capital," he mused. "I suppose that would not pose an insurmountable problem for Graham." He turned back to me. "Who stole the coffin?"

"I think it was someone in this firm, Ishmael."

"Who?" Richardson leaned forward. "And why?"

I explained the code in the bottom of the coffin and how it led me back to Abbott & Windsor and the billing records for the Graham Marshall personal matter.

"I see two possible scenarios," I continued. "First, one of the four lawyers in those billing records stumbled onto what Mr. Marshall was up to and decided to take over the Canaan network when Marshall dropped his own involvement in it. If Marshall suspected something like that, then that would explain the clue he wrote in the coffin." I shook my head. "But that scenario has problems. If the guy wanted to use the Canaan system for his own schemes, he would have to wait until Marshall died for fear that Marshall would find out what he was doing. But how could this guy know when Marshall would die?"

"He had a severe heart problem," Richardson said.

"I know," I said. "His widow told me there was a chance his artificial valve was defective. But even so, he still could have lived another twenty years. By then those Canaan thugs would be long gone."

"You said there were two possible scenarios," Richardson prompted.

I nodded. "The second one is even creepier. It assumes that Mr. Marshall had an assistant here at the firm. An assistant, or a successor that he was grooming. If so, maybe Marshall started having second thoughts about the guy he selected. Maybe he worried that his successor might try to use the Canaan system for his own schemes. If so, what could Marshall do to stop him? He couldn't go to the police, since he would end up incriminating himself in the process—assuming he could even convince the police to believe him. Instead, maybe Marshall left the clue in the coffin in the hopes that we'd discover who the successor was and stop him before he did anything else with the lottery." I thought it over. "Maybe Marshall even included incriminating evidence against that guy in the documents he buried in the coffin."

"Dodson?" Richardson mumbled. "Pemberton? Charles? Goldberg?"

"Those four are the most obvious suspects. Or at least three of them. I can't believe Benny has anything to do with it." Because if he did, Joe Oliver's troubles were nothing compared to Cindi's and mine.

Richardson was clearly shaken. "But why steal the coffin?"

"Not the coffin. Just the documents. Whoever did it must have thought the documents would implicate him. Or maybe he just feared that discovery of the Canaan lottery would ruin whatever he was planning to do with it. He must have found out about the codicil. Once Marshall died, he moved in, dug up the grave, and destroyed what he thought was the only evidence. His mistake was not putting the coffin back the same night, so that when the firm dug it up, it would find only a skeleton."

Richardson frowned. "Harlan Dodson learned of the codicil before the grave robbery."

"True. And he knew the firm had hired me to investigate," I said, mulling it over. "Maybe it spooked him into action before he had found a skeleton to put in the coffin."

Richardson shook his head. "Harlan Dodson? I can't believe that. But I can't believe any of this."

He paused. "Marshall would hardly be the first person to believe that life is a giant lottery. But to take that belief one step further, to decide that because man's life is ruled by chance . . . that man can therefore rule chance . . ."

We were both silent.

"Follow your logic," he finally said. "Say that Marshall had a motive, as bizarre and, frankly, as incredible as it seems. He believed that he had an ancestor from Canaan, Massachusetts. And the year 1985 had a unique significance to him. But what is his successor's motive?"

"I don't know," I said. "Greed? Power?" I paused. "What's going on now seems very different from Marshall's version of the Canaan lottery," I said. "There's nothing random about the targets or the events anymore." I paused. "This isn't a lottery anymore."

"Then, what *is* it?"

I hesitated. "I assume you know that Mr. Marshall didn't die in the office."

Richardson nodded.

I told him about the search of my apartment. I explained the attempt to kill Cindi and concluded with the extortion letter and the videotape of Cindi and Joe Oliver. "Someone out there—or someone in here—has seven damaging videotapes and a network of henchmen to carry out years' worth of extortions."

"My God," Richardson sighed, his shoulders sagging. "And you say the young lady is still alive?"

I nodded.

The color had gradually drained from Richardson's face. He had become an old man before my eyes. I watched Richardson draw circles on his yellow legal pad. Finally, he looked up. "What can we do to stop it?"

"You and the police have two different pressure points," I said. "One is the men on the el; the other is the lawyers who show up in the billing printout. I think you need to bring in the police for the first area. Tell them there's a blackmail scheme involving some prominent lawyers. Tell them it has to be kept confidential. I have the name and address of one of the men on the el. A guy named Rossino. And I can be a pretty good probable-cause witness. Good enough to help the police get an arrest warrant. Maybe the police can get Rossino to talk. If so, he might be able to identify the guy who's running the lottery. And even if Rossino doesn't talk, maybe the police can hold him in custody for a while. To give us some time. As for the lawyers on the printout—Dodson, Pemberton, Charles, and, uh, Benny—someone should ask each one what he did for Graham back in 1985. I shouldn't be the one to talk to them. If one of them really is involved, he'll get suspicious when I talk to him. Each of them knows I'm working on Graham's estate." I paused, formulating the plan. "You need a good low-key excuse to find out what they did. Some misdirection might help too."

"How so?" he asked.

"One of them had the coffin returned with a dog's skeleton in it. Let's let him think it worked. You should leak word that I've finished my investigation. Tell Harlan that he can go ahead and break the trust if the family agrees." I paused. "Finally, we have to bring Cindi Reynolds in out of the cold. Secretly. Whoever did this thinks she's dead. We need to have the police protect her and keep things quiet for as long as possible."

Richardson seemed to perk up some. He leaned forward and pushed the intercom button.

"Yes, Mr. Richardson," said the voice over the speaker.

"June, tell Earl Woods to come down here right away. And then see if you can get Fred Daniels from the mayor's office on the telephone." Richardson turned back to me, growing more animated as he spoke. "Earl is the firm administrator. I will inform him that we are trying to wrap up Marshall's affairs and that we need to determine whether the time these four attorneys spent on Marshall's personal matters back in 1985 can be billed to any client. I'll have him provide me with a written report by tomorrow. Earl will realize on his own that he should speak with each one of them. We will see what he discovers."

Richardson's secretary buzzed to tell him that Fred Daniels was on the line. Richardson picked up the telephone and immediately re-assumed the mantle of managing partner of Abbott & Windsor. He worked the conversation gradually around to the point, and—after calling in a few chips and reminding Daniels about the mayor's tough stand on white-collar crime and how the FBI loved to horn in on Chicago police matters and steal the limelight—asked Daniels if he could help out with a delicate investigation involving attorneys with ties to the Democratic party. Daniels agreed to talk to the chief of police about assigning a special investigator to the matter.

Richardson hung up. "I will call the chief in about thirty minutes," he said. "That should give Daniels enough time. Do you have a preference as to an investigator?"

I thought about it. "How about Kevin Turelli?

He's a homicide detective now down at Eleventh and State."

Richardson nodded and jotted Turelli's name on his legal pad. "I shall have Mr. Turelli contact you directly Rachel. You will have to keep me advised of *everything* from here on. I am determined to keep this matter under tight control." He looked at his calendar. "Are you free tomorrow afternoon around two?"

"I think so."

"I shall arrange for a private room at the Mid-Day Club. Let's meet there."

36

I SPENT THE REST OF Monday afternoon at my office catching up on other cases and working on my trial brief. Paul had called while I was over at A & W that morning. I tried his number twice, but no one answered. I remembered that he had said his big paper was due on Monday. I wondered what was important enough for him to call me at the office.

Kevin Turelli called that afternoon to inform me he had been assigned to the Canaan matter. Ishmael Richardson clearly had pull down at City Hall. We spoke for almost an hour about the case. At the end of the conversation Kevin decided to get an arrest warrant and pick up Rossino late that night.

Harlan Dodson called at 5:30. "I assume you've been told that the Canaan investigation is terminated."

"Yes. Once the coffin turned up, Mr. Richardson decided that enough was enough."

"Good." Dodson's breath rasped in the telephone receiver. "I'd prefer to keep all copies of your notes in my own file on the estate."

"Fine."

"Should I send over a messenger today to pick them up?"

"Give me some time to put them in order, Harlan. I'll drop them off at your office."

"How long?"

"A few days."

"Can't you get them here sooner?"

"No. They're a mess and I've got lots of deadlines to meet in other cases. I'll get them to you, Harlan. Don't worry."

I could hear him breathing. "Fine," he finally grunted.

"What are you going to do now?"

"I don't follow you."

"The Canaan legacy. Are you going to try to break the trust?"

"I've conferred with Mrs. Marshall and the probate judge. I'm certain we'll find a satisfactory resolution. That need be no concern of yours anymore, Miss Gold. We'll handle the details."

"Okay."

"Be sure to deliver *all* of your notes. The firm appreciates your efforts in this matter."

Mary had waved good-bye while I was on the phone with Dodson. She left her *Sun-Times* in the wastebasket. I took it with me and scanned the personals section during the cab ride home. No entries for Canaan.

Cindi had been to the grocery store that afternoon. By the time I got home she had made a tossed salad and pasta with pesto sauce. I told her Detective Turelli would be picking her up in the morning to get her story.

After dinner we watched the Cubs play the Cardinals on television. The Cardinals lost in eleven innings. Both of us were exhausted when it was over. My answering machine had two messages from Paul and one from Benny. I was too tired to return them. Cindi and I were asleep by 10:30.

Tuesday morning was uneventful. August is a slow month for Chicago's lawyers. Most of the judges are on vacation, which means trials generally don't start until September, and motions frequently are reset to be heard when the judges return. Depositions are difficult to schedule—particularly in cases involving several lawyers—because of conflicting vacation schedules. I spent the morning catching up on correspondence, drafting a few discovery requests for one of my trademark cases, reviewing two videotapes (Exhibits 1 and 2 in an upcoming copyright trial), and running down some points of law at the Chicago Bar Association's library for a brief due in one week in an appeal of a preliminary injunction.

Mary had finished typing my dictation tapes on my Canaan investigation, which were now current through yesterday. The typed version was close to two hundred pages long. She left early for lunch to drop off one copy in a special box at the post office. We kept the original and the other copy in my office safe. If anything happened to me, she was to send one copy to Ishmael Richardson and one copy to Detective Turelli. My level of paranoia had been rising steadily.

Cindi called from my apartment at noon.

"How'd it go?" I asked.

"Grueling. I spent the whole morning with two police detectives downtown. They interviewed me about everything. I guess my dental records hadn't arrived yet, though they'd already identified the dead man. And they had received a missing-persons report on Andi Hebner."

"What are they going to do?" I asked.

"They asked me not to make any public statements for the next couple of days. They want to do some poking around without letting anyone know I'm still alive. One of the detectives—that Turelli you told me about—he's acting real fatherly. He called my insurance company and explained everything but told them that he wanted the matter handled discreetly and kept in strictest confidence for the next several days."

"So what's going to happen?"

"One of the detectives drove me back here to pack my clothes. It'll take at least a month to fix up my condo. The insurance company's paying for all that. The police are putting me in the Park Hyatt under an assumed name and they're going to post a couple of plainclothes cops in the hotel for the next few days."

"Sounds good."

"I'm checking in this afternoon. I'll call you with my room number as soon as I have it."

"Please do."

"Rachel, I can't thank you enough for all you've done."

"I'm going to miss having you as a roommate. So will Ozzie."

"Listen, as soon as I get settled in the hotel I'll figure out how to sneak out and help you on this Canaan thing."

"Don't even think of it, Cindi. The best thing we can both do is just cooperate with the cops. They're taking over the investigation. Call me tonight."

Just as I hung up there was a knock at the door to my office. It was Detective Kevin Turelli.

He held up a McDonald's takeout bag. "I brought us lunch," he said. Kevin Turelli was a stocky man of medium height. He had a round, ruddy face and thinning gray hair.

"Great. I'm starving."

He sat down and started pulling stuff out of the bag. "Quarter-pounder with cheese ... regular fries ... chocolate milk shake ... and an apple pie."

"You trying to fatten me up, Turelli?"

He grinned. "Nothing wrong with a zaftig woman. Mamma thinks you're all skin and bones."

When I had briefed him yesterday, we had both agreed that the first step should be to arrest Rossino, the man from the el.

"We got the arrest warrant yesterday and picked him up at his apartment last night," Kevin said. "Charged him with murder and extortion. I let him stew in jail overnight and started grilling him this morning."

"And?"

Kevin wiped his mouth with a napkin. "He started singing. When it was clear there was a lot he knew, I dropped some hints about working out some sort of deal maybe giving him immunity. I've got a dick and an assistant state's attorney with a stenographer taking a statement from him right now. He waived counsel."

"What did he tell you?"

"He admitted stealing the videotapes from Reynolds's safe. He's a little vague about the explosion, but I think he'll come around on that too. Yesterday Bomb and Arson found some sort of timing device behind the stove in Miss Reynolds's apartment. As near as the bomb squad boys can tell—and they may know more already—the timer was triggered when someone opened the front door. Thirty minutes later, *boom*."

"Who hired Rossino?"

"He claims he doesn't know. He told me about an elaborate communications system, with alternating blind drop points. He says he never met with the person or persons at the top and wouldn't know how to contact them if he had to."

"What about the ones he works with?" I asked.

"Well, there're apparently four of them. Rossino thinks there used to be six, and that the others dropped out, or died, or just moved on. Rossino doesn't know. He doesn't even know the names of the other three operatives, even though he's worked with them in the past on other Canaan projects. That's one of the rules. No names."

"How long has he been doing it?"

"Since about 1985. Two or three times back then. Once or twice a year since then. He gets paid four or five grand each time. In cash. It's part-time work for him. Like I told you, Rossino is a small-time hood with a string of priors."

"How do the four of them communicate?" I asked.

Kevin removed the lid from his drink and took a big sip. "Rossino says the initial contact point changes each time. Sometimes it's a post office box. Sometimes it's a locker at the Greyhound station. Sometimes it's a mailbox in an abandoned apartment building. Each time Rossino acts as the messenger, the next contact point is in the package he gets. The package includes a description of the job and the identification number of the Canaan person who is supposed to do it. Let's say the job is to tape an envelope of cash to the bottom of a drawer in a filing cabinet in an abandoned warehouse. Honest to God, Rachel, that was one of Rossino's jobs. Well, that time one of the other Canaan operatives acted as the messenger and picked up the package. The instructions were to give the package to Canaan Six. So the messenger put a personal in the *Tribune* directed to Canaan Six, telling him to meet at an el station at a certain date and time, usually after midnight. That's another rule: Communicate through the personals column and exchange the package on the el trains."

"Why the personals?"

"Maybe so the head guy can monitor what they do. Anyway, that guy meets Canaan Six—which is Rossino—at the el station and gives him the package. Then the messenger goes back to the drop point to pick up his money. Rossino takes the package, which includes instructions for the job, the envelope he's supposed to tape to the filing cabinet, and—in that case—the key to a post office box at one of the post offices in Uptown. Two weeks after Rossino completes the job his money is waiting for him at the post office box. Then he's supposed to check the post office box at least once a week. He keeps doing that till there's another package. It could take months. When he gets the next package, he becomes the messenger and one of the other Canaan operatives gets the package up on an el platform." Kevin paused to finish his milk shake. "Pretty clever, huh?"

"What have they done for Canaan?"

"Rossino claims he doesn't remember most of his jobs. But he's had some weird ones. Last year he had to mug a certain trial lawyer. Beat him up and rob him. He remembered another one from late 1986. He had to break into the law offices of Bentley and Singer, remove an entire file drawer of documents, and plant two phony memos in one of the firm's correspondence files."

"My God, you mean that was a setup?"

"What was?" Kevin asked.

"Don't you remember that big scandal? Judge Henley ordered Bentley and Singer to produce some expert's reports in the middle of trial. It turned out the documents had been destroyed?"

Kevin said, "Oh, yeah. I remember now. Didn't they haul Bill Bentley up before the Illinois Supreme Court on disciplinary charges?"

"Suspended his license for six months," I said. We were both silent for a moment. "Does Rossino know where the next drop point is?" I asked.

Kevin nodded. "He's not supposed to, but he peeked in the envelope. It's a locker at Union Station. We've got it staked out."

I thought about it. "It could take months," I said. "Whoever's running the show probably doesn't do this more than three or four times a year."

"What about the Joe Oliver situation?" Kevin asked. "Won't they make another move on him?"

"Maybe. But our blackmailer might want to let Oliver squirm for a while. Can you imagine what kind of wreck Oliver would be if he'd gotten that videocassette and extortion note?"

"It almost makes you feel sorry for Oliver."

"The poor guy," I murmured. "What do we do now?"

"The ringleader is the target. We don't want to spook him, or he'll walk away and never be heard from again. We'll keep the Rossino arrest quiet for as long as we can. But word is gonna get out before long. Rossino has mob ties. He'll probably bring in some mob mouthpiece who'll start raising hell in a couple of days, even if we do give him immunity. We've got Miss Reynolds under an assumed name over at the Park Hyatt with round-the-clock security. But that can't go on forever, either. We gotta do something in the next few days, Rachel, or the big fish is going to swim away."

I checked my watch. "I have to meet Ishmael Richardson and see what his investigation turned up. I'll call you later, Kevin."

'Okay. But be careful, Rachel. This is a kinky case. Remember, you don't know for sure who your friends are."

"I'll be careful."

Walking across the Loop, I prayed that Ishmael Richardson's investigation had identified the blackmailer. I wouldn't feel safe again until whoever it was had been stopped.

37

"THE POLICE DON'T KNOW WHO it is," I said to Ishmael Richardson. I had just finished briefing him on what I had learned from Kevin Turelli. We were sitting across the table from each other in a small private room off the main dining area of the Mid-Day Club. "What did Earl Woods find out?" I asked.

Richardson reached inside his suit jacket and pulled out a folded sheet of paper. "His notes show a correlation between what each of the attorneys did and one of those newspaper articles. When did those people discover the money in the filing cabinet?"

"Around September twelfth," I said. By now I had memorized the dates of the four newspaper articles.

"Mr. Goldberg did a research memo in August

1985 for Graham on the rights of the finder of treasure trove."

"Oh," I said softly. Treasure trove is an ancient legal term that originally referred to buried treasure discovered by someone other than the original owner of the treasure. Over the years the term has come to mean any gold, silver, or money that's found in a concealed place. To qualify as treasure trove, the money must have been hidden for so long that it seems likely that the original owner is dead. For example, money taped to the bottom of a drawer in a filing cabinet in a long-abandoned warehouse in Evanston. "What did the memo conclude?" I asked.

Richardson looked at the notes. "Apparently, Mr. Goldberg found an Illinois statute governing the matter. The finder has to file an affidavit in court and then the county clerk has to cause a notice to be published for three weeks in a newspaper. If the original owner fails to claim it within a year, the finder becomes the owner."

"Finders keepers, losers weepers," I said. "So Graham wanted to be sure that the couple who bought the cabinet would be able to keep the money. Benny's memo told him that they could."

Richardson nodded. "So it would seem."

"What else?" I asked.

"Kent Charles had several meetings with the accounting firm of Barnaby and Lewis to go over their security procedures for the beauty pageant."

"Beauty pageant?"

"Barnaby and Lewis tabulated the votes of the judges at the Ms. United States Pageant in 1985. Kent Charles said he wrote Graham a memorandum setting forth all of the security procedures."

"Clever," I said.

Richardson smiled. "Earl Woods was proud of this one, because Barnaby and Lewis was one of Graham's clients. Earl thinks we can bill them for Kent Charles's time."

"What did Cal Pemberton do?" I asked.

"Calvin Pemberton recalls that he had a couple of meetings with people from Athena Publications."

"The people with the typo," I said.

"Correct. But Pemberton was unable to remember what the meetings were about." Richardson frowned. "Earl made an interesting discovery in Calvin's office."

"What?"

"Graham's missing dictionary. It was sitting next to Calvin's computer terminal."

"Cal took it?"

"He told Earl he was looking for a dictionary late one evening and found one at the top of an open box in Graham's office."

Was that all there was to the missing dictionary? "What do your notes say Harlan Dodson did for Marshall?" I finally asked.

"He vaguely recalls something having to do with Midway Airport. Dodson's brother is a pilot who flies a corporate jet parked at Midway. Graham Marshall wanted Dodson to obtain some information from his brother. Unfortunately, Dodson can't remember what it was."

I looked over Richardson's notes. "You're right. The dates all match," I said. "Each lawyer finished his project about a month before the event happened. What did Marshall tell them? How did he get them to work on these matters?"

"Partners do this all the time. Graham did not need an excuse to assign attorneys to work on his personal matters." Richardson stood up and walked to the window. He stared out toward the lake, hands in his pockets. He turned toward me. "At this point I'm through caring what Marshall did. What I want to know is who's doing this now. Is it someone in my firm?"

"It sure looks like it," I said.

Richardson stared at me. "He has to be stopped," he said. "What do you suggest?"

I could feel myself being sucked back into the case. "We don't have much time," I said. "Once he finds out about the arrests or about Cindi being alive, he'll know someone is onto him. If he gets spooked, he'll drop Canaan altogether and we'll never find out who it is. Let me set up another meeting with Kevin this afternoon. Maybe with Cindi too. See if we can brainstorm a plan."

"Let me know. I want to be there."

On my way back to my office I ran into Kent Charles and Cal Pemberton on Clark Street near City Hall. Both of them were carrying briefcases.

"How are you, Rachel?" Kent said.

"Good," I said. "You guys just leave court?"

Kent nodded. "Discovery motion up in Law Division."

Cal cleared his throat. "I heard you finished your work on Graham Marshall's estate."

"Yep," I said. "Guess I have to stop billing you guys. How'd you find out I was done?"

"Harlan Dodson mentioned it to me this morning," Cal said, eyes averted.

Kent chuckled. "Well, did you solve the mystery?"

"Finally," I said. "The matter is closed."

Kent smiled. "Was I any help?"

"A little," I said, and winked. "But not enough to share my fee."

"You could always pay me back by letting me buy you dinner," Kent said. "How about this Sunday? Maybe we could go out on my boat in the afternoon and have dinner afterward."

"It's a deal," I said. I had to act as if things were back to normal.

Kent smiled. "Great. I'll give you a call. We'll plan to go out in my boat around three."

"Sounds wonderful. See you guys later," I said.

"Take care, Rachel," Kent said. "See you Sunday."

As they walked on past I heard Cal Pemberton ask Kent Charles, "What mystery?"

I couldn't hear the response.

38

I called Kevin Turelli and Cindi from my office and set up a meeting at Cindi's hotel room at six P.M.

"We have to come up with some sort of plan for the cops fast," I told Cindi. "Maybe the four of us can dream up something."

"Great. I'm going stir crazy in here. The cops won't let me out of this room."

"Whoever did it must have known that you kept videocassettes in the safe behind the picture," I explained. "We have four suspects."

There was a pause, and then Cindi said, "Give me their names."

I did.

Another pause. "Cal Pemberton," she said.

"Pemberton?"

"Twice. About a year ago."

"Any of the others?"

"I don't think so, Rachel."

"How did Pemberton get your name?"

"He said someone from the firm told him about me."

"He say who?"

"He may have. I can't remember."

"Did you have any other clients from Abbott and Windsor?"

"I don't think so, Rachel. Graham and Cal. I think that's all."

"What do you remember about Cal?"

"Enough. He was a real weirdo."

I felt a chill. "How so?"

"It was like the guy had a split personality. The second time I was with him he was a completely different person than the first time."

"What do you mean?"

"Well, the first time he was real subdued. He had a lot of trouble doing it. Making love, you know. He took a lot of work. Afterward, after the first time, he asked a lot of questions. Not about sex. He was really curious about the business end of things. How I got customers, how I decided how much to charge, how I handled the income-tax end of it. That sort of thing."

"Did he ask you about videocassettes and where you kept them?"

"I'm not sure." Cindi paused. "I can't picture it in my memory, but I wouldn't be surprised if he did. He asked about everything."

"Did he want his own videotape?"

"No. We didn't make a videotape."

"What about the second time?"

"It was awful. He wanted to tie me up and try some rough stuff. He was a totally different person. I told him I didn't do that stuff. He got furious, tried to tie me up anyway. I fought him off and kicked him out. I tell you, I was a little scared. I told him I never wanted to see him again." She paused. "And I never did."

I thought it was over. Cal Pemberton? "Well, I'll be over at six," I said. "See you then, Cindi."

Mary poked her head in my office with a handful of message slips. "One of Mr. Richardson's secretaries called to say he'll be a few minutes late. Benny Goldberg called too. He's in his office. Also, that Paul Mason called again."

"Thanks," I said. Paul would have to wait. I had too much else to worry about without adding Paul and whatever he was after. Benny Goldberg? I shook my head. It just couldn't be Benny. I dialed his number.

He answered the telephone, as usual, with, "Talk to me."

"Hi."

"Rachel! What's happening, girl?"

"Not much," I said.

"Any new leads?"

But then again, how could I be certain? "Not yet," I said, "I'm stumped for the moment."

"What about the guy from the el? Rossino. You going to have someone talk to him?"

"Maybe."

"You and I could do it, Rachel. See if he'll talk."

"I don't know. It's too dangerous."

"Yeah. Maybe you're right. I hear they've closed the Canaan file, anyway."

"I gave Ishmael my report yesterday," I said. "Now that the coffin's back, I guess they decided they didn't need anything else."

"What about the other grave robbery?"

"Probably vandals," I said, waiting for his reaction.

"Yeah, maybe so. Well, sit tight for the next few days. I'm leaving town Thursday. I'll be back late Friday. You going to the hippo's funeral on Saturday?"

"Yep."

"We can try to figure it out after the funeral. We might want to go to the police on it, anyway. At least for Cindi's sake. She can't stay dead forever."

"Where are you going?" I asked.

"Down to your hometown."

"St. Louis?"

"Yeah, I'm looking at documents tomorrow and deposing their expert, a structural engineer, on Friday. I got some terrific background dope on the guy. I'm going to drill him a new asshole in that deposition."

"How're things at the firm?" I asked.

"You're going to love this, Rachel. These guys here are like vultures picking at bones. Earl Woods dropped in this morning to ask me about some project I did for Graham Marshall a few years back. They want to see if they can figure out some way to bill it to a client. Can you believe this place?"

"What kind of project?"

"Something on abandoned property. Marshall told me one of his kids found some jewelry or something like that. He wanted to know if he could keep it. I told Earl Woods they'd never be able to bill anyone for that time."

Don't you make the connection, Benny? "Well, have a good time in St. Louis," I said.

"See you on Saturday."

* * *

"We're going to have to lure this guy out into the open," Kevin Turelli told Cindi and me. We were sitting around the small conference table in Cindi's hotel room. "The way I see it, we have two, maybe three days. After that he's likely to hear Rossino's been arrested."

Cindi stood up and walked to the window, her hands in the front pockets of her new jeans. She turned toward us and said, "Well, he's operating right now with some pretty serious misinformation. He thinks I'm dead and he thinks no one knows he stole the videotapes. He assumes Joe Oliver got that extortion letter. And he doesn't know that Rossino got arrested and confessed. Maybe we can use that misinformation against him."

"We have to figure out how," Kevin said. He stood up, took off his sports jacket, hung it over the back of the chair, and sat down again. He had a gun in his shoulder holster. "I just can't make this guy. Muggings, setting up Bill Bentley with the document destruction scheme. And now this extortion number." Kevin shook his head.

"But not extortion in the usual sense," I said. "It looks like he doesn't want money from Joe Oliver. He just wants to make him squirm."

Cindi said, "He wants to make them all squirm. Power's what this guy's after. Power to screw up people's lives, throw them off balance. Believe me, I've dealt with plenty of power-hungry lawyers. They're into control—over clients, witnesses, jurors, other lawyers." She shook her head. "What we need to do is figure out who this blackmailer would love to have power over."

The answer came immediately. "Ishmael Richardson," I said. "Of course! If our guy is a lawyer at A and W, then Ishmael Richardson is the ultimate source of power: managing partner of Abbott and Windsor."

"You might have something there, Rachel," Kevin said.

Cindi sat down on the bed, frowning. "Maybe. But how do you turn Ishmael into bait?"

"How about this?" I said, the idea forming as I began talking. "Joe Oliver has the extortion letter, and he's desperate, right. Put yourself in his shoes. How can he stop the guy? Offer to trade him the videotape for something even more valuable. Offer to trade him for another videotape." I looked at Cindi. "A videotape of Ishmael Richardson and you."

"Me?" Cindi asked.

Kevin frowned. "I don't know."

"Cindi's dead, right?" I said. "Killed in that explosion as far as he knows. So a tape with Cindi can't be a fake."

"Me and . . . Ishmael Richardson?" Cindi asked.

"Richardson would never agree," Kevin said, standing up and walking over to the window. "Never. No way. Forget it."

"But Ishmael doesn't have to actually do anything," I said. "Don't you see? Joe Oliver offers a trade to the blackmailer and then tempts him by giving him a sample of the tape. Just the beginning. Cindi on the bed, telling Ishmael to join her. And then the tape ends. Just a teaser. That's the bait. Then Joe tells him if he wants the rest, he has to trade his copies of Joe and Cindi for the original of Ishmael. And if the blackmailer goes for the bait, you can arrest him when he makes the trade. Don't you see? We could make the videotape here. Tonight."

Cindi and Kevin stared at me. After a while Cindi started to smile. "It might work," she said.

Kevin shook his head. "It's not logical. Put yourself in Joe Oliver's shoes. That's what our guy will do. How does Joe know our guy is going to give him all the copies of the videotape with Joe in it? How does Joe know our guy will keep his end of the bargain?"

"Joe doesn't," I said. "That's the beauty of it. Don't you see? Joe can't be sure our guy won't keep an extra copy. That's why he'd insist that the exchange be done face-to-face. So he can find out who the extortionist is. Then Joe will have some leverage too. Our guy can't use his tapes of Joe or Joe will blow the whistle on him. And Joe can't try to blow the whistle on our guy because our guy will release his copies of Joe in action. It becomes a Mexican standoff."

"Not bad," Kevin said.

Cindi held up her hands. "Hold it. How is Joe Oliver supposed to have a videotape of Ishmael and me? Isn't our mystery man going to wonder about that?"

Kevin scratched his head. "Well," he said, "he'd be more suspicious if he thought you were still alive. Since he thinks you're dead, he'll be convinced the videotape is authentic. He may not even wonder how Joe got the tape. I've dealt with extortionists before. They're ready to believe others are just as devious as they are. And our guy obviously knows that Joe Oliver is one tough cookie. He'll probably convince himself that Joe bought the tape from you or snuck it out of your apartment one night when he was there. Or maybe he'll think you accidentally gave Joe the wrong tape. Believe me, if we're right about our mystery man, he'll be so eager to get the videotape of Ishmael that he won't care how Joe ended up with it."

"You're probably right," Cindi said.

Kevin shook his head. "Wait a minute. Once we get the tape of Richardson and Miss Reynolds, how do we contact the mystery man?"

I didn't have an answer.

"I know!" Cindi said. "We have four suspects. We send each one a note from Joe. A short cryptic note that only the real one will understand."

I thought it over. "Won't work," I said. "How would Joe know who to send the note to? How does he know who the suspects are? If he sends a note directly to the right one, the right one will get spooked. And even if he doesn't, the chances are that one of the others might tell him about the duplicate note he got. 'Look at this crazy note I got,' one of them might say when he shows it to the real guy. The real guy will know immediately that it's a trick."

Cindi lay back on her bed, her arms behind her head. "Rats," she said.

Kevin leaned back in his chair and stared at the ceiling.

"Of course!" I said. "The personals column. He'd put a message in the personals. A personals message to the videotape extortionist, whoever you are."

Cindi sat up. "I like it."

"And you think our guy reads the personals?" Kevin asked.

"Chances are he does," I said. "After all, that's how his Canaan operatives communicate with each other, right? He probably checks the personals all the time to make sure they aren't going into business for themselves."

Kevin finally smiled. "I like it," he said.

"So do I," Cindi said. "Let's nail that bastard."

Her telephone started ringing. Kevin answered it. "Hello? Fine, send him up." He hung up and turned to me. "Ishmael Richardson is coming up."

Kevin waited out in the hall while I explained our plan to Ishmael Richardson.

He didn't say yes and he didn't say no. He didn't say anything until he asked, "How do you propose to get this sample into his hands?"

"I don't know yet," I said. "We'll figure out some drop point and then put it in the personals message."

Ishmael turned to Cindi. "How do you feel about this, young lady?"

"This man tried to kill me, Mr. Richardson," Cindi said. "He killed two people in my condo. He broke into Rachel's apartment and almost killed her dog. Now he's trying to destroy Joe Oliver, and he'll destroy me in the process. He'll ruin any future I might have. I think Rachel's plan might work. I'm willing to try it, sir."

Ishmael nodded slowly.

"I don't know what else we can do," I said. "You'd never be visible on camera. It'd be just Cindi talking. She'd mention only your first name."

Ishmael rubbed his chin. Cindi and I were silent. He finally stood up and walked over to the telephone. He dialed a number. "June," he said, "I'll be at 555-2020 until about ten tonight. Room 847." Still on the telephone, he turned to me and winked. "It looks like I may be tied up for a while."

KEVIN HAD ARRANGED FOR THE police to bring video equipment to the hotel and had sent a woman police officer over to Water Tower Place to pick up a sexy outfit for Cindi. She had returned fifteen minutes ago with a Marshall Field's box.

Cindi was in the bathroom, having already positioned the video camera at the foot of the bed. Ishmael was sitting on the couch fiddling with a cuff link. Kevin Turelli was out in the hall. By agreement, I would witness the proceedings and operate the camera. There would be no one else in the room except for Ishmael and Cindi.

The bathroom door opened. Cindi stood in the doorway, barefoot. She was wearing a semi-transparent red teddy cut high on the hips and a black garter on her left thigh. "Well?" she said as she turned slowly. From behind, the teddy was cut even higher, exposing both cheeks. From the front, her nipples and belly button were clearly visible through the filmy material. She looked down and said, "I could use some Neet." A few blond curly hairs poked out of both sides of the lower V of the teddy.

"You look super," I said.

Cindi reached back into the bathroom and pulled out an oversize bath towel, which she wrapped around her body, sarong-style.

Ishmael cleared his throat. "All set?" he asked.

"I think so," I said, turning to Cindi. "This is the On button?" I asked, pointing to a button on the camera.

She nodded. "Make sure I'm in the frame before you push it."

"What is the script?" Ishmael asked, still seated on the couch, trying to look relaxed.

"We'll open with Cindi alone on the bed," I said, "facing the camera. She'll talk into the camera, say something about how she's lonely, and then she'll say your first name and ask you to join her. That's when I'll stop the film."

Ishmael frowned. "We want to make sure we bait the hook, correct?" He seemed to perk up.

I nodded.

Ishmael said, "Lyndon Johnson once told me that the best way to destroy a man is to catch him in bed with another man or with an animal. I am afraid I must draw the line at animals. After all, I am a trustee of the Lincoln Park Zoo." He smiled. "However, if we want to guarantee that the hook is properly baited, we should add another man to the bed along with Miss Reynolds."

Ten minutes later we were ready to roll. Cindi sat in the middle of the bed, her wrists handcuffed in front of her and one of the spaghetti straps of her teddy off her shoulder, exposing her left breast. She held a second set of handcuffs, the cuffs open, in her left hand. Seated next to her on the bed was Chicago Police Officer Thomas O'Brien, the beefy, moon-faced young cop who had been stationed on guard in the hotel room next door. He was in full uniform and attempting to keep a straight face.

"Ready?" I asked nervously, peering through the viewfinder. Cindi was in the middle of the camera frame; Officer O'Brien was to her right. I never expected to be making my debut tonight as a porno filmmaker.

Cindi nodded, looking down.

"Roll 'em," I said, pushing the On button.

Cindi looked up slowly, her eyes wide. She ran her tongue around her lips. "Ishmael," she said in a husky voice, "Officer O'Brien says that I've been a very naughty girl. He says I have to be punished because I'm such a bad, bad girl." She held her handcuffed wrists up, the second pair of handcuffs dangling. "Officer O'Brien says that naughty girls have to be spanked." She closed her eyes and then slowly opened them again. "Come over here, Ishmael. Spank me."

"Cut," I said, turning off the camera. "Perfect."

"Here," Cindi said, shoving her handcuffed wrists toward Officer O'Brien. "Take these off of me."

Officer O'Brien took the key off his belt and unlocked the handcuffs. Cindi got off the bed and walked quickly to the bathroom. She slammed the door behind her.

"That'll be all, Officer," I said to O'Brien.

"My pleasure, lady." He had a big grin on his face.

"If you breathe a word of this to anyone, Mr. O'Brien," Ishmael said, "I will personally see to it that you are transferred to the graveyard shift at O'Hare Airport."

O'Brien's eyes opened wide.

"Do you understand me?" Ishmael said.

"Yes, sir." O'Brien left.

Kevin stuck his head in. "Everything go okay?"

"Fine," I said.

"Where's Cindi?"

"She's changing," I said. "Give us a few minutes alone, Kevin. Okay?"

"Sure. I'll be out here."

Ishmael and I reviewed the videotape twice on the small viewfinder screen on the camera. It looked good. Ishmael watched as I tried to dismantle the video equipment. I couldn't unhook the camera from the tripod.

"Rachel," he said, glancing toward the closed bathroom door, "perhaps I should speak with her."

"No. I should," I said. "Maybe you could wait outside."

Just then the bathroom door opened. Cindi was dressed again in her blue jeans and pink cotton T-shirt. Her face was taut. She took a deep breath. "Let's go, guys. We have work to do."

But at 10:30 P.M. we were still stumped. Ishmael had left an hour before to meet in private with Joe Oliver to explain what had happened and what was planned.

Cindi, Kevin, and I were seated around the table in her room, having just finished our room-service dinners.

"There has to be a way," Cindi said as she poked her fork at a decorative orange half that looked as if it had been cut with pinking shears.

The problem was how to get the videotape teaser to the mystery man. We had to pick a drop point that would allow him to pick up the videocassette without the fear of being seen. The obvious choices were no good. A post office box, a locker at the bus or train station—he would be too visible, too conspicuous. It had to be someplace he knew he couldn't be spotted by a plainclothes cop.

"It has to be a private place in a public spot," Cindi said. "Somewhere where there's lots of traffic but where you can be private."

"A movie theater?" Kevin asked. "No," he answered himself. "He wouldn't know who was watching him in the darkness."

"How 'bout a bathroom?" Cindi asked. "A public bathroom, like out at O'Hare."

"Where would you put the videocassette?" I asked.

Cindi answered, "Tape it behind a toilet. Tell him which stall to look in. Like that scene in *The Godfather*."

I thought that one over. "Not bad," I said. "But not foolproof. What if someone else finds it before our guy? Some other guy goes into the toilet stall, happens to see it, and takes it with him because he's curious. By the time our guy gets there it's gone."

We mulled it over until Ishmael called at about eleven P.M.

"I spent an hour with Joe Oliver," he said to me over the telephone. "He is quite upset about the whole situation. I made him understand that my interests are parallel to his. He has agreed to co-operate."

I told Ishmael that we still hadn't solved the drop-point problem.

"The bathroom idea has possibilities," he said. "I'll think it over tonight. We should meet in Miss Reynolds's room tomorrow morning at eight-thirty. Time is of the essence here."

Kevin offered to drop me off at home. He went out into the hall to confer with the plainclothes cop handling the night shift.

"You okay?" I asked Cindi.

"Yeah. The whole thing got to me real bad while we were making the film. But I'll be okay, Rachel. Let's hope the cops get that bastard, and then I can get my life back together."

I gave her a hug. "We're going to do it, Cindi."

Kevin drove me home in his unmarked car. He came up to my apartment and searched each room with Ozzie and me in tow. Ozzie and I walked back down with him to his car.

"See you tomorrow morning, Rachel," Kevin said.

"Thanks, Kevin." I kissed him on the cheek.

I walked Ozzie to the end of the block and back while Kevin watched from his car in front of my apartment.

"I'll wait till you get upstairs," he said. "Flick your lights twice when you get up there."

I did, and heard Kevin's car start up and pull away.

There was another message from Paul on my answering machine. I dialed his number, let it ring ten times, and hung up.

Before I left Cindi at the hotel, I had asked her

about Paul Mason. "No," she had said. "Never had a client that matched that description. And I certainly never had an English professor from Northwestern."

40

<hr>

IT WAS A QUARTER TO nine Wednesday morning. Kevin, Ishmael, Cindi, and I were back in Cindi's hotel room. I had just told them my idea.

"In a sanitary napkin disposal?" Kevin asked.

"There's one in every stall in every women's bathroom," I explained again. "It's big enough to hold a videocassette. No one *ever* looks in there, so there's almost no risk that someone else might find it. It's a perfect hiding place. A closed box in a private toilet stall in a busy public bathroom."

"But how does he get to it?" Kevin asked. "Do you expect him to go in drag into a ladies' room at O'Hare?"

"No," I answered. "He could send a girlfriend. Or just find some woman at the airport and ask her to do him a favor. Or maybe pay her to go in there and get it for him. It's perfect. She walks into a private toilet stall in a crowded bathroom, takes the videocassette out of the sanitary napkin disposal . . . which reminds me." I turned to Kevin. "You'll have to put it in a plastic bag . . . to protect it"—I blushed—"from the rest of the stuff there. Anyway, she takes the videocassette, puts it into her purse, walks out, and meets our guy in some private spot at the airport and hands over the videocassette. There must be dozens of women going into those toilet stalls every hour out there. There's usually a line during the busy hours. She goes in and goes out, just like anyone else. No one knows she took it. No one sees him, and his assistant is completely inconspicuous."

"It's a great idea," Cindi said.

I said, "We just need to make sure the cleaning crew doesn't empty the disposal before she picks up the videocassette."

"No problem," Kevin said. "I can work that part out. We can keep the cleaning crew out of there for hours."

"Let's get the personals message written," Ishmael said.

"Already done," I said. I passed around the message I had worked on last night when the idea came to me in bed. "Now we need to come up with a message from Joe Oliver to the mystery man. We can have it typed on Oliver's stationery and put it in the videocassette jacket along with the videotape."

"Joe Oliver has to insist that the exchange be done face-to-face," Kevin said, "so we can nail him when it happens."

"How quickly can we get the personals message into the newspapers?" I asked.

Ishmael checked his watch. "We have about four hours before the afternoon editions go to press," he said. "I know the publishers. I'll handle that part. It'll run this afternoon and in all the morning editions. Set the drop for tomorrow afternoon."

Joe Oliver came to my office at two P.M. to sign the note that would be included with the videocassette. Mary had typed it on a sheet of Oliver's stationery that he had furnished by messenger that morning. Ishmael had approved the text at noon.

"Hello, Joe," I said as he walked into my office. He was wearing dark-rimmed glasses, a blue blazer, and gray slacks.

Joe Oliver nodded curtly. "Where's the note?" he asked.

I handed it to him. It was typed in all capital letters with a space for his signature at the bottom:

IF YOU LIKE THIS PREVIEW, YOU CAN
TRADE FOR THE FULL-LENGTH VERSION,
STARRING ISHMAEL RICHARDSON.
YOUR COPIES OF ME FOR MY COPY OF
RICHARDSON. YOU NAME WHERE AND
WHEN. BUT ONE CONDITION: WE
EXCHANGE FACE-TO-FACE. WHEN I
KNOW YOUR IDENTITY, WE HAVE
MUTUAL ASSURED DESTRUCTION.
UNDERSTAND? IF I DON'T RECOGNIZE
YOU, THE DEAL IS OFF.

Oliver read it through twice without comment and then, pulling out a gold fountain pen, signed his name in a diagonal scrawl at the bottom of the page. He looked up at me. "Ishmael said you intercepted the videotape," he said in a nasal monotone.

I nodded.

"Did you watch it?"

"Yes."

He took off his glasses and slipped them into the inside pocket of his blazer. There were bags under his weary eyes. "I want to meet him face-to-face," he said slowly. "I don't want some Keystone Kops operation. You understand?"

"Even if he goes for the bait," I said, "he'll still be worried it might be a setup. He'll try to arrange the meeting in a secluded place—where he can be sure that the police won't be around. Don't worry, they won't be visible. But they'll be there to protect you."

"The police can come in later," Oliver said. "But I have to meet him face-to-face. Alone."

"Joe, the odds are good that he'll try to kill you. You can't do this on your own."

Oliver stared at me, his face expressionless. I had seen him do that to hostile trial witnesses on cross-examination. It worked in court, but it didn't work today. The effect of the dreaded Joe Oliver stare was lost on someone who had seen him on videotape naked and tied to the bedposts with pink scarves. "I assume he will try to kill me," he said in his deliberate monotone. He breathed deeply through his nose. "That's why I want to meet him alone."

"You aren't the only victim, Joe. He tried to kill Cindi Reynolds. He actually killed two people in that explosion. He's a dangerous man."

Oliver remained stone-faced. I sighed and said, "You don't want to cooperate, fine. We can junk the operation, and eventually he'll give those tapes to your family and friends. Is that what you want? You're not the only one who's been hurt. I'm a victim too, and I'm not going to let you screw this up. You understand? Damn you, Joe. You can either trust the police or you can get out of here and we'll forget the whole thing."

Joe smiled at my anger. He stood up. "Call me when he picks up the videocassette. I'll call you when he contacts me. Don't worry, young lady."

As soon as Oliver left I called Kevin. "Kevin, you're going to have to watch out for Oliver. He may try to turn free agent on you. You may have to put a tail on him."

I spent the rest of the afternoon trying to dictate my Canaan investigation notes. I wanted to get the rest of the story down—to make sure there'd be some record of all this. Just in case.

But I couldn't concentrate. Last night I was filming a porno flick. Today I had arranged a "high noon" encounter between Joe Oliver and the blackmailer. This wasn't what they prepared me for in law school. I stared at my Dictaphone and then reached forward to buzz Mary.

"What's up?" she asked, poking her head into my office.

I sighed. "I'm bushed."

Mary studied me. "How 'bout some fresh coffee?"

I gave her a sheepish smile. "That sounds great. Bring us both a cup. I could use some company."

Harlan Dodson called around four-thirty to ask why I hadn't yet sent him my files on the Canaan legacy. I told him that I'd been busy on other matters and would send them over in the next few days. He made a vague threat about informing Ishmael Richardson about my dilatory behavior and hung up.

By six P.M. I found myself dictating the same sentence over and over. I decided to pack it in and go home. A warm bubble bath and an early bed sounded wonderful.

I picked up the afternoon *Tribune* on my way to the subway station and found the personals message as I waited for the northbound train:

> To Video B-Mailer: Will exchange my tape for yours. Mine is better. For sample, go to ORD, Term. 3, Main Level, SW Wom. Bthrm., Stall 3, San. Napk. Disp. Thurs. @ noon. Joe O.

The sanitary napkin disposal in stall number three of the women's bathroom in the southwest part of the main level of Terminal 3 at O'Hare Airport. Tomorrow at noon. Go get him, Kevin.

Ozzie came trotting out of my bedroom when I opened the door to my apartment. I froze in the entranceway. My bedroom light was on. Backing into the hallway, I grabbed for the umbrella hanging from the closest doorknob.

As I drew the umbrella back with both hands, Paul Mason strolled out of my bedroom. "What are you doing here?" I demanded.

"Whoa," Paul said, his eyes wide. "It's just me, Rachel." He put his hands in the air with a sheepish grin.

Ozzie walked back to Paul, his tail wagging. Paul kept one hand in the air and patted Ozzie on the head with the other.

"Answer my question, dammit. What are you doing here?"

"Hey, relax," he said. "I've been leaving messages on your damn answering machine for three days. I finally gave up and decided to come over to show you what I found. Your landlord's gone, so I came up here." He smiled. "My key still works. I was afraid you'd had the locks changed when we broke up."

"You just come barging into my home? Damn you, Paul. You've got no right to do that."

"Hey, I'm sorry. Okay? Relax. I wouldn't have used the key if I thought you were in here. I knocked on the door, shouted your name. You weren't here." He shrugged. "So I decided to come in and leave you a message along with the stuff I found." He rubbed Ozzie on the head. "Old Ozzie was sure happy to see me, weren't you, boy?" Ozzie was sitting in front of Paul now, his tail flopping.

I walked into my apartment. "Give me that key," I said, holding out my hand.

Paul dug a hand into the front pocket of his jeans and pulled out the key.

I took it from him. "Don't you ever do that again. Ever."

"My mistake, okay? Let's drop it. Listen, I've got some great stuff to show you. Then I promise I'll leave." He raised his hand. "Scout's honor. You're going to love it."

I shook my head, trying to force back a smile. "You are really a jerk," I said. "Okay, what do you think you have?"

"*Think* I have? May I remind you you're talking to someone who probably knows more about Sam Spade and Mike Hammer than anyone in this country."

"Give me a break, Paul. Reading about detectives isn't the same as being one. I've read *Big Two-Hearted River* about ten times, and I still can't bait a hook." I was standing just an arm's length away from Paul, close enough to pick up the familiar scent of his cologne. I was torn between an urge to kiss him and an urge to crack him over the head with the umbrella. I wasn't strong enough to do the latter; for the moment, at least, I was strong enough to resist the former.

"You want proof?" Paul asked with a wink. "Look at what I left on your desk."

I followed him into my bedroom. He lifted a large envelope off the desk. He had scrawled a brief note to me on the outside.

"I was down in the microfilm room at the library all afternoon yesterday and all morning today," he said as he tore open the envelope. "I started with 1985, keying in to the week or so before each of those four newspaper articles." He shuffled through the glossy photocopies. "Look what I found."

He handed me four photocopied pages from the classified section. Circled in red on each page was a Canaan message in the same format I had found—each with the name of an el or subway station, a time (always after midnight) and a day.

"So they used the same system back then," I said.

"Exactly. So then I tried 1986 and 1987. I didn't have time to check all the newspapers. It's incredible drudge work just going through one set of microfilm. I stuck with the *Sun-Times*. I found three—two in 1986 and one in 1987." He handed them to me.

I stared at the Canaan messages. They were proof that someone out there had carried on the lottery, or at least used the Canaan communica-

tions system, after 1985 *but before Marshall died.*
I looked up at Paul. "Good work," I said.

"You better believe it. But here's the best part."
He pulled a folded page of newsprint out of the
envelope. "I tried to call you on Sunday about this
one. Look what appeared in last Sunday's *Trib.*"

It was the same Canaan message Benny Goldberg had shown me out at Maggie's place last Sunday—the message that led to the discovery of the
extortion scheme. But that wasn't what caught my
attention. What did was on my desk, right next to
where Paul must have placed his envelope before
I walked into the apartment. Last night I had sat
at my desk trying to think of a drop point for the
fake videotape of Ishmael and Cindi. I had
sketched out my thoughts on a yellow legal pad.
When Paul handed me the page from the Sunday
Tribune, I saw those notes. No doubt Paul had seen
them too—before I got home.

Near the top of the first page of the legal pad I
had written *Canaan.* Below that were the words
*Joe Oliver—how to get Ishmael videotape to extor-
tionist???* The rest of the page, and the two following it, contained random notes, arrows, words
underlined or circled, words and phrases crossed
out. It was all too easy for someone clever to figure
out.

I looked at Paul, who was smiling proudly. He'd
have to have seen those notes.

"That was just a couple of days ago," Paul said.

"Huh?"

"This message in the paper. Hell, I was half
tempted to go down to the Grand Avenue subway
station myself to see what happened. I probably
would have if I hadn't had the deadline on that
paper I was writing."

I nodded, feeling numb. "Yeah. I wonder what happened down there."

"How are you doing on your end of the investigation?"

"I'm basically done," I said. "The coffin turned up."

"No kidding?"

I shrugged. "There was a skeleton inside. Whoever did it probably bought a skeleton and put it inside. But the law firm was satisfied. They're going to break the trust and close the investigation."

"Just like that?" Paul asked. "They don't want to find out what's going on now?"

I shook my head. "I guess not. Ishmael Richardson decided that enough was enough."

"God, lawyers are hopeless. This is great stuff, and all they want to do is get back to their cases."

"Me too," I said. "I've had it."

"Well, I'm going to keep poking around. I might surprise you, Rachel."

I stared at him. "It won't be the first time," I said quietly.

Paul checked his watch. "Listen, I've got to run. Another faculty meeting. We're getting geared up for the fall semester."

I followed him to the front door.

"So I'll see you tomorrow night," he said. "Around five."

"Tomorrow night?"

"That function at the aquarium. Remember?"

"Oh. Right." Last week, when Paul had spent the night at my apartment—or at least part of the night—in a moment of gratitude for his being there I had asked him to come with me to a cocktail party this Thursday at the Shedd Aquarium.

"Take care, Rachel."

"Bye, Paul."

I made myself a salad, walked Ozzie, had a bubble bath, and went to bed early. But it was a long time before I fell asleep.

41

I WAS EATING LUNCH WITH Cindi in her hotel room on Thursday when Kevin called from the airport.

"He got the videocassette," Kevin said.

"When?" I asked, checking the clock on the nightstand. It was 12:45 P.M.

"Don't know for sure," Kevin said. "I sent a policewoman in there ten minutes ago to check that Kotex box in stall number three. The tape was gone."

"No suspects, I guess."

Kevin laughed. "We got plenty of suspects. There must have been five hundred gals in and out of there since noon, and they all had purses."

"What next?" I asked.

"We wait for him to make a move. See if he's really gone for the bait. Joe Oliver is supposed to get in touch with me once our mystery man contacts him. We'll take it from there." Kevin chuckled. "Ishmael must have a lot of clout at the smart shop. I'd like to know who his rabbi is down there."

"Why?" I asked.

"I just got a heavy car assigned to me for this operation."

"What's a heavy car?"

"An unmarked squad car with two coppers trained in special weapons and tactics. Pump-action shotguns, high-powered rifles."

"Wow."

"Look," Kevin said, "if this guy goes for the bait, he might try something wild—like knocking off Oliver. And even if he decides to let Oliver live, you know we won't be able to move in until the last minute. I just hope that jerk Oliver cooperates."

"Are you going to keep an eye on him?"

"You bet. I have a plainclothes cop stationed over at his law firm. And I've got his schedule for today and Friday from his secretary. He's in the office today till five-thirty. Then he's going to some cocktail reception for a new federal judge over at the Shedd Aquarium. Tomorrow he's got an oral argument at ten over at the Daley Center, then he's got a lunch meeting at the Yacht Club, and then he's got some plaintiffs' steering committee meeting in his office for the rest of the afternoon. Tomorrow night he's got reservations for two at Gene and Georgetti's on North Franklin."

"I'll probably see him tonight," I said.

"Where?"

"At the aquarium," I said. "Abbott and Windsor is giving the cocktail party. They sent me an invitation. You remember Bill Williams. This is A and W's big send-off for him."

"Well, keep an eye on Oliver tonight, Rachel,"

Kevin said. "I doubt he'll be contacted before the weekend, though. Our mystery man is going to plan his next move carefully. Still, I'll assign one of the heavy cars to surveillance over at the aquarium. They can follow Oliver home after the party."

"I'll call Joe and tell him the tape was picked up," I said.

"Good. Keep your fingers crossed, Rachel."

"So he picked up the tape?" Cindi asked when I hung up.

I told Cindi what had happened, then dialed Joe Oliver's office number.

"Mr. Oliver is on a long distance conference call," his secretary told me. "Can I take a message?"

"This is Rachel Gold. Tell him that the videocassette was picked up today around noon. He'll know which one. I'll be back at my office in an hour if he needs to talk to me." I gave her the number.

"So the police are taking over?" Cindi asked.

"At last," I said. "Kevin has got a whole S.W.A.T. team as backup."

"When does he think the guy will make his move?" Cindi asked.

"He doesn't know. Maybe not until next week. Maybe longer." I stood up. "I've got to get back to my office."

Cindi reached into a plastic bag and pulled out her black wig. "I'm going out too. Kevin said I could if I wore this. I'm going to take a walk around Michigan Avenue with a plainclothes cop."

"Take care of yourself, Cindi."

"You too."

We were both jumpy when we parted.

* * *

Kevin called me with the bad news at four P.M. "He didn't go for the bait."

"How do you know?"

"Oliver got a message delivered to him ten minutes ago."

"From who?" I asked in frustration.

"We don't know. It was in a plain envelope. Apparently delivered to the mailroom at Oliver's firm. No one knows who dropped it off."

"What did it say?"

"Short and simple," Kevin said. " 'You keep your tape, I'll keep mine. No trades. I'll be in touch soon.' "

"That's all?"

"Yeah. I guess it's back to the old drawing board on this one."

"Damn," I said, my spirits sagging.

"For what it's worth, I thought you came up with a hell of a plan, Rachel."

"What are you going to do now?" I asked dully.

"Don't know. Guess there's not much we can do until the extortionist makes his next move."

"But that could be weeks," I said, fighting my disappointment. "Or even months."

"I know. But we don't have a choice. It's his move now, not ours. Talk to you later."

I sat alone in my office, staring out the window, numb. The trial brief still needed work, and it was due tomorrow. I tried without success to force myself to work on it.

Mary stuck her head in a little after five P.M.

"Don't forget that cocktail party at the aquarium, Rachel."

"You taking off?"

"Yep," Mary said. "I'm meeting Tom over at the

bandshell in Grant Park. We're going to have a picnic and listen to the concert."

"Sounds like fun," I said, trying to pump some enthusiasm into my voice.

"See you tomorrow," Mary said.

After she left I leaned back in my chair. Joe Oliver would be there tonight. Chances were good that Harlan Dodson, Cal Pemberton, and Kent Charles would be there too. Benny wouldn't. He was down in St. Louis on that deposition.

There was a rap on my door. It was Paul Mason, looking almost like a lawyer in his khaki suit, blue button-down shirt, and blue rep tie. I'd gotten dressed up for the occasion too.

"Ready?" he asked.

I forced a smile. "I guess."

42

THE SHEDD AQUARIUM IS ONE of my favorite places
in Chicago. I had first been there twenty years ago
with my father, who had taken me to Chicago for
a weekend. Just three weeks ago I had taken Katie
and Ben there. While Katie and Ben had watched
the sharks, I had stood transfixed before the tank
occupied by the moray eels—three green monsters
peering out of the caves in the rock formations in
their tank. As I watched, one of them had slithered
out of its cave. It slid along the glass, a penny-sized
gill hole puckering and unpuckering below its
puffed neck, wrinkles and creases running down
the length of its body. As it moved past, it had
turned to me with dull, milky eyes and opened its
V-shaped jaws to reveal rows of gray daggers.

"Here we are, folks," our cabbie said.

Paul paid him and we stepped out onto the walk-
way leading up to the aquarium. It was a beautiful

summer evening. To my left, highlighted against a blue sky, was the Chicago skyline.

The Shedd Aquarium sits on a small hill at the base of a finger of land that juts out between Monroe Harbor and Burnham Harbor. Rows of anchored sailboats swayed in the water on both sides of it. In a city of tallests and longests and biggests, the Shedd Aquarium is, naturally, the world's largest aquarium. Up close, it looks like a Greek temple. Farther back or from the side, its octagon shape is revealed.

Paul and I walked up the two flights of marble steps. As I searched in my purse for my invitation, I heard my name being called. I turned to see Benny Goldberg bounding up the steps toward me.

"What are *you* doing here?" I asked.

"Why wouldn't I be?" Benny's face was flushed and he was panting from his jog up the stairs. "Jesus, my heart's beating like a rabbit." He looked at Paul. "Hello, Professor."

"You said you were going to St. Louis," I said. "You said you were leaving last night after work." I did some quick calculating. It was Thursday night. Benny was supposed to leave Wednesday night. The personals message to the video extortionist appeared in the Wednesday afternoon papers—the edition Benny usually bought.

"They canceled it yesterday afternoon," he said. "It's rescheduled for next week, same time." We were walking up the steps. "Ever been to a party here?" Benny asked.

"No. You?"

"Once."

"How did the firm pick this place?" I asked.

"One of the partners is a big wheel over here.

On the board of directors or a trustee or something. Harlan Dodson, I think."

I paused at the door. "Dodson?" I asked.

Benny frowned. "Or maybe Kent Charles. I'm not sure. Anyway, we had the firm Christmas party here. It's kind of a neat place for a party."

We handed our engraved invitations to the guard at the door. A few lawyers were chatting in the large high-ceilinged lobby area inside. Two white-coated bartenders were visible through the Doric columns at the far end of the lobby. The bar was set up just to the left of the Coral Reef Exhibit, a ninety-thousand-gallon circular glass-paneled tank in the large rotunda of the building. During the day a diver enters the coral reef tank from above and hand-feeds the sea turtles, sharks, and reef fish while talking to the spectators through a microphone in his diving mask.

Bill Williams, the guest of honor, was standing to the right of the bar, his back to the Coral Reef Exhibit, shaking hands with well-wishers. He was a lanky, bald-headed man, slightly stooped, with a quick smile and a hearty laugh. He was patting Joe Oliver on the back as Paul and I approached.

"Thank you, Joe," he said. "That's excellent advice." Williams saw me and grinned. "Hello, Rachel. So glad you could be here." Joe Oliver nodded at me, unsmiling, and walked away.

"Congratulations, Judge," I said, extending my hand.

He covered it with both of his large hands. "Thank you, Rachel. And please, it's still Bill for one more week. How have you been, dear?"

"Can't complain," I said. "I'm busy and I have interesting cases."

"Wonderful. I sure as heck miss you, Rachel.

You did some doggone fine work for my clients. We all miss you."

"Thanks." I introduced him to Paul Mason and watched as the two shook hands and chatted.

During my early years at Abbott & Windsor I had been one of the only associates willing to work on Bill Williams's cases. Bill was an old-fashioned lawyer in the best sense of that phrase: good-natured, patient, and generous. Those same qualities had made him easy prey for the Young Turks at A & W, who methodically stole his bigger clients and saw to it that his partner's share was cut. The more ambitious young associates, with their seismographic ability to detect the most subtle shifts in the firm's hierarchy, avoided Bill Williams and ducked his assignments. By the time I left A & W, he had been effectively isolated within it; his persistent good cheer only made him seem more pathetic. When a judicial slot on the federal bench opened, the firm had used its political muscle to kill two birds with one stone. The cocktail party was an attempt to send him off with some residue of good feelings about his former partners.

"I'm looking forward to having you appear before me in court," Bill Williams said to me.

"So am I, Bill. So long as you just read my briefs this time. You aren't allowed to edit them up on the bench."

He burst into laughter. Bill Williams was a meticulous editor of briefs. He would edit and rewrite and edit and hone and edit and polish until— and sometimes beyond—the court's filing deadline. "I promise I won't touch them," he said.

"Just read them and accept them as the gospel truth," I said with a grin.

He laughed again, and then someone else caught his eye. "Hello, Bob! How the heck are you?"

Paul and I walked toward the bar. Benny intercepted us, carrying three drinks. "I got you both a drink," he said.

"Thanks," I said, taking mine.

"Somebody's gonna try to pick her up in that outfit," Benny said to Paul.

"What's wrong with the outfit?" I asked. I was wearing a crisp cotton off-white oversize shirt-dress cinched at the waist with a wide leather belt.

"Nothing. You look gorgeous, as usual," Benny said.

Kent Charles seemed to appear out of nowhere. "I agree," he said. "Hello, Rachel. Hi, Paul." He nodded at Benny. "Hope you enjoy yourself here," he said to me.

"You leaving us already?" Paul asked.

"Have to." He pulled a ticket out of his shirt pocket. "I have a ticket to a concert up at Ravinia. André Watts is playing *Rhapsody in Blue*. Then I have to get ready for an oral argument in the Seventh Circuit tomorrow."

"You have a minute?" Paul said to Kent. I watched as the two walked out. Kent paused at the door to shake hands with two lawyers from Sidley & Austin who were coming in.

A few of the younger lawyers from A & W joined Benny and me near the entry to Gallery One. There are six galleries of fish tanks at the aquarium, radiating from the rotunda like wide spokes on a wheel. Each is about ninety feet long and thirty feet wide, with high-arched ceilings overhead. The lighting in the galleries is low, and the gallery walls are lined with illuminated fish tanks set into the walls like portholes.

After about twenty minutes of idle chat I excused myself from the group, claiming I needed a refill on my drink.

"Get me another bourbon and Coke, Rachel," Benny said.

I nodded and walked back toward the bar. It was getting crowded now. Bill Williams was still standing near the Coral Reef Exhibit, surrounded by lawyers and glowing from the attention. I spotted Harlan Dodson, drink in hand, talking with another lawyer near the entrance to Gallery Six. I wandered around the rim of the Coral Reef Exhibit and found Cal Pemberton, sipping from a bottle of Beck's and staring at a large sea turtle that was resting on a coral ledge. Cal and the turtle were at eye level, staring at each other motionless.

I decided to find Joe Oliver. I wanted to get a better fix on what he planned to do now that my plan had failed.

He wasn't near the bar or in the rotunda. I walked slowly around the outer edge of the rotunda, pausing at the entrance to each of the galleries. There were lawyers in each gallery—some chatting and others looking at the exhibits. No Joe Oliver. For that matter, no Paul Mason. I came around full circle and looked in the main lobby. I didn't see Joe or Paul. I walked to the front entrance of the aquarium. Neither one of them was outside.

I walked back inside the aquarium and made another quick circle around the rotunda, looking into each gallery. Dodson was standing in line at the bar. Cal was still communing with the turtle. Benny was still talking with his group.

"Have you seen Paul?" I asked Benny.

"Yeah. I saw him go into one of these authorized-persons-only doors about five minutes ago. I think it leads upstairs. Hey, where's my drink?"

I walked slowly down one of the galleries, trying to imagine why Paul would go upstairs. It was just like him—always poking his nose where it wasn't supposed to be. All that was upstairs, as far as I knew, was the entrance to the fish tanks. I paused in front of a tank occupied by four large, flat, zebra-striped tropical fish. They moved stiffly through the water like inverted Mikasa serving platters.

There was a huge shark tank at the end of the gallery. It took up the entire back wall. Three gray sharks, their gill slits quivering, swam slowly in and around a splintered ship's hull on the tank floor. No Joe Oliver. Just as I started to turn, one of the sharks glided down to the bottom and nudged a small black object with his snout. The black object slid two feet along the floor of the tank as the shark moved on.

I looked closer. I bent down to make sure. It was a videocassette. A videocassette on the floor of the shark tank. I squinted up to the top of the tank and caught my breath. At the far upper left-hand corner of the tank a hand hung limp in the water.

43

I DIDN'T EVEN THINK OF going for help. I just knew I had to find out if that hand was Paul's. I ran back down the length of the gallery and found a metal door marked AUTHORIZED PERSONNEL ONLY. It was locked. So was the door in the next gallery. I hurried past that gallery and spotted another door. It was slightly ajar. I pulled it open and ran up the narrow concrete staircase, two steps at a time.

I stopped at the top of the stairs, my heart pounding, and tried to get my bearings. I was above the fish tanks, somewhere over the galleries. The floor vibrated from the metallic drone of pumps. I stepped forward, ducking under a bundle of large orange pipes overhead. I remembered reading somewhere that there were seventy-five miles of pipes in the Shedd Aquarium.

I was standing at the head of what looked like a long narrow laboratory. Along the floor against both sides of the room were the open tops of the large fish tanks I had been studying from the gallery below. Most of the tanks had low guardrails around them. Down the middle of the room, interspersed among various pieces of equipment, were smaller fish tanks on steel platforms—two tanks, then a lab table, three more tanks, then a deep metal sink, two more tanks, and then an upright white freezer. Two large sacks of Purina Trout Chow were leaning against the wall to my right.

I walked over to the first open tank on the left and peered hurriedly down into it. Only yellow and red fish, darting back and forth in the water.

I told myself the shark tank should be at the far end of one of the galleries to my right. I made my way as quickly as I could down the long room past other fish tanks and paused at the end, peering in both directions down the narrow passageway toward the adjacent galleries. I didn't see anyone. Please, God, don't let Paul be dead. I took a deep breath as I started down the passageway.

I had never seen a dead man before. Except in the movies. They look a lot deader in person. At least Joe Oliver did. I felt a flood of relief—it wasn't Paul—followed by a wave of nausea. Oliver was flat on his back in a puddle of blood near the shark tank, his legs splayed apart. His left arm hung over the rim of the tank and into the water up to the wrist. His shirt and suit jacket were stained dark red. His sunglasses hung from one ear sideways across his face, exposing an open eye. The odor of human feces filled the air.

I staggered back against the wall, fighting the urge to vomit. I took several deep breaths and then, still queasy, moved back to where Joe Oliver's body lay. There was a videocassette on the floor near his left knee. He had a pistol in his outstretched right hand. There was a note pinned to the lapel of his suit jacket. I bent down and read the typed message:

> To my friends and family:
> I cannot go on
> living a lie. I
> apologize to all
> for my weakness.
> Joe Oliver

I stared at the note, and then at the bullet wound, and then at the gun. A gray dorsal fin glided slowly past Joe Oliver's arm and slipped below the surface of the water. There were six bloody footprints on the concrete floor leading away from Oliver's body toward a narrow corridor. The first two prints were dark red and blurred, the next two were lighter, only partial prints, and the last two were barely visible, just heel splotches.

Above the drone of the water pumps I heard water splattering into a deep sink. The noise seemed to come from an area beyond the gallery. He must be cleaning up, I thought. I stared at the videocassette. The splattering noise stopped. Turning, I scanned the room for cover. I was standing behind the shark tank now, at the far end of the room. Water bubbled to the surface of the open tanks in the floor. No place to hide there. But down the middle of this room there were steel tables and deep sinks and small upright tanks. Maybe I could hide under one of the tables.

Footsteps approached from down the corridor. I dashed around the perimeter of the shark tank and into the middle of the room.

That's when I saw Paul Mason. He was crouched under a steel table about two-thirds of the way down the long room. He was staring at me wild-eyed, with no sign of recognition. The look on his face stopped me in mid-stride: It was pure huddled fright.

Before I could move farther, from behind me the footsteps entered the room near the shark tank and stopped. I gripped a table, my legs unsteady. I waited, my shoulders hunched.

"Hello, Kent," I said finally. I turned around slowly.

I was all too right. Kent Charles was standing by Joe Oliver's body. He had a wad of wet paper towels in one hand and a dark leather briefcase in the other. His eyes narrowed, and then he smiled. It was a sub-zero smile.

"Hello, Rachel," he said, his voice calm, almost matter of fact.

"It's over," I said, struggling to control my voice.

"Over?" He frowned. His suit jacket was off and his shirt-sleeves were rolled up to his elbows. "What's over?"

"You and Canaan," I said.

"Ah. Canaan." He came around the shark tank. "Marshall's little pet." He dropped the paper towels on the floor and rested his briefcase on the corner of a deep sink located halfway between the shark tank and where I stood. We were about thirty feet apart, separated by the middle row of tanks, sinks, and steel tables.

"We know about you and Canaan, Kent."

He shrugged. "I have no idea what you're talking about."

"Joe Oliver was a setup," I said. "There's no videotape of Richardson and Cindi Reynolds." The corner of his mouth twitched, but his face remained impassive. "Cindi's alive," I continued, "and the police arrested one of your Canaan thugs. He confessed. We know about the faked gas explosion in her apartment. We know all about your Canaan schemes." I took a deep breath, trying to keep my voice calm. "The cops are waiting downstairs." Why hadn't I called the police? I grasped the table to keep my hands from shaking.

Kent stared at me, his eyes narrowed.

"Why did you kill Joe?" I asked.

His eyes glared. "Self-defense. I called that prick this afternoon. Two hours after I sent him the message that the deal was off. Thought I'd catch him off guard. I disguised my voice. Told him to meet me up here at six-fifteen. He came up here on time, but when I asked for the tape, he tossed it into the tank and tried to pull a gun on me. I had to shoot him."

"You were going to shoot him anyway," I said.

He shrugged. "Maybe. But not in the chest."

"Why did you search my apartment?" I asked. I had to keep him talking. To give Paul a chance to do something.

"To see what you'd discovered. Paul told me you kept a lot of your work at home." He smiled. "And to shake you up a little. Maybe scare you off." He shook his head. "Guess I underestimated you. When did you figure out that I was the one who broke into your apartment?"

"I guess just now. I had a lot of suspects, and you were one of them. If it makes you feel any better, Paul was another one. But I started to wonder about you when you answered Paul's phone that night. You said you'd be right over—that I was just five minutes away." I paused. "Yet you'd never been to my apartment before. How would you know it was just five minutes from his?" I glanced quickly around the room. I couldn't see Paul from where I stood.

"Not bad," Kent said. "Of course, Paul could have just pointed out your street one time when we were driving by."

"I know. And that's what I told myself. I didn't want the killer to be anyone I liked." I shivered. "You searched my office too, didn't you?"

Kent raised his eyebrows.

"What did you find in my—"

"Enough to know I'd have to keep an eye on you," he snapped.

"What was in the coffin?"

Kent shook his head. "It's a good thing I found out about the codicil in time," he said. "Ishmael tried to keep it all hush-hush, but that buffoon Dodson was so worried about covering his ass that he told me all about it. He wanted me to know that he had nothing to do with drafting it."

"What was in the coffin?" I asked again.

"Four newspaper clippings, a photocopy of that Canaan book, and a computer printout from 1985. The printout had everything Marshall did back then: times, places, names, the lottery system, the whole thing. My name was in there several times."

"What did you do with it?" I asked.

"What do you think?" Kent smiled. "I fed it all into the firm's paper shredder." He had his hands on the briefcase.

"Where'd you buy the dog skeleton?" I was running out of ways to keep him talking. When was Paul going to make his move? And when was someone downstairs going to look into the shark tank and see Joe Oliver's hand? It seemed hours since I'd come up here.

"A small rendering plant on the west side."

"What about the second grave robbery? Was that just meant as a red herring?"

He nodded. "You do good work, Rachel. I'll give you that much."

"How'd you get involved in Marshall's lottery?"

Kent laughed. "*Marshall's* lottery? He'd be flattered to hear you say that. It's not *his* lottery, Rachel. He's not the only one." Kent clicked open the locks on his briefcase. Was his gun in there?

"He recruited me," Kent said. "It was on a business flight from London to Chicago in late 1985. Both of us had had pretty much to drink. He told me the story of the original Canaan lottery. A couple of weeks later we were out in L.A. together. That's when he told me what he had done. He had decided that I would be his successor. I was the perfect choice. We did a few together in 1986. He let me try a couple on my own in 1987." Kent paused. "I took over completely when he died."

"Took over?" I said. "You didn't take over. You completely perverted it. Look at what you've done—extortion, murder. That's not the Canaan lottery."

"So what?" he answered, his voice rising. "Graham Marshall set up his elegant little Canaan network, got his rocks off by playing God, and then walked away from it. Walked away!" Kent's face contorted with anger. "You should have seen Bill Bentley's face when he walked into court that day to tell the judge that the documents had been destroyed. I sat at defense counsel's table and told myself I was finally even with that asshole." He shook his head. "You can't imagine the kind of crap Joe Oliver's pulled on me in the Canterbury securities case over the last two years. I was going to let him twist in the wind for a few years. And that's what I'll do with the others. Do you realize I even have a videotape of a judge with that hooker? Unbelievable stuff. Do you have any idea what I'll be able to do to that guy?" He reached into his briefcase. "And you're not going to ruin it for me." He was holding the gun. "I've wasted enough time on you. Don't threaten me with cops. There aren't any down there. You think I'm some kind of moron? Get over by Oliver."

I didn't budge. My dress clung to me, damp from perspiration. "You can't get away with this, Kent," I said, trying to keep my voice steady. "They might believe one suicide, but if you shoot me, it's murder. Let's go downstairs. You can tell the cops that Joe Oliver tried to shoot you. With a good criminal lawyer you might get off."

"C'mon, Rachel," he said in an exasperated tone. "Don't try that bullshit on me. No one even knows I'm here. Remember? I left an hour ago. I made sure plenty of witnesses saw me leave too. Including your boyfriend. And I did leave. I went down to the harbor, got my boat, and came back. I anchored it out back and came in the back way. I have my own set of keys. Out of the perks of volunteering for the aquarium's annual capital drive. I'll leave the same way. My car's up at Belmont Harbor. I'll be at Ravinia by the intermission. Now, quit stalling and get over here." He gestured with the gun.

I moved slowly toward the shark tank, wondering where Paul was. He was nowhere in sight.

"It's a shame, Rachel," Kent said as I approached him, dragging my heels as much as I dared. "I thought I threw you off the track. The firm would have been proud of you. Too bad about us, eh? I was looking forward to our boat ride this weekend. What a shame I'll have to ruin your pretty dress," he added sarcastically. "You should never have come up here. Never." He raised the gun.

"You know who really set you up to be discovered?" I said. "Graham Marshall."

"You're crazy."

"He obviously realized he'd made a horrendous mistake getting you involved. That you didn't care about the Canaan lottery. You just wanted to use the system for your own little schemes."

Kent smiled. "You underestimate me, Rachel. Graham never suspected a thing. He thought I was totally committed to the lottery."

I shook my head. "You're blind to the obvious, Kent. Marshall was two steps ahead of you, even from the grave. He set up that codicil to make sure someone dug up the coffin. He couldn't blow the whistle on you while he was alive, since he'd incriminate himself too. So he made sure he could nail you after he was dead."

Kent was frowning. "Then he failed. I outfoxed him by digging it up myself."

"Wrong," I said. "You destroyed the documents but you didn't destroy the coffin. And what you didn't know was that Graham left a clue in the coffin. I followed that clue right back to you." I paused. "It looks to me that Graham had the last laugh."

Kent scowled, his jaws clenched. "That son of a bitch," he hissed. He quickly regained his composure. "But I'm one step ahead of him now." He gestured with the gun. "Stand over by Oliver. *Now*, goddammit."

I looked down at the gun in Joe Oliver's limp hand as I moved toward Kent.

Suddenly there was the sound of water crashing.

"Duck, Rachel!" It was Benny, down at the other end of the room. He had taken the coiled fire hose off the wall and turned it on. He was holding the nozzle with both hands and spraying a thick arc of water toward us. "Get away from her, you scumbag!" Benny shouted.

Kent Charles spun toward Benny and fired his gun. The shot was high and to the right, ricocheting off a pipe.

"Holy shit!" Benny shouted, and dropped the hose.

Kent Charles started down the narrow aisle between the fish tanks toward Benny. The hose was whipping back and forth on the floor, spraying loops of water across the room. I dropped to my knees and tried to pull the gun out of Joe Oliver's cold hand. I couldn't get his thick finger out of the trigger slot. I looked up at Kent, who was now twenty feet away, his back to me, moving in a slow crouch down the aisle after Benny. I raised the gun in Joe's hand, aimed at Kent's back with both hands, and pulled hard on Joe's trigger finger.

The recoil from the gun knocked me backward to the ground. Joe Oliver's handgun slid along the concrete. I scrambled after the gun. When I looked up, Kent was hobbling away from me to where his gun lay on the floor near a large fish tank. He was bleeding from the middle of his right thigh, his hand over the wound. From a sitting position I aimed again—my hands shaking—as Kent slipped on the wet floor just a few feet away from his gun.

He reached for the low guardrail in front of a fish tank as I finally forced myself to pull the trigger again. Click. The gun was empty.

With a sob I got to my feet and ran toward Kent, who was reaching for his gun. He turned toward me, holding on to the rail for support. I threw Oliver's gun at him. Kent ducked, raising his arm for protection. Oliver's gun bounced off his arm and plunked into the fish tank.

As I backed away, Benny charged down the aisle, growling. He lowered his shoulder and rammed into Kent just as Kent picked up his gun.

It seemed to happen in slow motion. The force of the blow knocked Kent over the low rail in front of the tank. The gun flew up out of his hand and bounced off the back wall as Kent pitched backward into the water, headfirst.

I ran to the tank and stared down at the churning water. I could barely make out the figure of Kent Charles thrashing underwater. Benny and I stood there waiting for Kent to come back up. Only then did I notice the yellow Danger signs on the guardrail and on the wall behind the tank.

He didn't come back up. Not until the fire department squad pulled his corpse out of the tank an hour later.

As it turned out, there were eyewitnesses in the gallery below: two attorneys from Winston & Strawn. They had been sipping white wine in front of the moray eel tank when Kent Charles plummeted into the water headfirst. According to them, Kent's right hand slid into one of the small caves, apparently startling the inhabitant. The moray eel clamped down on the wrist and held tight. One of Kent's flailing legs struck another moray eel, which grabbed hold of its prize. The third eel joined in the free-for-all and pulled Kent's other arm into its cave up to the elbow. The two attorneys stood horrified as Kent Charles slowly drowned on the other side of the glass, his eyes wide, his arms and leg yanked back and forth in a macabre tug-of-war.

Benny had run downstairs to call the police. I stood by the railing above the moray eel tank. Kent had stopped thrashing a while back. He was still upside down in the water, his body jerked occasionally by the eels. Looking down through the water, I could see the crowd of gawkers jostling for position in front of the viewing window below. I thought of poor Bill Williams and how his long overdue moment of glory had been ruined by this grisly disruption.

"Terrific work, Rachel."

I turned. Paul stood before me with a forced grin. I stared at him. "What the hell were you doing up here?"

"I guess I was one move ahead of you. I saw your notes about Joe Oliver when I was at your apartment. Then I saw that message from Joe in the personals—the one about the videotape. I put it all together, and I kept an eye on Joe downstairs. When he snuck up here, I followed him. I saw the whole thing." He shook his head. "Boy, I can't believe that my friend Kent—"

"Your friend was going to kill me," I said.

"I know. I couldn't believe it. I was trying to plan some sort of distraction, when Benny barged in."

"Kent was going to kill me." I shook my head. "You didn't do a thing to stop it."

"Hey. I'm telling you, I was about to do something. Knock over one of those empty aquariums. Something like that. Give you a chance to escape."

I stared at him. "If Benny hadn't showed up, I'd be dead. And you'd *still* be hiding under that table."

"No. You've got it all wrong, Rachel."

"I came up here to save *you*, Paul."

"I was going to help you. I really was." Paul tried on another smile. It looked more like a grimace.

I had lost interest in the conversation. "Forget it. Go back to your make-believe thrillers."

I turned and walked toward the stairway leading down. "Wait a minute," Paul called as I reached the stairway. "Where are you going?"

I paused at the top stair and then slowly started down. I didn't look back.

44

ALL THINGS CONSIDERED, THE GRAVESIDE ceremony that Saturday was handled with dignity and restraint. The coffin rested on four cinder blocks spray-painted black. It was at the edge of the open grave, encircled by two thick steel cables. The cables were held taut from above by a large iron hook attached to a long hoisting cable. The hoisting cable rose overhead to the derrick of a diesel-powered crane parked behind the coffin. The derrick towered high over the grave, casting a long cross-hatched shadow through the middle of the large crowd.

Maggie stood by the side of the enormous grave. She wore a black dress, white pearls, and black pumps. Gus presumably was naked inside a pine coffin the size of a Ford van. Two male representatives of the zoo's board flanked the coffin, looking more than a little out of place. Gus's keeper—a young woman in a gray zookeeper uniform—stood next to Maggie and occasionally wiped her eyes with a handkerchief.

Maggie delivered the short eulogy into a battery of microphones, mini-cams, and cameras facing her across the open grave. "Heavenly Father," she recited as the cameras clicked and whirred, "we know that not even a sparrow falls without your knowledge. Comfort the survivors of Gus. Give them reassurance that he is happy with You in Heaven."

Maggie stepped back and nodded toward the crane operator. The engine started with a deep roar, and the enormous reel began to turn. All eyes were on the coffin. The cables tightened, the wood creaked, and then the coffin was off the ground, swaying slightly two feet in the air. Four workmen, two on each side, guided the coffin over the enormous rectangular hole. One of the men signaled to the operator with his fist. We watched the huge pine box sink slowly into the earth.

Maggie waited until the cables were removed from the coffin and hoisted high above, dangling and twisting against the blue sky. She walked over to the mountain of dark soil at the edge of the hole, picked up the shovel, scooped out some dirt, and tossed it into the hole. The clods of dirt clattered onto the wood below. Maggie handed the shovel to the zookeeper, who scooped some dirt, tossed it into the hole, and handed the shovel to one of the zoo's board members, who looked at the shovel as if it were a dead snake.

Gradually, a line of mourners formed. There were children and men and women of all ages in the line, which wound through the gravel pathways of the cemetery. Some were dressed in black, others in shorts and T-shirts. One by one they stepped forward, took the shovel, and scooped dirt onto the coffin below. One little girl in a white pinafore and black patent-leather shoes dropped a long-stemmed red rose into the hole.

Cindi, Benny, and I waited for Maggie by the chapel. She came walking toward us, followed by a mob of reporters, cameramen, and photographers. The reporters were shouting questions and jabbing microphones at her.

She turned to face them at the chapel door. "Give me five minutes, boys, and then I'll be happy to answer your questions." She looked at us as she opened the chapel door. "Come inside," she whispered. "These vultures give me the creeps."

We walked through the Slumber Room. While the others moved on into Maggie's office at the rear of the chapel, I paused at the little coffin. It was on the wooden bier in the middle of the Slumber Room, where Maggie had placed it that morning after Cindi, Benny, and I had arrived.

The three of us had come early with a sack of doughnuts. Maggie had put on a big pot of coffee when we arrived, three hours before the funeral. As the four of us sat around the table sipping coffee from thick cream-colored mugs, I filled them in on what had come to light in the thirty-six hours since Kent Charles's body had been pulled out of the eel tank.

"The police got a court order and opened Kent's safety deposit box yesterday afternoon," I explained. "They found all seven videocassettes, plus two more copies of Joe Oliver's tape and the fake one of Ishmael and Cindi."

"What about the rest of the Canaan network?" Cindi asked.

"There's no more than four others, and probably just two," I said. "Detective Turelli is going to arrest them one at a time. He'll place a personals message to one each week. Set up a drop point at an el station after midnight, just as if it's business as usual. When Canaan One or Canaan Four or whoever steps off the train and walks over to the man with the package, he's going to discover that the messenger is a police detective."

"Did Kent finance this Canaan stuff out of his own pocket?" Benny asked.

"I don't think so. Tyrone Henderson has been running some computer searches through the Bottles and Cans disbursements files. He's turned up some oddball expense requests from Kent Charles over the past two years. Ten thousand here, ten thousand there—for payments to nonexistent court reporters and experts and litigation support outfits. It looks like enough money to finance the operation, and yet it was small enough to get lost in the Bottles and Cans expense files."

"How did Kent find out about the videotapes in my wall safe?" Cindi asked.

"Cal Pemberton told him. The police questioned Cal yesterday. It was Kent who sent Cal to you about a year ago, when Cal complained about problems with his wife. Later, when Kent asked him how it went, Cal told him that Cindi would even keep a videocassette for him if he wanted. After Marshall died, Kent decided to go for the tapes in your apartment. When he found the one of you and Joe, he hatched his blackmail scheme. He saw it as a chance to get even with Joe Oliver."

"How the hell did Rambo know to come to the rescue?" Maggie asked, gesturing toward Benny.

I smiled at Benny. We had spent most of Thursday night down at police headquarters answering questions. Benny had been furious with me for cutting him out of the investigation. I had come up with an explanation that sounded lame even to me, but I swore to myself that I would never let Benny know that he had once been a suspect.

Benny grinned. "I was thirsty. Rachel was supposed to bring me back a drink. When she didn't come back, I went to find her. I had just come around the corner when she went charging up those stairs. I followed her up there but got lost in all those damned corridors and passageways. By the time I reached her, there was Kent Charles pointing a gun at her. I didn't know what to do. I grabbed that fire hose, unrolled it some, and turned on the water full blast." Benny smiled and leaned back in his chair. "The rest is history. Face it, girls. You're looking at a stud with the biggest balls this side of the Pecos River."

We all laughed. "One thing I don't understand," Cindi said. "What was the videotape Joe brought to exchange? There was no real videotape of me and Ishmael."

"That's my favorite part," I said, smiling. "Kevin Turelli fished it out of the shark tank yesterday morning. Five years ago Joe Oliver represented the plaintiffs in a giant securities fraud case involving some bonds and notes issued by a Mexican gold-mining company. It looked like a sure winner for Oliver, with possibly fifty million dollars in damages. He had a contingent fee arrangement, which meant he might get as much as ten million in fees. Graham Marshall represented the main defendants, and did an incredible job. The jury awarded only three grand in damages. Joe Oliver ended up with almost nothing. When it was all over, Marshall took Oliver and his wife out to dinner and gave him a little memento of the case: a videotape of *The Treasure of the Sierra Madre*. Oliver kept it on a shelf in his office. That was the videotape he brought to the aquarium. The one he tossed into the shark tank before Kent's eyes. The videotape that Kent thought was the mother lode itself."

We had been interrupted by the crane operator, who had wanted to know when he was supposed to lift Gus's coffin.

And now Gus was buried. The Canaan coffin would be next, after the crowd left. I ran my hand over the smooth coffin lid and moved on to Maggie's office. Benny handed me a plastic champagne glass as I walked in, and then he served champagne to everyone. We all raised our glasses.

"To Gus," said Benny. "May he rest in peace up there in that big jungle river in the sky."

They all looked at me. I held my glass a little higher. "To Cindi, Benny, and Maggie," I said. "My three buddies."

We buried Canaan late that afternoon. There was no ceremony. Maggie handed the coffin to one of the workers and told him to bury it. She knocked once on the coffin lid and said, "You better stay put this time, boy." We watched the workers put the coffin into the hole and cover it with dirt.

The Closing

THERE'S A COLD WIND BLOWING in off the lake. It shudders the windows in my living room. Ozzie is curled next to me on the couch, sound asleep. The Farmer's Almanac says we're in for a long, bitter winter, and I can believe it. The first frost came in October. We've had snow already, and it's still three weeks to Thanksgiving.

Last month I finally finished my Canaan journal. I sent a copy to Ishmael Richardson, along with my investigation notes and a three-hundred-dollar refund on the retainer. My cover letter stated that the package contained a complete copy of my Canaan file.

It didn't. I still have the three-by-five index card.

Benny left Abbott & Windsor on October first. He starts at DePaul Law School after the first of the year. He sent me a postcard from Puerta Vallarta last week.

Cindi Reynolds landed a job as a model on a WGN game show, and I helped negotiate her employment contract.

Maggie Sullivan remains one of my clients. We're going to trial next spring in a contract dispute with one of her coffin suppliers.

I haven't seen or talked to Paul Mason since the night Kent Charles died. I doubt he wants any reminders of the night. For that matter, neither do I. I suppose he's still entrancing his students with the gutsy exploits of Sam Spade and Lew Archer.

Julia Marshall, Graham's widow, called last week to ask about the final results of my Canaan investigation. I'm going to meet with her tomorrow afternoon.

Ishmael Richardson suggested that I not tell Julia Marshall everything I found. After all, her husband is dead and life goes on. But I think she deserves to hear the full story. And when I tell her, I'll probably give her the three-by-five index card.

It's sitting on my coffee table as I write this. One corner is dog-eared and there's a pinhole near the top of the card.

I found it in a New York City bookstore five weeks ago. I had been down on Wall Street for a deposition that ended at noon on the second day. I took a cab up to Greenwich Village to meet a friend for lunch. I was ten minutes early, so I poked my head into the bookstore next door.

It looked promising: no best-seller tables up front, no cardboard displays, no computer section, no swimsuit calendars. Just floor-to-ceiling bookshelves; long, narrow aisles; three serious browsers; and a coffeepot near the back.

By the coffeepot was a message board crammed with thumbtacked messages—some on scraps of paper, others on index cards, and a few with a row of tear-off tabs with telephone numbers on the bottom. Feeling a surge of nostalgia for my schooldays, I sipped black coffee from a paper cup and scanned the requests for rides (to Boulder, to Swarthmore, to Santa Fe), the pleas for lost cats, the offers to sell (a brass bed, a Cuisinart, an espresso coffee machine).

The elderly proprietor up front, bent low over a slender volume of Wallace Stevens poetry, had no idea who put the messages on the board and couldn't care less who took them off.

I took one off. None of the browsers noticed. I replaced the thumbtack and put the index card into my purse. On the flight back to Chicago I thought again of how Kent had laughed when I called it Marshall's lottery. He's not the only one, Kent had said.

The message on the index card was printed in black ink in neat block letters:

CANAAN NO. 671
DROP POINT L
2:00 A.M., WEDNESDAY